The Vermilion Bridge

Books by Shelley Mydans

THE VERMILION BRIDGE

THE VIOLENT PEACE (With Carl Mydans)

THOMAS

THE OPEN CITY

The Vermilion Bridge

by Shelley Mydans

DOUBLEDAY & COMPANY, INC.
GARDEN CITY, NEW YORK
1980

ISBN: 0-385-03547-0
Library of Congress Catalog Card Number 79-7804

PRINTED IN THE UNITED STATES OF AMERICA
FIRST EDITION

For *Kay Tateishi*

Who kindled my interest in things Japanese

AUTHOR'S NOTE

Japan in the eighth century, like Japan today, was in the late stages of assimilating a great foreign culture. At that time, and for the century preceding it, the superior civilization the Japanese aspired to was that of T'ang China—much as in the nineteenth and twentieth centuries they have been absorbing the advanced technology of the Western world.

As Noël Coward so succinctly put it, Japan is "very small," China is "very big." And during the period in which this book is set (A.D. 710–70) Ch'ang-an, the Chinese capital, was the cultural center of the world, inheritor of twenty centuries of artistic and political development. Under the T'ang Dynasty (A.D. 618–907) Chinese influence extended throughout East Asia and from Persia in the west to the little-known mountainous islands of "dwarf people" to the east. Japan before that time had been almost completely cut off from the world, a nation organized by clan, lacking a formal religion or a written language.

Contrary to some current opinion, Japan has probably borrowed less of foreign cultures over the course of history than many other countries—a result of long periods of self-imposed isolation as well as simple geography. But in the two outstanding instances when the Japanese have come in contact with more ancient or more successful cultures they have taken to them so voraciously they seem to swallow them whole, although after a period of digestion they tend to eject that which is truly foreign to them.

In much the same way that in the mid-nineteenth century

the long-isolated samurai of Tokugawa Japan observed the military and economic power of the West with some astonishment, the clan leaders of the seventh century peered across the waters of the Yellow Sea and were amazed. And like the subsequent Japanese governments of the late nineteenth and twentieth centuries who set themselves to learn all that was useful to them in the social structures and industrial techniques of Europe and America, the Imperial Court of the eighth century adopted almost without reservation the religion and philosophy, arts and sciences, political and economic structure, even the technique of writing, from the far older and bigger Chinese nation.

By the end of that century—as by the end of the twentieth—they had absorbed what they could utilize of that superior culture from abroad. And by the tenth, when the T'ang Dynasty came to an end, they had already discarded much that did not fit their native character and were proceeding with their own unique history.

In this book I have tried to portray that period when Chinese influence was at its height and Japan's first (Chinese-style) capital was the city of Nara in western Honshu. A strong central government had been consolidated under sovereigns who were both gods incarnate of the Shinto belief and heads of a vast Chinese-style bureaucracy. Concurrently, the Buddhism that had been imported from China and Korea reached a peak of influence under the encouragement of these same sovereigns and became, in effect, the state religion.

By that time, the educated Japanese of the Court had begun to utilize their newfound written language, employing Chinese characters to record the first histories of their nation, the *Kojiki* (Record of Ancient Things) and the *Nihongi* (Chronicles of Japan) and to compile the first anthology of poetry, the *Manyōshū* (Collection of a Myriad Leaves), and I have used these sources as well as the detailed chronicle of the years from 700 to 790 which is called the *Shoku Nihongi* as a basis for my book. I also used, from materials in writing at that time, some sutras (teachings of Buddha) that were popular in Nara, some Shinto prayers of the same period, and some descriptions of high ceremonies that are preserved in the *Todai-ji Yoroku* (Records of the Todai-ji Temple) and the *Engi-shiki* (Supplementary Civil Code) of two centuries later.

Of course I consulted a great many works by later authorities, among which I would single out M. W. De Visser's exhaustive study, *Ancient Buddhism in Japan.* But because I wanted to try as far as possible to experience that unique time and place without relying heavily on intervening interpretations, I attempted to stay close to those early books. Also, I spent many days in Nara in an effort to absorb the aura of the place and the ancient temples there and to examine some of the personal belongings of Emperor Shōmu that amazingly have been preserved over these twelve hundred years. And I did take a course in early Buddhism and the Lotus Sutra from Professor Senchu Morano of Risshu University.

But my primary sources, as I say, were those first Japanese books and I am greatly indebted to the scholars who translated them. I relied on W. G. Aston's translation of the *Nihongi,* Donald L. Philippi's translation of the *Kojiki* and some *norito* (Shinto prayers), the Nippon Gakujutsu Shinkōkai edition of the *Manyōshū,* and G. B. Sansom's translations of Imperial edicts from the *Shoku Nihongi.*

Because the whole of the *Shoku Nihongi* has not been translated into a modern language, I leaned very heavily on Robert Karl Reischauer's splendid study, *Early Japanese History,* for the basic chronology of my story and employed two Japanese scholars, Fujimura Haruo, a student of the period, and Ide Etsuko, an interpreter, to make oral translations for me of specific important episodes about which I wanted a great deal of detail.

I am also deeply indebted to Professor Allan Grapard of Cornell University, who read the book in manuscript and made many very valuable suggestions and corrections, although I alone am responsible for the interpretation of events and for any errors.

Since this is a novel that I hope will interest general readers, I have of course strayed from an exact and scholarly study. However, all of the characters, with the exception of the lady-in-waiting, Shihi, are historical personages taken directly from the chronicle.

I have great respect for myth and legend and have incorporated them in this book. Some, such as those concerning the origins of Japan, were well known in the eighth century. Others, like the legend of the Old Man of the Mackerels, and the account of the High Priest Gyōgi's mission to the Isé Shrine, were recorded in later centuries. However, there is a deep seed of truth in all of them. Also, I have put into the mouths and letters of my characters verses from the *Manyōshū* that were written by poets of the period.

In one instance only, I have deliberately changed the historical record. According to the account of the time, the doctor-priest Dōkyō first met Empress Shōtoku when she was at the Hora Palace in the year 761. Because this book is a novel and for reasons of artistic unity and tension, I have introduced him in the Palace at Nara many years earlier.

All Japanese names are written with the surname first. In early times they were generally written with the preposition "no" between the names, as in Kibi no Makibi, but in more recent years the "no" has been omitted, and as I am aware of the difficulty that Japanese names present to the average American reader, I have tried to simplify things by using the last and first names only in most instances (as in Fujiwara Nakamaro) as well as by avoiding most changes in titles.

I have included in the Epilogue a few facts of the history that followed the period of the book but it is of additional interest that the Fujiwara family succeeded in infiltrating the Imperial line until, in following centuries, they became virtual rulers of Japan. And in our own time a distinguished member of that family, Prince Konoye Fumimaro, a Prime Minister during the years before World War II, upheld an ancient and honorable Japanese tradition by committing suicide after the arrival of conquering American troops when he was notified that he would be charged as a war criminal.

Larchmont, New York
June 1979

A maiden walks alone
On the great vermilion bridge . . .

She trails her crimson skirt.
Her cloak is dyed blue
With the herbs of the mountain.

Has she a husband young as green grass?
Does she sleep single like an acorn?

—from the *Manyōshū*, eighth-century
collection of Japanese verse

The Vermilion Bridge

CHAPTER I

Now with the change of times
Nara has become
An Imperial City that was.
Grass grows in the streets.

—from the *Manyōshū*

On the night of the tenth day, Second Month, in the fifth year of Jinki (A.D. 729), a company of Palace Guards was sent to surround the mansion of the Great Minister of the Left, Prince Nagaya-Ō. It was a heavy-clouded night, very cold. Sometime after midnight, late in the hour of the Rat, a thin spring snow fell briefly and the soldiers bunched themselves under the curved roof of the massive outer gates. They saw no lights or movement in the wide court or the heavy shadow of the mansion's spreading roofs.

Next day the Imperial Questioners came to examine the Great Minister. They were all men of power: two Imperial princes and the senior member of the ascendant Fujiwara family.

When they left, Nagaya-Ō escorted them as far as the inner court and knelt in a formal bow, his head bent almost to the ground. Because of his rank his Court gown was the color of wisteria. When snowflakes lit on it they melted into purple spots.

The questioners climbed into their high-wheeled carriages and were drawn away by the grooms to the outer gate where the oxen waited. Then with their guards and banner carriers they moved off behind the long wall of his residence.

Nagaya-Ō sat back and rested his hands on his thighs. He watched the floating snow grow thick again, one large flake and then another. They drifted slantingly across the stout red pillars of the gate and seemed to disappear against the whitewashed wall before they showed up white again on the dark twisted trunk of the plum tree.

"All is illusion, says the Buddha." The new teaching of the Sanron priests. "Everything exists within the mind. Men observe appearances and disappearances and call them life and death."

The blossoms on that gnarled old plum tree had reached their full bloom yesterday. Now they were falling with the snow. At one time Nagaya-Ō had drunk wine with his friends and floated plum blossoms in their cups while they made poems.

In my garden plum blossoms are falling.
Or are they snowflakes
Swirling from the sky?

"Everything changes. Nothing remains unchanged." That plum tree he had brought from the old Palace when the Empress moved her capital here—nineteen, almost twenty years ago. That great move to Nara when this mansion had been dismantled, pillar and plank all numbered by the artisans, and dragged on sleds and floated down the river to rise and stand here in this new city.

"Everything changes . . ."

Inside the house, seated where he had faced the questioners, Nagaya-Ō summoned his four sons. He had been charged with sorcery, with practicing magic against the life of the infant Heir Apparent, with treason. The punishment was death. Better to die by one's own hand than suffer the shame.

The boys sat stiff and silent before their father. Kashiwade, Kuwata, Kazuragi, Kagitori, each took the poison cup as he was handed it. When at last they lay stretched out together on the floor, Kashiwade holding the youngest to him, tears on his face, the father took the cords that bound his most beloved books and strangled them. Then he went behind the curtain-screen of his own room and hanged himself.

Kibi his wife, mother of these four sons, came running along the covered walk from her own pavilion with her hair disheveled and her feet bare. The women running after her sobbed and cried aloud.

That night in the Imperial Palace which was across the city, at its very heart, the little Princess Abé no Himé woke to see the shadow of a man hanging from the ceiling beam. He hung between the place where she was lying and the raised platform of her mother's bed-space in the center of the room. When the wind moved, the hanging man swung in the pale wash of the curtains, back and forth.

She lay rigid, staring at it a long time. Then when it faded—perhaps the dawn had come—she crept across to her mother's bed and slipped in. She was ten years old and had only recently reverted to this childish habit.

The infant Prince on whom the Great Minister had practiced his black magic (as her mother said) was her baby brother whom she dearly loved. "He is so dear," she often said. "He is so adorable!" She was a winsome little girl, and delicately framed, but excitable.

The two were the children of Emperor Shōmu and the beautiful Fujiwara Lady Kōmyō who was his consort. Although the boy was not the first of the Imperial line (just the year before Lady Hiro had borne the Emperor a son) he was the first by Shōmu's first and recognized wife whom he loved and leaned upon. And his father made him Heir Apparent almost at his birth.

Abé, the daughter, had been born when her father was still Crown Prince. Until she was five she lived with her mother in her grandfather's rambling mansion in the city's eastern ward and her father had visited. It seemed to her, when she remembered it, that she had been the center of that world.

She remembered such special days as the Iris Festival when she must have been two or three and her mother's ladies filled the rooms with sweet-flag blossoms and hung spice bags on the pillars to ward off evil. That evening when her father came from the Palace he wore a special cap made of iris leaves and a bright Court costume of peacock brocade.

She remembered how he picked her up, all rustling silk, and began to count her toes.

"You will spoil your sleeves." Her mother was laughing, though her face was hidden by the white moon of her fan. "She's a wriggler."

"Never mind, you will sew them for me." But he put her down.

Later they were reciting poems in the dark, the men in the garden sitting below the wide veranda steps, and she with the ladies in the room. She was resting heavily in her mother's lap, letting her head fall back and her eyes glaze over as she listened to the voices in the dark. They were laughing, and her mother roused her, whispering a message that she did not understand, or had forgotten now.

She could only remember the laughter and the whispers telling her, "Go on, go on," as they pushed her out into the moonlight under the wide sky. The pointed tops of the veranda posts were higher than her head. They gleamed like silver, and the bamboo leaves were like little polished swords. She had to sit on each step as she went down.

She remembered the strong arms that had caught her up, the musky perfume of silk sleeves, the low endearments of male voices, and how she was sent up again, kneeling on each step, to trot across the porch. She remembered, in that vaguely rustling, flower-scented room, how she was passed again from arm to arm, from lap to lap. They hugged her, pressing their cheeks against her mouth and breathing into her ears. "Tell me, tell me," they whispered. How happy she had been to find her mother!

Then, when she was five, the Old Empress abdicated and her father became Emperor—Sovereign of the Heavenly Sun-line of the Yamato Court—and she was moved with her mother to the consort's palace in the northern sector of the Imperial Palace grounds. She had never been out of the halls and gardens of the old Fujiwara residence and the prospect excited her almost beyond control.

The day of the move was a lucky day: the first of the Monkey in the Third Month (what they called the "Ever-Growing Month") in the first year of Jinki. (The year-name, Jinki, had been given in honor of a rare white tortoise found at the time of her father's elevation.)

The city of Nara was still quite new. The spring green willows along Nijō Street were scarcely higher than a man. And as they slowly rode along it in their gabled Chinese carriage, her mother held her tightly so as to stop her quivering and pointed out the way the streets ran east to west and the avenues north to south, just like the famous city of Ch'ang-an in China.

Someday Nara, too, will be a great world capital, she said. And foreigners will come from far away. She spoke very tenderly, stretching the words out, faar awaay.

As they approached the long wall of the Imperial Palace grounds, Abé saw the massive side gate with its high double roof, and while they were carried through the outer precincts in their palanquin, she peeked between the curtains and caught a glimpse of the smooth white pebbles of the parade ground and the speckled light of the budding trees by the long colonnades.

The Palace was new then too, though some of the buildings had been moved from the old Imperial residence across the hills. These were thatched with thick brown cedar bark like the old pavilions in her grandfather's house. But the roofs of the Emperor's wide-winged residences and ceremonial halls were curved and tiled in the Chinese manner, and the pillars were painted Chinese red.

Her mother's pavilion, where they were taken, was light and elegant with brocaded ribbons on the rolled veranda blinds and patterned rugs on the floors. There were covered walks to the eastern and western wings and many gardens.

In the large southern garden there was a lake with floating islands and a bridge with a long curved roof. Little red carp lived under the lily pads and when Abé clapped her hands they came swimming up to her and made round mouths in the water. Sometimes in the winter months cushions of snow lay on the roof and the water was smooth and black. In the spring, when the sun was rising and shining through blossoming trees, the water turned pink. Always it reflected the long line of the railings and the curve of the roof.

It was across this bridge that her father came to visit them. If he came at night they didn't see him and only knew by his tapping that he was there. He never sent a messenger. In the daytime it was different. Then there were high Court nobles surrounding him, making a procession. When she ran to the veranda to watch his coming, Abé knew him instantly among them all. There were his narrow shoulders and his lean high head with the wing of his cap standing up in silhouette. He was very tall. And when he came out from the cover of the bridge the light from the water reflected in his face, giving it a bright and quizzical look.

Always, whether he came at night or in the daytime, whether they sat in lamplight or on the mats where the sun came striped through the window bars, he asked to see her writing before she was sent away. That was their game. And while he sat beside her, watching with inquiring eyes, she tried to imitate her mother's strong, firm characters. The brush felt large and clumsy in her hand. She could never write like her mother. The ladies said she must calm her spirit first, but that only made her nervous.

One day when she was ten years old, Lady Shihi told her that she could expect a brother. Shihi had been with her mother since they were both girls, and although she came from the provinces, she had been in the capital so long that she had acquired the accent and the airs of a woman of culture—"above the clouds," as the Court people sometimes styled themselves. Just recently, since Abé's old nurse had grown too ill to be useful, she had assumed responsibility for the Princess.

Now she was smiling, nodding her head and looking closely into Abé's eyes. Her mother always spoke of Shihi as though she were beautiful. "Shihi has such lovely hair."

"Soon we shall have a little prince in the house." She smiled, but she was worried, that was clear. The very look in her eyes was frightening.

"There is nothing to worry about," she said. "All the signs are right."

By the signs, Abé knew she meant the reading made by the diviners in the Bureau of Yin and Yang. The hexagram had been *Ching,* Symbol of Source, which was good. But later it warned of danger:

". . . *the site of the town may be changed while the well undergoes no changes . . .*

". . . *the water of the well never disappears and never increases; all those who come and all those who go may draw and receive the benefit . . .*

". . . *but if, before the rope has quite reached the water, the bucket is broken—this is evil . . .*"

The reading was apt. The city had been moved but the Yamato line remained unbroken and unchanged. Now the rope was descending to the water. A son was to be born. The prediction sent a thrill of fear through the Court. "*If the bucket is broken . . .*"

Every precaution was taken. Hundreds of priests from the city's shrines and temples and wandering monks from the countryside were summoned to ward off demons. Abé's four strong uncles, her mother's brothers, came themselves to hang white curtains in place of the bamboo screens. The servants had made up the bed-space with its hangings all in white and put up another, like it, for a substitute so as to confuse the evil spirits.

Abé was not allowed to approach her mother's bed. "Don't bother my lady now!" Shihi looked distracted. Her face was shiny under its white paint and tears had reddened her lids.

But when Abé pouted, ready to cry herself, Shihi patted her roughly, as though in sport, and worked up a little smile. "This is no time for tears! A happy occasion surely! A propitious time! You will see."

That night Abé woke to screaming outside the shuttered windows. The priests were shouting, shrieking with all their might to scare away demons. Beating their drums. And inside, her mother's ladies were strewing rice for luck. They were dressed in white, and when they flung their arms wide, pale gray shadows wavered after them.

Abé retreated to the standing screen by the door. It had two little spotted deer on it and was her favorite hiding place. There she curled up, listening fearfully until at last she dozed. When she awoke it was midmorning and the noise had stopped. The air was full of sun-motes and the floor was crunchy with rice. She was amazed to see both men and women wandering by, oblivious to one another, dazed with relief. She sprang up and someone saw her, bent to her smiling, and told her to be happy now, a baby boy was born.

They named the baby Moto-Ō, and in celebration of his safe delivery the Emperor declared a general amnesty and sent gifts of fine hemp cloth to every child born on that day—a soft day on the Nara plain when the rice fields that encroached upon the still unfinished capital were being harvested. The tawny ears hung drying in long rows and in the evening the surrounding sacred hills were lined in purple mist.

When he was five weeks old his father gave him the title of *Kōtaishi*, Heir Apparent. He might have been the forty-sixth Emperor of Japan; his lineage could be traced directly back to that first August Ancestress, Amaterasu Ōmikami, who was the sun. And when he reached the age of seven-times-seven days he was taken to his father's ceremonial hall to be presented. Before that it was forbidden for the Emperor to see him.

Shōmu was childishly impatient during the waiting time, sending messages at all kinds of inconvenient hours. Was the baby healthy? Well formed? Did he show any signs yet of his mother's beauty? Princess Abé had been told she looked like her father.

On the morning of the forty-ninth day the roofs were covered with frost. A wash of silver rimmed the blue-green tiles. As soon as the shutters were opened Abé ran to the veranda, holding her fists clenched in her quilted sleeves and hopping from foot to foot. "It is more beautiful than snow!" she cried.

Her mother called to her, "Little silly, come and put your feet here under my robe before the frost bites you."

She ran in, ducking through the curtain to the scented warmth, and would have lain there, nestling in the quilted garments by her mother's side, but already a message had come from the Emperor, "Today's the day!" and with it the fragment of a poem written on frosted paper:

Though I tread the earth,
My heart is in the skies . . .

Someone poked at the curtains and called, "Come, little lady, don't hold up the day." It was Lady Shihi and Abé knew that if they ignored her she would thrust her hand through to pull her out. She always felt that she could take any kind of liberty.

Her mother laughed and pulled the covers away, and Abé crawled through the curtains and went to stand by the brazier where her clothes were being warmed. Her undertunic smelled of sweet basil when she slipped it on and the silk of her quilted jacket was soft and warm. They had changed to winter clothing when the season turned, but everything she was to wear this day had been made especially new. Her jacket was cherry-colored lined with willow green and her trousers were of heavy white shantung. Her girdle and her shoes were embroidered with birds and butterflies. What she liked best was the little scent bag tucked into her belt.

Her mother was carried in her indoor palanquin across the bridge and down the long veranda walks and sheltered corridors to the Emperor's Palace, but the soft cloth boots of the ladies following went sliding over the wooden floors as though to polish them. Abé was almost lost in the midst of their crimson trousers and the panels of their skirts. Like them she wore the flowers they had made for the occasion perched upright on her head. They danced above her as she trotted to keep up.

They went very quickly, but the Emperor had already risen when they approached and Abé, peering from among the skirts, saw him stride forward and then lean and look into the palanquin. He was not at all as dignified as she had seen him in this room before. He didn't even try to hide his eagerness. Instead he laughed, looking around among the ladies and then to his wife. "If I am impatient, it is because he's ours."

The ladies affected not to notice but took the baby to the cushions that were laid out for him beside his father's seat. They folded back the wrappings that had covered him and then retired behind the curtain-screens where they would not be seen.

To Abé the room seemed smaller than before, when she had come here on the Chrysanthemum Festival with the young girls of the Palace. Then she had walked, it seemed, in a very long procession to her father's seat to bring him the traditional gift of small white trout. Then it was night and all the gentlemen of rank sat watching, and the lamplight shone on her father's brocade robe. Now the room was divided by many hangings and by the standing screens that could be moved about for warmth or privacy.

The baby's little couch was laid in front of one of these. It had trees and flowers made of birds' feathers on it, and a poem in strong black characters. The baby lay there on his back, waving his arms and legs and staring blandly at the waffled canopy above him. He was a placid baby, but when his father knelt to touch him he seized the outstretched finger with surprising strength.

Shōmu was delighted. "He has got hold of me and won't let go!" He turned in wonder to his wife, showing her how the baby clung to him.

Kōmyō sat radiant in the center of the room. Her sweet round face was pale as a peony, her softly brushed-in eyebrows like moth wings, and on her cheeks she wore small plum-flower marks of dusty blue. Her robe fell from her sloping shoulders into scarlet folds on the rug. She nodded, smiling softly, bending her head to arrange the long sleeves in her lap.

She had been given to the Crown Prince when they were both fourteen, placed in his Court by her father, Fujiwara Fuhito, to become the future Empress. And she had won and held his love, for she was the stronger of the two, the cleverer, better calligrapher, and even more pious than the pious young Prince. Certainly she was more beautiful, her beauty was famous. And if her lineage was not as exalted, her family was more powerful. She was a Fujiwara.

Shōmu looked at her in wondering adoration, as at some Buddha smiling its secret smile. Then he turned back to his son. The baby still held him and he said again, "He won't let go. He knows me!"

Abé had followed her mother and sat pressed beside her. Her feet tucked under her were like little nesting birds, and she smiled in unconscious eager imitation of her father's smile.

Shōmu moved his finger gently back and forth, still held in that small prehensile grip. "Strong man as I am . . ." he murmured, leaving the verse unfinished. Everyone knew the reference and the implication that his son, like the pine of the poem, would grow stronger than he. The ladies, listening, nodded to one another.

Abé glanced at her mother, a quick bright look. "He's very strong," she whispered, "isn't he?" Kōmyō nodded, and she scrambled forward to kneel beside her brother and peer into his face. The baby waved his free hand aimlessly and she poked her own small finger against the closed pink fist. "He has got hold of me," she cried, though he had not. Nor had he taken his solemn empty gaze from his father's face, where he had transferred it from the ceiling. "He has got hold of me and won't ever let go!"

"Overeager," said the ladies, squinting through the screens. It was often hard to approve of the Imperial Princess.

The Emperor looked at her mildly and back again at his son. A perfect boy, perfectly formed. Not a blemish. There had been talk of evil omens at his birth . . .

CHAPTER II

Despite the fears and clamor that attended his delivery, the birth of Moto-Ō had been quite normal. And as he lay clutching his father's finger, returning his father's earnest gaze with a wide unblinking stare, he looked like any healthy, seven-week-old mortal child. There was no sign of the mysterious divinity within him. But the divinity was there. It was his heritage from his first August Ancestress, Amaterasu Ōmikami.

She herself, the August Ancestress, had been born of her father's left eye. The moon was born of his right eye, and that fearful god of storm and destruction, Susa no Wo, had leapt full-furied from his father's nose. Susa no Wo was the ancestor of the Izumo people and he had been banished from his sister's presence after a number of heavenly transgressions: breaking down the dikes between the rice fields, flaying a horse backward, defecating under the throne-mat of her ceremonial hall. And like their god, the clans of Izumo were denigrated and put down, pushed back by the dominant clan who sprang from Amaterasu as they ascended into the plain they called Yamato, pushing back their mountainous and forested boundaries.

All this was myth and ancient history. But it was written down just fifteen years before the birth of Moto-Ō by scribes who had to borrow Chinese characters to do it, for they had no written language of their own. Some of the modes of thought in this first history of Japan were Chinese also, as were the forms of government that had been adopted by the Yamato Court, the system of land distribution and taxation, the Buddhist religion and Confucian ethics, the arts and architecture and city planning—all in brilliant emulation of a civilization that surpassed all others in the eighth-century world, that of the T'ang Dynasty in China.

But the legends of the August Ancestors were Japanese, tales that came floating through the mists of memories, preserved by a people who did not know how they had come to these mountainous and quaking islands and presumed that it must have been from heaven when they were gods. Such treasures of the heart are incorruptible by any foreign influence.

Princess Abé learned the history of the Ancestors before she learned to read. There were attendants in the Court who, though they were low-ranking, even of common stock, were gifted with such intelligence that they could repeat aloud whatever they were told. It was said that whatever struck their ears was kept forever in their hearts.

A woman named Piyeda Aré was one of these. Her manner when she appeared before the Imperial Family was subdued, and her hemp cloth coat was acorn-gray, suitable to her station. Abé couldn't remember that she had ever seen her eyes, for she kept them fixed on her hands laid formally in her lap as she recited.

But her voice was beautiful, sometimes coming from her chest, sometimes from her throat as it rose and fell over the ancient words. When she finished and bowed low over her knees, the sweat dropped from her face onto the floor.

What Abé learned from her was that at the beginning of heaven and earth there were three deities whose forms were not visible. Next, when the land was young, resembling floating oil and drifting like a jellyfish, there sprouted forth something like reed shoots. From these sprang further deities, also invisible, until there were seven generations. This was the Age of the Gods.

At this time the heavenly command was given to two of the deities: "Complete and solidify this drifting land!" So these two stood upon the Heavenly Floating Bridge and lowered the Heavenly Jeweled Spear into the brine below, stirring it with a churning-churning sound. And when they lifted it up again, the brine that dripped from the tip of the spear piled up and became an island. The names of these two deities were Izanagi no Mikoto and Izanami no Mikoto. They were brother and sister.

Izanagi and Izanami descended to this island and there erected a heavenly pillar in a spacious palace. Izanagi spoke to his spouse asking, "How is your body formed?"

"My body, though it is well formed," she replied, "has one place that is formed insufficiently."

Then Izanagi said: "My body is formed with one place that is formed to excess. Therefore, I would like to take that place in my body which is formed to excess and put it in that place in your body which is formed insufficiently and in this way give birth to the land. How would this be?"

"That will be good."

"Then let us walk around this heavenly pillar and meet and have intercourse. You walk around from the right and I will walk around from the left."

They circled the pillar and when they met Izanami exclaimed, "What a handsome young man!" And Izanagi said, "What a lovely maiden!"

They began to procreate, and together they brought into existence all the islands and their natural phenomena: rivers and harbors, mountains and plains, trees and the wind. But when Izanami gave birth to the fire deity, her genitals were burned and she fell sick and died.

Izanagi, following his sister-wife into the land of the dead, did the forbidden thing and looked at her. Maggots were squirming and roaring in her corpse.

He fled in horror, pursued by the hags of the dead, and went to purify himself of this corruption. It was then, when he bathed in the pure river, that the ancestral deities of the clans were born. Among the last, when he washed his eyes, there came into existence Amaterasu Ōmikami who was the sun.

When he saw her, Izanagi rejoiced. He took off his necklace, shaking the beads so that they jingled, and gave it to her saying, "You shall rule over the Plain of High Heaven."

In the course of time, Amaterasu sent her grandson to rule over the Land of the Reed Plain far below. It was a land of darkness and disorder where many spirits darted about like fireflies at night and buzzed like summer gnats in the day, where stones and stumps and the bubbles of the water all had the gift of speech. She gave him the Three Sacred Articles, the mirror, the jewels, and the sword, and he descended, cleaving a cloud-path through the sky, to a mountaintop in Kyushu.

After many years again—1,792,470 years exactly—there began the Age of Men when Emperor Jimmu, descendant of that god, was guided across the water by a bird-man riding a tortoise's back and through the mountains by a giant crow until, after many encounters with strange earthly deities, he came to a fair valley encircled by sacred hills. Doubtless it was the center of the world, so he built his palace there and established the power of the Heavenly Sun-line on the Yamato Plain.

Emperor Jimmu was the first of all the emperors of Japan. He lived 137 years. Little Moto-Ō might have been the forty-sixth, but he lived less than a year.

When the baby first fell ill they said it was nothing. No need to be alarmed. Yet Abé remembered clearly the fear she felt that night when she heard him cough. Earlier she had heard a deer call, out beyond the northern gate where the trees began, a call so lonely that she had crept into her mother's sleeping place. It was later that she heard the baby cough and woke to see the glow of lamplight in an unaccustomed place. There was the sound of murmuring, and shadows grew on the curtain beside her head. She reached out for her mother and found the coverings flat. And after that she could not move. When she tried to call out, no sound came. She lay in terror, paralyzed, and heard that small metallic sound: the baby coughing.

Next day the sun was shining and the doctors said it was no more than a sort of croup. The herbalist ordered a little ginger to be mixed with his food and soft-boiled leeks to improve his appetite if he languished. But later, when the Master of Medicine came from the Yakushi-ji temple he looked more grave. He was a student of Chinese medicine and prescribed what he called the divine herb, the root of the ginseng plant. He also suggested that it might be wise to call an exorcist.

The Emperor was alarmed. He ordered 177 images of the Merciful Goddess Kwannon to be made and 177 copies of the Sutra of the Golden Light to be distributed and read in all the temples of the inner provinces, with processions of drums and banners around the Buddha images one full day.

During the summer months the little Prince grew worse. He was no longer fat and it was pitiful to see his little breastbone rising and falling rapidly in the warm, clove-scented breeze of his nurses' fans. On the tenth day of the Tenth Month, the Godless Month—that time of year when the ancestral gods were absent—the Emperor held a special ceremony for the health of his little son: a Meeting to Liberate Living Beings. All the ladies and the noble gentlemen of the Court opened the cages of their singing birds and insects and set them free. Even in the distant countryside, hunters and fishermen were taking in their traps and nets and letting loose their hawks and cormorants.

Abé went into the garden and untied the thread from the leg of the little russet sparrow she had tamed. His fluttering made her clumsy and she took a very long time. The shock of their little struggle, his scratchy flapping and his frightened flight, made her cry out. He had left some tail feathers in her hand! When she ran weeping to her mother, Kōmyō smiled to comfort her and smoothed her hair. "You mustn't cry about your little bird. He will be free and happy now. That is your good gift to him."

Of all the teachings of the Buddha, her mother spoke most often about charity. Almsgiving was the first of the six virtues every true follower of Buddha must practice. Whenever she came into possession of new rice lands or taxes from additional households because of a rise in rank or a special gift, she always made over a portion to a temple or temple hospital. She was so generous, so pure, as Shihi frequently said, she was like a bodhisattva in her lifetime, a living saint.

Now she told Abé about the loving charity of the Buddha Sakyamuni. Sakyamuni, when he lived as a man, she said, was like a footprint of the Eternal Buddha in the world. He was the embodiment of selflessness. And that is true charity, she said. Furthermore, in all his previous lives he had practiced good. Otherwise, in all the aeons of his incarnations, he could not have reached Buddhahood. Could Abé understand that?

Then she told the story, holding her daughter close, of the Buddha in an early life and the hungry tiger. "He was walking with his brothers in the wood," she said, using the special voice she used for holy things, "when they came upon a mother tiger with her cubs trapped in a deep ravine. The tiger was starving, and the cubs too would die if she did not find them food. The brothers felt pity. 'What are we to do?' they asked. And they answered, 'There is nothing we can do.' But the Blessed One took off his coat and handed it to them saying, 'Take care of our parents.' And then he flung himself into the ravine and stretched out his body so that the tiger and her cubs might eat and live."

The story so frightened Abé that she hid her face for a long time. "That is true charity," her mother said. And Abé, behind the blackness of her clenched eyelids, wished that she could be a bodhisattva too, and fling herself into the tiger's jaws. But the vision of yellow fangs and torn red flesh, the imagined smell of meat, was too horrid and she shuddered.

"There is nothing to be afraid of," her mother said. "Why must you be so tense?" Not for the first time recently, there was impatience in her voice.

It was the next month that the baby died.

The funeral rites were so extensive they exhausted the whole Court. During the farewell procession to the Gate of the Scarlet Bird the Emperor nearly collapsed. Everyone down to the

Fifth Rank junior grade was there and wept for pity. No one could see if the Consort in her curtained palanquin was weeping, but her ladies said she had withdrawn into herself.

On the forty-ninth day, when the baby's soul would be finding its new resting place, the Hossō priest Rōben came to the women's pavilions to comfort the mother. The year had turned. A wind blew down from the mountains and across the sky and the sound of the wild geese riding it was like discordant bells.

Abé was resting with Lady Shihi when he came, and her mother was hidden behind her screen of state, though you could see the glow of her lamp where she was reading. The incense candle burned with the scent of aloeswood, telling the hour after dusk.

When Rōben stood in the entrance he seemed to bring the last light of the evening with him, though the ceiling was lost in blackness. He was a brilliant, gifted man, and an artist. It was said that he had been snatched up by an eagle when he was two years old and deposited on the steps of the temple where the High Priest Gien of the Hossō sect was in residence, and Gien adopted him and taught him until he became a Buddhist priest himself.

Now, as he stepped into the scented rooms, he brought the fresh air with him, although his face had a somewhat pallid cast and his expression was somber. When the attendants had set out cushions and a lamp for him and he was seated by the Empress' screen, the lamplight shimmered on his bronze silk shoulders and made a rim around his shaven head.

Abé saw her mother's lamp go out. Now it was dark behind her screen and no one could tell if she was listening or if she had retired, and for a long time no one spoke. At last Rōben began to tell a story, a parable.

"Once there was a young woman named Kisagotami, the wife of a wealthy man, who lost her mind because of the death of a child. She took the child in her arms and went to the Buddha who was staying at the temple of Jetavana. The Blessed One looked on her with sympathy and said, 'To heal the child I need some poppy seeds. Go and beg four or five poppy seeds from some home where death has never entered.' "

He paused to let the lesson take effect, but when there was no answer he went on: "And so the poor demented woman went out and sought a house where death had never entered, but she found none. There was no such house."

He paused again, but still there was no sign from behind the curtain and after a time he repeated with more emphasis, "There is no such house.

"At last she was obliged to return to the Buddha. In his quiet presence her mind cleared. She understood the meaning of his words. She took the baby away and buried it and then returned to the Buddha and became one of his followers."

Abé found the story so sad that she flung herself into Shihi's arms, and Shihi, holding her, could feel the little winglike shoulder blades moving convulsively. But from behind the screen there was no sign. Only silence.

When Rōben went to see the Emperor he found him still in the muslin robes of mourning and with his face so pale and distraught it was impossible not to be moved. It was at the time of the morning roll call, just before dawn, and Shōmu lay half reclining with his head leaning on the armrest of his couch. To Rōben he looked like a child or a doll, much smaller than he knew him to be, with his wrinkled clothes and his hair sprouting fanlike from the loosened comb.

The Emperor was grieving for his son. But Rōben knew, and all the high Court nobles knew, that there was more to it than that. Ever since the eminent statesman Fujiwara Fuhito had given his adolescent daughter to the young Crown Prince, the goal of their union had been to produce a son. There was no fixed rule to the line of succession, and throughout history both male and female sovereigns had ruled with equal strength. But a certain pattern had been set by Shōmu's grandfather: that the line descend to an Emperor's own son or grandson, and if the boy was under age that the throne be held for him. In this way the sovereignty was held for Shōmu's father by his grandmother. And in Shōmu's own case, after his father's early death, it was held first by his grandmother and then by his aunt. It had seemed to him a serious filial fault not to produce a son.

Some of the Court had tried to comfort him by reminding him of Lady Hiro's boy, a bright and endearing infant now having passed his first New Year. A son by a second wife or concubine would be acceptable. But Lady Hiro's boy was not a Fujiwara, and the pressure of that family was very strong. Moreover, Kōmyō's hold on his heart was such that he could not picture any child but hers as the *Kōtaishi.* It was his dream, his determination—and hers too—that the next emperor should be their son.

That was why he had made Moto-Ō the Heir Apparent even before he saw him. And that was why, in the following months as the child grew in strength and beauty, his gratitude to his wife increased—as did the subtle pressures of the Fujiwaras to reward her.

When the baby was ten months old, therefore, he had an edict drawn up by the secretaries of his Central Ministry announcing the elevation of his consort to the First, the full Imperial Rank:

"*Inasmuch as an Imperial Prince has been born as heir to the Heavenly High Seat,*" they wrote, "*He was pleased to appoint the Lady Fujiwara, who was the mother, to be Empress.*"

But when the edict was presented to the Grand Council there were objections. Such an elevation was unprecedented. Prince Nagaya-Ō, the Great Minister of the Left, pointed out that only those of Imperial family could occupy the Heavenly High Seat. And the Fujiwara family, he reminded them, was not of the Imperial clan, being descended from a lesser deity as was written in the Record of Ancient Things. Nagaya-Ō himself was an Imperial prince, grandson of an emperor, as well as Great Minister, and the others listened and came around to his way of thinking.

Now Rōben sat by the Emperor's couch trying to comfort him. Nearby, some of the nobles of high rank sat ready to be of service. Since these were men of venerable age and many of them princes, they were not compelled to keep a rigid silence or formal pose and some of them whispered, some nodded on the verge of sleep. In a dark alcove priests were reading a sutra, their voices muted.

The younger officers who were on duty in the Court drooped in their places by the door and some, half hidden by a pillar or a screen, shifted from time to time and stifled yawns. But some, like young Fujiwara Nakamaro, took their duty very seriously and sat immobile through the long night hours.

When a man like the Great Minister observed Nakamaro something like wonder filled him. There he sat, firm as a stone, his face set sternly and his brows pulled down. His hands which he rested on his knees were clenched into fists so that his heavy shoulders were thrust forward.

Nagaya-Ō himself sat by a pillar close to the Emperor's couch. The lamp in the bracket above his head cast hollows in his cheeks and he looked frail. He gazed at Nakamaro, half amused, then closed his eyes.

At the sound of the roll call some of the young men rose, bowed stiffly, and withdrew, though Nakamaro stayed unmoving in his place. The Emperor stirred and straightened as he heard the twang of the bowstrings and the calling of names in the dew-soaked yard, the sound of footsteps as those released went home. He looked around the room with swollen eyes. There was an imprint of the embroidered armrest on his forehead.

Nagaya-Ō opened his eyes, though he did not lift his head. He saw the pale young face and the red imprint on his brow, so pitiful. He spoke to comfort him, using the words of a familiar verse:

> "If my sorrows are too heavy
> to be shared with friends,
> How shall these shoulders carry them
> alone?"

Shōmu turned to look at him. The verse brought another to his mind. He knew the poet well and that he had written it on the death of his own son, "born of us two, our dear white pearl." With an effort he recited the envoy, though his voice was strained. He had not spoken for many hours and his listeners were moved to tears.

> "So young, so young, he will not know the way.
> Courier of the world below,
> With offerings I beseech you,
> Bear him on your strong back
> Along the road to heaven . . ."

The poet's child had slept between his parents like the three-stalked plant, the bud between the bracts. It was a long time since the Emperor had shared his bed. He turned and asked for his writing box and took a sheet of heavy pine-bark paper. He waited while a boy-servant rubbed the ink stick on the stone. Then, dipping his brush he wrote: "Perhaps he is already carried on that strong back . . ." It was time for the little soul to find its new habitation . . .

He sighed and hastily wrote below:

> Even the wild ducks skimming
>   the shore of the pond of Karu
> Do not sleep alone . . .

He folded the paper and looked around for a proper messenger to carry his letter to the women's palace. Then he saw young Nakamaro, sitting so stolidly by the door, and beckoned him.

CHAPTER III

As Nakamaro crossed the bridge to the women's quarters the thud and scrape of his heels on the boards brought the carp gliding to the noise. The sun was rising and a silvery haze hung on the water. Transparent rays came slantwise under the narrow roof and lit on the bright green silk of his Court costume, freshening it. There was no sound but that of his own steps.

He did not break his stride but went on steadily, the letter tucked in his belt. He had come this way to visit his aunt's pavilion many times. As a boy he had been welcome to come and go in the women's rooms. Now that he had passed the age of manhood—he was eighteen—he was constrained to be more formal and await a summons or send a request for an audience. But as he was on a mission for the Emperor, he trudged on stolidly.

He took the incline to the veranda walk at that same steady pace, eyes straight ahead as though on some mountain trek, and was startled to have his cousin Abé suddenly run at him. She stopped abruptly, as surprised as he, and blurted out a greeting. "We are all very sad here," though she looked less sad than flustered. "Why did you come?"

She had knocked against a tub of *hagi* flowers by the veranda rail and some of the scattered blossoms had stuck in her hair. Her greeting was so abrupt that Nakamaro scowled as he stared down at her. Why was she running about in her nightclothes?

"Don't frown," she said. There was a curious pleading in her eyes and Nakamaro really looked at her for the first time. The Imperial Princess, after all, was one of a dozen little cousins in and around the Court.

The tiny, fragile flowers trapped in her hair were wet with the dew and already curling in upon themselves. She brushed at them quickly, pushing her hair from her forehead with her palms.

She is quite charming after all, Nakamaro thought, with the scattered blossoms trembling on the narrow shoulder of her little gown and lying about her bare feet on the boards. There was an eagerness, and yet a childish vulnerability about her. "How old are you?"

"Almost eleven."

Almost a woman. But there was something breakable about her, easy to crush. He found the thought disturbing and hoped that she would grow to be more like her mother.

"I have a message from the Emperor," he said as he brushed past her.

For Abé the morning had been unpleasant. She had waked early to the sound of the roll call far away on the parade ground. It was a strong, comforting sound and she sprang up and ran to see if she could peek at some of the men dispersing, coming along the east walk toward the headquarters of the Guards. But it was dark, the shutters were still closed, and she bumped into things as she ran barefoot through the shadowy room. She had forgotten they were in mourning. And she had blundered into the alcove where some of the ladies were sleeping, dim mounds of coverings and tangled hair.

Before she could back off, Lady Shihi rose and angrily seized her by the shoulders and spoke into her face: "Little girls should be obedient and gentle," while they all lifted up their heads in the dark to stare.

She turned and ran from them—and she had torn a corner of the curtain as she ran. Another bad mark. In dismay she spun around to see their dark shapes rising, staring after her. And she had turned again and, pushing on the heavy door, had run out onto the veranda in the silver dawn. And there was Nakamaro!

He was coming toward her and she saw his shoulders rocking to his stride. The wings of his Court cap jogged above his ears, and he was frowning. What is wrong with me? she thought wildly, staring up at him. His eyes were like those flat black stones from the Otomo shore. They didn't tell her anything, and he looked away.

At the door he stopped to peer inside. It was like night in there. Across the room, behind the curtain of his aunt's resting place, a lamp was burning. The feel of the dawn had just begun to penetrate and he saw dim figures of attendants moving about. He tapped and waited, tapped again, until at last someone came, moving reluctantly and hiding her sleep-smudged face with her sleeve.

"I have a message from the Emperor," he said. He handed it to her and as she turned away he stepped inside.

Abé crept after him and slid behind her favorite screen that stood beside the door. As always, she felt safer there, comforted by the deer. They stood with their noses almost touching over a flowering bush and were like sisters, she thought, whispering secrets.

Nakamaro felt quite sure his aunt would receive him if she was awake. He was her favorite nephew, the second son of the eldest of her four brothers, and in spite of the bluntness of his face with its smooth full eyelids and broad cheeks, he had a clever and intuitive mind and a tenacious sense of purpose. In that, he took after his famous grandfather, Fujiwara Fuhito, who had held the power behind the throne of five sovereigns and steered the tortuous line of succession through nearly half a century. Through it all, Fuhito had guarded his own position as the powerful head of a powerful and growing family of Imperial ministers and consorts. Four of his sons held high positions in the Court and he had given two of his daughters to two successive emperors to become their recognized wives: the eldest to Emperor Mommu and the younger, the beautiful Kōmyō, to Mommu's son, Shōmu.

Of all the cousins of the next generation, Nakamaro was perhaps the most ambitious. His elder brother, Toyonari, was both bright and winning, and this had sharpened Nakamaro's competitive nature but had taught him caution. At eighteen he already held the Fifth Rank upper grade, and was a captain in the Inner Palace Guard. His duties were not so military as ceremonial; there was little need for military men when he was young except for an occasional expedition against the barbarian Ezo in the far north or the Hayato tribesmen in the west. And a young man of good family with so promising a career was not sent so far from the Court.

He would have made an excellent soldier had the times been warlike for he was a natural commander, and with his strong back and stocky legs, he was an expert horseman and excelled at the archery games, shooting both from the saddle and on foot. And when he played at football or danced in the Court festivals, he showed an unexpected grace and dignity. Even when he entered his aunt's room in the darkness and crossed to the mat that had been put down for him, he had that same control: head poised, back upright, and fingers straight at his sides.

From where he sat he could see through a crack in the curtain. The colors of the garments piled about glowed and shifted in the lamplight when he moved his head. He glimpsed the sloping shoulder of his aunt's soft robe, the long line of her hair as it fell beside her cheek. Her head was turned away. He assumed that she was reading the letter and that he was to wait for her reply, but she did not call for her writing box.

He was surprised to hear her murmur, "Later." Then to him: "Nakamaro. Do you know the nine causes of untimely death?" The pause was very long before she prompted him: "In the Sutra of the Master of Medicine."

He did not. Although he was well educated in the Chinese classics and Court practices as well as all the arts, he had left the reading of sutras to the nuns and priests. He knew of his aunt's scholarship, but not that she had actually been reading so difficult a book. Even the priests seldom read more than a cursory page or two at the rituals, as he understood it.

"Not yet," he stammered, wondering if she really expected it.

Why should he read the Sutra of Yakushi, the Healing Buddha? He had never felt ill.

Kōmyō turned in his direction and he caught the glimmer of her face, round and pure as a melon in moonlight, before she turned away again and the black hair curtained it. "Nine causes of untimely death," she repeated.

He waited, trying to divine them, until she spoke again.

"First, there are patients who die for lack of medicine." Her voice changed and she added, "But he had the very best—from China and from our own gardens. It could not have been lack of medicine."

Nakamaro scowled as he had scowled in the Emperor's rooms. There was too much grief. "Please do not grieve," he said.

"And there are those who are put to death for punishment." She spoke as though she had not heard him. "And those from drunkenness. Some die by fire, some by drowning. Some are killed by wild animals. Some fall from a precipice. Some die from hunger or thirst."

She had spoken rapidly in her clear, cool voice, but now she paused for a long time.

The silence was disturbing to Nakamaro. He was accustomed to having his aunt read his thoughts, but he could not read hers. What was she trying to say?

"You don't ask the ninth cause."

"Weren't there nine?" He felt that his question was stupid, and he was not accustomed to feeling at such a loss. But she had spoken so very rapidly. He shifted where he sat, like a small boy.

"Some are killed by magic spells or demons."

"Well, of course." Of course there was magic, possession by evil spirits. That's what the exorcists were for. It was obvious she was thinking of her son with all this talk of dying. But he was a baby. What sort of demon would have entered so small a child? "But he was a baby."

"He was the Heir Apparent."

Perhaps it was possible. Nakamaro was dubious. Perhaps there was jealousy, a jealous spirit. Moto-Ō, of course, had been selected over Lady Hiro's little son, but that was expected. Even if the Emperor had favored her, it was unlikely he would think of putting her son forward. "Yes, there is jealousy," he said. "But it would seem unlikely that her son . . ."

"No, no. Not that one." As usual she had read his thoughts. "She has neither the skill nor the power. She is of no consequence to me."

With her quick movement he had sensed the weight of her hair as it shifted with a faint whisper on the bed garments, and he smelled the scent of patchouli, like the scent of violets.

"There is only one man who hates me and has the power. The Great Minister of the Left."

What was she saying? Nagaya-Ō? It was true he had the power. But vindictive, cruel? A man so respected? So devout a Buddhist and a poet of such learning? He stared at the crack in the curtains, trying to see her face. She had said demons and magic spells. Yes, the Prince was skilled in all kinds of Chinese lore. It was possible . . . But such a man?

Again she read his thoughts. "You do not know what sort of man he is. I have a report." Her voice remained as light and cool as before. "Only recently the Great Minister was seen at the Gango-ji temple when the priests were offering food for the poor. He was aloof, as usual, and carrying his ivory rule of office, and although the priests welcomed him he responded very briefly and did not say why he was there.

"A wandering homeless monk came up to him to beg. And the Prince without a word of warning struck him on the head! I was told that the poor monk stared at him a long time without speaking. The blood was oozing from the cut where the Prince had struck him. He said nothing, but there was prophecy in that look. There is no doubt among those who saw this that the Great Minister is a cruel and bitter man."

Nakamaro's feeling for his aunt bordered on awe, but even so he found her story difficult to believe. A man of such rank, such reputation, to act in this manner. Was it possible?

When he left he passed his cousin hiding by the door. She seemed so tremulous, looking up at him, that he wondered if she had overheard and whether she understood. Pausing, he spoke rather brusquely, although she had not asked, "There is nothing to be afraid of," and walked on.

It was not long after this—on the tenth day of the Second Month—that two men came to the Palace with information that Prince Nagaya-Ō was engaging in heretical practices and that he plotted to usurp power. Their rank did not permit them to enter the inner Palace grounds, so their message was carried by Nakamaro, who was on duty.

Immediately the City Guard was put on the alert and messengers dispatched to all the barriers outside the capital. And at midnight a company of Palace Guards was sent to surround the mansion of the Great Minister of the Left.

When the plum blossoms
Have fallen,
Are not the cherry trees
Ready to bloom in their place?

After the death of Nagaya-Ō the spring and summer went by. The cherry blossoms followed the plum and the lotus rose from the mud, until it was the season for "the flowers that blow in autumn fields." That is to say it was the Eighth Month when an Imperial Edict was proclaimed before a large assemblage in the Great Hall of the Eight Ministries.

As the day was warm, the bamboo shades had been rolled up and a dry breeze brought the shrilling of cicadas into the room. All the Court from the Fifth Rank upward had been assembled, each in the place that was marked for him. Their costumes ranged in color from the light blue of the lowest rank, through the shades of light and dark green, red, and grape color of ascending ranks to the deep purple of the highest. To Abé, looking out at them, it was like a garden.

She sat on the dais beside her mother and the Emperor but somewhat apart where she could watch them through the tears of her excitement. Their feet were hidden beneath the pyramids of their layered robes and their hands in the folds of their sleeves. Only their faces, beautifully painted, looked out expressionless.

The Emperor wore a crown of thin gold leaves with a rock crystal shaped like a rising sun. Its rays were made of silver wire hung with pearls and coral tube-beads and gilded copper balls. Her mother wore carved flowers made of jade and ivory and her scarf was of the gossamer silk that they called dragonfly's wing. They were so beautiful that many in the hall besides the little Princess wept. And then their radiance, seen through the prism of tears, was truly godlike.

The edict had been prepared by the officers of the Central Ministry and was read by the acting Prime Minister. The words he spoke were as though spoken by the Emperor—Imperial words chosen for their antiquity and elevation. And he placed his voice high in his throat, dropping his chin and filling his chest with air before each phrase. Then as he raised his head the sounds issued forth prolonged, authoritative, full of ritual music—though his sibilants were sometimes lost in the cicadas' shrilling.

"He commands, saying: Speak the words of the Sovereign to the August Children and to Ye, O Princes and Ministers . . ."

And recited how the Emperor had now been six years on the throne and it was not good for him, the Lord of the Realm-Under-Heaven, to rule alone, but even as in heaven were the sun and the moon and on earth the mountains and rivers, so must the head of government have his helpmate.

Further, as he recalled, when the Fujiwara Princess was bestowed on him, his mother had admonished him: "Are all women alike? No, I remind you, when you take this woman remember the minister her father who served the Sovereign House for many generations with a pure bright heart. And if she is without mistake and without offense, reward her."

Therefore for six years he had tested her and found her without fault. And now, before this august gathering, he bestowed on her the full Imperial Rank of Empress, so that together they might rule and govern the Realm-Under-Heaven.

He finished and sat silent in his place and no one moved or made a sound while the slow drums began the ceremonial music. Some, while the wavering melodies of the flutes and the *shō* rose up and wandered off in the warm air, remembered Nagaya-Ō and his fate and kept their eyes cast down.

Only the little Princess, feeling some aura of doubt waft through the room—or perhaps some unremembered, unnamed fear, the words "untimely death"—began to shake.

"Why do you suppose she does it?" Nakamaro asked. He said it quite carelessly, talking to Shihi. But he was disturbed by Abé's extreme sensitivity. He could see that her parents had in mind to make her the Heir Apparent. "You saw in the Great Hall . . ." His voice trailed off.

But Shihi only answered in the same careless tone. "I wonder. Why, do you suppose?"

"What sort of unfriendly spirit could it be, I wonder."

"That's what I wonder too, if it *is* a spirit." She didn't look at him. "She has always been a high-strung child, you know. So I only say *if* it's a spirit. There is no certainty at all!"

Neither mentioned the Great Minister of the Left nor the name of his wife Kibi who had starved herself, nor the four boys. But it was whispered around the Court that their spirits were restless. The ashes of the mother and the sons had been properly interred with all the rites and mourning ceremonies suitable to their rank, but the bones of Nagaya-Ō himself were sent away because the remains of criminals could not be kept within the capital.

The urn with the ashes and small bones were sent to Tosa "to be forgotten" as the order read, but they did not rest there and the people of Tosa suffered. During the next rainy season there was flooding and a cave-in of the lands along the coast. Some of the fisherwomen burning seaweed there for salt were crushed. Next year there were earthquakes coming from the northeast quarter, and still later a large thunder-tree floated in to land and caused a pestilence.

In Nara Lady Tachibana, the Empress' mother and widow of Fuhito, fell ill and the doctors could not put a name to it. They called the exorcists and hung the room with charms. And when the old lady neither spoke nor moved nor opened up her eyes, Kōmyō lay down beside her in the curtained bed and held her in her arms all day and night.

After the death and mourning period she went very often into the little alcove of the West Pavilion where Lady Tachibana's personal shrine was kept and prayed before it, stretched out on the floor. Abé sometimes went after her and sat quietly, her face full of longing. As she had grown into adolescence under Shihi's hand she had calmed somewhat, but sometimes she laughed without reason and at other times fell silent with a pensive face and the tears came welling from her heart, though she could not say why.

When she followed her mother into the little shrine room she felt comforted. The shrine stood on its pedestal with the doors swung open to reveal the Amida Buddha of the Infinite Light. He sat on his lotus-flower throne with his hand uplifted gently as if to say, Do not fear, and the beautiful bodhisattvas who attended him stood poised on their long-stemmed lotus buds as though entranced. The tiny images of the newborn souls floating into his Western Paradise on the screen behind him were almost lost in the shadows of the box, but the gold of the Buddha, smiling and dreaming so peacefully, seemed to glow. Be not afraid.

I am not afraid, Abé assured herself. Nevertheless, she did not like to search the rooms for her mother and find her gone—or find her, after all, like this: just the dark blue of her mourning costume and the black scarf of her hair spread out along the floor.

There were evil omens that year, and unseasonable rains, until at last the bones and ashes of Nagaya-Ō were taken up from Tosa and moved to Kii no Kuni to be buried among the tombs of ancient emperors where they were quiet. And after a time things returned to normal in the capital and the Empress' household.

CHAPTER IV

When Abé was fourteen her mother gave her a small pavilion of her own. All the buildings of the Empress' palace had been refurbished and the offices enlarged after her elevation, and the rooms she selected for her daughter were in the sheltered east wing with its little garden. It was connected to the main pavilion by a covered corridor and a long protecting wall, but something about the way the sun came late over the low roof line made it seem remote. However, the Empress kept close watch on it. And Shihi was always there.

Five young ladies, girls of her own age, were brought to live with the Princess as her waiting women and companions. They were all well bred, the daughters of Court nobles and officials of high rank, and each brought with her one male and two female servants as was the regulation.

Kōmyō selected them for their elegant deportment and good looks and she would have liked it if her daughter could have had the same young years that she had when all the gay and important people came to her father's house and the young men vied to catch a glimpse of her before she had been given to the Crown Prince as his first wife.

Of course, she reflected, with a small ache in her heart, such a life was impossible for Abé. Other things were planned for her. It can't be helped, she thought. There is no help for it. But it saddened her when Abé asked her eagerly about the future and she had to remind her that our destinies are fixed for us in our past lives.

Shihi was more explicit when Abé, drooping by the veranda rail, complained that all the others had their admirers and that letters came for them but not for her. "You should be grateful to your parents for who you are!" she said. She felt that Abé must have accumulated a great deal of merit in her past lives to have been born into her position, for in her opinion the Princess had not shown much virtue in this one. "How can you question your mother's plans for you?"

It was amazing to her that a mere girl like this should have such elevation in her future—and to question it! Men were not important in Shihi's life and her own marriage had been brief. "Look at your great-aunt, the Empress Dowager," she said sharply, "and speak her name with awe. Did she go mooning for a man? Did she marry when she held the throne for the Emperor your father all those years?" She stood there in the long corridor beside the garden waiting for an answer until Abé shook her head.

There was a young willow tree in the garden, the weeping kind that trailed its slender branches into the pond. Shihi was not much given to poetry but the lines came to her mind, "Where the spring mist slowly drifts, the warbler in the green willow tree . . ." Something about the way the Princess stood with her head bent and one slender hand on the railing . . .

It struck her suddenly that the girl had grown quite lovely in these past few months. She had softened and that thin tense body, those skinny arms, she thought, had rounded. We shall make something of her yet, she thought, taking credit.

It was true that Abé had learned to walk when she wanted to run and to cover her teeth when she laughed, but the effort had left a tension in her, a kind of inner vibration, and no one could be quite certain that she wouldn't cry out suddenly, or turn and laugh. Many people were uneasy in her presence but at the same time they were drawn to her by that very hint of the unexpected.

She was leaning over the railing both because she would like to have run from Shihi and the conversation that gave her pain and because she saw someone across the garden she would rather talk to. Shihi, seeing her gaze, gave a quick smack of her tongue. It was the little Lady Saisho whom Abé favored but she did not.

Saisho was a small, somewhat disheveled girl with a quaint way of speaking and a round sunny face. Some of the other young ladies whom Kōmyō had gathered were so very shy and finely bred that the slightest attention so embarrassed them they were close to tears. But Saisho had been able to approach the Princess and even laugh with her from the very first. Her father was a distant cousin of the Empress, and Saisho had been brought to the Palace when he was selected as an envoy to the Court of T'ang and sent to China in the embassy of 732. She felt herself, perhaps, a little above the others. At any rate, she had made herself the Princess' favorite friend.

Now Abé watched her as she stood by a tub of trailing wisteria on the porch of her pavilion. She must have been aware that the color of her sleeves with their persimmon lining contrasted elegantly with the lavender blooms. She was arranging the branches in an intense, preoccupied way with her little head bent forward earnestly.

She is waiting for me, Abé thought. She gazed across the garden at her, at the veranda with its pretty flowers, and at the open rooms beyond. Her very own court. All the screens had been rolled up and the floor of the long gallery beyond the threshold of the narrow porch had been polished so that it shone like wax. She could look through the open curtains to the inner room where her own pale screen of state looked cool and clean and the freshly woven rice-straw mats were like airy floating islands.

How charming it is! she said to herself, her mother's voice in her ears. How very *elegant!*

It was, in fact, a very small pavilion, a mere appendage to the Empress' grand palace, but with its little garden it was charming and because so many young, just-blooming girls were gathered there, it had about it a sense of something impending, a quivering in the air.

Notes and sentimental verses—frequently folded into knots around a flowering stem—arrived by messenger for one or another of the young ladies almost every day. Some were quite frivolous, with no purpose other than to show off a witty phrase or fine calligraphy. But some were more serious, written with the hope of a liaison. Shihi set herself to supervise them all, keeping a balance between courtesy (the minimum courtesy at least of a reply) and caution.

(The men whom these young ladies actually saw—apart from those they might observe, peering through the curtains of their carriages at some parade or temple festival—were the Empress' major counselors and senior officials who had business at her Court. And of course the doctor-priests who could come and go in the women's quarters as they pleased.)

Abé, as she looked at Saisho across the garden, knew she was waiting for her and that she had a secret. She has received another letter, she thought, and before Shihi could catch her sleeve she had moved away. Saisho always shared her letters and was always amusing in her comments on the young man who wrote her.

For a long time she had been receiving messages from one, Fujiwara Hirotsugu, whom she scorned. Hirotsugu was the awkward and superfluous one among the many Fujiwara cousins and she laughed at his letters and never answered them, although she often left them lying about where others might find them. She said his ill-formed characters looked like bird tracks and that his verses were preposterous. They did not deserve a reply, she said. But he persisted over the months.

Shihi scolded her for a shameful lack of manners. "He will think we don't know how to behave here in the Princess' palace." She would have liked to see Saisho married off. "You must make an effort."

"The only effort I intend to make is to avoid everyone who bores me!" Saisho said this with a little lift of her chin as she turned away and glanced at Abé from the tail of her eye. At the sudden small explosion of Abé's laugh, Shihi left the room.

One time a letter came attached to a sheaf of field flowers.

When the messenger had left she took it to a shaft of light coming in from the veranda, for the bamboo blinds had been let down and the room was full of evening—almost time for lamps. She made such faces over it, holding it up and squinting, pursing her mouth, that Abé demanded to see it right away. They were alone together and she handed it across. "It isn't his own, you know. He copied it."

"Poor man," Abé said, still smiling.

"But why does he persist so, when I do not care!"

"It is probably just the work of his karma, something from the past," Abé said. "It's nothing he can control."

Saisho held the letter to the light, scattering the field flowers over the floor as she handed it across for Abé to read.

> "Though I am chided like a horse
> That crops the barley grown across the fence,
> I love and love—
> Never can I halt my thoughts of you!"

Saisho was watching her with a small smile ready, and Abé looked up and laughed. Could it be that he knew—or didn't know—that privately they had decided that Hirotsugu looked like a horse? They had seen him once at the archery contest and each had noted to herself the horselike quality of his long narrow face with the prominent teeth pushing out between his lips. At first they had said nothing, but it had come out in their secret conversations. "Like a horse laughing," Abé said. But Saisho, squealing, had corrected her. "Not laughing, cropping the grass. I've heard he has a very solemn disposition."

Now Abé said, "Do you suppose he knows?"

"He hasn't the wit for that. It is pure blunder."

Hirotsugu, as everyone who knew him said, was forever blundering. He was a very earnest young man, very ambitious, and resentful of correction—pushing for what he thought was due him without the tact or talent to win others to him.

Abé felt a twinge of sympathy. "He seems to live in a real agony of desire."

"But how can I answer such a thing?" She took the letter back and pushed it carelessly under a cushion where it would certainly be found. "Don't light the lamp!" she said suddenly.

It had grown dark and Lady Shihi had come in. It was her turn to light the lamps today, and she had entered without ceremony. To her the Princess was still a child.

"Don't light the lamp," Saisho repeated. "We like the dark."

"Then you'll have to light it later by yourselves," Lady Shihi snapped.

"It won't be necessary. We will be on the veranda."

"You may sit on the veranda if you like!" She turned to Abé. "You will please tell me when you are retiring. Some of us would like some sleep, after all."

"You needn't wait up," Saisho said.

"Young lady, it is not for you to speak for the Princess. She knows well enough that it is my responsibility." She caught the gleam in Saisho's eye. "And you needn't use that tone with me."

Abé too had seen that quick defiant look and it made her pause. She was learning to check her impulses and she had found it pleasanter to avoid quarrels. So she spoke soothingly, "Just for a little while, it's so close in here. You won't mind, dear Lady Shihi, for a little while?"

"Just remember that there are people waiting."

"Yes."

"It can be very tedious."

"We know."

Saisho had already slipped out onto the veranda, and when Abé joined her she saw that the fireflies were gathering in the dusk, winking their faint green lights in the dark foliage. The sky made a pale blue rim above the trees, but under the willow by the pond it was already night.

Saisho turned to her abruptly. "Let's have a firefly hunt."

"Now?" She jumped up and Saisho jumped up too.

"Why not? We don't have to wait to organize a hunt. It's always so stupid with so many people. Cramming ourselves into the carriages. And Lady Shihi is so bossy, calling out to everyone not to fall into the river! It spoils the mood."

"By the river?" Abé laughed.

"Not by the river. What are you thinking of? Right here. By the pond." She went quickly down the steps and along the path toward the little willow tree. Abé could see the glimmer of her summer robe moving swiftly in the dark. Beyond her the arc of hemp grass where it leaned over the pond was dotted with blinking lights. They were so beautiful, she thought, so coldly pure. And yet so unpredictable. Who could tell when they would stop or start? Suddenly she felt how much she loved them and she hurried down into the garden.

She paused for a moment, feeling the warmth of the night sky over her. There was no breeze, but a faint scent drifted from the hemp grass and she opened her arms to let the smell perfume her sleeves—like the poet-priests, she thought, gazing up into the sky, who scent their robes with the wind from the lotus pond.

Saisho called to her and she started, brushing the hair from her temples with that quick flat-handed gesture that remained from her childhood when her hair was short, although her hair was long now, almost to her heels. She wore it like the ladies of the Court, bunched at the top and with a long cascade falling down her back and bound with a cord between her shoulder blades. When she ran it swayed in a thick black streamer against the silk of her gown.

Saisho had caught another firefly and put him in her sleeve. A tiny glow appeared and disappeared through the thin material. How quick she was! To Abé their silent erratic flight was bewildering. She believed that she was as eager as Saisho to catch one in her hands—and yet, was it better simply to watch them, they were so beautiful. She stood perplexed and Saisho called out in the dark, "You have to be quick." She had caught another. "I have five," she called. "How many have you?"

At her feet Abé saw one nesting quietly. His glow was steady, only faintly pulsing like the slow breathing of someone deep in sleep or the long fluctuating notes of the *shō*. She stooped and put her hand out, watching him fixedly.

Suddenly she heard the sounds of the men dispersing after the evening roll call and the twanging of the watchmen's bowstrings against their elbow guards like the sound of a gourd being struck. She straightened among the fireflies and listened.

Saisho was clutching at her sleeve. "Someone is coming!" she whispered. Together they scurried across the garden and up the veranda steps and hid themselves behind the bamboo blind.

A man came walking casually, swinging his shoulders, past the long veranda walk and the light from the Empress' rooms. They peered around the screen to get a glimpse of him. "He's coming this way!" Saisho hissed. He had stepped down into their own little garden and was coming along the path.

"Oh, it is only Nakamaro," Abé said. But they kept quiet when he approached.

"Why isn't there a light here?" Nakamaro asked in a loud voice. "Have you all gone to bed?"

"He doesn't stand on ceremony," Saisho whispered, putting her face close in the dark. Abé could feel the sweet breath on her ear. The smell of the garden was still about them, caught in their clothing and their hair. It gave the night an air of strange adventure.

Now he had climbed onto the veranda and was sitting down, arranging his clothing and breathing loud enough for them to hear. How casual he was!

He began to tap on the lattice with his fan—not two feet from their faces. Saisho put her sleeve over her mouth and her shoulder trembled. What a situation!

"Why doesn't somebody come?" Nakamaro said at last. "I have some important news."

"What?" Abé asked, while Saisho bit on her sleeve to keep from squealing.

"Is that you?" Nakamaro asked. "Why are you sitting there in the dark? I would have thought you might answer me when I came all this way. Where is the Nakatomi girl? Is she there with you?"

What a way to speak, "Nakatomi girl," Abé thought. He thinks he can ignore the courtesies because I am only a child. She answered him coldly. "Why do you ask?"

"Well . . . It's very uncomfortable out here," Nakamaro said abruptly. "Why don't I come inside?" He could hear the rustle of the girls retreating and frowned in annoyance. He had never known his little cousin to be coy—although, in fact, he realized, he hadn't seen her in many months. Perhaps she has reached that stage, he thought, remembering his first wife when he married her, full of sudden changes. "Never mind. You can hand me a cushion. Is Miss Nakatomi with you?"

"Yes," Abé said. She slid a cushion onto the veranda and drew back.

"And something to eat."

"There is nothing here. The servants have gone to bed."

"At this hour? It is very early."

"Well, they are very old." She only said this for the sound of it. It wasn't true.

"And no one knows the news?"

"What news?"

This was not at all as Nakamaro had pictured it. He had thought of a warm reception in the young Princess' court . . . a girlish eagerness, perhaps . . . gratitude . . . "Well," he said at last, "it's only that the embassy's returned." He tossed the words off carelessly and sat staring up at the sky. Saisho's little gasping shrieks coming out of the dark at him were like the squawking of some raucous bird. Not at all the adoring looks, the little hands serving bean cakes that he had pictured.

"My father?" Saisho squealed. "Has he come? And who else? Where are they now? Will we see them soon? Tell us everything, dear Captain. Oh, it is so kind of you to come. Tell me about my father. Is he in the capital? Is he here?"

"Are you finished?" Nakamaro cut across her words. "Of course they are not here. The envoy's ship has put in at the island of Tanegashima, and a second ship has been sighted. That is all."

"Is the second ship my father's? Is he safe?"

"I suppose so. They will be setting out for Kyushu soon, I imagine. When they reach headquarters at Dazaifu we will hear more." Then he changed his tone and asked in an insinuating voice, "Are you anxious to see your father?"

"Well of course," Abé answered for her. It was obvious. Why ask?

"And then you can be married, eh?" He was still speaking to Saisho in that teasing tone.

They had thought Hirotsugu's infatuation was a secret, but the way Nakamaro spoke made them realize that it was an open joke among the cousins.

"I shall never marry!" Saisho cried out haughtily.

Abé glanced at her with a flash of anger. Of course she will marry . . . someone . . . sooner or later, she thought, now that her father is returning. But not I.

Nakamaro gave a little sound, but except for that they sat in silence for a long time and Abé wondered if he intended to say more. She could hear him making himself comfortable. Why did he remain if not to tell them? She felt her impatience rising but her curiosity was stronger, so she controlled her voice. "We would like to hear more about the embassy. If you please."

If you please. She sounded like her mother, Nakamaro thought. That same light, calm authoritative voice. She must have grown up while he wasn't looking. Her voice and manner seem to have developed quite a charm, especially in contrast to the pert-voiced Nakatomi girl. He liked women with a little self-control, though not so cool as his wife, perhaps. It was said in Court that his taste was low because of the kind of waiting women he spent the night with. But he chose them, frequently, without much thought to their wit or beauty but because they were convenient and were careful of his clothes and never wept after him.

"It is a long time since we have talked," he answered thoughtfully. "You must be quite grown now."

He seemed to move a bit. Was he trying to look at them? They were certainly not prepared to be seen, dressed as they were and all disheveled from running about the garden.

"Surely you didn't come to talk about my size, or even my age."

"Yes, you are right." He paused, and she felt that he was still staring at her.

"If you have no more news . . ."

He sensed that she was withdrawing and said hastily, "I came all this way to tell you about the embassy and you keep me waiting outside here with the bugs. At least I should think you might have the interest to stay here and listen."

"We are *very* interested in the embassy. You know that!" she burst out. Her voice was childish once again and made him smile.

"Very well," he said soothingly, as though talking to a child. "The messenger arrived at Court this evening. He reported that the ship of the Great Envoy had arrived at Tanegashima and all aboard survived. They made the trip straight back from China, where they were well received. They have brought many gifts. The ships the Chinese Emperor provided are even larger than our own, or so he said . . ."

Abé remembered the day the embassy set forth. It was her first trip out of Nara—across the passes of Mount Ikoma to the port of Naniwa. She had glimpsed the edge of the sea then, bright with waves, and the four red ships of the embassy riding the water.

At the Sumyoshi shrine she performed her first ceremonial duty as the Princess Imperial, presenting the sacred offerings of wine and mulberry cloth. And afterward she had sat on the high seat they had built for her and felt the sea wind moving her clothes. Below her on the sanded court the ritual dancers entertained the gods, slowly turning, rising, lifting their shining sleeves and dipping their bright bird-helmets east and west. And meanwhile her prayer went up to her deity-ancestors to keep the people of the envoy safe.

The ceremony lasted through the rise and swell of the tide. Then with the turn the four small ships cast off, trusting themselves to the unknown ocean, hoping to find safe landing somewhere along the coast of China five hundred miles away.

Now after three years they were returning.

"They are bound to bring back many interesting things." After another of his long silences Nakamaro was speaking again. He had stretched out on the veranda, making himself at home, and was lying with his hands behind his head, his head on the cushion, looking at the sky. "What do you like best of the things from China?"

Abé did not answer. She was thinking of the ships and of the men.

"The scents," Saisho said.

"And you?" Nakamaro was no longer interested in what Saisho thought. Her name and circumstances—and Hirotsugu's infatuation—had made him curious. But now he had heard her voice his curiosity had shifted to the Princess. "And you? What do you like best?" He wondered if she would answer as a child or a woman.

"Books," Abé said. She was not sure why she had said it. She too liked Chinese scents. Or she might have said games, or images of Buddha like the Amida of her grandmother's shrine. But she said books. Was it to please Nakamaro? To capture his approval? Her voice had an odd quality in her own ears when she said the word.

"Books? That's interesting. What books do you like?" There was a kind of amused condescension in his voice, an intimacy, and it was closer. He had rolled around as if to look behind their screen.

Abé drew back. The voice, the intimacy caught her by surprise. It was as though her body had been brushed by moths, leaving the tingle of their touch on her skin.

"What books?" And when she did not answer, "Which books? Why don't you tell me? Are you shy?"

"No." She was not shy, certainly. But why did she feel like this?

"Then why don't you talk to me a little? Why won't you tell me?" And when she was silent, "Tell me."

Tell me. Tell me. The echo of the words brought a dim memory of men's strong arms, their perfume and protection in the night. It was delicious and she waited for him to speak again.

"If I knew what books you like," he coaxed, "I could bring them. Wouldn't you like that? Would that please you? What books shall I bring?"

It was the same tone he had used when he said, Tell me. As though he said, Do you love me? Nakamaro!

Saisho had taken her hand in the dark and squeezed it. What should she say now?

For a long time there was silence. Then suddenly he jumped up and was standing with the shadow of his bulky back to them. He was looking off across the garden. Had she annoyed him?

"I must be going now," he said in that loud casual voice that he had used before, and they heard his feet on the path as he walked away.

"Has he gone?" Saisho said at last. She still held Abé's hand and now she took it in both of her own. "I think he likes you," she breathed.

"He is just a cousin. He has known me all my life."

"What difference does that make? He likes you, I am sure. Didn't you hear his voice when he spoke to you?"

"About books." Abé pulled her hand away. "He spoke to me about books." She rose abruptly. "I am going to tell Shihi we have gone to rest now, that she needn't worry."

Saisho rose hastily but she did not follow. It was better to stay away when the Princess' mood changed and her voice took on that tone.

Nakamaro had no settled destination but he walked as usual with that steady trudge through the garden and turned away from the bulk of the Empress' pavilion to follow the covered walk to the main Palace grounds. He could not go home because his house in the East Ward lay in a direction that was forbidden by his calendar today. And he was not inclined to visit the waiting women of the Emperor's bedchamber—though he realized his feet were taking him toward their residence.

He stopped, squinting up into the sky. It was dusted with stars and the scalloped line of the roof tiles cut a clean black border across it. Below him a firefly winked in the bush clover by the wall. He sat down, crossing his legs and tucking the skirts of his trousers under him. Deliberately, he fixed his eyes on the darkness of the foliage. When he caught the faint green flash of light—the little insect showing itself for an instant to his gaze—he felt a thrill as though he had glimpsed the face of a beautiful woman caught unaware.

She was growing up, he thought. Sometimes she spoke with the voice of a child. But when she spoke like a woman, the tones had entered his ears like the feel of honey tickling his throat. He made a little grunting noise of surprise as he realized how she had roused him. He remembered her eyes as a child, full of questions. He had not given them much thought before, the little Princess' eyes: without defense, translucent, very dark. One could look through them into her soul if one chose. Simply to hold her face between one's fingers and look down into them, one could force his way in deep . . .

He rose and stood a long time in the darkness of the walk, his broad back straight, head bent a little, hands flat along his thighs like a soldier under reprimand. His well-muscled body did not move, even his breath seemed stopped. Then he turned abruptly and walked back the way he had come.

When he reached the lattice screen where he had left her it was dark within. He tapped very softly with his fingernail and after waiting, listening awhile, he crept around it softly and got down, inching his way on his knees and feeling the mats and cushions that were left scattered on the floor. He heard a sigh, someone turning in her sleep, and crawled in that direction until his hands encountered the edge of a sleeping mat and the soft contours of a reclining form.

Someone sat up and gave a little squeak. It was one of the younger waiting women who was on duty in the room.

"It's all right," Nakamaro whispered, knowing that it was not. "Just let me speak to your lady."

The girl was frightened out of speech. The heavy bulk of his presence and his soft breathing seemed to paralyze her and she stared through the dark unmoving.

"It's all right," he repeated impatiently, giving the girl a push. She scrambled away like a small frightened animal and Nakamaro looked around in the dark for the curtains of the Princess' bed.

Abé woke at the sound of the little scuffle and lay perfectly still, feeling the presence of a man in the room. All at once, without warning, the thought of Nakamaro and the sound of his voice came flooding to her mind. Immediately she was ashamed. What was she to him? But it was he, she knew. She could hear him moving tentatively near her bed and smelled the warm scent of his clothes as she had smelled it when he settled himself on the veranda.

"Where are you?" he whispered, and she bit her lip. "Is that you?" He had heard a rustle.

But it was Lady Shihi, whom the waiting girl had roused. She came bustling, hissing, "What are you thinking of?" She knew right away that it was Nakamaro. "This is not some ordinary household where you may presume yourself welcome at any hour!"

Nakamaro decided to face the matter boldly. "I had thought we might talk a little," he said calmly, though in a very low voice. "We were conversing earlier . . ."

"Indeed, conversing! And what shall I tell Her Majesty about this conversation!"

"Quite harmless, I assure you. Harmless," Nakamaro murmured. "As you know, Lady Shihi, I am not a man to do anything improper."

Shihi, feeling that she had successfully averted a calamity, began to breathe. "I would like to believe you, Captain," she said, staring at the handsome outline of his head and shoulders as they emerged from the dark. She had always been friendly with Nakamaro. "I do believe you. But this is no ordinary household, as you know. This is no ordinary lady with whom you claim friendship. This is the Princess Imperial, as you know."

"I know, I know of course. The Princess Imperial must be protected. But she is not a child, you know. Surely she can speak for herself."

But Abé had grown suddenly cold to their conversation. She was uncomfortable with what she felt for Nakamaro—this strange fear and desire—twice in one evening! She was sure that she did not like him very well. And his presence now, how embarrassing! She pulled her cover up over her head and stopped her ears so that she would not hear them talking.

"Of course she can speak for herself if she has a mind to," Shihi said. "At a proper time."

Nakamaro realized that this formidable dame intended to keep watch, but still he lingered, partly to preserve his dignity and partly in the hope that the Princess would indeed speak for herself. "There is no need for you to keep us company," he said stiffly.

"And leave you to your designs?" Shihi was hissing once again. "What of my poor young lady?"

"I only want to talk with her." Nakamaro inched a little toward the curtain. "You don't intend to shield her all her life . . ."

"And you appoint yourself? You will surely get into trouble, young man, if you go on this way."

Abé had lifted the cover for an instant and almost laughed to hear these words. Nakamaro a young man! He was married, a father, almost ten years older than herself!

"Not at all, not at all. My intentions are quite honorable," Nakamaro murmured, while his hand groped for the curtain's edge so that he might part it.

But Abé, feeling the air stir, let out a little moan, and Shihi cried out, "Here! No more, sir! Her Majesty gave me charge of my young lady and she is not a plaything for a man. You have forgotten her position. It is time for you to go!"

"Well, I had thought that we were friends," Nakamaro said in his most touching voice, speaking at the curtain. "But Lady Shihi wants to throw me out, and I see that you will do nothing to protect me."

Protect him! What did he mean by that? How odd. How strange it all was, Abé thought. She was silent. And when Shihi, too, said nothing, a kind of penetrating stillness filled the room until the sound of a mouse in the ceiling grew very loud. At last Nakamaro rose to his feet and with what dignity he could summon groped his way from the room and the pavilion.

CHAPTER V

Abé did not want to wake when daylight came. She lay with her robe still covering her head until Shihi roused her with a note from Nakamaro. Her face was warm and pink, softened with the puffiness of sleep, and even Shihi felt a pang at her budding beauty when she looked up over the covers, her dark eyes shining with the depths of night between their smooth and slightly swollen lids. How very delicate yet warmly tinted her skin was, how moistly glistening the thick hair.

At the sight of the note she was flooded once again with those conflicting feelings of arousal and aversion. His close proximity had frightened her. But to be desired, to be desired at last!

The only one she told was Saisho, whom she summoned right away, and Saisho was delighted. But Shihi had decreed that there could be no question in this case of answering the letter.

As for Nakamaro, while he was still of two minds whether to send a second note, circumventing Lady Shihi if he could, or perhaps attempt another visit in the hope of better luck, the Empress sent for him and told him in her charming way—for he was still her favorite—that she and the Emperor himself kept watch on their daughter and he was not to trespass.

Later, when Abé made her morning call to her mother's

rooms, Kōmyō spoke lightly in her small cool voice of all that had happened as she heard it from Shihi, smiling placidly while she looked down at Abé and thereby diminishing to a trifling incident that strangely stimulating and yet troubling arousal in her daughter's life. "You must think of it as a dream, a dream in the night and nothing more," she said. "I have spoken to Nakamaro."

Now the interest of the Court turned to the news of the embassy. There was little enough yet, nor would be until the ships reached Kyushu, the westernmost of the main islands. And even then there would be no more than sketchy reports until the weary men themselves arrived in Nara several months hence. Meanwhile the ladies and Court gentlemen spoke vaguely of what they knew already of the great world beyond and speculated avidly on what they did not know.

Abé, at fourteen, could comprehend China and the great capital of Ch'ang-an, the exotic gifts the envoys would bring home, and the strange foreigners who might accompany them only as they touched her own life from time to time. It was not ignorance. Her education had begun when she was five years old with the Confucian classic on filial piety. She had read it frequently since then, had copied it, learned much of it by heart. She knew of course that it was Chinese, but she thought of it simply as universal wisdom. Confucius did not bring the reality of China to her mind any more than did the images of Buddha that had come from there.

She was not consciously aware when her hair was dressed that the style was copied from the T'ang Court ladies' though if anyone had thought to mention it she would have known it all along. And of course she knew that when she practiced on the lute she sometimes tuned it in the Chinese mode. But Ch'ang-an was simply a name to her, a symbol of elegance.

The embassy she knew because she had gone to Naniwa and glimpsed the red ships starting out. And she had seen many foreigners. The embassies from the kings of Silla and Paikche across the straits came to the Court with tribute almost every year. (When Abé thought of the presents these men brought she called them tribute. The bales of silks and brocade costumes that her father's envoys took to the T'ang Court she spoke of simply as gifts.) And there were many families even in high Court circles who boasted of foreign blood. Still, it was not the same . . .

When she thought, "not the same," the weight of her own inheritance settled down on her. She should have felt grateful, or exalted, she knew that. Only it was a little lonely to be alone . . .

When Shōmu received word that the envoy's ship had at last reached Hakata—the entry port to the empire on Kyushu—he ordered thanksgiving services in all the provinces. In every temple drums were beaten, flowers strewn, and processions of banners circled the Buddha images, while in private houses the parents and wives and children of those who were safe bowed and clapped their hands to their family gods and piled up offerings before their shrines.

In Hakata when his ship landed the envoy knelt and put his palms and forehead to the ground. His face was burned by the salt wind and it was wet with tears. Many times he had lost hope of seeing home again. The mast of his ship had snapped in a typhoon, and the ship of the vice-envoy was missing forty men. As for the other ships, they had not been sighted.

Three years ago when he set out, the four ships had carried six hundred men and he had known, as they all knew, that the chances were that two hundred would return. Two hundred might stay on in China and the rest be lost to illness, pirates, storms, and the demons of the sea. They had sailed without chart or compass, one hundred and fifty men in each small ship: the envoy and vice-envoy with their junior officers, their doctors, Shinto chaplains, Buddhist priests all sharing deck space with the secretaries and interpreters, students and student-priests, while around them the captain and his crew—the navigators, engineers, carpenters, and seamen—worked to keep the ship alive and the soldier-bowmen crouched below.

They had landed, beached, at widely separated points along the China coast and made their way across the alien land to the Court of the T'ang Emperor in Ch'ang-an. Now, in the journey home in the Chinese ships, they had been caught by the typhoon and plunged into the heaving heart of the sea. It had been forty days from the time they left the yellow waters of the Yangtze estuary till they came, miraculously saved, to Tanegashima. And now, at last, they were home.

Two of the men who came ashore at Hakata were returning to their homeland after eighteen years abroad. They had gone to China with the embassy of the Old Empress in the first year of Yoro, 717.

One was a small man with a curiously appealing face, rather knobby with prominent cheekbones and wide eyes and the wispy beard of a scholar. His name was Kibi no Makibi and he had gone to China as a student at the age of twenty-two and was returning now a learned man bringing gifts for the Emperor that he had gathered during those years spent at the center of civilization.

The gifts were a reflection not only of his Chinese education but of his own wide interests and bright mind. There were one hundred and thirty volumes of books ranging from history and government through philosophy and medicine to Chinese etiquette and Court procedure, each on its ivory roller with identifying tabs in green, vermilion, yellow, purple, and indigo. There were also musical instruments and scores; ingenious pitch pipes, drums. There was a solar calendar and an incense clock, an inlaid gameboard for a new game of skill and bows and sounding arrows with tips like lotus bulbs.

He stood now, feeling the ground tip under his feet, while he watched the laborers bring his chests and boxes from the ship. His eager face turned first to the ramp down which they staggered and then to the dockside and he called out to them to take care. He liked the way they bent their knees under the loads and chanted to keep their spirits up and made jokes. True Japanese.

"True Japanese!" He turned to the man beside him, the priest Gembō who like him had gone out as a student in the old embassy. He had returned after those eighteen years with a chest full of sutras and the purple vestments of a High Priest of Buddhism. The robes had been bestowed on him by the T'ang Emperor himself, an extraordinary honor. There was not a priest in Japan who had been granted this costume of the highest rank.

"Harmonious." Kibi was looking back at the lines of workmen and the way they helped one another. "Sympathetic." He was delighted to be home.

When Gembō did not answer he repeated, louder than before, "True Japanese!"

Gembō looked down at him. "What else?" he said. He was a tall man with a small head and a way of looking out from beneath very heavy eyelids that implied superiority, though it might have been merely his height. At times he could open his eyes wide to reveal a piercing, knowing look.

He and Kibi had seen little of each other in Ch'ang-an, as Kibi spent his time in the capital and Gembō with the priests in the mountain temples, but they were compatriots after all, and when they came together they spoke without formality like old friends. Now, when he said "What else?" to Kibi he looked down under his lids, but Kibi went on smiling while he watched the men. He was unaware that even as he stared at the laborers on the ramps he was being stared at by the villagers behind him. Gembō, though he was quite aware, chose not to notice.

To the people of Hakata, however, if these two seemed strange, at least they were not foreigners. What made them gape and laugh aloud were the fantastic men from distant lands who had returned with them—men with big noses and outlandish clothes. Too bad to have no more than a glimpse of them before they disappeared into the great box-carriages the governor had sent and were carried off to Dazaifu to be gazed at.

Dazaifu was the government headquarters and military outpost on this island nearest to foreign lands, and here the travelers were welcomed and—because of those foreigners—

discreetly screened until permission came for their journey to the capital.

There were among them two noted Chinese Buddhist priests, a famous prelate from India, a Persian doctor, and a tiny Annamite master of music and dance. The last three were the most exotic foreigners who had ever landed here. But if they were the objects of wild curiosity, they were themselves as curious about Japan.

As they proceeded through the island-studded waterways and the rough countryside toward Nara, they questioned Kibi (always courteously, masking their dismay) about his native land:

"What is that sort of gateway for, like a big bird roost?"

"What do those papers mean that are folded there so neatly?"

"Why do you use oxen for your carriages, not horses?"

"Our horses are for riding," Kibi smiled. "The 'gateway'?" They had passed a little Shinto shrine, a weathered torii on a pine-topped knoll. And there had been a sacred spot marked off by thick straw ropes hung with the folded strips of mulberry paper that symbolized offerings. How should he put it to these foreigners, how explain?

"Something awesome lives there," he said hesitantly. "A higher spirit . . ."

"Awesome?" they echoed, staring up a small worn path as they passed by. At the top stood two unpainted uprights joined by a flat crossbar. "Fearful?" The place was no more than a gentle rise in a quiet, empty field. "Some spirit to be placated? . . . Perhaps at night? . . ."

"Not placated exactly. Reverenced." What was the word? It was odd to realize how ignorant these learned men were in this respect. "Something of a higher nature touches us, you know. And we are made aware . . ."

"Gods?"

"Yes, gods you might say, but not as we know the Buddha."

"There seem to be a great many of them. In almost every field . . ."

Yes, Kibi thought, they are in the fields and in the sacred mountains, and in our homes. Suddenly he remembered his mother's hearth and her kettle. In fire and in water. And in our ancestors too, in a different way. It was difficult, impossible, to define the feeling he had had in childhood of a life lived among higher spirits, the reality of things unseen.

How to explain the mystery of that world, the awe and the sense of gratitude, the permeating presence of the *kami* of his youth. "We are a happy people," he said lamely, "so we are grateful."

They did not press him. They could see quite clearly how the people lived, the miserable dirt-floored huts, the worn old women permanently bent from working in the fields, the naked children, and the men with their scrawny shoulders bowed under towering loads. And yet they had to grant there was a gentle, even merry spirit among these Japanese, a smiling sense of peace.

And they had learned from months of association with him that Kibi no Makibi was not a man to be taken lightly. Kibi with his erudition and his clever mind had become a name even in Ch'ang-an. Because of their respect for him, some slight respect was added to their curiosity about the little far-off island of dwarf people that had produced him.

Their first view of the capital was from the side of Mount Ikoma where the forest stopped, and it had shown the little valley in its most tender season, softly green. Here and there were patches of golden rape-flower or the deep pink of legumes, and where the rice seedlings had been planted, silver water gleamed between the bright green shoots. On the far hillsides wild azalea made a froth of pink and white, and above them like reflections in the sky lay small white frothy clouds.

The city itself, encroached upon by fields, was tinted these same colors, for the willows gave a skim of green to the avenues, and late-blooming cherries dropped their petals on low roofs. To the foreigners—as they remarked aloud—it was an entry into a new world. Here was an ethereal city, touched by the softest spring, capital of an unknown and exotic people. And yet there were familiar things. The curved roofs of the city gates, the long straight avenues, the blue-green tiles of the palaces were all echoes of Ch'ang-an. But to find them here in this gentle valley—here beyond wild mountains on an obscure island in the middle of the sea!

"A centerpiece of civilization . . ." someone said. And Kibi, standing near, heard the unvoiced thought: "set in a wilderness." And when they continued on in the great procession that had been sent to escort them, and had entered the city through the Rajōmon and saw the central avenue stretching out—three miles to the Palace gate—he wanted to laugh with them at the presumption. This was not Ch'ang-an! But again, he wanted to weep for his remembered boyhood and his home.

He gazed up the broad, tree-bordered thoroughfare and remembered suddenly the saplings planted at spindly intervals along the muddy road when he had left. He looked for the clutter of construction sites where the mat sheds of the carpenters had leaned in the drifting rain—and he saw instead that there were gardens and warm houses behind the long earth walls.

When he was a boy he had frequented those worksheds, seeking out the foreign artisans among the foremen there, observing the rituals through which they taught their skills to their Japanese apprentices. It was then he had first heard of the Court of the great T'ang and the fabulous city of Ch'ang-an. Now he knew it of his own experience, with the familiarity of years. He knew the honey-colored light of its hot summers and the blue line of the mountains over the northern wall. He knew the life of the jade palaces and the conversations of learned men behind the moon gates of their flowered courts.

Over the years he had met with Buddhist missionaries who had traveled from India across the southern seas, and with Turkic Manichaeans, and Nestorian Christians and many other strangers who like him had come from around the world to that capital of culture on its broad gold plain at the heart of a continent. And now as he rode in the slow procession through this town of his, this home, built with such energy in this gentle valley at the end of the road, he thought back to its prototype, golden Ch'ang-an, and smiled.

Within the Palace he found that he was treated like the foreign guests, with deference and elaborate courtesy. This gave him an unpleasant feeling, for he had never considered himself anything but Japanese. But after a time some of the government officials with whom he dealt explained, smiling apologetically, that he had the patina of China on his speech and bearing. It was as though they said he had a smudge of dirt on his clothes—for all their admiration of things Chinese. After he became acclimatized, they assured him, he would be like one of them. But this too he found disquieting. He was no longer quite like them nor ever could be.

This was the man whom Kōmyō selected to be the tutor for her daughter: Kibi no Makibi, a man not of the capital but of a proven brilliance. It was an innovation to have such a man at Court.

Kibi himself was caught off guard by the appointment, not quite sure of himself in this context. When the summons came from the North Pavilion, he asked what he might expect of his royal pupil and was told, in confidence, that he might find the Princess eager but unpredictable, and sometimes difficult. How, "difficult," he asked. But the answers varied.

CHAPTER VI

On the bright spring morning when he was first escorted to the Empress' pavilions, Kibi was pleased to be greeted quite informally and assured that as tutor he would always be welcome. "Her Majesty is very intellectual." The senior lady who said this was speaking of the Empress, but she led him quickly through the pillared rooms toward an alcove where he was to meet the Princess.

The Empress' reputation was well known—for her charm as well as her intellect. Someone in speaking of her had used the verse, "If she but turned and smiled she cast a hundred spells." But of course he did not expect to be received by her so soon. Indeed, he was surprised to see her ladies sitting nonchalantly with their books and games and sewing work and surmised that he was to be put in the category of the doctor-priests who came and went without formality in the women's pavilions. A strange convention, he thought wryly. These men were no eunuchs.

The Princess was seated behind a standing screen—a curtain of thin silk on a persimmonwood frame—and he could see the outlines of her figure. She seemed very slim; her sleeves hung in a straight line from her slender shoulders. Ah, she is of the old-fashioned type, he thought. Again a poem came into his mind: "The brook was pure at the mountain source . . ."

Standards of beauty had changed in these recent years. He supposed that the T'ang Emperor's new concubine had much to do with it. (His mind had gone back to China as it often did.) He was told that Empress Kōmyō had the pure round flawless face and full plump figure that was favored there—and now here, he had noticed since his return. His impression of the daughter was of a maiden out of some old tale.

He waited a little for her to speak, but when she did not he recited a poem rather softly, looking off to one side. He did not want to seem too forward or to provoke that "difficulty" that people spoke of.

"Today the people in China
Float their little boats for pleasure
And sing songs . . ."

He chose this verse because it was the third day of the Third Month, the First Day of the Snake. Time for purifying oneself in flowing streams.

"Yes." She spoke quietly, but he thought he heard some surprise, even humor in her voice. "We too celebrate this festival. Of course."

"My mind went back to China."

"Mine went to this morning!" That morning she and Saisho had made small wooden dolls and marked them with their flaws and shortcomings and thrown them into the stream as she had done every year that she could remember. Now she was purified—or so she hoped—and ready for new things. That was why this day was chosen for the new tutor, this learned man from China. Having heard him speak as though she were a child, she thought perhaps she need not be afraid of him.

She had had many teachers before now. The very first was the old professor from the university who had come to her grandfather's house when she was five years old to conduct the ceremony marking the beginning of her education. She had worn the crimson trousers for the first time, and he had stooped before her to tell her the story of the dutiful son from the *Book of Filial Duty*, reciting the stanzas in a rolling voice.

"With sports and embroidered robes he amused his parents."

Since then she had learned it all by heart, of course, and had gone on to master much more of the Confucian doctrine and the *Thirteen Classics*. But the story was still vivid in her mind.

It was the same old teacher who had asked the opening question: "Do you know by what virtue the good emperors of old made the world peaceful and the people to live in harmony, the inferior contented under the control of their superiors?"

Abé had not known, and the professor answered for her, as he expected to: "The duty of children to their parents is the fountain from which all other virtues spring."

Then he had told the story of Lao Lai Tsu who lived in the Chou Dynasty so long ago, a man so old that he had lost nearly all his teeth but whose devotion to his parents was such that he stopped at nothing to make them glad. "At times he pretended to be a little child, dressing up in brightly colored clothes and frisking and cutting capers in front of them." The professor had waved his fingers in faint imitation of the old man's capers and some of the ladies present had raised their fans to cover their secret smiles. But to Abé it was all quite real and she listened solemnly as the story went on.

"Sometimes he would take up buckets of water to carry to the house and pretend to slip and fall, kicking up his heels and wailing. This made his mother happy and she laughed and clapped her hands.

"This was the way old Lao forgot his own age in order to make his parents' last years full of joy."

The professor had looked earnestly at Abé as he added, "If Lao Lai Tsu had not been so sincere, do you think his love for his parents would have been worthy of our imitation?" And when Abé, in her new trousers, stared back at him, he shook his head. "No, we must always be sincere in our love for our parents and strive to please them."

Though she had said nothing, Abé understood the lesson very well: Children should bring their parents joy. And as she grew older and sometimes sensed a sadness in her mother, or some distraction, she tried to do as old Lao had done, crawling and rolling on the floor and making baby sounds, but her mother was not amused. Was it because her love was not sincere?

The sting of that memory often returned to her, making her wince even as she grappled with the intellectual difficulties of the *Book of Changes* or the *Book of Rites.*

Now she wondered what this new teacher would ask. She felt she was well prepared in the classics and in poetry. She was ashamed of her calligraphy but proud of the way she played the lute. And she felt quite certain he would not concern himself with her drawing and embroidery and mixing of incense.

However, Kibi did not ask her any questions but only talked for a little while about China, feeling his ground. Then when he learned she liked to play the lute he promised to bring her one from Ch'ang-an so that he could hear her play.

It was not until the Fourth Month, seventh day, that the Bureau of Yin and Yang at last announced a propitious date for the envoy to return his Sword of Office to the Emperor and conduct the formal presentation of the foreigners. The whole Court was in a flurry over the event. No one, not the oldest official—not even the Empress Dowager—had seen men from such distant lands before. Of course even Abé knew of the Indian High Priest by reputation. It had taken years to persuade him to make the journey. But she did not know what an Indian might look like. And those who had seen the Persian doctor and the little man from Annam reported that they were truly astonishing.

Shōmu himself gave orders for the refurnishing of the halls. Everywhere new screens were set out and new curtains hung. In the gardens the streams and flower beds were rearranged. Because of the unseasonable rains the blossoms had fallen early and the gardeners were set to fastening paper blossoms on the cherry tree by the steps to the Ceremonial Hall.

As Princess Imperial, Abé would be present at the ceremonies, though she would not take part. "You are not to be seen," her mother warned, "but you may sit in the alcove by the door to the banquet hall. From there you can watch the proper Court etiquette for such occasions."

"Oh, may I take Saisho with me?"

"A few of your young ladies. But you must not move or make a sound. These are distinguished men from distant civilizations and they will be approaching the Imperial High Seat for the first time. We must be sure that everything is correct."

"You are not to laugh," Shihi chimed in.

"Why should we laugh?"

"And no fidgeting. You must take nothing to drink the day before and confine yourselves to a little dry rice on the day. There will be no bucket handy."

"I am not a child."

"Am I to call you a lady?" Shihi stared pointedly at Abé's face, which she had not powdered, and her eyebrows which she refused to shave.

"You are to address me as Madam." When she was angry, Abé's eyes filled with tears and the tears made her angrier still. Shihi arched her neck and put her head back, laughing in an artificial way, and Abé snatched up a scarf as the nearest thing at hand and threw it. Although it floated harmlessly between them, Shihi backed away as though it were a sword. "Careful, careful!" she called out.

"Oh, you are hateful!" Abé cried. But when Shihi left, she sank down by her mother full of remorse.

"You must be more considerate of Shihi," Kōmyō said. "She is growing old and quarrelsome—as I am."

"She is nothing like you!"

"Oh yes, though I try to hide from my mirror it does no good. Shihi confronts me with my image."

"Oh, never, never!" Abé took her mother's hands and kissed them. "Never like Shihi. You are so beautiful!" She looked up into that soft and perfect face with an open adoration that made Kōmyō smile.

"Oh well," she said, gazing down into her daughter's eyes. She looked a long time, very softly, then she said, "You shall have a new costume for the ceremony. An aster robe, I should think, with a blue lining. And you shall wear a crown of flowers that we will make together." She smiled again. "Would you like that?"

Abé nodded, shifting her eyes away. She is looking for some sign of beauty in me, she thought. Something to praise. She was not aware of the special vibrancy that made her beautiful any more than she understood the fine articulation of her bones—those fragile ivory-colored shafts of her slender fingers or the amazing intricacy of her small wrists—nor could she begin to comprehend the quick electric currents of her mind that gave such animation to her face and speech. She did not know that when she looked away from her polished mirror where she stared solemnly that her eyes glinted and her mouth quivered with expectancy any more than she gave conscious thought that inside her mouth were small white teeth washed with silver saliva and a warm pink restless tongue. In fact, she knew nothing about herself—and disapproved.

"Oh yes, I would like that!" She sat up, smiling quickly, brushing the hair out of her eyes and in that way hiding them.

Everyone of rank was to have new clothing, whether they were to attend the ceremony or not, and some of the Court gentlemen sent boxes with the silks of their robes and trousers to be sewn and scented by special friends. To some of the ladies this was familiar work and they went about it without comment. But others smiled and turned pink.

My very soul, it seems,
Has stolen into every stitch
Of the robe you wear.

Abé rose and went out on the veranda. Soon Saisho came and sat beside her looking very glum. A wicker box of clothes had come from Hirotsugu with a pleading note. When it first arrived, Saisho had jumped up in a fluster and cried out: "Who could it be? I have no lovers!" So they had all been looking at her when she saw the name on the note.

After that she had shut the case and simply stared at it. She would not touch the cloth until they pleaded with her not to be unkind. If he meant nothing to her, that was neither here nor there. Lady Shihi even snatched the trousers from the box and thrust them at her, but she merely scowled and jerked the cloth about and sewed the seams up in big stitches, not even caring if she got things back to front.

The very worst of it was that she knew—perhaps they all knew—that Hirotsugu would not have dared so intimate a gesture if he did not have the approval of her father. And the more worldly of them knew that the vice-envoy would surely welcome this connection with Hirotsugu's family. So Saisho was scowling, close to tears, as she sat by Abé looking out across the garden.

There were some men there moving rocks beside the pond and planting shrubs. They were country men from the annual work-tax levy who had been brought in to do the heavy jobs under the supervision of the gardeners. The noise of their rough speech and common laughter came across the water. They seemed as strange as foreigners to Abé and she stared at them, but Saisho sat frowning at her lap as though there were nothing in the world worth looking at. She was not aware of her drooping head or the misery in her face until Abé said quite suddenly, "Do you love me, Saisho?"

She looked up, startled and ashamed. How beautiful the Princess was!

"Do you love me?" Abé asked again. And when Saisho nodded wordlessly, wiping away her tears, she said, "Let us make a pact. Let's say that we will always love each other no matter what comes between. And even if we are parted, we will always remember that."

"I will always love you," Saisho said. "I will always love you! And I don't want ever," she went on, her voice breaking into a wail, "I don't want ever to go away."

But they both knew, of course, that very soon she would have to return to her father's house, perhaps to be married.

Nakamaro had stayed away from the Princess and the women's pavilions at the Empress' request. But on the day the foreigners were presented he caught a glimpse of the young ladies as they passed up the steps from the small garden of the Imperial Council Hall to the Ceremonial Hall of the Eight Ministries.

The Princess looked very charming in a crown of flowers and with her head bowed modestly beneath the billowing umbrella that her attendants carried. But then, the others were quite charming too, holding their round fans delicately before their faces and trailing the long panels of their skirts. He wondered vaguely why he had been so unaccountably attracted.

The girls went on and up the steps and into the side alcove that had been allotted them. It was far behind the rows of high Court nobles and officials who took their places to the left and right of the Emperor's High Seat, and because of the pillars and the screens in front of them, they could not see the Emperor or the great procession that was approaching across the outer court. But, to their amazement and delight, they saw the foreigners.

Leaning sideways to peer around the screens and crowding one another so that the scents of their garments rose in a mingled essence, they watched each stranger as he was escorted forward to be presented.

First were the two Chinese priests, big men, but not remarkable. But then the Persian doctor came—so fantastic in his conical hat and his long dangling curls! And then the tiny Annamese master of music and dance. He wore a bright pink tunic and red leather shoes! So charming!

Tears of wonder stood in Abé's eyes so that she saw them swimmingly as they passed by. Baromon Sojo, the Indian priest, the famous holy man, went undulating forward in a haze of orange robes. Such a dark and polished face! Such a nose! At the sight of that nose she drew back in a rustle of soft silk and looked at Saisho unbelievingly, her fan against her mouth.

It was different when the Japanese went by—the envoy quite magnificent in his ceremonial robes, and the vice-envoy too. Saisho, when she saw her father, raised her little chin. It was as though she had been an orphan until now, and here was the proof of her family, her rank.

Because of this she was caught off guard when she turned again to see the tall priest, Gembō, approach the throne. He was wearing the purple vestments of the highest priestly rank that the T'ang Emperor had given him, and the light fell sharply on the fine dome of his head and the golden borders of his long trailing sleeves.

To be sure he walked with assurance, Abé thought, and such robes had not been seen before in Japan, but what was the need, she wondered, for Saisho to stiffen so. She had laughed at the Indian holy man, at the little Annamite. But now the fan before her face stopped its quivering. Perhaps her breath itself had stopped, she was so still.

If the foreigners seemed strange to the young ladies, all of Japan struck the foreigners with amazement. Sometimes they questioned Kibi no Makibi, making him wince. On his return to Nara he had been disturbed to find an emphasis placed on elegance and a grand air as an indication of a man's virtue and education. Observing some of the high Court nobles he said to himself, "The man of honor thinks of his character, the inferior man of his position."

He was fond of such aphorisms and his own standards followed the Confucian pattern: "Virtue is the denial of self and the response to what is proper." "The superior man seeks what he wants in himself, the inferior man seeks it in others." And so on.

Still, it was disconcerting when such men as the Persian doctor thought to flatter him by remarking that in all his travels he had never encountered such "emulative talents." To encounter here, he seemed to say, so far from anywhere, this little replica of the great T'ang!

They were walking in the colonnade of the long Waiting Hall and Kibi turned his head away to gaze at the vermilion pillars and green window bars on the whitewashed gallery across the court. Patience, he thought. For how many years had he talked of his home to these men he met in China? Still they persisted in finding it amazing.

The Persian, catching something in Kibi's air, amended quickly, "After so long a journey . . ."

After so long a journey he had expected to find freaks or barbarians perhaps? Was not Japan as equally the center of the world as Persia? The others had spoken in this tone as well. The words they used were complimentary, and yet they buzzed a little. They remarked on the "diligence" with which the proper forms were followed. They found the people "courteous" and "clean." Had they expected to find dirt in the corridors? They were amazed, they said, to see such "energy," such "progress." Was there something, perhaps, they found a little comical?

Of course it was unthinkable that their remote, polite curiosity should denigrate the Emperor himself. But they felt quite free to comment on the Court and government.

"Is not the structure of the government patterned on the Chinese?"

"Quite so."

"Then what is this 'Department of Shinto' that seems to hold equal power with the Grand Council itself?"

Kibi smiled. Surely they were aware that the Emperor and all the high Court nobles could name their ancestors among the gods. Surely they understood that the welfare of a nation did not depend on men alone but on their accommodation with heaven. But aloud he only said, as though in apology, "It is our religion, you know."

"And your Emperor, of whom I speak with great respect"—the Indian priest was talking—"is he not head of your secular government as well as your religion?"

"As you say."

"A heavy burden?"

"Ah, perhaps . . ." Of course, it was obvious that the sovereign was burdened with the demands of both. How could it be otherwise?

Still smiling with deceptive affability, Kibi reminded them that in every nation it was the Imperial responsibility to care not only for the welfare of the people but that the winds and rain came in their proper seasons and the five grains ripened at their appointed times.

And as for the special problems of Japan, he did not want to frighten them but felt compelled to mention that the seas and skies were sometimes turbulent. "We Japanese," he smiled, "live all our lives with earthquakes and typhoons."

They did not let it go at that but pressed him to explain why although the government was, as you might say, copied from the T'ang where Court officials were selected on the grounds of merit, here it would seem that of the hundred men or so, as they were told—that is to say, of the Fifth Rank and up—who were allowed at Court all but a little handful were members of a few great families.

Yes, yes, he was quite aware that in Ch'ang-an even a poor boy from the provinces, given the proper education, could pass the examinations and rise up to the highest rank. And no, it must be admitted, here it was not quite the same . . .

What a painful conversation!

Kibi's smiling acquiescence broke out into laughter and he felt sweat on his palms. "We Japanese put too much stress on family! Too much tradition!" He stopped abruptly, though he kept the smile, and they went on to talk of other things. It did not cross his mind to tell them that he himself had reached his present rank through merit.

Alone, the foreigners were more candid. They had thought that with the envoy and with Kibi whom they had known through many adventures that they conversed quite freely. But alone together—even though they came from different lands—they heard their own voices fall into normal tones and realized there had been tension.

"What do you think of this Fujiwara family?" the Persian doctor asked. "The Emperor himself is a Fujiwara, is he not? Through the maternal side?"

"It is a very distinguished family." The priest was more careful.

"And the Empress, she is his mother's sister, I understand." In all his travels he had not come across a society so ingrown. "They seem quite tolerant of incest."

"The Emperor is a devout and earnest man. Sincere." The priest was frowning but the doctor did not mind. "He follows the Eightfold Path with diligence."

"Ah, diligence!" How diligently they had tried to suck his knowledge out of him. But not for nothing was he known as the Secret Healer. "Nevertheless, devout or not, the Emperor has been surrounded by this powerful family."

"It is not unusual for a ruler to choose his own men to advise him."

"Not unusual. But in this case the sovereign has not chosen men for their proven ability, not even from the most ancient families, but rather from a family that has crept in next to him and chosen among themselves!" It was his job, the doctor said, basic to his profession, to be observant. "And I have observed this."

The little Annamite took up the conversation, looking at the Persian with eyes that took in everything and told nothing in return. "You seem to have observed their government quite closely. But where would you say the ultimate power lies?"

"Yes, I have observed them," the doctor said. He was not insensitive to their hostility but he was used to being lonely in all company. "I have observed that the Imperial Advisers, those seven most powerful men close to the Emperor, include three brothers—sons of that famous statesman Fuhito—and one half brother. And the Great Minister of the Right is yet another brother.

"I observe, furthermore, that the Empress is their sister. *And* I have learned that her elevation followed the downfall of a certain prince—a prince, be it observed, who was not of that famous family and, indeed, opposed it. Taking these things together . . ."

"The Emperor is a devout and well-studied Buddhist," the priest said stubbornly. "Loving and well loved by his people. He is supreme." He turned away. The doctor was a Westerner after all, a Zoroastrian, and his mind was tuned in the Western way to the rivalry of good and evil and the practicalities of the world. A very learned man in his own field, but inclined to point the finger at the obvious while ignoring the true nature.

He himself had found in Emperor Shōmu the spirit of a bodhisattva. Indeed, it had been a moving experience for him to find the possibility of a true Buddha-land developing. The Emperor and the priests together . . .

Although the priest said nothing more, the dancing master could not let the Persian rest with the last word. "If I understand you, you are saying that the Emperor's advisers are more powerful than he?"

"Working toward power."

"And the Empress? A Fujiwara, as you say . . ."

"Already powerful."

"Yes, she has great strength. The women are strong. Perhaps *that* is the ultimate source of power: the mother figure, the mysterious female. The country was once ruled by priestesses, you know."

The Persian's mind went to the politics of the harem. "Their women? They do not take many wives. Although they seem to be quite free . . ."

"That is not my point. I am speaking of their strength. And their strength they draw from their women. This is what *I* observe." He smiled politely. "Perhaps they are even afraid of them."

"Afraid?"

"Because of that dependence, you know. There seems a most extraordinary bond between the mother and child. I think I see here more than I have ever seen the hidden female power."

"Perhaps, perhaps." The doctor had no notion what he meant. "Of course each man must have a favorite among his wives and concubines. We are all human, after all, no matter the nationality." He smiled his rather surly smile.

"He may have many wives and mistresses. But only one mother."

"You are stating the obvious. But that is all behind the screen. What *I* was speaking of was the power to make decisions, to seize control. I will make a prophecy," he went on, conscious that his arrogance annoyed them all but too sure of his diagnosis to withhold it. "At the moment we see in this isolated and impotent little land a sovereign claiming some similarity to the great Emperor of the T'ang. But can we seriously make such comparison?

"And we see around him four strong men, all of one family, all sons of one formidable man, all ambitious, closing in. Before long, let me predict to you, they will be the rulers of Japan."

This thought was evidently in the mind of the vice-envoy when he started negotiations to give his only child to a son of Fujiwara Umakai. He had been frightened for his life many times on his long journey and concerned for the welfare of his daughter. She would be safe, he felt, in this powerful family.

So it was that not long after this, when Abé sat with Saisho in the long gallery one autumn evening sorting dried wild flowers for a game of "comparisons," that Saisho, with her head bent, not even looking up, said, "I shall be leaving soon."

The marriage had been arranged and she had the Empress' permission to go home.

The smell of summer meadows rose from their fingers as they parted the white *kikyo* blossoms from their tangle of long stems. A moth had come into the room and was softly circling the lamp, but they went on working quietly, listening to a bell-cricket out in the dark garden.

Without inflection, as she had been schooled, Abé said, "I know."

Their supple hands continued to move expertly among the flowers and their long hair fell as black and thick in the shining light as it had ever done. But like the shadow of the moth, something of youth passed over them and was gone.

Now Hirotsugu's letters went to the house of the vice-envoy —and were answered. And one night when he sat outside in the darkness, playing his awkward flute to a clouded moon, he took up courage and stepped inside and sat down next to the young lady's bed-curtain.

Since he could think of no better words to express his longing, he spoke out bluntly: "I should like to see your face."

It was not pleasant for him to hear her crisp voice answering:

"Then come and see it. It is plain enough for anyone who wants to look."

Nevertheless, he moved around to where she was reclining and lay down next to her and took her in his arms and spent the night there glumly making love.

Next day, when he sent his morning letter, he sent as well a formal application to her father for the "union of our two great families." And the vice-envoy, eager as he was for this connection with his more powerful cousins, gave his quick assent.

In this way Saisho became a married woman and her heart grew small and hard as a salted bean.

CHAPTER VII

The Persian doctor, now established in the Bureau of Medicine, knew the human body and the human mind, perhaps, but not the forces outside man's control. For shortly after the last ship of the embassy arrived—having encountered evil winds and illness—a pestilence broke out in Hakata. In the following months it spread throughout Kyushu and in the next year, which was the ninth of Tempyo, a young emissary from an embassy to Silla that had failed (because of illness) came to the capital to report.

As was the regulation, he submitted his account to the Controller of Envoys, Fujiwara Fusasaki. Soon after that, Fusasaki woke one morning hot and very thirsty, complained of headaches and a pain in his back, and in a few days watched with horror the dark spots appear upon his skin.

The smallpox, which had crept from hut to hut, from fishing village to farm hamlet in the far countryside, was now let loose in the red-pillared halls and wide pavilions of the Palace.

Ten days later, on the seventeenth of the Third Month, Fujiwara Fusasaki—first of Kōmyō's four brothers—died.

Emperor Shōmu suspended all Court functions. He ordered the priests of every province to make images of the Healing Buddha and read portions of the Ninno Sutra to stop the pestilence.

In the Empress' pavilions the women clustered together, keeping the lattice windows closed and the hanging screens let down. To Abé, who had moved into her mother's rooms, it was as though they lived in a dark silk cocoon. The doctors made them sprinkle crystals of camphor on their sleeping mats and wear scent bags of dried storax to ward off the pestilence, and Lady Shihi was forever tossing grains of something she called dragon seeds into the braziers, so that the air was very heavy.

The days were so enclosed, so tedious, that Abé longed for Saisho, who might at least have brought some gossip or thought up some little games. But there were few diversions, and the only people to go in and out were the doctors and the priests.

One night toward the end of the Fourth Month she felt so restless that she rose and wandered down the length of the long gallery and into the far corridor of the west wing where her grandmother had lived. She had not been there in a very long time and she was surprised to see that one of the new sliding panels had been put at the entrance to the alcove where her shrine still stood. She paused outside it, wondering who was there, for she heard a man's voice murmuring.

At the end of the corridor the shutter had been left unlatched and a strip of cool night sky showed through. She went to it and put her face up recklessly, breathing in the air. Outside, in the soft haze of a quarter-moon, a spray of late-blooming cherries made a froth of white.

She drew back and went again to the door of the shrine room and knelt down and slid the panel back very gently, only an inch or two. A man was sitting cross-legged before the shrine. Over his habit he wore a fine silk stole and her first thought was for his elegance. He seemed for a moment like a higher being, someone from another world. It was as though he had no substance and no weight, as though he floated there. The candlelight in the haze of incense fell very softly on the pure line of his head and his perfectly cut profile, and for the few seconds before he turned, Abé felt his image come into her eyes like an intruder, come with a sort of penetrating blow through her unguarded eyes to lodge deep in her heart and mind.

He had been reciting spells from the Formula of the Peacock, gazing up into the shrine and sometimes, when he came to certain passages, lowering his forehead to his fingertips. When he heard the sound of the sliding door he had just looked up again, and as he turned, his expression was still abstracted and his lips parted.

Abé slid the door shut and drew back. But she had seen the dark arch of his eyebrows and the flat molding of his cheeks, the curve of his parted lips. How terrifying! And yet she wanted to laugh. In her eyes was still that feeling as though they had drunk him in, and on her lips a softness she could taste. She did not move but sat and listened, holding her breath, half laughing, though it was not a laugh.

The priest, whose name was Dōkyō, sat staring at the door. He had not seen who the intruder was, merely a glimpse of color and a white startled face, but in her hurry Abé had caught a corner of her sleeve between the panel and the jamb and it lay now in a pool of crimson on the polished floor. The expression changed on Dōkyō's startled face as he looked down at this.

Yuge no Dōkyō—Dōkyō of the Yuge family—had come to the capital to study under the famous Hossō priest Gien, and his disciple, Rōben. Before that he had studied medicine in the province of Kawachi, where he was born, for the Yuge family, although ancient, had merely provincial standing.

He had been raised, a shining little boy, in the dark cavernous rooms of his family's ancestral home. At night the rats ran in the heavy thatching of the great cumbersome house. It might have been called a farmhouse, and the buildings scattered around the spacious courtyard of packed earth did the duty of farm buildings. But in spite of that, it was an ancestral hall.

There were many little brothers in the old house, but Dōkyō, being the eldest, was the pearl. And when he was eleven years old his head was shaved and he was dedicated to the Buddha so that he might study with great teachers and enter the capital and even the Imperial Court—not as a provincial as his father had, scorned for his country ways, but under the world-spanning wings of the Buddhist brotherhood.

It was only during the frightful months of the smallpox epidemic that he, like so many other priests and doctors, was summoned to protect the Imperial Family. The duties he had assigned himself in the women's quarters were continuous prayer and fasting with the recitation of the proper spells at appropriate hours. The practice kept him in a state of light-headed exaltation, so that the appearance of a woman's face, shimmering white in the darkness of the corridor so close beside him, flashed on his unprotected consciousness like a dream of Amida's heaven.

Then the door closed and he was left with that little length of sleeve, that glowing crimson silk with its delicate pale lining catching the candlelight. And while he stared at it as though not comprehending, his hand reached out for it.

For a moment he held it as though his hand did one thing while his mind was occupied with quite another. And while he held it he recited in a voice so low it was almost silent,

"Well I know that this human body of mine
Is insubstantial as foam . . ."

This in reference to his Buddhist belief, but then in a stronger tone he went on,

"Even so, how I wish . . ."

For Abé it was as though the tug on her sleeve had sent a little train of sparks up her arm, and she sat horrified, delighted. What would happen next?

There was silence until he spoke again, his low voice hoarse with feeling, "Tell me who you are."

Who am I, Abé thought. Who am I? He would not have recognized the Imperial scent, all smothered as it was with camphor and the smell of storax. Perhaps I am a woman like any other.

He was still holding her, and the feel of his hand through the length of her sleeve, though not so rigid, not so intense in its tug, acted on her like some paralyzing drug. She sat still.

Then he began to talk and to persuade. "If you will but let me hear your voice . . ." And when she did not answer, he pleaded, "I do not even ask to see your face again, though the memory is like a dream . . ."

How amazing, he thought, how amazing that simply being close, with this door between them, should arouse such feelings. All his life since childhood when he had renounced the world he had tried to follow the Buddhist precepts and to escape the lure of women. On a few occasions, since he was healthy and very beautiful, girls of the city had tempted him into meaningless encounters, but never had he felt this wild desire.

"Perhaps as you do not know me," he went on softly, "you think that it is my habit to engage in affairs of this sort, but I assure you . . ." Again he paused, although the pull on her sleeve never wavered. "And yet, although my vows forbid me, and the barrier of our separate ways of life is far more solid than this frail door between us, something beyond my power to control . . ." He stopped as though emotion had overcome him.

He thinks I am one of my own ladies, Abé thought. Or as one thinks of a courtesan! She found that she was smiling as she thought, He thinks that it is *he* who is unapproachable . . .

She sat there with her free hand to her smiling lips when suddenly the door slid open and he was before her. He seemed so overcome with feeling that his eyes were luminous and his cheeks wet with tears. How beautiful! she thought, even as she shrank back quickly into the darkness and, almost crablike, fled away from him.

Afterward, when she relived that moment, she could not say if it was out of confusion that she had withdrawn to the end of the corridor beneath the window rather than to the gallery where she would be safe. Perhaps it was fated, perhaps she had no choice. And there was such a flurry of excitement in her brain, such paralyzing sweetness in her veins, that it seemed to her she had made no choice at all. She was simply there, beneath the open window and the slit of moonlight that came through.

Instantly he followed and came close to her, so close that the scarf end of his stole lay across her lap and she could feel his presence burning hot. He had his hands upon her garments as though to pull her toward him when he recognized the Princess with a shock, and hesitating, drew back on his heels.

"Forgive," he said, "forgive . . ." But still his eyes were shining in the dark and he looked directly at her.

She put her hands up, covering her face, but she did not move. And in a somewhat calmer voice he went on earnestly. "Ever since I first decided, when I was a boy, to follow the Eightfold Path, I have diligently lit the sacred fires and prayed daily for the health and safety of the Imperial Family . . . I never dreamed to presume upon the sacred person . . ."

He saw that she was not averse to him, not cowering away, nor cold, but she was trembling like any other girl, with her face hidden and her elbows tight. And her silence, her gentle trembling, he realized, was not so much from fear as from expectation.

Tentatively he raised his hand as though to touch her, saying in a lower voice, appealingly, "Surely an inescapable fate has brought us here together—I who have vowed a life of purity and you, beyond mortal reach. Surely the passion that so shakes my heart must rise from the frustrations of a thousand former lives."

He paused and Abé waited, waited for what he would do next.

When he spoke again his voice had sunk to a choked whisper. "Tell me you feel as I do, that we are together in the power of an overriding fate . . ." And when she did not answer, he reached out and took her sleeve as though to pull it from her face. But instead her whole body leaned to him, following the tug of his hand. His arms went out, so that their sleeves were overlapping, and as they fell together onto the bare floor, the moonlight through the open crack fell on the moving, heaving mass of their robes.

Their mingled scents rose in the cool night air and the sound of their breathing, of his whispered passion, of her small hissing moans, were like the sound of silk on silk as he untied the sash of her under robe.

Long afterward they lay in tears, turning their heads as they lay side by side so that they breathed into each other's mouth, and tried to hold back the knowledge that the dawn had come. He would have risked everything, death, he said, for one more hour. But she rose, and when he half rose to go after her, she pushed him back. She felt that she should speak, or he should, but they were silent, and she moved like an old woman, tottering past the door to the shrine room, back toward the world.

When she turned to look at him, he was lying down again. His clothes were gray in the gray dawn and his arms were covering his face. He is weeping, she thought. Oh, how odd, how odd, that he should lie and weep while I walk away.

She herself was weeping so that she could hardly see, and sobs were coming from her heart into her throat. But she held the sound in as she went, bent almost double with her disheveled garments all about her and her long hair hanging down, back along the dimness of the gallery to her own bed-space.

Next day her mother sent for her but she did not go. And when the Empress sent again to inquire, she lied and said that she was in a retreat—reading the Sutra of the Healing Buddha for the health of the Court, she said—and could not break her vow of solitude to visit anyone for several days.

Having written this, she lay back and stared at the ceiling. She had never lied to her mother in her life, her mother who was the closest and the dearest person in the world to her. She had tried very earnestly never to disappoint her, never to do anything to displease her. But although she told herself these things, as though to shame herself as she lay on her back, her face expressionless, she could not summon any feeling of remorse.

Finally, when the sun had risen high enough to make a pattern of the lattice on her bed-curtain, the letter that she waited for arrived.

"You cannot know the torment that I suffer, remembering that I raised my eyes to you and spoke unguardedly. I believe it was the work of an evil spirit that led me to such transgression. And my punishment shall be to feel the pain of a forbidden love throughout this life, perhaps into the next . . .

"Having met you in a dream
I feel myself dissolve,
Both soul and body,
Like snow in a darkening world . . ."

And he added: "Please believe me that in all my life I never thought that I should fall in love. Now that I have—and know that it is hopeless—I am desolate."

After Abé read this, laughing and crying over it, she hid it in her clothing and fed her heart on it until another came. It was attached to a spray of weeping cherry, pale as shells, the cherry that had been outside the window where they lay. It was very brief:

"Do you suppose that it was meant in heaven that we should meet as in a dream and never again?" And the verse:

"I thought myself a strong man
But the sleeves of my garment
Are wet with tears . . ."

She wanted to write him: "What will you do now?" But the thought was frightening. What if he came to her in the night? The scandal! Nor did she really want her body to be used like that again, the frantic whispering, the feel of his fingers everywhere, the urgency, the pain. She did not want that. But she wanted him. How beautiful! she thought again. How beautiful he was.

So she wrote nothing, though he wrote again, several times. Until at last a message came:

"I am returning to my home. I cannot now remain in the

capital, so near . . . I have asked Buddha to help me accept this loneliness, this longing, this inescapable fate . . . I know now that before you I am nothing. And that is as the gods intended. It is right, it is correct, it is as it should be. I am nothing. I am your slave . . ."

It seemed to her as she read this that he raved a little and she was glad. It was not right that he should have overwhelmed her, dominated her as he had. Rightfully, she should have been the one to dominate and he to crawl to her and press his forehead to the floor. Visualizing this, she ran her tongue along her lips, half smiling, till she read the verse:

> "When clouds above me
> Banner the sky at sunset,
> I sit paralyzed.
> This is what it is to love
> Someone who lives beyond my world."

She felt mollified. He did appreciate . . .

She found that she was planning a next meeting, what she would say to him and he reply, how they would look together, what she would wear, when suddenly the realization struck her that he had gone. He had gone away! She rose up in her bed as though to find him, and when she peered between the curtains it was dawn. The dawn bells were tolling and she remembered how they sounded on that morning—only three days ago?—and the pain of parting, the excitement, and the exquisite pain. She had been alive then, every part of her. Truly alive.

Such restlessness possessed her that she turned and turned again within the bed-space in a kind of false exhilaration, a frantic dance. Then she called for her writing things and sent them away again, and for her clothes and had her attendants dress her and went precipitately into the main pavilion and then back again, for the ladies were not prepared to receive her, and lay down and then rose again.

She did not venture along the corridor of the west wing until evening of the third day, after her incessant wanderings through her mother's rooms and corridors had caused comment.

"Have you lost something?" Lady Shihi asked. For she had a look of expectation in her face, as though behind each pillar or standing screen there might be something she was searching for.

At last at sunset ("when the clouds make banners in the sky," she thought) she went along the gallery and turned at the corridor. Seeing the window at the end, she stopped. Something dealt a blow straight at her body where it was most vulnerable and she bent double. Then on her knees she crept to the door of the little shrine room and listened breathlessly, her eyes wide, but there was no sound within it and no light. And when she slid the panel back she saw the emptiness, the quiet corners filling up with dusk. The doors to the shrine were open and the golden Buddha smiled.

She wished with desperation that she had not come, to put so positive an end to it, to look with her own eyes where she had dreamed he might be, and find nothing. She put her palms down flat upon the floor as though to feel for something or to conjure up. But nothing happened and she put her head down and wept bitterly.

CHAPTER VIII

Gradually, as the days went by, the feeling died. The pain grew thin and failed to nourish her. The encounter was so brief, so alien that it formed a sort of skin around itself, like a cyst, and lay in her mind in a quiet way until it was as though she had forgotten.

At first it had not been so. At first the pain alone, as well as the memories her senses carried—the touch, the feel of his voice in her ear, even the still-remaining sweetness in her veins—kept her alert to her own person, kept her alive. But as the days and then the weeks, the months went on, her dreams had less and less vitality, her feelings faded, and the lively pain that had sustained her died.

Sometimes her mother, watching her anxiously, asked if she felt ill. But she felt nothing and she smiled and said that she was well. Their fear of the smallpox was no longer real to her and she was unaware that if her face flushed with a sudden memory, or she sat forgetful with her head drooping during a conversation, or lay too long in bed, a thrill of fear shot through them all: was she ill? had the pestilence arrived?

During the last of the summer months the famous priest Gyōgi came to the capital. He was not welcome among the aristocrats of the Court because his immense popularity with the common people made them uneasy. He was a big and active man and of the two fields of Buddhism, the field of worship and the field of compassion, he had chosen the latter, as much, perhaps, because of his excessive energy as his warm heart.

He seldom rode or took a cart when he went around the country, but walked like a common man. He was an inspiration to all artisans and artists and the temples that he built were full of splendid images. Whenever he saw or heard of things to be done he did them: dredged out harbors, shored up dikes, dug wells, built bridges, anything to help the farming people and the poor. Often with his own hands he carried the earth or placed the timbers for a bridge, slipping his arms out of his sleeves and tucking his hem into his belt so that he worked bare-legged and bare-backed like an indentured laborer or slave. At those times his clothing looked the way his vestments were designed to look, like the ragged clothes of the poor.

Now, when he appeared at the Hall of the Central Ministry in the Nara Palace, the pattern of black borderings on the bronze silk of his robe took on a formal elegance and he brought his big voice down to the tones of the supplicant.

He had been in the countryside, in the homes of ordinary people—the people the Emperor called his own—and had seen their suffering. He pleaded for them among the officers of the Court, and when he left, Shōmu instructed the doctors of the Bureau of Medicine to draw up a proclamation for the people's use, informing them of the symptoms to watch out for and the treatment. Gembō attended their consultation, and the Persian doctor, though he did not understand a word they said, and many of the local doctor-priests. But Dōkyō was not there. He had gone into retreat, it was reported, at a mountain temple near his home. To pray for the health of the nation, it was said, and the Imperial Family.

Gembō came late and took the opportunity to lecture them on the famous discourse in Vimalakirti's Sutra. "Come, gentlemen," he said, "the human body is transient, weak, impotent, frail, and mortal."

He had begun, and had their interest. He looked around at them where they were seated, each at his little desk, then closed his eyes and tipping back his head recited on. "An intelligent man never places his trust in such a thing. It is like a bubble that soon bursts. It is like a plantain tree that is hollow inside. It is false and will be reduced to nothingness in spite of bathing, clothing, and nourishment. It is a calamity!" He opened his heavy lids to be sure that they were listening. "It is subject to a hundred ills . . ."

"Yes." It was a very old Court physician who had ventured to interrupt. "Yes, yes. And so we must proceed."

"It is transient and sure to die!" Gembō concluded, looking straight at the old man. Then he took the seat that had been kept for him, making no apology for being late—whether from arrogance or absentmindedness they did not know yet. He was new to them.

Now that he was seated there was silence, one of the many long ruminative pauses throughout the night, for this was a formal meeting to produce a consensus of all their ideas and experience, and there were more such silences than there was talk. At last, after many hours of consultation they wrote this:

> The name of this disease is the Red Pox. The symptoms are similar to the common chill and fever but in three days there will be a rash and red eruptions. The patient may burn so much with fever that he will ask for water, but it should not be given.
>
> Keep the patient warm and bind his stomach with a cloth. Do not lay him on the ground but on mats or clothing spread out on the floor—as there may be no proper bedding in the peasants' huts.
>
> Feed the patient thin rice gruel or millet soup three or four times a day. If the peasants do not have rice enough, a portion from the government granaries should be given them and the quantity recorded.
>
> Do not feed him fresh fish, cold food, fruits, or fresh vegetables, though he may hold toasted sea grass or powdered salt in his mouth. Even twenty days after recovery he should abstain from these things or he may develop a dysentery from which

> not even the famous Chinese doctors of antiquity could cure him.
>
> Never give pills or powders sold by passing strangers. Pure certified ginseng brew alone is safe to drink and may bring the fever down.

This proclamation bore the Imperial seal and the official stamp of the Grand Council. Copies were made of it in all the provincial capitals and circulated through the countryside. Six copies went to the barrier guards at the strategic roads leading to the capital. There travelers paused and felt their cheeks for fever as they read the posted notices. Few were allowed to proceed into the city. But it was far too late.

All through Nara and within the Palace itself men and women showed the fearful symptoms, even those who had the best of care—the warm beds and the ginseng and the special reading of sutras by the priests.

The Emperor and his family were spared, but many of the high Court nobles, the most exalted ministers whom he leaned upon, came down exactly like the poorest peasant in his dirt-floored hut: burning with fever, calling for water, feeling the nausea and the cramps until the Red Pox overcame them and they were gone.

In the Sixth Month the Imperial Adviser Fujiwara Maro died.

In the Seventh Month, his brother Muchimaro, Great Minister of the Right.

In the Eighth, the last of the four brothers, Umakai.

Not until cooling weather came did the pestilence subside. And on the day of the Chrysanthemum Festival, when they dared to come together in little groups, the people of the Palace looked about them and realized that there had been no new case for many days. Slowly the Court took up its old routine, its problems and its pleasures, healing over with new appointments the gaps in government left by the death of friends.

Now the power of the Fujiwara family passed to the next generation: eighteen young cousins, sons of those four powerful men. Playmates and competitors from childhood, they masked their rivalries and drew close during this period of consolidation.

Only Hirotsugu with his new wife and newfound feeling of importance openly competed for position. He was the awkward one of Umakai's six sons, the butt. When he began to push himself above his elder cousins, it was convenient for them to put him down. On their suggestion, a place was found for him and a post created: Junior Assistant Governor of the Government Headquarters in Dazaifu.

Saisho said she could not abide the provinces, she could not go with him. For the time her husband stayed in Dazaifu she would be at the Palace once again. Wasn't that the best plan? Surely their separation would not be long, she smiled. And he could not expect her to cross the mountains and the sea. She was afraid of boats. She could not understand what made them float. Supposing they should sink? He could see that it was best for her to stay behind.

He would speak to the proper people at the Imperial Household Ministry, would he not? And to someone at the Palace Attendants' Office in the Empress' quarters? Princess Abé would be glad to have her back, she knew. "And I will wait for you, and send you letters, and tell you everything that is going on." She was determined to be in Court for the New Year celebrations and with a flurry of admonitions and vague promises she sent him off.

She arrived at the Princess' pavilion on the day of his departure, but being more given to impulse than to careful thought, she brought elaborate presents for all the ladies—even for Shihi, a boxwood comb. This time she would be pleasant to everyone; the Princess would not be the only one to love her.

So the bundles were untied and the boxes opened and the floor was strewn with deep-dyed and second-dipping silks and finely printed hemps. Kneeling among them she brought out incense pots and toilet kits, writing cases, picture albums, books, turning her little face up, laughing, close to tears. But even as they bore their gifts away, the others let their faces drop. This was a dark time in the Palace with so many to mourn. She should have been more sensitive to that.

Moreover, Saisho was dismayed to find the whole tone of the Court so greatly changed. Abé herself she found subdued, withdrawn. And of all the many New Year festivals that she looked forward to, only the ceremony of the Young Herbs was kept, and that without joy. Everyone just ate a little of the rice gruel with its seven lucky greens in the privacy of his own rooms. (This year of all years it was wise to ensure one's health.)

Because promotions had already been made to fill the posts left by the Fujiwara brothers and the others who had died, there was no banquet for the Announcement of New Ranks. The Emperor simply appointed Tachibana Moroé, a gifted and upright man from the powerful Tachibana family, to take the place of Muchimaro as Great Minister of the Right. Moroé was the son of Lady Tachibana and Kōmyō's half brother. But whereas she controlled herself with a gentle voice and soft face for the world, he practiced a more rigid self-control so that his demeanor was somewhat stiff, and late in life (he was now fifty-four years old) he became almost a figure of awe in the Court and Shōmu came to lean on him above all others.

Some of the Fujiwara cousins of the next generation were moved up in rank as well, and Abé had been named the Heir Apparent. Saisho thought perhaps that this new and exalted post accounted for the Princess' solemn manner—even her dullness, as she perceived it. Still, she thought, it would be a very long time before she might actually become the sovereign. It was unreasonable of her to be so withdrawn. Besides, she had heard—though of course it was only gossip—that when Lady Hiro's son, Prince Asaka, grew older the Emperor might change his mind. The boy was beautiful, they said, and already quite accomplished at ten years old. Everyone loved him. And with the Fujiwara power broken, so they said, the Emperor might decide on him instead. But in the meantime Abé had become so serious it was hard to find entertainment in her Court, and Saisho moved restlessly from room to room looking for some distraction.

One cold day when the black needles of the pine trees stood against a hard gray sky she came upon the Princess and her tutor, that learned man from China. They sat face to face with a metal brazier on the floor between them and their books unrolled in their hands. From Saisho's angle they were in silhouette against a small barred window, two bent figures like ink drawings on a ribbed fan. Sometimes the teacher leaned his wrist to warm it on the rim of the brazier, or took the long handling-sticks to rearrange the charcoal. Otherwise they sat quite motionless with the steam of their breath rising up between them as they read aloud.

The lesson was in Chinese. They were reading a book of poems, and while Abé picked her way through the difficulties of the script the professor helped her. He treated her almost like an equal, Saisho thought. Rather presumptuous! They were reading a poem by Li Po. Saisho knew that much. Everyone knew a little of Li Po or they would not be in the Palace, after all, among sophisticated people. Li Po was the most sympathetic of all the Chinese poets, everyone agreed.

The lesson went on, slowly, conscientiously. How dull the Princess and her professor were after all! There they sat, bent forward over their books, almost as though they were building something together. How intent they looked, quite comical! Like people seeing how many of the new *go* stones they could balance on one finger. Saisho was very good at that. But that, at least, always ended in a burst of laughter.

Suddenly, as though at the memory, Saisho laughed aloud, a little chirp of mirth. Quickly she put her hand over her lips. But she was dismayed to see not only the professor but Abé herself turn to her with the same serious, questioning, somewhat disapproving look, and she shrank back behind a pillar as though struck.

Actually, Abé was not so much disapproving as embarrassed. Why should her friend have burst out in such a foolish way? She had felt such a lift of the heart when Saisho returned. She had wanted so desperately to have her for a friend, even a confidante, to tell her everything. But it had not worked out as she hoped. There was a strain between them.

Now as Saisho ducked behind the pillar like a child who has been slapped, Abé felt such a sudden pang, such a pull of the old fondness, that the tears came to her eyes. She blinked and quickly took up her book again and stared at it. But her feelings were so absorbed with Saisho, trapped behind the pillar, that she could not focus properly and the strokes of the characters blurred and jumped on the page.

Kibi waited, glancing up from his own book once or twice in expectation. He saw that she had the place, and by her bent head knew that she must be reading, but she was silent. The book trembled. What a child the *Kōtaishi* was in many ways. He was not used to dealing with girlish sensitivities. He fixed his eyes on the poem once again and waited, thinking of other things. In his eyes too the ink strokes blurred against the pale blue paper with its flecks of gold . . .

He had met Li Po, that giant of a man. He had talked with him on his balcony beside the river where the peach trees bloomed. He knew the look of his big hand with the brush and the accent of his voice.

When at last he raised his head and turned it toward the window, Abé glanced up at him. Through the mist of her confusion and the tears standing in her eyes, she saw the ridges of his cheeks and the knob of his brow picked out in the cold light. Years later, when she knew him better, when she had sent him back to China and when he had returned with white hairs in his beard, she realized that in that early time when he had been her tutor and she first saw his face, he had been in his prime. But now, as she saw the worn look that he turned upon the window, she thought him old.

When he spoke it was in a quiet voice as if he was reciting for himself. And he did not take his eyes from the window and the gray sky beyond:

"I am endlessly yearning
        to be in Ch'ang-an . . .
Insects hum of autumn by the gold brim of the well.
Heaven is high, earth is wide;
        bitter between them flies my sorrow.
Can I dream through the gateway, over the mountain?
Endless longing
        breaks my heart."

It was not the poem they had been reading but simply one that had come into his mind.

When her teacher had left her, Abé sent a note to Saisho with a reference to their old-time selves, hoping to appease her if her feelings had been hurt. More than ever she needed a close friend, but Saisho kept her fan before her face as she approached and was slow to speak, using a tiny voice as though she had become very shy in the presence of the *Kōtaishi*.

"What do you think of me?" Abé burst out. "Am I so very changed?"

"They say you are learned, madam."

"Do you think so, Saisho?"

"Who am I to say? I have no learning."

"Who is 'they,' then?"

"Everyone, madam."

"And what does everyone say then? Tell me."

Saisho paused a long time, sitting stonily behind her fan. "They say: 'The Princess is very studious. The Princess is very devout. The Princess' Court is very intellectual.' "

"Do you think so, Saisho?" she asked in a small strained voice. The picture was not attractive. "Is that what you think too?"

Saisho's fan came trembling down and she burst into tears. Leaning forward with her small round face all wet, she looked up into Abé's eyes. "I think that it is dull!" she cried. "And oh, it is too bad. It is too bad for you. It shouldn't be!"

She toppled headlong into Abé's lap and sought her hands to press them on her wet cheeks and mouth. Abé, leaning over her, felt such a pain of anguish that she said aloud what she had often said within her heart, "It hurts."

The two had come together briefly but it didn't last. Abé was occupied and Saisho bored. She had no talent to make friends with other women, and certainly no inclination to sit alone and dream about a distant husband. More and more often she went to the Empress' pavilions, where she felt there was more life.

Often there were more priests than Court officials there, but although they did not make such a splash of color, the doctor-priests especially, who had the freedom of the ladies' rooms, were quite entertaining. Most fascinating of them all to Saisho was the High Priest Gembō, who had been in China but did not make such a fetish of it, Saisho thought, as the Princess' tutor.

He was a favorite of the Empress too, though he was often rather careless of the formalities and certainly unpredictable in his conversation. But he had come with such honors from the T'ang Court that she had granted him sustenance lands from her own holdings when the Emperor made him Patriarch of the Hossō sect. He was the head of the Northern Branch as Gyōgi was head of the Southern. He made his headquarters in the Kofuku-ji temple, but he was more often at the Palace, either in the little chapel that had been built for him or in the Empress' pavilions.

Saisho thought he was extremely ugly but she loved to watch him. She often said a priest should be good-looking. Otherwise how could he expect the company to keep their eyes on him while he read the sutras or recited the prayers? It was too tedious if he was fat or old or fidgeted with his clothing. He should sit straight and keep his chin aloft, as Gembō did, and his voice should be full of resonance, as his was—though he was so ugly.

She kept her bright eyes on him, for he fascinated her. He had a way of sitting with his head thrown back as though immersed in lofty thoughts. But then, when one least expected it, he turned it quickly toward the person who was observing him and pierced her with a sharp glance under his heavy lids. It was as though there were no curtain in between them—neither a screen nor wall of propriety. This she found out.

When she returned to her place in the Princess' apartments she wrote dutifully to Hirotsugu. She liked to remind them that she was a married lady. And when a letter came from Dazaifu she cried out, "It is from my husband!"

She wrote him bitterly of Kibi no Makibi and said he scorned the old ways and was forcing on them everything Chinese. And she wrote admiringly of Gembō who was so often at the Empress' Court, and whom the Emperor admired too, she said. He was a great and holy man and brought all kinds of improvements . . . Everything was changing—except herself, of course, who remained as he had always known her, lonely for his return . . . When she wrote these last words they were so hastily stroked in, with the brush almost running dry, that he could scarcely read them.

By the end of the year Lady Saisho was, if not a favorite, a woman of some prominence. She was perfectly aware that she had neither the learning nor the beauty to match the others of the Empress' ladies. But she had something that they lacked. She was original, and she was daring. And because of her own restlessness she invented new diversions, putting her ideas forward happily, without regard for decorum.

During the rainy season when everything was dull, she proposed a visit to the craftsmen's shops in the Bureau of Artisans where they were making tiles. To see the fires, she said. What an odd idea! But they went. And the next New Year, when it was time for the Feast of the Young Herbs, she said they should all go to the countryside to hunt the herbs themselves. "Why leave the pleasure to the officers of the storehouse every year? They can never appreciate the beauty of young growing things as we can . . ."

But Lady Shihi said there was no precedent. "Ladies of the Court have never taken part in the herb hunt. You would exhaust yourselves besides."

"But we have often gone picnicking . . ."

"Whoever heard of picnicking in the snow!" Lady Shihi laughed.

"But there is no snow! There is no snow!" Saisho glided to the veranda door. Though there had been a light fall in the night, the moist earth was now dark and soft and a low mist lay on it. Perfect for finding the little shoots of spring.

Gembō, who was sitting near the Empress' screen of state, looked at Saisho with the light behind her and no curtain in the way. Her hair was looped beside her ears and the rim of her scarf stood out very delicately around her neck. With the Empress' permission, he said, he would invite the ladies to the gardens of the Kofuku-ji, where he was sure they would find some pretty grasses.

So Abé and Saisho and six others of the younger ladies squeezed into two small basket-carriages and were driven through the muddy streets to the extensive temple gardens where they searched out the little sprouting shoots and tight-curled ferns and were served an elegant Buddhist meal of vegetables.

On their return they found the Empress' pavilion full of visitors, for word of their strange excursion had spread. It was like old times, Saisho felt, with the young men in their beautiful New Year's costumes and some of the senior ministers as well. Great Minister Moroé arrived to announce that the Emperor himself would come to taste their gruel, and the Empress sent word that she expected poems from them all reflecting on their outing and the tender shoots they found. How splendid! How successful it has been! Saisho exulted. And heedless of the wet stains on her sleeves or that the hem of her skirt was muddy, she sank down only half hidden by a screen to watch the gentlemen.

The other ladies disappeared as quickly as they could. They knew the tone these parties took when there was too much wine. And even when the Empress called for them, they crept back silently and took up safe positions in the shadows.

When the Emperor entered, the nobility of his person almost stifled Saisho. He was wearing a magnificent Chinese cloak of grape-colored brocade with a crimson robe and soft white under robe and his trousers were willow green. He walked in rather swiftly, observing them from his height, and his manner was so jovial that they felt at ease.

Having seated himself among the gentlemen, he tasted the gruel which the cooks had made and remarked on the fragrance of the herbs—such tender hands had picked them. Then he lifted the silver wine cup and drank from it before he sent it around from man to man, each one making a verse before he drank. But after it had gone around for the third time the verses grew less elegant and sometimes boisterous and he rose, still smiling placidly, and left them to join the Empress and go off with her hand in hand.

Abé loved parties and all sorts of games, but she was afraid of drunkenness and already this gathering was turning rowdy. Softly she stole behind her mother's screen, where she could watch in safety, her eyes glistening with a mixture of apprehension and delight. Some of the men were so amusing! But then others . . .

One of the middle counselors tilted the cup so far when he drank that she could see his throat move up and down. Amazing! When he finished he spoke out in a loud and ragged voice:

"If I could only be happy in this life
What would I care if in the next
I become a bird or a worm!"

Then looking around the crowded room, "Let us all get drunk," he said.

Someone started a clapping game and she wished she might join in, but just then young Momokawa, usually so solemn, knocked over a stand of winter oranges and laughed so raucously he lost control while others scrambled after them across the floor. How hot they looked. How red their faces were!

It was really beginning to be alarming, Abé thought, when an old minister from the Board of Censors lost all his dignity and sense of place. Standing up to call attention to himself, he took up a slender pitcher and held it out between his legs while he started a vulgar song. Lady Shihi let out a startled shriek and her face was full of outrage as she rose, backed off, and scuttled from the room. How comical she looked, Abé thought, but at least she had escaped. Some of the other ladies were less full of fire and sat with their hands within their sleeves and their eyes cast down.

Saisho, she noticed, was neither so energetic as Lady Shihi nor so quiet as the others. And when the cup was passed to her, she had not the sense to take those little closed-lipped sips of the more experienced ladies, but swallowed down the wine until the powder on her face was caked and her damp hair, already in disorder from the day's excursion, clung to her flushed cheeks and neck.

Abé watched her in alarm. She had fallen forward with her hands supporting her on the floor and was slowly shaking her head. But when she rose no one attempted to stop her. Only Abé seemed to notice as she walked with small stiff steps and careful dignity, sidling a little sideways now and then, and putting her hand to steady herself against a pillar as she rounded it to pass behind the hanging screen that curtained off an alcove.

In the gap between the pillar and the screen, Abé saw Gembō sitting alone, as though he waited. His back was very straight and his hands were on his knees and his head high in his characteristic pose, but his eyes were open.

She watched as Saisho approached and sank down facing him, quite close, and saw him reach his hand out silently and pull at the neck of her robe. Then his hand went sliding down upon her breast as though it knew its way there and had been there more than once.

CHAPTER IX

The dread Imperial command
I have received: from tomorrow
I sleep with the grass,
No wife being by me.

–Mononobe Akimochi,
on being dispatched
as a frontier guard
to Kyushu.
From the *Manyōshū*

Hirotsugu felt that his appointment to a meaningless distant post was the working of some sort of plot against him, though he could not exactly place the blame. He knew for certain, though, that his cousins, warm with their wives and daily at Court, were happier than he.

He had ridden southward with his chin across his shoulder, looking back at what he deemed the center of the world. Dazaifu he thought of as its farthest outpost, isolated and uncivilized. He wrote to Saisho that he had slept with grass for his pillow, but in actuality the bell-token that he carried as a Court official had provided him with at least a roof and fresh horses at the government posting stations and ferries at the waterways.

And Dazaifu, when he arrived, was not the lonely stockade he had pictured but a good-sized city with streets laid out like home.

It was a military city, though, an army post, and he begrudged it any charm. The earthen walls were high and thick, with watchtowers at the corners and the massive double gates. The wide and barren streets were full of soldiers. And on the mountains to the west the long walls of the hill-forts curved to the rim of the sky.

He knew Dazaifu's history. It had been built by Emperor Tenchi nearly a hundred years before to repel invaders after the great sea battle when the T'ang navy overwhelmed his own. Before that, for many centuries, the Japanese had kept strongholds in Korea. But after the battle the treacherous men of Silla had joined with the Chinese to push the Emperor's forces off the peninsula. Fearing that they might follow and attack him in his own land, he had built these defenses here on the most vulnerable of his home islands.

The invaders never came, and the Emperor made his peace with the Chinese. But from that time on the embassies to Ch'ang-an had to go the long and perilous way across the open sea rather than skirt the Silla coast. And the fortifications on Kyushu were kept up and strengthened to this day. As far as Hirotsugu knew, that sea battle was his nation's only defeat, and it rankled that he should be posted to this place of its reminder.

When he presented himself to the governor he was given quarters furnished in a hopeful imitation of his residence at home. The governor was kind; he was a homesick man himself. But he was old and Hirotsugu young. Their conversation flagged. There were few duties for a junior assistant governor and the days were empty.

His cousins said that Hirotsugu lacked a sense of fitness, that he was irritable, full of foolish notions, difficult. But he thought, when he considered this, that on the contrary he was calm and reasonable. Perhaps, he thought, he saw more than the others did, was sharper and more aware of currents in the Court that they could not perceive. Take the smallpox: Was it not possible that the disease was planted in the Court? Brought for a purpose by some enemy? By whom he could not say. And he had no proof. He only knew what happened: four Fujiwara brothers dead within a few quick months!

Was his own exile part of this same plot? Hirotsugu thought of these things while he explored the city. Nothing to see. Earth walls, brown soldiers, dust in the wide streets. He rode out to the mountain forts and climbed the ramparts to the highest point. The firm stone walls went spilling down the mountainside like the ribs of a great fan. The sunburnt young commanders said they could withstand the weight of China and the Silla dogs combined. But the valley that they overlooked was silvery with water sluices running down the hills, and calm. Where was the point of danger?

He rode out farther, into the territories where the local people lived and to the port of Hakata on the coast. Nothing but fishing vessels bobbing quietly on the soft water, no foreign ships standing off on the horizon. Why should there be?

He took a company of soldiers and rode south, to the southernmost province of the island, and spoke to the headman of the Hayato, those tattooed people who had been so difficult to subdue. They were friendly enough to him, though they seemed proud. He had been told they were descendants of the August Ancestors, but born in the midst of fire. In their own legends their gods came from the sea.

He questioned them severely as to their loyalties. The history of their rebellions was very long—and it was recent too. Not twenty years before, they had killed the governor from Nara. Even though Hirotsugu had been only a boy, he remembered when their delegation came to the Court with restitution after they were put down. The Imperial Cavalry had been drawn up on the parade ground to impress and intimidate them. Hirotsugu, nine years old, had stared with more absorption at those five hundred huge matched horses and five hundred full-armed men than he had at the Hayato. But now that he saw them once again he remembered the blue tattooing on their folded arms and their impassive faces, all alike, when they had watched the cavalry.

He questioned them but he found nothing, and he rode back to Dazaifu unsatisfied. He felt some danger hovering, but he could not locate it.

Once in a while a letter came from Saisho: "The men from China are changing everything . . . Kibi no Makibi is a favorite. Everyone listens to what he says and he makes fun of our old ways . . . I am not at all happy."

Sometimes gossip drifted down: The Emperor had made a visit to the private residence of the Great Minister of the Right, Tachibana Moroé. An almost unprecedented honor. How high he had risen since the deaths of the Fujiwaras!

More often, official dispatches came from the central government: instructions to the governor to draw up maps of the districts under his control; instructions to reduce the number of district officials—there are too many in the bureaucracy eating the people's rice.

Again from Saisho: "We have been entertained by the Patriarch Gembō, who condescends to teach us the latest Chinese fashions . . . There was a full moon and it was delightful . . . Our lives have become full of interests once more . . ."

And again an Imperial dispatch: instructions to prepare reports for the itinerant inspectors who were being sent to investigate all local governments and the condition of the people.

"It is another of those new ideas that have been brought from China," Hirotsugu said when the governor told him to prepare for the inspectors. "The government is being run by foreigners."

The governor raised his eyebrows. "Foreigners? The instructions came from the Ministry of Central Affairs as they always have."

Hirotsugu did not reply and the old man pressed him: "What foreigners?"

"Men who have been too long in China."

He said no more, but something was building.

Saisho wrote: "The Patriarch lectured us on a sutra and it was not so dull as you may think. We had a maigre feast of vegetables. The Patriarch has great influence on the Court. Perhaps I shall turn myself to serious study, you see I am quite changed . . ."

While Hirotsugu pondered this, his head between his hands, a new directive came from the capital: The government in every province is instructed to build a seven-storied pagoda in its guardian-temple grounds. All Buddha-images that were previously ordered for these temples must be completed without delay. By Imperial order, two thousand men and women are to become monks and nuns. Additional rice fields are to be set aside for their sustenance.

Hirotsugu snorted when he read this. More of the nation's wealth and energies, more rice fields, even more human beings diverted into the hands of the Buddhist priests! Who was responsible?

Someone wrote in confidence, giving no name: "Hirotsugu: The Patriarch Gembō debauches the ladies of the Court. Your wife is not above reproach."

Now he knew where the danger lay. Perhaps he was not the only one who saw it. Some murmurings of discontent had reached him. But only he, he thought—even at this distance—had the keen perception, had the bold courage, to take action.

He wrote a letter of strong criticism to the Grand Council, constructing his opening sentences with elaborate care but swept headlong at the end by his emotions:

> Since the beginning of heaven and earth our Sovereigns, Gods Incarnate, have ruled this land of Yamato trusting wise counselors. For six long reigns the Sovereign House was served by a loyal minister. Six Sovereigns, ruling from the High Throne, trusted and listened to this excellent man who served with a pure heart and a bright heart obedient to their wishes, until his very death. Such was the Great Minister Fujiwara Fuhito.
>
> What has become of the family of this minister whom six Sovereigns trusted? Had he no wise, obedient sons?
>
> He had four sons.
>
> These four strong sons are dead. And I myself, a humble member of that loyal family—I am in exile. Why?
>
> The God Incarnate Emperor Shōmu, whose name I write

with awe, has been betrayed! New men with foreign notions swarm through the Court. New temples eat the people's land. The Patriarch Gembō eats the heart of the nation. He is not to be trusted. Kibi no Makibi is not to be trusted.

Priest Gembō and that Kibi, who is of low birth anyway, must be expelled from government. Old ways must be recovered. Beware. I write this in the sincerity of my heart.

The letter was not answered.

In the far end of the western wing of her palace, in the rooms her mother had once occupied, Empress Kōmyō was talking alone with Nakamaro.

"We have not seen you recently as much as we would like." Her voice was gentle as it always was, but this was not light conversation.

He pleaded illness and she glanced at him. He looked robust as ever, though his face was deeply marked by the smallpox that had attacked him too.

"I'm glad you have recovered, for I want to talk to you."

As usual, his tongue was slow in the presence of his aunt, and she continued, "The signs are evil and there are evil plans afoot, I think. But what is your opinion?"

This was the Eighth Month and there had been no rain. The Patriarch had ordered sutra readings at the Kofuku-ji but his prayers brought no more than a brief fine spray of rain. All month the water in the lake had given off a noxious smell and now it was covered with small white grubs. Their mouths were black. That is why the Empress had moved to this back corner of her palace complex.

But more troubling was the knowledge that the drought was a reflection of bad government. The Emperor was distressed. Perhaps he should make a pilgrimage. Perhaps the capital should be moved . . .

Suddenly there was purpose under the Empress' light voice. "We have had reports, accusations. There have been threats. The name of our family is evoked."

Yes, he had heard, Nakamaro said.

"Who is involved?"

"No one. It is only Hirotsugu acting alone."

"And you do not think that Hirotsugu, acting alone you say, is dangerous?"

"He is a fool. This is not the time."

"What do you mean by that?"

What Nakamaro meant was that although Hirotsugu was undoubtedly a fool, his complaint about the Patriarch was well taken. He himself was troubled by the priest's growing influence and galled by his arrogance. And he did not like to see the amount of land and goods that were going from the Court into the temples. He would like, at a judicious time, to reverse that trend. But Hirotsugu, being a fool, and evidently under some delusions too, had blurted it all out. Not only had he sent his idiotic letter to the Grand Council but several notes and messages to the family. He seemed to want them to take action, but it had been decided in confidential talks not to act. Better to wait, the feeling was, and see.

His face remained as disciplined as ever while he quickly thought: How much did his aunt know of their deliberations? How far did her sympathies lie with the priests? How much with the family? Or did she see any conflict? He had never been able to sense his aunt's reactions, though she seemed always to know his thoughts. She need not have said, What do you mean? She knew.

"There is some feeling, here and there, perhaps, that the priests are powerful . . ."

"Should they not be?"

Nakamaro did not blink. "They should."

"Are we not good Buddha-people here at Court? Are there those here who think we should not strive to make a true Buddha-land of our ancient realm? Are there men under our protection who are so unfilial as to criticize the Emperor for piety? What sort of loyal subjects would these be? I call them traitors."

"I am sure there are none . . ."

"Did you see your cousin Hirotsugu's letter?"

"I laughed at it."

She seemed almost to laugh. "Yes, he is a very foolish man. If there are no others . . ."

"There are none."

"Be sure of that."

"I will."

Hirotsugu, acting alone, spent the month riding out again: to the mountain forts where the young indentured soldiers, far from home, were restless; to distant villages steeped in traditional ways where isolated men were easily touched by fear; to the southernmost provinces where the Hayato kept their grievances. Even among these backward people of Kyushu, his name was powerful and his earnest horselike face looked trustworthy.

He told them that they had no choice but to join him in a protest to the capital. Danger threatened from foreign influences, and who knew better than they, here on Kyushu, the peril of letting down one's guard to foreigners. Petitions and forewarnings had done no good. They must take up arms together and convince the government to remain loyal to the old ways. He did not oppose the Emperor. Far from it. He supported the throne, which was itself in danger. And he had letters from his powerful family . . .

His belief in all this was unshakable and he persuaded them. By the month's end he had the promise of ten thousand men.

Emperor Shōmu made a progress to the village of Kuni on the Kizu River, where he knelt down and faced the four directions and then prayed to heaven and there was rain. It rained for five days and the country people praised him for his virtue, wishing him ten thousand years of life.

When he returned to Nara he appointed Ōno Azumando as his Great Sword-bearing General and instructed him to muster sufficient men to put down Hirotsugu and the army he had raised against the government. There were more men under arms in Dazaifu than in the capital and all the inner provinces combined, for it was only on Kyushu—that point of entry for invading foreigners—and in the far north where the barbarian Ezo were kept at bay that the empire had need of soldiers.

But Azumando was a seasoned captain. He had made many forays into the northern wilderness and built the stockades and the fort of Taga-jo that kept the Ezo back. He had been an Imperial Investigator during difficult times, and although he was a taciturn man, lacking in the graces of the Court, he had recently been appointed an Imperial Adviser to fill a post left vacant by the Fujiwara deaths.

In two months he had his army: seventeen thousand men. He had raised them, scraped them up, from the elite of the Palace Guards and the magnificent horsemen of the City Guard, from the forced-labor contingent in the capital who were drafted each year as tax duty but were seldom trained, from this year's and next year's tax draft in the inner provinces, and from musters he called up in the provinces on his way.

The Guards of the advance party wore suits of scale armor beautifully laced with red and purple cords. The lacquered neck-guards of their helmets flared out beside their cheeks like the wings of birds. The sheaths of their swords were dusted with gold, and their quivers were of woven wisteria. The men of the capital labor force had each been issued a seven-foot birchwood bow and thirty bamboo arrows with iron heads. But the rest of the army carried a mixed assortment of old weaponry drawn from the government storehouses in outlying districts.

So they went straggling through the mountains and across the sea, carrying their tents and caldrons, drums and horns and pipes, flags and banners, spears and halberds, long bows and short bows and scythes and knives. Some were in armor, some in hunting cloaks, and some wore cloths around their loins. Very few had ever faced an enemy, but with Azumando at their head they felt themselves invincible.

Azumando was a small man, thick in the body and short in the leg. But his reputation gave him stature, and although men did not like him they felt safe in his command. Behind his heavy, somewhat brutish face, he had a decisive mind. It was said of him that he was tender with his wife, but that was all the tenderness he had. He had never felt fear and was contemptuous of pain, both in himself and others. With these qualities he forged a hodgepodge crowd into an army.

When the last boat reached Kyushu's northern shore, Azumando rode to the shrine of the God Hachiman at Usa, a Shinto deity sympathetic to the Buddhism of the Court, and in the name of the Emperor made an offering of a fief of twenty houses and sacred treasure from the Imperial Shrine. The god spoke to him through the mouth of his priestess, saying: "The army you seek has left the fortress and has hidden in the hills." Therefore, though it puzzled him, Azumando was not surprised when his scouts reported that Dazaifu itself was occupied by only a token force and even the hill-fort of Ono-jo was very lightly held. He made no comment, but commanded that the fort be taken. From that height he would have the advantage and proceed from there.

Hirotsugu, hearing reports of the army that was coming against him, had devised a plan. He would go forth to meet them boldly. He would not hide away in the fortress. He would surprise them in the open before they were prepared. He would entrap them. He would meet their captain and subdue him. He would scatter them, and when they were scattered the Hayato could pick them off. He had not been able to consult the Hayato chieftains but they had left a liaison man with him. He could coordinate their movements when the time came.

When he was told that the enemy was converging on the hill-fort and that Ōno Azumando, the Great Sword-bearing General himself, was in command, he smiled. "I know Azumando," he said comfortably.

Then he thought a little, considering his situation. He had about two thousand men with him, he thought. The Hayato were somewhere off behind—though he could send a message to them easily, he said. He did not know exactly where the men from the villages were. Given these facts, he told his captains, it would be better to do nothing until the Hayato, who were in reserve, so to speak, should join them. Then he would feint and draw the enemy after him—into the devastation of their flying arrows! He looked at the Hayato liaison captain who was at his side, but the man said nothing.

They waited until the sun was almost overhead and still there was no word from the Hayato or from the villagers. And no news of the enemy, until, at last, when the waiting had become almost unbearable, they saw a row of figures on the fort wall, the first of the Imperial Army.

Well, they are very few, Hirotsugu thought. Perhaps the reports had been exaggerated. He looked around and showed his long teeth to his officers in a confident smile. But when he looked again the wall was crowded, and along the crest of the hill the upright bows of the Guardsmen were thick as sedge grass.

Among the banners Hirotsugu saw the crest of the Fujiwara family and was dismayed. He had sent them word. He had tried to warn them. They must have been deceived—or had they deceived him? He thought it was understood that they would not oppose him. And there were the family banners! There were their gilded antlers rising above their helmets—like his own! Suddenly the sky seemed wide and he felt very lonely.

Then, as he looked with anguish at the men arrayed against him, his family banners, and those golden antlers slowly turning in the sun, a thought came bursting into Hirotsugu's mind: I have been betrayed by my own family, and now I shall be betrayed by my allies here in Kyushu too. My life is lost, he thought. Perhaps he should challenge Azumando here and now. The decisive clash . . .

Carefully he put his helmet on and tied the bows. He did not look at his companions because of the tears in his eyes as he drew the reins in and started down the slope. The horse went quietly, picking its way through the steep gullies, swaying its rump, and the men from both armies watched it and watched Hirotsugu's helmet nodding slowly as he went.

He reached the bottom, paused. They could see him peering up. Then without waiting he turned around and started back, the bay horse scrambling on the loose stones, heaving his rider jerkily, until they reached the top.

Hirotsugu's long pale face was calm as he approached. "I

have reconnoitered," he said solemnly. "We must wait for the Hayato and attack tomorrow."

During the night the Hayato deserted him. Their liaison man, having observed Hirotsugu's little foray down the hill, withdrew into himself. And by evening the captains he had selected from the Dazaifu garrison were urging conciliation. They too had felt their hearts sink at the spectacle.

At midnight he sat alone beside the outpost hut he called his headquarters. His troops were scattered, finding bivouac where they could, and his officers lay sprawled out in the darkness of the hut, their heads against the wall.

He was thinking, he said, planning strategy. But there was a stone inside his chest, and a white moon cast long-fingered shadows through a spindle tree nearby. He tried to read some portent in their lines. Whom could he trust now?

He had not meant to challenge the Emperor! he thought wildly. He was not a traitor! Didn't they know that he was only trying to save the Court from men who would pollute it with their foreign ways? He had made that very clear to them. Why did they come after him, his own family?

Thinking these things, his head between his hands, he did not hear the troop approaching till they were almost on him. He sprang up, shouting to his men, and some scrambled after him as he ran through the hut and bolted through the window while others, better trained for war, snatched up their weapons to defend themselves.

There was a short, halfhearted skirmish in the dark, just long enough, and by the time Azumando's men burst through the door there was no one there.

As dawn came up, Hirotsugu counted. He had a company of twenty-six men. His troops were scattered and the Hayato had disappeared. He looked around him at the empty hills, the ominous cloud-forms in the sky. "We must be careful of a trap," he said. Then, reassuringly, showing them his teeth again—that smile, "There is no need to worry. We will turn westward, toward the coast," he said. "We can rally there."

But when they came to the coast there was no talk of rallying troops, of turning to fight. All the way he had explained to them, and explained again, that there had been a misunderstanding, some sort of plot. Sometimes he spoke of enemies of various kinds with whom he could not grapple, of traitors, false allies, even of foxes or gray badgers who might turn themselves into the likeness of a general so as to lure men into false steps.

A cold and foggy wind was blowing from the sea and dark brown bands of seaweed heaved in the green waves. Froth bounded up between the rocks and went hissing down again. They stopped and peered across the water. Here was the edge.

Off in the harbor the fishing boats were coming in, a sign of storms ahead. But Hirotsugu knew he had no choice. It was difficult to keep his spirits up. He had sent scouts back but he did not wait for their report. He knew Azumando would be after him in force.

"We will go to Tonra Island," he said quietly. "There are friendly people there." He remembered hearing of a prince who had come with tribute from Tonra once. It lay off to the west, not far perhaps. He did not know.

But it did not matter. The fishing boat that they commandeered took them no farther than a few miles off the shore when the storm blew them back. And Azumando's men were waiting on the low rocks of the coast. They moved in one direction, then the other, to match the course of the tossing boat as it shifted with the waves. The wind tore at their hair and cloaks so that they looked like ragged animals. And they held their arms wide as they fell and rose, staggering and slipping on the seaweed-covered rocks.

They seized the gunwales of the boat as it came slamming in. They shouted, roared their battle cry, beat on the water as they drew their swords. Hirotsugu heard them over the cries of the fishermen trying to save their boat and the oaths and grunts of effort as his own men leapt to the shore. Even the seagulls screamed aloud and the water hissed on the rocks. Only he was silent, hearing everything.

When it was over, this small war, they seized him, bound him, put him on his horse. They were exultant. But when they looked at him, disgraced, with the line of his narrow body dark against the clouds, his elbows pinned behind his back, and his long head drooping, they found he was too pitiful to watch. After a glance, they turned their eyes away.

CHAPTER X

At the time of Hirotsugu's capture, Abé was with the Emperor in the small, dark, opulently decorated "Hall of the Third Month," the Sangatsu-do, in the Todai-ji temple grounds listening to a foreign priest expound the difficult sutra of the Kegon sect. "The Great-Wide-Square-Buddha-Flower-Wreath-Adornment," he proclaimed, lifting the sutra scroll to the dome of his high brow. "The first of all the Buddha's teachings, spoken before he took into account the ignorance of his listeners, the nescience of men. A teaching full of wisdom, but too deep for human understanding . . ."

Nevertheless he had come here, Abé thought with awe, to read it to them and explain!

Every day since Shōmu had dispatched his Great Sword-bearing General to confront the rebels, he had come to this new hall on the hill, bringing his wife and daughter and members of his Court, to hear the sacred words. He hoped in this way both to deepen his own understanding of the Buddhist mysteries and to protect his suffering nation from rebellion and disease.

Therefore when the messenger from Dazaifu returned to Nara to report Azumando's victory and Hirotsugu's capture, he found the Emperor unavailable. And as he wandered somewhat dazedly around the Palace he was intercepted by his cousin

Nakamaro, who found in him a source of news—therefore perhaps of power—and escorted him to his own mansion.

This messenger whom the Great Sword-bearing General had selected was Hirotsugu's own young brother, Momokawa, a mere youth. But Azumando had discerned in him something of his own stubborn strength.

"So he ran away. So he ran away," Nakamaro said when they were seated. "So he ran away and then allowed himself to be taken." He wished that Hirotsugu had somehow disappeared. He was an embarrassment and a disgrace.

"Yes. He bungled everything."

"Who captured him?"

"Someone in the Guards. He was blown back to shore, I understand . . ."

"Where is he now?"

"They were bringing him to Azumando's headquarters. I didn't see him. I have come to find out what is to be done with him."

"The Emperor is at the Todai-ji, at the Third Month Hall. They are expounding a sutra there, you know. He goes there every day, and the Empress and the Princess."

"Every day?" Momokawa wondered when he would be allowed an audience. He had thought they would be anxious for his report. So important. And he the messenger. But to find them calmly visiting the temple every day . . . "Going to listen to the priests every day?"

"This particular doctrine is very difficult."

Momokawa could not tell from his tone whether his cousin approved or disapproved. "Yes. Well, I brought the news . . ."

"There was no battle of any kind? No encounter?"

"None. Nothing. A few skirmishes, but he was not involved. He said he meant no harm! Then he betrayed the Hayato and they left him. After that he fled." Momokawa still had one foot in Kyushu. He had been dispatched so quickly to the capital that he assumed it was a great responsibility—and yet, no one had quite defined his message. "What will they decide to do about him, do you suppose—Hirotsugu. Has the Emperor been very angry?"

Nakamaro looked at him. He's tired, he thought without compassion. He did not like competition from young cousins. "Not so angry as the Empress," he said. "She regards it as a stain on the family. She has decided to give her father's lands to the Todai-ji temple in restitution."

Momokawa blinked. Even Hirotsugu had not dreamed that their grandfather's wealth might be given to the priests. The fiefs which had been granted to the statesman Fuhito included the fields and produce of five thousand households—a good portion of the family wealth.

Nakamaro watched the red flush creeping up Momokawa's eyelids as he tried to steady himself. It was a shock, he knew. He intended it to be. He himself had made his own adjustments since he had spoken with the Empress. It was not only useless but self-defeating to raise objections, he realized, especially after Hirotsugu's folly. The Imperial tide was running strongly in favor of the temples and this was not the time to swim against it. The Empress was the moon that pulled the tide, but she was also his best hope for further promotions.

He wondered how soon Momokawa would come to these same conclusions. But he felt comfortable, watching that young angry face, that this rather heavy-footed cousin would never be a favorite at Court.

"Perhaps you would like to refresh yourself?"

Nakamaro's wife had brought them wine and red bean cakes. She was his second wife, a woman easy to overlook, small, plain, with a self-deprecatory manner that gave no hint of her high family connections and considerable intellect. But she was ambitious for her husband and her sons, and she could read Nakamaro's mind and manner and knew when he had visitors worth hearing. In the guise of hospitality she had brought the trays with her own hands and now she lingered, fussing over the dishes.

"The Fujiwara lands? To a temple?" Momokawa stammered out.

"Yes, the Todai-ji." Nakamaro still spoke in that offhand tone. He waved his wife's hands from the pitcher on his tray and poured some wine. "It is to be the headquarters-temple of the nation, so to speak." He drank. "And every province is to have a guardian-temple full of monks and an atonement nunnery for nuns under its jurisdiction." Only that small phrase "full of" gave a hint of his feelings.

Momokawa, when he had been with the army in Kyushu, had felt nothing but the purest indignation and contempt for his elder brother. Now things were not so clear in his mind. There seemed to be complications in his feelings. There were various circumstances he had not taken account of. Of course he would never question the Empress. Impossible. Loyalty was the groundwork of his being and he had never seen the need for anything more. And yet it might be possible to question . . . He stood up.

"And of course the temples will need sustenance lands," Nakamaro went on calmly, fitting the stopper into the pitcher's narrow neck, "for the cost of construction and the maintenance . . . the completion of the pagodas too, of course . . . and the images . . . the reliquaries, the sutra halls, and so forth . . ." He had little humor, but it amused him to see Momokawa shifting his feet before him, uncertain whether to sit down again. "So this is an opportunity for the Empress to remove the blot on the family that Hirotsugu has made. What does Azumando intend to do with him?"

The question came so swiftly, with no change of tone, that Momokawa's answer was no more than a short wordless noise. Then he went back to the subject of the temples and his grandfather's lands. "But if there are to be so many monks and so forth, in so many temples—and the Todai-ji at the head. Why, it would rival the Court itself!"

"Yes."

"But the Emperor . . ."

"The Emperor appoints the priests." Nakamaro looked up sharply for the first time. "The Emperor builds the temples. The Emperor provides the lands. I don't imagine you question an Emperial decree?"

"Never. Oh no!" Momokawa sank down on the mat.

Nakamaro gazed at him a long time before he repeated his question about Hirotsugu's fate. There had been such a strengthening of Buddhist influence these past few years that he supposed the Emperor would balk at taking a life. He would send that stupid rebel into exile, he supposed. If the decision were in his own hands he would have him executed. It was simpler that way, better for everyone to have him out of the way, forgotten. And knowing Azumando . . .

"Did Azumando send you for instructions from the Court?"

"Yes, well, he sent me to report."

"And after that?"

"Why, to return again . . ."

"With instructions?"

"Why, I suppose . . ."

"You will not see the Emperor for several days at least."

"Well, the Grand Council . . ."

"You were instructed to report to the Emperor?"

"Yes, well . . ."

"He will not want to be disturbed."

"No."

"So you will wait?"

"Why, if you say so . . ."

"And Azumando. Azumando, do you suppose he'll wait?"

At first Momokawa was not sure what his cousin meant. But he saw his brow pinch up a little as though it were a smile and knew he wanted him to wait, and that Azumando would not wait, and that way it would be taken care of.

In the temple Abé sat in earnest concentration, gazing up at the priest on his high sutra-platform under its wooden canopy. Outside, when she had been carried up the steep path to this hall, the opaque mist of dawn had stood between her and the trees. Now, in this dark interior, a mist of incense rose between her and the tall gold image of the Kannon Bosatsu that was worshiped here. The pale blue smoke went spiraling up beside the copper lotus flowers and gilded banners and spread a veil scented with sandalwood before the goddess' face.

The priest's bald head was lighted by his sutra-reading lamp.

"When we speak of the Ten Bodies of Buddha," he was saying, "we do not speak of separation but of One. For these Ten Bodies of the Three Worlds mutually blend . . ."

He was indeed an awesome man, Abé thought. Rōben had brought him from Korea to expound this difficult doctrine. Rōben himself, while eminent, was not so awesome, she thought, even though he had founded the Todai-ji temple and built this hall on the hillside and was closest to the Emperor of all the Buddhist priests. It was Rōben who first had visions of a network of guardian temples that would spread throughout the provinces with the Todai-ji at its heart. And with his own hands he had made the gilded Kannon that stood before her now, rising in the dark.

The foreign priest was speaking of the Ten Bodies that make up the Three Worlds. "What is meant by that?" he asked. And answering: "In the First World there are Three Bodies. In the Second World there are Six. The Third is the One Body of the Absolute Reality of empty space.

"Now let us take the First World. Here the Three Bodies are: The First, that contains all forms of beings that are born alive, or born from eggs, or from moisture, or from causes that we do not know. The Second contains all phenomena, all things and places. And the Third is the Body of all work and its reward.

"These Three Bodies make up the First World, that of illusion, of material things. For as we know, all space, all time, all matter are illusions."

Abé shifted her gaze from the priest to the merciful Kannon with her many arms for helping those in need. The head and the jeweled crown were far above her in the dark. There were twenty thousand jewels, Rōben said, but she could not see them. Instead she watched the golden arms that seemed to move and ripple in the wavering light. A loop of cord hung from the third right hand. It was used to capture stubborn souls who refused salvation or were thought to be beyond it.

Suddenly she thought of Hirotsugu. Could that little loop of cord reach him, she wondered. Save him? She did not really want him saved. A hateful man. But of course one must not take the life of any living thing, even a man like Hirotsugu. But on the other hand, if it were up to her . . .

The priest was talking about the sutra now, and about other sutras and learned commentaries, wandering through the gardens of his erudition, extemporizing. Rōben had promised that when he preached a great illumination would issue from his mouth and words like flowers form upon his lips. Abé stared at him, entranced, while he lifted up his head and spoke, elaborating on his elaborations.

". . . so that anyone who hears this sutra, either standing or sitting down, that person—merely from the mass of merit resulting from that hearing—will become at the time of his next existence, the owner of innumerable carriages—of carriages that are yoked with bullocks, or with horses, or with elephants, of vehicles yoked with bulls, of celestial aerial cars . . ."

Glorious images formed in Abé's mind.

". . . and if someone—a young man of good family, or a young lady—says to another person, Come, friend, and hear, and if that other person is persuaded to listen, were it but a single moment, he will become the reverse of dull, will obtain keen faculties, will have wisdom . . ."

Abé allowed herself to lower her chin. The words were sometimes hard to follow and the priest sat very high. The Kannon was more comfortable to watch. Rōben said this image was especially dedicated to men with troubled minds. Her father had been troubled these past few months, and his health suffered. His burden of responsibility is too great, she thought.

The priest continued his exposition. "He will have wisdom. In the course of a hundred thousand years he will never have a fetid breath. He will have no disease of the tongue. He will have no black teeth, no unequal, no yellow, no ill-ranged, no broken teeth, no teeth fallen out. His lips will not be pendulous, not turned inward, not gaping, not mutilated. His nose will not be large or wry. His face will not be long, not wry, not unpleasant . . ."

Again Abé thought of Hirotsugu. What was to become of him? Certainly he could not stand against Azumando's army. And what must she do with Saisho in her disgrace? People said that she should let her go, should send her away, although her mother was kind and had said nothing yet. Some of the Imperial Advisers spoke of moving the capital to a more propitious site, and if that happened she was sure she could not take her, scorned as she was. That foolish Saisho, little Saisho whom she loved . . .

"Mark!" the priest cried, and Abé's eyes flew up to him. "Mark how much good is produced by a man's inciting but one single creature to hear this sutra. He shall never be ill-favored but on the contrary his tongue, his teeth and lips will be delicate and well shaped, his nose well shaped, his face perfectly round. He will receive a very complete organ of manhood. He will have many advantages . . ."

The golden voice went on. And Abé, straining her neck, watched anxiously for the illumination.

In Dazaifu, General Azumando ordered the Guards to form a hollow square on the parade ground. Overnight the sky had cleared and the rain had seeped into the hard-packed earth. By the walls, the long shade cast by the early sun was damp, but in the open yard a layer of soft dusty particles had formed though it was hard as iron underneath. In the center of this barren yellow square a red cloth had been laid out like a rug.

Azumando stood on the broad steps of the hall, half in shadow, half in the sun. The light fell hard on his leather boots and the tip of his Great Sword in its sheath, but his broad torso and bare head were hard to see. To the squinting soldiers, although his features were not clear, the ferocity of his controlled emotion showed in his stance and the quivering of his hair-knot ceremonially tied at the crown of his head.

When Hirotsugu was led out they were relieved to see he had regained his dignity. However, his elbows were again bound at his back so that his figure seemed extraordinarily long and thin. He was allowed to make his last obeisance in the four directions before his guards came forward to press him to the ground.

Azumando stepped into the sun and Hirotsugu, seeing his

approach, made one wild look around the yard—at the yellow walls, the line of the hills, the blue, blue sky beyond—before he bent his head.

Some thought, as they looked on, that there might have been more ceremony. Or there might have been more questioning and consultation, word from the capital perhaps, before such summary execution. Some felt, despite their fear of Azumando, that the executioner lacked height. They felt uncomfortable to see so squat a man poised over that lean bent figure.

But when he slipped his right arm from the sleeve of his surcoat, baring his knotted shoulder and the muscles of his neck, and when he drew the Great Sword from its scabbard in one long sweeping gesture, raising it high in both his hands, he seemed to grow and tower in the sun.

He brought the sword down with a whipping noise and a grunt of exerted breath. The sounds of the crack of bone and the soft thud of the severed head, the scrape of the sword tip on the ground were almost simultaneous.

CHAPTER XI

Emperor Shōmu, struck by the calamities of epidemics, drought, rebellion, had turned increasingly to the Buddhist priests for help. More and more often during the past year he had had sutras read and abstinence days proclaimed. He had ordered the building of pagodas and of guardian temples and nunneries in each of the provinces. He had increased the number of monks and nuns by many hundreds. Thousands of artists and artisans had created images of Buddhas and bodhisattvas, deva kings and guardian gods in bronze and wood and clay and dry lacquer at his command. Still there were crop failures, disease, unrest. And he himself was not well.

For a full month after the rebellion and Hirotsugu's death he continued to visit the hall on the Todai-ji hillside and listen to the foreign priest expound the Sutra of the Kegon sect. He put his heart and his whole being into it.

It was clear to many who observed the Emperor's sincerity that he had accumulated many merits in his previous lives. Even in this one he tried to emulate the bodhisattvas in his selflessness and compassion. He was deeply troubled by Hirotsugu's execution, although his advisers—even his gentle wife—assured him it was for the best.

Progressively as he sat day after day in the dark hall, with his eyes fixed and unseeing on the haze of gold beyond the incense smoke and his ears half tuned to the voice above him, he felt himself grow less and less attached to the life of this world and nearer to the truth of Reality. And one day, suddenly, through the thicket of the foreign priest's expounding, he heard a clear call from the Buddha straight to his heart.

Thunderstruck, he heard the words: "I am Roshana Buddha and I live in the Lotus World. I am surrounded by one thousand petals, each petal being a world. And each of these worlds contains a hundred million other worlds, with suns and moons and Buddhas of their own. The Buddhas of these thousand petals and of these hundred million worlds are transformations of myself. They dwell in me and I in them. I am the source and origin of all, and my name is Roshana."

A piercing ray of illumination entered Shōmu's mind. This was the Eternal Buddha whose form encompasses the whole of all creation, the universe. And he perceived that all things in this universe touch upon one another, reflect one another, influence one another ceaselessly. If one single being in this universe is enlightened, he perceived, all are illumined. If one dies, all are diminished.

With this, a dazzling vision rose in the little room, swelling the confines of the walls, lifting the smoke-streaking ceiling. It was a golden image of this Buddha on his lotus throne with every petal etched to contain a world and every world containing many more, so that the compassion of this Buddha flowed into every particle of his domain, and in every particle the Buddha could be seen!

Had Shōmu been a man of less earnest character, he might have kept this vision to himself and retired to a monastery where in the quiet routine of a monk he might have deepened further this understanding and prepared himself for his future life. But he was the guardian of the people's welfare and the land's prosperity. He was responsible.

Kingship was based on the virtue of the king. This had been taught him very thoroughly when he was Crown Prince and they kept him waiting till he was twenty-two.

"If any king upholds my teaching," Buddha said, "and

brings it to all classes, high and low, I will protect him from ill health and bring him peace of mind."

But more than that, and more important, Shōmu knew: "I will protect his cities and make his people glad. In the time of his sovereignty the earth shall be fertile, the climate temperate, the seasons follow in their proper order. The sun, moon, and the constellations shall continue in their regular procession. And no meanness shall be found in human hearts."

Truly a great responsibility. So for the sake of his people, Shōmu thought, for the sake of the land, he must continue to serve Buddha and to rule with a pure bright heart.

But he was still troubled by the implications of rebellion, and furthermore, his advisers from the Bureau of Yin and Yang—those concerned with the prevention of calamities—agreed that it would be wise to move the capital. Perhaps the configuration of the Nara Plain, the flow of water, and the line of the hills were inimical to health and peace. Perhaps in a more propitious site things would go better.

Shōmu instructed Tachibana Moroé to inspect the village of Kuni on the Kizu River northeast of Nara. The river was broad and full of water and Mount Wazuka sheltered it. Moroé was satisfied and after consultation built a palace there. And in the First Month of the following year Shōmu held court there for the first time. By the Tenth Month all the palaces were completed, the streets made wider, and the marketplaces moved from Nara. And on New Year's Day, 742, the last of the government offices were transferred. Kuni was now the center of the empire. Nara was left behind.

When Abé first saw Kuni she was in two moods. She was eager to see the new city and her eagerness was tinged with an irrational hope—or not so much a hope as a kind of tingling in her heart—that the beautiful priest from Kawachi might be there. She did not think about it, merely felt it, but her eyes were bright and her face eager as she peered from her palanquin. When they crossed the river snow was falling, floating downward in great leisurely flakes.

Constantly as falls the snow,
Ceaselessly as beats the rain,
Ever thinking, I have come . . .

The roofs of the palaces were bleak and low, striped by the falling snow. He would not be there. How foolish to have thought so. Her life would not change.

The other mood, the sadness, washed through her heart. How hard it had been to leave Nara, to leave her childhood, to leave home. How sad to come away without a friend.

Saisho was left behind. She knew it would be so. She squinted at the low roofs through a blur of tears and snow. It was as though each tender flake paused for an instant in a tiny draft over the water's surface before floating on to touch and melt and disappear. A little death.

She thought, indeed, how like a human life it was to drift, to float, and vanish without a sound.

Her pavilion had been prepared for her very beautifully. Her favorite standing screen was here, with the twin deer on it. The garden was small, enclosed, and had been planted with little pine trees for the season—some black, some "female" with soft reddish bark. She was amused to see the gardeners in their stiff straw capes still working there, shifting the rocks around the pond and clearing out the weeds. They worked bent double and the piled-up snow formed little saddles on their backs.

When in a few days she had settled in, she went to her mother's pavilion, following the covered walk by the long garden. The snow had changed to rain and now was running off into the gutters in muddy streams. She thought in contrast that her own little garden with its rocks and tiny pool, its leaning pines, was far more charming and just right for her.

"Yes," her mother agreed with her. "Your garden was planned with the utmost care. And I hope you enjoy your rooms as well. A great deal of thought went into them."

Abé smiled. "My own deer screen is there. Yes, it is all quite lovely."

"Nakamaro planned it, did you know?" Her mother searched her face. "He took care of everything."

"Indeed!" Abé was amused. "I wonder that he would have taken such an interest. Did he plan all the palaces?"

"Just yours."

So, Abé thought. Just mine. Her mind went back to that night so long ago when he had sat beside her curtain and she had felt his hand creep underneath. How frightened she had been. What a child she was!

She wondered if she should make herself available to him now. Was that what her mother wanted?

Kōmyō, as usual, read her thoughts. "I am thinking of your health. It is not good for a woman to spend her life deprived of such intercourse. People will say you have an incubus."

Abé had heard this kind of talk before. It did not frighten her. But why had her mother changed, she wondered. Had she discovered the secret of the Kawachi priest and did she sense her longing? Was she afraid there might be others? Her mother was almost magical in her intuition and, indeed, some god might have told her. She seemed to know everything.

"Are you less afraid of Nakamaro than of the others?"

"There must be no others!"

How cruel her voice could be and yet remain soft! Or perhaps it was never cruel at all, but only that Abé loved her with such unguarded tenderness that the slightest chill felt like a piercing wind.

The snow had definitely turned to rain. It had rained for more than a week when, late one dim green afternoon when Abé sat alone in her small gallery looking out through the curtain of transparent drops that fell from the low eaves, Nakamaro was announced.

She was neither glad nor sorry but felt instead an unaccustomed calm settle in her heart. She would receive him, and they would talk alone. She raised her fan before her face in a perfunctory way. She really did not care. And when her maid had set a cushion for him in the middle of the room and then withdrawn she turned around to look at him unblinking.

She remembered the first time she had seen him—or the first

that she recollected—and she spoke from that memory suddenly, without introduction: "I remember you in a green Court costume, Nakamaro, and a very frowning face!" She smiled, though she looked away again into the wet garden, for she had observed how somber he had grown and how rough and pocked his face was in the rainy light. How alien he seemed. A man like a stranger.

Nakamaro did not answer. It was not a welcome thought. A green robe: Junior Rank. For a long time now he had held high positions in the Court and thought of himself as an important man. At last, feeling the need to answer, he muttered that he too remembered—"when I was a boy."

She laughed, although she was aware it was not kind to laugh. She made enemies that way. "No," she said quickly, to retrieve the laugh, "but I remember you also at the archery contest when you captained the West Team." (The West had won that year.) "And one time leading the procession to the Kasuga Shrine." That freezing night with the torches flaring. She did in fact remember him, though she had not been much impressed at the time. Others had found him very handsome and he had been talked about.

"Do you miss Nara?"

"Yes," he said, though in fact he had not given it any thought. He had been too busy here in Kuni.

"I do not miss it. I am very happy here. In my beautiful pavilion. With my garden . . ." Was this what her mother meant for her? She fell silent as she turned away from him.

Nakamaro had been told he was wanted in the Princess' rooms. What was the purpose, he wondered. And why were they left alone? He shifted his position so that he could see more clearly the tender line of her slim shoulders against the light. A dim glow came from the garden and the rain fell through the needles of the pines like fine silk threads.

If she had been keeping him at a distance with her inconsequential talk, Nakamaro thought, what was the meaning of her silence? She had lowered her fan into her lap and the air between them seemed to grow thick with tension.

Still with her back to him she asked abruptly: "Are you afraid of me?"

Nakamaro, to his intense surprise, discovered that he was. "Not at all," he tried to laugh. "Should I be?"

"So many people are, it seems, for one reason or another." There was a long pause while Nakamaro waited for what would come. "So I am glad that you are not."

Her voice was so flat that he could not tell if there was irony in it, but as she continued it seemed to warm a little. "I would like to have a friend to whom I could confide—everything."

She did not turn, but surely it was an invitation. Very cautiously he moved forward till he was next to her. Together they looked at the garden, at the rain and the green pines. On each long needle a clear drop formed, trembled, and fell down. Her breath seemed calm enough, but Nakamaro felt his own begin to falter and grow warm in his throat.

After a time she turned to look at him and her face was there before him, shockingly lovely.

Nakamaro had grown cautious in his sexual activity, though he was only thirty-three years old. His ambition in this field, as it was in others, was to assume full mastery and control. In the past, in order to achieve the power and the calm he thought enhanced his lovemaking, he had sometimes practiced a kind of meditation recommended by the Chinese manuals to bring the forces of yin and yang into close union.

He had spent some hours seated on a special stool and breathing deeply in an effort to form a center of power beneath his navel that would sustain enormously prolonged and satisfying sexual experience. But he was not by nature meditative and he had never achieved that special power. This made him somewhat nervous about his virility.

Furthermore, he had always believed that the act of sex was strengthening to a man. But recently, from the *Code of the Jade Chamber* and other manuals that Kibi no Makibi had brought from China, he had learned about the danger of too frequent ejaculation. Impotence, the Chinese experts warned, was almost always due to overindulgence and the squandering of one's seed. So it was better to contain oneself . . . though, on the other hand, as everyone knew . . .

Such contradictory thoughts and impulses impeded Nakamaro as the Princess turned her face to him and whispered very softly, so that he hardly heard, "Do you want me?"

Automatically he lifted his arms to her, removing her scarf from her shoulders and then encircling her to untie her sash and loosen the layers of her robes. He rose to his knees to unfasten his own clothes, thinking she would not know how to help, but she reached out and took his belt from him, and then her hands went in around him, feeling his skin.

Together they sank back on the floor, and as he leaned over her, struggling with doubt, the warm scent of her flesh, released when her garments parted, was almost overpowering. Her face was calm, unmoving in the rain-reflected light. Staring at it, he removed the boxwood comb and the long pins from her hair and ran his fingers close against her scalp.

Surprisingly this roused him with a stab of such desire that he regretted sharply that he had had another woman only that morning. Could he afford to lose his seed twice in so short a time? And if he was to be so moved by the mere touch of her hair, would he be able to refrain? She showed little sign of passion, and except for the glisten on her face, he might have thought she was oblivious to him. On the other hand, it was the very calm with which she accepted him, the languor of her small soft body that excited him almost beyond control.

As the manual instructed, if a man must save his seed, he raised his head up sharply when he mounted her, and ground his teeth. Opening his eyes as wide as they would go, he looked first to the left, then right, then up, then down, while he clenched his muscles against ejaculation, safeguarding his virility from dissipation.

When she stopped moving and lay quiet under him, he removed himself and held her in what he meant to be a comforting embrace. It was not his habit to linger after making love and he felt awkward. They lay so quietly, unnaturally still, yet not asleep, that their breathing seemed to rake the room. He felt he must say something, but what to say? He chose a verse he felt was apt, speaking it close to her ear.

> "How steadily I love you,
> You who awe me like the surge of waves
> On the coast of sacred Isé."

She opened her eyes and turned to look at him, a quiet look. He could not tell what she was thinking. But he was surprised to find he did feel somewhat awed. He let his mind touch on the fact of her sacred lineage.

"I feel unworthy," he began. He was in some ways sincere. "Why would you give yourself to me . . ."

But the humility of his tone was so unlike him that she stopped him, smiling faintly, as she said, "My mother wanted it."

Although this liaison lasted many years, with many shared triumphs as well as bitter times, and even mutual affection now and then, Nakamaro never forgave those words so softly spoken.

A shock of rage went through him and he rolled away and stared at the ceiling for a while, hearing the rain outside and the rustling of the Princess' garments as she pulled them into shape. She seemed to be taking it all so calmly! He was not used to this.

After a while he rose and went to the veranda. The steps to the garden glistened and the smell of the pines was strong. He would have liked to leave now. Out of the question. The Imperial Princess was not a woman you could leave in the middle of the night. But what to do with the long hours till the cock should crow?

He turned. She had risen on her elbow and was watching him. "Shouldn't you be lying down, keeping warm?" Abé knew the proper etiquette of the bedchamber. Although it was not part of her formal education, it was commonly studied by Court ladies, often in her presence. And it was written in the *Manual of Lady Mystery* that a man should roll on his right side after love and cover his jade-stem with his hands to keep it warm.

Even more concerned for his virility than his pride, Nakamaro came back and lay down. Their clothing overlapped as they lay side by side as though they were true lovers, and they slept a little, forming a quiet bond.

Abé woke to hear him murmuring the proper phrases for a lover taking reluctant leave. There was the faintest feeling of dawn in the room and she heard him say that he wished the morning would never come, and that he could not stand the hours till they should meet again. But even as he spoke he was preoccupied with feeling about amid their tangled clothing for his hair-cord and his fan. Then he was up and pulling on his trousers, cinching the belt around him hastily.

"I had better not be found here," he said, making for the door. It was standard usage for a visitor when he was overtaken by the day and the house was stirring.

"Nakamaro," Abé said, rising. "Nakamaro." He stopped. "Nakamaro, let us be friends."

He turned and saw her little figure standing in the dark, and for the first time thought of her other than as his cousin, the *Kōtaishi*, who had caught him off his guard. He thought of the sweetness of her yielding, the fragrance of her hair, of an inner quality that fled from him even as it led him on, so that he wanted to pursue, to catch, to hold—to damage? He stared at her.

He saw that she was waiting and recalled himself. "Yes, friends," he said. How strange a word! "You honor me." Then, baffled by his feelings, he murmured once again the standard words that he was loath to go. And then he left.

His next-morning letter was correct, though somewhat stiff. He could have got it from a copybook. Abé laughed aloud when she read it. And then, hearing her own voice and the harshness in it, she folded up the letter and lay down and wept.

CHAPTER XII

All this time—during the consultations over the move to Kuni, the purification of the temple there, the farewell to Nara and the great procession north—the image of the Roshana Buddha sat before Shōmu in his dreams.

He longed to make it real, to set before the world this vision of the Eternal One. But he wondered if he could live to see it done. He was very tired. And it would be costly, it would need tons of tin and copper, and where would he find the gold? There was no gold in Japan. And would the people willingly give their taxes and the labor of their hands? And would the August Ancestors be angered?

After his Court had been installed in the new palaces he summoned the priest Gyōgi from the countryside. It was the first time the big priest had entered the Imperial presence, but Rōben suggested that he knew the people and would be honest in his advice.

Gyōgi seemed to bring the scent of the country into the darkened room and in the expansiveness of his person Shōmu was comforted. He told the Emperor that the people loved him and loved all the Imperial Family, and because of that love they were willing to accept the Buddhist Law. But there were some old-fashioned people too, the Emperor must understand, who were jealous for the sake of the Ancestral Gods. They held the misconception that the Buddha was a foreign god, a rival. Therefore he recommended that the Emperor request the help of the God Hachiman at Usa once again.

Shōmu's gifts to the shrine at Usa (a brocade cap, copies of two sutras written in gold, eighteen novice monks, and five blue horses) were rewarded with a message from the god's priestess that Hachiman would be pleased indeed if a great statue of the Buddha were built to protect the nation.

Still Shōmu hesitated, for there were puzzling omens all through the year. Lightning struck and thunder rolled in his new Palace at Kuni, and after that there was a comet more than ten feet long. But on the other hand, a three-legged sparrow, a propitious sign, was presented to the throne. He made a journey to the ancient capital at Naniwa and began to refurbish the old Palace there. And when he returned he went to Shigaraki, where he thought he might build his Buddha. Then he sent again for Gyōgi.

When he saw the holy man he felt his tensions ease, and Gyōgi listened to him quietly, absorbing the Emperor's worries. Shōmu was forty-one years old and the priest seventy-two, but Gyōgi's face was ruddier and his spirit more vigorous.

The Emperor was not well. His eyes troubled him. When he looked at Gyōgi he had to squint, and this haze before his eyes made it difficult for him to see clearly what he should do . . .

Did he dream, then, as he gazed at the broad sunburned face before him as through a film of silk, that Gyōgi offered himself as an Imperial emissary to the fountainhead of the Heavenly Sun-line? Did this priest of the people say to his Sovereign that in his own rough, humble person he would take with him a relic of Buddha as the Emperor's offering and make supplication for him to his August Ancestress in her Grand Shrine at Isé?

The Isé Shrine is the golden heart of the mystical body of Japan, the resting place in Yamato of the Goddess Amaterasu. There, in an ancient forest, across a sacred bridge, beneath giant cryptomeria and camphor trees, behind four barrier fences, and within a shrine of pristine cypress wood, lies the round bronze mirror that the goddess gave to her grandson Ninigi when he descended to the Land of the Reed Plain at the dawn of time. "This mirror," she said, "have it as my spirit. Worship it just as you would worship in my very presence."

Is it possible that Gyōgi went there, seventy-two years old and traveling on foot? Is it possible that he passed beneath the outer torii gate and crossed the arch of the bridge and was met there by the Shinto priests in their gleaming white silk robes? Did he follow them along the gravel path by the translucent stream and turn and climb the moss-grown steps and come at last to the small covered gateway in the barrier fence and there sit down and wait? Did he keep a silent vigil there through seven days and nights, enduring the weather of the Month of Frosts? Some think so.

Perhaps he entered into Shōmu's dream and lived it for him, seated outside the barrier gate under the open sky. He had given the relic to the attendant priests. Would the goddess accept it? Would she give him an answer to take back? He waited.

A curtain hung between him and the opening of the fence. He could see no more of the shrine itself than the slender horns of the crossbeams rising against the sky and under them a section of the close-packed thatch. There were no ornaments, no carvings, no colors but the pale gold of fresh cypress and the tawny sheen of the thatch.

Closing his eyes, Gyōgi tried to tune himself to his surroundings, waiting for any message he might receive. The feeling he absorbed was one simply of quiet, of serenity. Severe, perhaps, but not intimidating. Certainly he was in a presence that was awesome. This he was prepared for. But he did not feel threatened, despite his errand . . .

Was this the Emperor's dream? He held his head up, listening carefully. He heard no threat, no promise, no invitation to escape the sufferings of the world. What was being said to him, he wondered. Nothing. Only a silent permeation of the trees, the stones, the shrine. An unvoiced proclamation: "I am here." He waited.

At dusk he heard the sounds of wooden soles against the stones of the steps. A procession of the white-robed priests passed by him silently and disappeared behind the curtain. He saw that they were carrying in their outstretched hands small pyramids of fruits on wooden trays and earthen cups of wine and sacred branches of the sakaki tree. This was the day the Emperor tasted the first of the new harvest and in the Palace thanksgiving rites were performed. At Isé the priests were offering the great prayer of the harvest to the Sun Goddess.

Gyōgi felt the cold that precedes the darkening of night. The light and color left the forest and the line of the ridgepole faded. The noises of night insects and the little rustlings of grounded leaves seemed to intensify the chill. He heard the first tones of the chant behind the barrier fence, the appeal to the "Great Heaven-shining Deity Who Dwells in Isé."

Although the words were ancient, the voices rose and fell in familiar cadences. And as the music of them flowed into his ears, pictures of this land he knew so well emerged in his mind's eye.

". . . because the Great Deity has bestowed on him,
    the August Child of the Gods,
lands of the four quarters over which his glance extends
    as far as where the bounds of earth stand up
    as far as where the wall of heaven rises
    as far as the blue clouds are diffused
    as far as the white clouds settle down
by the green sea-plane as far as the prows of ships can go
    without letting dry their oars
by land as far as the hooves of horses can go
    with tightened baggage-cords
treading their way among the rock-roots and the tree-roots
    where the long road extends . . ."

Gyōgi had been meditating on Equanimity, pervading the four directions with his thought and seeking identity with all things in the universe through the penetration of his quietude, free of ill will. He had been roused briefly when the priests passed by but retained that open stillness.

Now, as he listened to the Shinto prayer a passage from the Sutra of the Golden Light came to his mind. "Every drop of water in the vast ocean can be counted," he recited to himself, "but the age of the Buddha, none can measure. Crush the Mountain of the World into particles as fine as mustard seed and we can count them, but the age of the Buddha cannot be measured."

The true reality, he thought, is not in seas and mountains. And although the power of a ruler—or his gods—may extend to the ends of the earth, the earth itself is insubstantial and of no consequence. "Just as in the vast ethereal sphere," he recalled the sutra, "stars and darkness, light and mirage, dew, foam, lightning and clouds emerge and vanish like the features in a dream—so must everything of shape and substance be regarded."

The sky was dark now, pricked with stars between the needles of the trees. He heard again the eerie voices from within the shrine enclosure:

". . . therefore will the first fruits for the Sovereign Deity
be piled up in her presence like a range of hills,
leaving the remainder for the August Child
tranquilly to partake of . . ."

He thought of Shōmu with his worried face, this weight of myth and history on his narrow shoulders, partaking of his little bit of rice so that the people of his nation should not go hungry.

Duty, he thought. He also had a duty to this land. And again the familiar words of Buddha came into his mind: "I am the father of the world, the self-born, the healer, the protector of all creatures. I, who know the course of the world, declare: I am he, the Buddha. And I consider: How can I incline those unbelieving men to True Enlightenment? How can they become partakers of the True Law?"

For seven days and seven nights Gyōgi sat at the shrine of the Sun Goddess, and in the end—was it a dream?—they came to him and told him that the goddess had been pleased to accept his offering. And through her priestess she had pronounced the words:

"The sun of truth and reality shines over the long night of life and death."

And when he asked how he should interpret this:

"The illumination of the sun is seen in the Roshana Buddha."

He rose and made his way down the stone steps and under the silent trees, across the bridge, and through the torii—did his feet touch the ground?—and all the long way back to Kuni.

Shōmu was waiting as he had left him. He had not rested for seven days. When he heard the words of his August Ancestress it was as though the muscles of his heart relaxed. That night he slept and in his sleep the goddess stood before him in a radiant disk. Her voice was a burst of light:

This land is the country of the gods; the people should worship them. But the Wheel of the Sun is the Great Buddha, the ultimate Reality is Roshana . . .

CHAPTER XIII

It was midnight on the eleventh day of the Eleventh Month in the thirteenth year of Tempyo (A.D. 742) when Amaterasu Ōmikami appeared to Emperor Shōmu. Next day he announced his plan to build a gigantic Buddha-image.

No one questioned his decree, but before the year was out a message came to him from his aunt, the Retired Empress Gensho, who lived in her own detached palace by the river's edge. She had not taken part in the affairs of government since she handed him the sovereignty after holding it so many years, but she reserved the right to do so. She treated the Emperor like a boy.

Dutifully he went to her, like a boy. The weather had turned very cold. The wheels of his winter carriage squeaked on the frozen road and the ice of the puddles broke into shards. Her garden was somber. No one had cut the trees back properly when this palace was built and a cold mist hung in the branches overhead. Even her hall was frigid. Shōmu felt the bite of the bare boards through his soft felt boots. He had left his Imperial bearing at the door and began to stoop his tall shape as he approached her.

The Empress Dowager was seated on a Chinese couch scarcely raised from the floor. Her legs were drawn up under her and one old hand rested on a metal brazier by her side. Her sparse gray hair was pulled up into a single hair-knot without ornament as though she no longer cared for her appearance. But her robe was of heavy silk damask with a phoenix and flower pattern, and the damask slippers placed on the floor in front of her were sewn with green jade ornaments.

She bowed her head to him as he went down before her. He was ashamed that he had neglected her since the move to Kuni. He realized almost with alarm that the last time he had visited this palace he had envied the old lady for the shade of her garden and the cool river breeze. That must have been half a year ago.

He glanced at her apologetically. She had leaned forward, her old hand twitching slightly on the brazier's rim, and a thread of clear water grew and hung immobile from the tip of her nose. For a moment he thought it was an icicle.

"We must see that you are moved to a warmer hall," he said.

"I should like to come to the Palace," she said. He remembered the mild tone of command that she always used. She spoke softly and things were done.

He felt his eyes shifting for a place to look. "The Empress herself will see to it. A warmer hall. The south garden . . ."

"My needs are very simple," she brushed him off. "But I must see to the ceremonies of the New Year."

Shōmu looked up at her apprehensively. Did she feel the ceremonies had not been properly celebrated since her departure? The drop was gone from her nose but her eyes were stern. He reflected that instead of growing thick and tolerant as some people do with age, his aunt grew thinner and sharper with the years. She was sixty-five, and except for the slight palsy in her hands seemed stronger than ever. He knew that she accepted the Buddhist faith but had heard that she found his own devotion too extreme, and unbecoming in the Sovereign Prince of Yamato. Now she seemed to be saying that he neglected the Shinto rites.

She had always been critical of the Buddhist priests, and especially of the nuns, he reflected. He remembered the many times when he was Crown Prince and learning to rule under her tutelage, when decrees had been issued forbidding priests and nuns to act wickedly. And often she had summoned the high priests to request that they teach their underlings the value of good deeds. He knew that she found him too soft in his piety when he was a boy. One time he had begged for the life of an upstart serving man who had pointed at her sacred person and she listened to him, staring at his tears with an august disapproval. But she had nodded, after all, and commuted the punishment from death to exile.

No, she had never criticized him openly. But censure surely seemed implied when she said she was moving to the Palace to see that the proper forms were kept. Perhaps she did not approve of his plans for the Great Buddha, but she did not mention that.

"I will see that your rooms are made ready. The Empress herself will see to it," he repeated. He rose, as if a moment's delay was out of the question.

"No need to bother Kōmyō," she said tolerantly, speaking of the Empress in the familiar terms of one who is both older and superior in rank. "My ladies have everything in order. I shall move today."

Princess Abé had never known her Imperial great-aunt as she had known her grandmother, Lady Tachibana. By the time that she was carried to the Imperial Palace that long-ago spring morning when she was six, the Old Empress had abdicated and moved to her own palace. But since they had come to Kuni and now that the Dowager had moved into a wing of the Central Palace, she was called upon more and more frequently to visit her. She had thought these visits would be painfully formal. She had noticed that her father often seemed hesitant, even to grow smaller in the old lady's presence. But with Abé she was quite lighthearted and kind.

They were together when the news was brought of Ōno Azumando's death. The cold spell had broken and for a few mild fleeting days they were having that gentle weather they called "little spring," so seats had been put out for them on the south veranda of the Dowager's pavilion.

It was late afternoon and the low red sunlight fell obliquely, casting a pale pink glow on the whitewashed walls and on their hands and faces. Even the caves and ridges of the old lady's face took on the rosy look of a child's.

The messenger sat on the path below, bowing and drawing in his breath as he talked, showing his deference to the exalted personage above him. He had reported to the Emperor and the advisers and now was sent around to give his information to the Dowager. It was she, after all, who had singled out Azumando for promotion and sent him north against the Ezo where he made his reputation. She remembered him, the stocky, somewhat surly junior officer in whom she had discerned the traits of a Great Sword-bearing General.

To her questioning the man repeated the little information that he had: Azumando as Her Highness knew, had returned to Kyushu when the government headquarters in Dazaifu was abolished and the Emperor needed a strong man to supervise the change of authority there. Then, absolutely unexpectedly, he died. Some said he had been killed, but no one living was accused. After investigation it was agreed there had been an accident, a fall from his horse. All that was positively known was that he was brought back to the fort with his neck broken.

While he was talking it seemed to Abé that the skies darkened. The old lady's face went gray. Looking up, she saw the edge of a cloud come sliding low across the sky, and all of a sudden she began to shake. It was as though a chill had crept inside her clothing and raised the hairs of her skin. But it was not Azumando that she was thinking of, with his head lopped sideways over his shoulder, but Hirotsugu—and that foolish Saisho whom she had loved.

Saisho had not come with her to Kuni. That was impossible, her mother said—though very gently. They had never been able to speak more than a stiff few words after her disgrace. Her mother said it was better not to see her, so she had not. She had not even said farewell, though she had waited in that rainy dawn behind the half-closed shutters and seen the grooms drawing the small palm carriage close to the veranda. And she had seen that forlorn figure, that little sodden drooping girl, creep across the porch. One person only was there to see her off. Lady Shihi! They did not speak.

Abé lived again the pull of her heart as she watched Saisho go. She should have run after her, she should have spoken. Weighted against this was her mother's reasoning: In her position it would not be wise. Now as she sat in the sudden chill of a fading winter sun, she felt the strain of that inner conflict, love against duty, as she had felt it that gloomy dawn when she watched Saisho go.

Waves of anguish made her shudder and her great-aunt turned and looked at her, a look not of sympathy but of appraisal. Was the Crown Princess, the Heir Apparent, emotionally weak? Why should the news of a soldier's death cause such shivering—unless, perhaps, as she herself half wondered, some evil influence had been at work. What had she known of that strange man Hirotsugu? Had she reason to think his spirit was restless? Had his ashes been returned with proper ceremony?

When the messenger had been dismissed she asked these questions, but Abé said that her shivering was only from the cold and, rather hesitantly, that she was remembering an old friend, a widow, who had been cast out. The memory made her sad for a moment, that was all.

Was she lonely then?

No, of course not, she had many ladies to attend her. Ever so many more since their move to Kuni.

But one special friend, like the little widow of whom she was so fond?

No, no one special.

The ex-Empress was not talking out of girlish curiosity, nor even kindness. There were several reasons for her move back to the Court. She was afraid that her nephew in his preoccupation with the Buddhist temples would neglect the old ways that protected the nation. She was aware of the power that his wife had over him and the power of the Fujiwara family. And she wondered if this girl, the *Kōtaishi,* when the time came for her to rule, would be dominated by the priests or by her mother's nephews. Had she strength of her own? Had she properly been taught a sovereign's duty to the August Ancestors?

She made two moves:

"I know a young lady," she said, "whom I can recommend for your household."

Abé hesitated. "Usually my mother selects the ladies of the Court."

"You are twenty-six years old, are you not?" She did not pursue this nudge toward independence but continued, as though it were her only thought: "The young lady whom I have in mind is somewhat younger, not too much . . ."

The cloud bank moved across the river and across the town and the last trace of fading pink died out. The old lady clapped her hands for her attendants and when she rose Abé rose and followed her, as she indicated, through the anterooms into her inner chambers.

Empress Gensho's rooms, no matter in what courts and palaces, always carried her distinctive odor: not only her own exclusive and Imperial blend of perfumes in the sachets of her stored clothing and the sharper scent of the waxy camphor cakes in her books and writing things, but above all and pervading everything the strong dry smell of the old-fashioned rush blinds that she preferred and carted with her everywhere.

Now, seated in the dim and rush-smelling room, she continued her conversation. "The young lady I have in mind might long ago have been your playmate. I regret that you have been kept apart. I blame your mother for that." Her old eyes were almost squinting, gleaming with speculation as she looked at the silent girl. She knew Kōmyō's power over her daughter, but she had sensed now and then a budding rebellion. "In fact," she continued, "it is the daughter of the Peony Court."

Tears came into Abé's eyes as they sometimes did when she was startled. "Peony Court" was the name given to the outer palace where her father's second wife, Lady Hiro, had been set up with her children. The daughter would be Abé's half sister, but she had never been allowed into the pavilions of the Imperial Palace that Kōmyō ruled. Abé had never seen her closer than their carriages might be drawn together in the crush of some festival or temple ceremony.

Perhaps this was unusual. Perhaps Kōmyō was less forgiving in her attitude than most wives. But Abé accepted it as she had from childhood when Prince Asaka was born to Lady Hiro so close to the time of her own little brother Moto-Ō—and now survived him by almost fifteen years.

"I shall speak to your father about it." It was as though she closed the subject, but she had in mind not only the sister but the young Prince her brother. He was the most beautiful of all of Shōmu's children, fond of hunting and perhaps a little wild but with a good intelligence. She had watched him grow, sponsored him in the archery contests and Great Thanksgiving dances when his mother pleaded for him, and very discreetly made sure that he had the proper education. There was always the possibility that Shōmu might change his mind and name this son as Heir Apparent in spite of the pressure of the Fujiwaras. It was best to be prepared.

Of course it was far more likely that this princess—intelligent no doubt, but unpredictable—would be the next sovereign. Perhaps very soon. Shōmu had been talking more and more about wanting to leave the world. He had always been a pious boy, she reflected, and now he was draining the country for the image of the Great Buddha—the Daibutsu—that obsessed him. She had approved his plan when he consulted her, but lately it had become his sole preoccupation it would seem, and when the construction was not going well he traveled restlessly in search of a better site: to the old Imperial capital at Naniwa that was now in ruins, to Nara they had so lately left, back again to Kuni and to the original site. It was unsettling for the Court and for the gods themselves. It might be better for them all if he should do as he longed and abdicate.

The Crown Princess had some feeling for the ceremonies, she had observed. It had been at her own suggestion that the girl presided over the farewell rites when the last embassy was dispatched to China, and she had been pleased to hear that she performed without fault. But she was disappointed to see that she was becoming, like her mother, an overzealous Buddhist and sentimentalist.

Now she realized that she had startled, perhaps even frightened her. Of a very delicate sensitivity, she thought, not disapprovingly. Rather than pursue the subject, she turned away and carefully, with practiced, slightly trembling old fingers, folded and smoothed the scarf she had been carrying. "The new year is coming," she said in an offhand way. "We must observe it with every solemn rite and proper ceremony, don't you think?"

Abé waited apprehensively. What had this to do with her half sister?

"The Obeisance of the first day and the Lesser Obeisance," the old lady listed. "The Bestowal of Ranks, the Ceremony of the Blue Horses, the Festival of the Young Herbs . . ." This last she herself had inaugurated when she established the Code of National Festivals in the third year of her reign. "And on the sixteenth day we must have the Poetry Dances that we used to have. This is a very pretty custom," she said, nodding at Abé with a softened face, "very ancient. We have neglected it."

Abruptly she began to chant, beating her cupped hands together. The soft palms made no sound but her voice was firm and even musical.

> "O the ladies of the Great Palace,
> Like quails donning their scarves,
> Like wagtails, their tails criss-crossing,
> Like garden sparrows bowing low . . ."

She stopped, still beating silently, and nodded to Abé to carry on. It was an old familiar song, recorded in the Record of Ancient Things, so Abé, picking up the beat of the soundlessly clapping hands, sang in a high sweet voice,

> "Today they appear like floating flowers
> That are steeped in wine—
> The high-shining ladies
> Of the Sun Palace."

What strength of will the old lady had! By the time the First Month ceremonies were concluded, young Prince Asaka was familiar in the Court. And during the Festival of Spring Prayer, when a hundred high officers from the Department of Shinto appealed to the deities for a good rice crop, the boy walked in the procession with his father—although for several years before this Shōmu had not gone himself but sent a substitute.

On the other hand—for she had not yet chosen her favorite—she arranged for the Crown Princess to take part in the Dance of the Five Seasons during the Iris Festival. Like the Spring Prayer, the dance had been neglected for several years although it was included in the Code of Festivals.

It was a very ancient dance and Abé entered into her training for it with a sense of awe. By custom it was performed by four Court dancers who had been schooled from infancy. But as the Dowager pointed out, it was not so much a matter of instructing the body as refining the spirit.

Because its history went back to the days of the gods, their first instruction was by a priest from the Department of Shinto. "In the first days of human history," he told them, "when Emperor Jimmu [speaking his name with awe] made his conquest of the Yamato lands, he came to the mountains of Yoshino, where the local gods, the Chieftains, greeted him. Breaking open the rocks they lived in they emerged from under the ground. They had tails and shone with an inner light."

Abé thought the priest quite handsome although his face was somewhat heavy and his manner slow. He had thrown a thick silk robe over his white priest's costume and the brilliant pattern contrasted nicely with the plain wood of the room. They were in the Shinto Hall of the Central Palace and there was a sense of purity, Abé felt, as there should be. Even the air in the garden seemed extraordinarily clear. A wisteria vine had been trained over the veranda and someone had cut a spray and draped it in a plain ceramic tub. That and a kaya-wood mirror stand were the only decorations.

The priest had been sitting cross-legged before them. Now he rose and grew more animated as he came to the heart of his story. "Many years afterward, many centuries, when thirty-nine emperors had sat upon the throne, thirty-nine gods incarnate, Emperor Temmu, who was the fortieth, fled to the Yoshino mountains from his brother's court for fear of treachery. And just as the Chieftains had risen up for Emperor Jimmu, the Spirit of the Mountain rose for Temmu.

"She rose and sang for him their ancient song, waving her long sleeves and singing, repeating it five times."

The priest shrugged off his outer robe and stood with his arms wide and his fingers stiff. And humming a long melody through his nose he waved his arms and turned and turned again. Sometimes he sang a snatch of words, very archaic. Abé strained to hear.

" 'Where the trees are growing, the great oak trees,' " she heard. And later: " 'We have made this wine . . .' "

Abruptly the priest stopped singing and stood still. "It goes on, of course. A very ancient song. But it was then, as the Spirit of the Mountain sang to him, that Emperor Temmu your ancestor"—he bowed to Abé—"composed this dance. The dance that you will learn. And it was then that he made the proclamation that the Yamato Court has lived with ever since." Again he put on his sonorous voice:

"In this Great Land of Many Islands, in order to control both high and low, keeping them ever tranquil, it is necessary always, ever peacefully, to have Ceremony Music and Dance."

Abé had spent several weeks in strict seclusion studying each motion of the dance. She had many teachers, but the one who inspired her was the little Annamite who had come from China. He taught her to find the balance and the concentration within herself so that the movements would flow smoothly and have meaning.

The day before the ceremony she underwent the purification by abstinence and did not eat or drink. And before dawn on the morning, when she rose, she stood at the window of the Shinto Hall and watched the procession from the Office of Sacred Dance as they carried the *koto* and the pipes and drums across the wide parade ground to the Ceremonial Hall. Their brightly colored figures and the sounds they made were muted by the early river mist.

Later, when she stood behind the curtain of the stage, she heard the voice of Tachibana Moroé reading the edict in her father's name: how the Emperor, recalling the proclamation of his ancestor and the dance that he composed, and wanting it to be received and handed on forever, had instructed the Crown Princess to learn it and now humbly present it to the Court.

From behind her the musicians moved out on the stage, rustling in their peacock-colored robes, and soon she heard the keynote of the *shō*, long-drawn and wavering, and then the flute and the plucked keynote of the *koto*. The voices of the singers rose, chanting the words, and then the clapping of the hands, first with the rough beat, then with the fine, and at last the music. There were four tunes, and with the fourth she moved out on the stage.

The dance began with a slow passage to the east and west, a lifting of the sleeves. She and the Court dancers slowly turned and softly raised their feet and placed them in a soundless stamp. For Abé the dance was something with a spirit of its own. It enveloped her. It drew the movements out of her the way a thread of silk is drawn from a cocoon—a motion never wavering and never breaking, never in haste.

To those watching, the Court dancers moved with exquisite control. But the Princess seemed to embody the August Ancestors, she seemed divine.

During the banqueting that followed there was still a glow in Abé's heart. The Empress Dowager commended her for filial piety, and the Emperor granted promotions of one cap-grade to the officers of her household and two cap-grades to her tutor, Kibi no Makibi.

He might have granted promotion to her dancing master, the little Annamite, too, Abé thought. But it was not her place to speak, and soon she had forgotten him in the music and laughter and the warmth of the wine.

Nakamaro came almost every night to Abé's rooms and for a time remained somewhat in awe of her. But the role did not become him and in a little while he persuaded himself that his age, his superior education (as he thought) and knowledge of the world, his natural leadership, made him her equal. And after all, if one were going to go by what the Buddhists said, men were always the superior, and in any case she seemed very pliant and willing to listen.

He enjoyed her presence—she was never dull—and although he felt no passion, it was obviously to his advantage to continue the affair. Emperor Shōmu's failing health and his preoccupation with his great Buddha-image made it seem likely that he might abdicate at any time. In a year or two, Nakamaro calculated, even a month or two.

He knew of course—it was common gossip in the Court—that the young Prince Asaka might yet displace the Princess as Heir Apparent, but he doubted that any influence could override that of his aunt Kōmyō. So he continued his secret visits with the thought of establishing a relationship that he could count on through the years.

For Abé the relationship was less calculating and more physical. She had not enjoyed the first night of their lovemaking any more than she had expected to. And even as she grew more experienced she felt little passion. And yet she found that she was absorbed in his personality. The scent of his clothes seemed to permeate her days. And once when she glimpsed him unexpectedly in a group of other gentlemen she was surprised and somewhat shaken to feel a sudden sweet, sharp stab in her loins.

After a month or so he came less often but she did not mind. They had grown to understand each other in that time, even to the motives that lay behind the roles they played.

Some of her ladies were disturbed, however. They could not understand. Was this a courtship? Surely it was more than just a passing affair. What did the gentleman have in mind? And how could he presume upon Her Ladyship this way?

Shihi spoke to the Empress about it. "This unseemly liaison."

"We cannot expect her to remain lonely all her life." Kōmyō's voice was sharper than usual. "Think of her health."

But Shihi did not like to think of this, given her own situation. "There will be talk," she said.

"All her young ladies are quite loyal, I am sure."

"They will say that Nakamaro is using her."

"For what purpose, using her?"

"Why, so as to be powerful, my lady, when she is Sovereign!"

"Well, and why not? Nakamaro is a level-headed man. Who would you rather see as an adviser?"

"Adviser, my lady? Adviser? More of a master, I should say. A man as strong as he, and ambitious!"

"There are some things, Shihi, that you really know nothing of. Do you imagine that I don't know what goes on in my own courts? Do you think I have no plans for the future? I know Nakamaro perfectly well. Very thoroughly. And I know what I want of him."

CHAPTER XIV

That same winter when the Empress Dowager had brought Prince Asaka into the Court she had introduced his sister, whose name was Fuwa, into Abé's household. The girl had come in the cover of an icy night, silently, with no attendants. Because of the wind they had not raised the shutters for several days and in the dense blackness everyone lay huddled under piles of clothing. Her coming did not wake them, for the only sound she made was the whisper of her skirt and the trail of her long hair on the floor.

Abé had curled herself around a brazier like a shrimp and burrowed deep against waking. But toward dawn it snowed, breaking the fierce grip of the cold, and she opened her eyes to see the gleam of white between the shutters. Her first thought was of Fuwa and her heart lifted. The Empress Dowager had promised her a friend.

There were several young ladies in her household who were beautiful, some who were accomplished, some entertaining. But none filled the empty space that Saisho left.

She sat up quickly. "Has she come yet?"

"In the night," they said.

"I would like to see her." She thought she would be lonely like herself.

"Perhaps she will be rather shy the first few days . . ."

"Nevertheless." And she asked for her writing desk and some ink to be prepared. Although they said, Yes, madam, the groove of daily duties outlined by the Empress ran deeper than their need to please, and she was wrapped in a fresh warm robe and her face and hair made ready for the day before the ink-stone was brought. And she had to push aside a breakfast tray in order to pull her writing desk to her. "I shall ask her to share my breakfast," she said while they looked doubtful.

She wrote the note quite briskly, using sharp characters to suit the day, and added the verse:

> Though we have not met by the brush fence,
> The snow makes a bridge . . .

She hoped this did not sound abrupt and appended in her own words that Fuwa must come and share her breakfast, for she intended to love her.

The answer did not come for a long time, and when it did it was extremely disconcerting: " 'Tread not the snow around the palace,' I have heard it said." And the remainder of the verse:

> Away, away, away,
> Tread not the snow!

It was a cruel rebuff. To bring up the past so forcefully! The ladies, sharing the note when Abé put it down, were shocked at the impertinence.

Almost an invitation to be sent away again, Abé thought. She would risk that disgrace! Perhaps the girl had come only on the insistence of the old lady. Oddly, she felt a twinge of pity for her, though she felt fear too, she could not say why.

Almost at once there came a second note, like an apology. The writing was exceptionally delicate. One could forgive the writer almost anything. And it said simply, "I am not fit to be seen. Please have patience with my uncouth ways."

When at last they met it was midday and the crust on the snow had a brittle sheen. Against its glare Fuwa's figure wavered, almost like a ghost. She was tall like her father and very slim. Her robe fell from her shoulders in a line so delicate that the ladies thought her character must be quite fine after all. She did not seem to walk as she approached, but glided.

What startled Abé was that when Fuwa reached her screen and sank down, she lifted her face in the full light, scorning to raise her fan. It was a beautiful face, a beautiful pure round line with a soft mouth and clear almond eyes—or would have been beautiful except that in her left eye there was a cast, a flaw like a beam of light through a rip in a summer curtain or a sliver of winter ice.

Taken aback, Abé gazed at the calm, delicate face so defiantly exposed, and a queer notion came into her head: I will survive her. It was merely a twinge of thought, soon gone. But its effect was to make her even more gentle than she had intended, and she called her "sister" and kept her by her often.

Fuwa had been in Abé's service for some time and everyone had grown accustomed to her ways when one autumn night when she was on duty in the Princess' rooms, she observed that Nakamaro came quite late in the evening and then departed long before dawn. Even before the first birdsound, she noted. Even before the trees emerged from the morning mist! When she glided to the window to peer after him, a soft unpleasant smile blurred her clear features as she watched the vague bulk of his figure hurrying away.

Her own lover fought against the dawn, whispering, pleading, returning time and again until she pushed him out. This affair was no more than a matter of politics!

Fuwa's lover, the man she was destined to marry, was Prince Shioyaki, the younger son of the Imperial Prince Niitabe. Niitabe was a formidable man, one of the questioners of that Great Minister of the Left who had hanged himself so many years ago, a heavily bearded man with a large voice. And perhaps it was this image of paternal power that fomented rebellion in his sons, for Shioyaki and his elder brother Funado were heedless impulsive boys and often in trouble.

As long as Prince Niitabe was alive he kept them in some control. But he died when they were approaching manhood, and what had been merely boyish pranks became serious in the eyes of the Court.

Not long after his father's death, Funado was promoted to the Fourth Rank junior grade and his friends planned a promotion party for him. The object of these parties was to make the guest of honor drunk, and from time to time they were forbidden by the Grand Council because of the noise, the lewdness, the broken furniture, and so forth. But since the Court had moved to Kuni there had been a loosening of regulations and Funado's friends—urged on by Shioyaki—took the chance.

The party followed much the usual course, and at the time of the first cockcrow Funado led a procession out to stop the morning drum so that those who were scheduled for Court duty would not have to leave. As usual, it was Shioyaki who was caught by the guards as he was creeping up the ladder to the drum. And as usual, he was the one called up for special punishment. It seemed to be inherent in his character that he be the one to catch the blame.

Though he might be the youngest in a group, or the last in line, it was always Shioyaki who was accused of inciting the others. And whether he was the ringleader or merely the scapegoat, he was the one singled out for censure. His elders seemed to see a gleam of mischief in his eyes even when he was innocent, whereas Funado managed to give the impression that he could do no wrong.

In fact, the two were fairly evenly balanced in their capacity for mischief and for sober achievement. But as they reached manhood the impression of Funado's reliability was reinforced by the solemnity of his growing beard—for he had inherited his father's hairiness—while Shioyaki's reputation clung to him, perhaps for no more reason than that his eyes had a merry shape and a gleaming blackness.

So it was that Shioyaki was caught in the drum tower and confined to his quarters while the others slipped back into the shadows and escaped. Once again promotion parties were prohibited. But Funado, whose promotion was the occasion for this latest one, was forgiven.

When Shioyaki was imprisoned in his rooms Funado often

came to visit him. It was a time when the seasons were turning, bringing the warmth of April with its wide white skies and pale blossoming trees. In the hills the deer had newly grown their antlers and young Prince Asaka, the Emperor's only son, had arranged a medicine hunt. Spring horns are a cure for many different ills, but Asaka's interest was not so much in the medicine as in the ride to the mountains and the beauty of the stags.

Funado stood in the long grass outside his brother's window, for Shioyaki's room was in the quarters for Imperial Pages, one of the many partitioned cubicles in the great warren of the Secretariat Hall, and its barred window looked out on a grassy corridor between it and the headquarters of the Palace Middle Guards. From there he might hear the party starting out, or even catch a glimpse of their bright hunting clothes when they passed beyond the eastern gate.

He was only trying to keep his brother's spirits up, for he knew how it would be for Shioyaki, stuffed in his little room, while the others rode away. He truly meant only to stay and comfort him. But somehow his fingers curled around the window bars when he peered into the room. And Shioyaki's fingers likewise curled around the bars. It seemed a kind of joke at the time, as he looked into his brother's bright black eyes, that their four bare hands could so easily loosen the wooden bars. There were always horses at the eastern gate. And Prince Asaka and the others laughed when they saw the brothers galloping to catch up.

Afterward, when they rode home, there were flower petals caught in their full-sleeved hunting cloaks and some had stuck sprays of blossoms in the quivers on their backs. Prince Asaka was radiant, and the others—even those far older than he—followed him deferentially. It was said that he was now his father's favorite and this motivated some, but others truly loved him for himself.

All of his influence with the Emperor, however, could not save Shioyaki, who was found guilty of Discord, one of the ten crimes that were not subject to amnesty, and sent away into exile for a year. It was shortly after his reprieve and return to Kuni that Fuwa spoke to him of Nakamaro's cool affair with the Crown Princess.

"It is just a matter of politics," she said. "He means to have a hold on her when she is Sovereign."

Shioyaki said he wished he could have a hold on Fuwa and he was smiling hopefully as he reached for her. But she pulled her hands away and continued, for she seldom smiled, "I said *when* she is Sovereign, but I should have said *if*."

"If?" Shioyaki was still smiling, lounging on his elbow, toying with her sleeve. "She's the *Kōtaishi*."

"Only because of her mother. Everyone knows that Asaka should be heir." It was not merely that the young Prince was her brother that she felt this way. "It is better for a man to rule. A man is wiser." She avoided his laughing eyes looking up at her. "A man is stronger." She said this not only to flatter Shioyaki, as she did almost automatically with every man she spoke to. She perfectly believed it although she herself was cleverer and stronger, very much stronger, than the man she spoke to, and though it was a fact of history that the land of Yamato had always prospered under female sovereigns.

"Well, of course if she has a son . . ."

"She will not have a son."

Shioyaki smiled. Already he was aware of Fuwa's uncanny faculty of foretelling the future. She had predicted his return to Nara almost to the day. "Well, a daughter then."

"I have told you. She will not have a child. No matter how hard Nakamaro tried, it has not happened. She is infertile. And now he has given up. His hope is only to control her. That is quite clear."

"Poor Nakamaro."

"If you say so. But I do not like Nakamaro and I do not trust him—though he is strong, you must admit that. But I do not like him."

"Who do you like?" He asked this rolling over onto his stomach and putting his face into her scented sleeves where he breathed loudly.

Perfectly composed, she bent her head and gazed at him. There was nothing new in the fact that he loved her or that she had accepted him. She had taken their months of separation calmly, as she took his return. What she wanted from him now was serious thought about affairs of state. (What she wanted in the long run—though she did not confide this to Shioyaki—was to be sister to the Emperor rather than merely waiting lady for the Empress.) So she persuaded him. And through him word was passed to those who might have special interest, that Fujiwara Nakamaro was establishing a hold on the *Kōtaishi*. And by the time it reached such influential ministers as Tachibana Moroé and Toyonari—and finally the Emperor himself—it had become a question: Who will rule the Crown Princess when she rules the land?

The question was only one of many that were troubling Shōmu. The frame of the Great Buddha that he was building at Shigaraki had collapsed and the builders did not know why. Also, the diviners had not been able to interpret a strange phenomenon when two stars had approached each other and receded four times in the space of a candle's burning. There had been drought again, out of season. And his eyes had suddenly grown worse. It seemed to him the gods must be displeased.

Perhaps the fault was in Kuni and he should move the capital again. He had been rebuilding the old Palace on the ancient site at Naniwa. And sometimes he thought with longing of a return to Nara. Remembering the poem, he said aloud, "The waving wisterias are in bloom . . ." The wisteria of Nara. But the advisers did not favor a move. They were thinking of the cost rather than the calamities. Nevertheless he continued to dwell on the possibility, and early in the Godless Month he summoned all his officials to a grand conference and put the question to them, but they were hopelessly split.

Try as they might to reach consensus, by the final count twenty-four of those in the superior ranks voted to remain in Kuni while twenty-three preferred Naniwa. And in the lower ranks the results were much the same. He sent Nakamaro to the markets to find out what the merchants thought. Perhaps, like him, they would prefer a move, sensing that the gods desired it. But Nakamaro brought back word that only one man voted for Nara and one for Naniwa while all the rest were content to stay in Kuni.

Shōmu listened wearily to the report. He had selected Nakamaro as one of the Imperial Advisers when they came to Kuni. Nevertheless he did not always trust him. He closed his eyes and opened them. So often a kind of gritty fog descended between him and what he tried to see. And around Nakamaro's sturdy figure there seemed to float an atmosphere of calculation, thick as incense vapor, almost palpable. He was Kōmyō's favorite, he knew. And now the Crown Princess also . . .

Abruptly he decided to visit Naniwa. Perhaps the sea air would improve his eyes. "I will go to Naniwa after the new year," he said. "And I will take Prince Asaka with me, he is so fond of the hills."

Nakamaro sat with his fists on his knees, his face impassive, eyes opaque. He understood the implication and his mind went to the future and its possibilities.

Shortly after the New Year Shōmu set out for Naniwa. Young Prince Asaka, now seventeen, accompanied his father, riding beside his palanquin.

On the second day of their journey, as the sun rose, clouds of five colors covered half the sky and a blue mist rose from the ground. No one could say if this was an omen, either for good or evil.

Shōmu, enclosed in his palanquin, was testing his tired eyes. He put his right palm over his right eye and stared at the heavy curtain swaying beside him. Its pattern was that of lion masks woven in muted stripes. Even with his right eye, which was the better one, it seemed somber. With his left it was ominous.

Quickly he leaned forward and pulled the curtain back. The strange light in the sky struck through the mist and he smelled the sea. He felt a little happier when he saw the flank of his son's horse and his foot, half hidden in the stirrup cone, swinging gently back and forth to the slow pace. He knew how the boy liked to follow the steep trails up the mountainsides and was touched that he should remain so close.

Asaka was not a calculating man. He was not ambitious as his sister was. Though he rode so close to his father, it was not for the impression it might make. He would have been content to follow a secondary role at Court, enjoying the games and festivals. However, others were ambitious for him and for this he was made to suffer. Perhaps there was something in a previous life that required punishment. It could not be helped.

Suddenly, while his father watched, Asaka's foot jerked back from the stirrup and the flank of his horse swung round. Why was the Prince turning? Was there some game to follow off on the hillside? Shōmu leaned out and saw the boy's legs jerk and straighten, and in a moment watched him slide from his horse like a stiff-legged doll.

That was the image that went through Shōmu's mind: the image of a little doll, the kind of wooden manikin that sly vindictive people sometimes carved to bring disaster to their enemies. He leaned from his curtains and stretched out his hand, whether to uphold or touch, and saw Asaka's bright face turning pale. He was still smiling, an incredulous smile that he, a horseman above all, should lose control like this. He almost laughed.

A flurry of people came between them. Horsemen rode up, dismounted, pushed their mounts aside. The sidling fat rumps of the horses and their swishing nervous tails, the wide-winged shoulders of the soldiers' uniforms and their wildly waving sleeves made a rushing and a thundering in Shōmu's eyes and he could not see.

Someone spoke to his bearers, hurrying them along, and guards moved close beside his curtains. Was there some danger? His litter bounced at a quicker pace, and the sight of Asaka's empty saddle, the knot of converging men, the flurry, vanished behind the trees.

Still incredulous, half laughing, Asaka was taken to the small Sakurai temple, the nearest resting place, and Shōmu instructed his bearers to take him there as well. Even before the rooms were set up properly for his comfort, he sent dispatches to the capital to begin services for his son's health. Six hundred priests read the Healing Sutra and carried their banners and earthen lamps around the sacred images till they were exhausted. He sent offerings of rice to the temples and sacred cloth to the shrines. He forbade the slaughter of animals and offered alms to widows and helpless solitary people and granted amnesty to prisoners. He was not able to see his son.

Asaka's smile had faded as he lay in the arms of his friends. He heard as though from far away their voices and the chant of the exorcists—even the loud cries of the evil spirit they had trapped in the medium. No matter what was done for him, the slow paralysis came creeping up his legs, up through his belly and his loins, to his lungs. He died on the third day, and when the news came back to Kuni the Court mourned for him.

"I think I shall go to the Koga temple and spend some days." Abé's voice was trembling. It seemed she had not been well.

"It will be unpleasant for you. In this cold."

"But one doesn't undertake such a vigil merely for pleasure. Isn't that so?"

"I will send Shihi with you then." Her mother looked at her with concern.

"You will make her unhappy."

It was a strange stiff conversation, hurtful to Abé who needed her mother's love. But in the past few days she had withdrawn herself from everyone and hardly spoken.

On the way to the mountain temple, as their carriage trundled over the bumpy road, Abé put her head down in Shihi's lap. It was as though she were afraid to go beyond the city's edge.

"Nothing to be afraid of," Shihi muttered, smoothing the dark hair. "Just a big baby."

But it was not the strangeness of the countryside that frightened Abé. Usually she was eager for new sights. It was what Nakamaro had told her, sitting with his pockmarked face in the bold sunlight, openly speaking of preserving the Sun-line for her.

Just as he said this, looking meaningful, his face had blurred and she had seen Prince Asaka's smiling face with a transparent brightness. Then, as she started, it turned pale and grim and floated off, leaving Nakamaro staring at her. "What's the matter?"

Perhaps it was just a cloud across the sun or the shadow of a windblown plant on the screen behind him, but it left her terrified.

"What is it?"

"Perhaps a cloud . . ."

"A cloud?"

He was looking at her closely with narrowed eyes. Did she only imagine an inner meaning in that look? Did she only imagine that she had seen Asaka's face with that light around it like a ring around the moon? No, she had seen it!

She felt her own face stiffen and she put her fan up quickly. No one must know. "It was nothing."

"Nothing?"

No use to lie to Nakamaro nor to tell him. Either way he would seek to dominate her, argue her down. So she said nothing more. And since then had hardly spoken.

"Come, we are nearly there," Shihi said. It was late afternoon and the temple stood in the shadow of the mountain, cold and forlorn.

I have come to the right place, Abé thought, as she sat up and looked out. The sunset bell was just ringing as their oxen pulled up at the gate and the sound of the mountain stream was loud. How dark it was under the trees as they climbed the long stairs to the temple!

Although the priests were not expecting them and of course were not told who they were, a room was made ready for them and the young acolytes brought lamps and braziers and later an adequate vegetarian meal.

Abé scarcely noticed any of these things as she prepared to tell the head priest her dreadful secret. It was late at night before she managed to whisper her request to him. "I fear I may have been responsible for someone's death . . ."

The old priest kept his eyes fixed on his page although, she thought, he probably is too old to read in this dim light. Very likely he knew the spells by heart. Then, glancing at the side of his bony cheek and his moving lips, she was afraid he might think she had done something unforgivable. "I was not there," she said hastily. "It was done . . . If it was done, it was without my knowledge."

"Well then," he said at last. And she saw that he had very mild old eyes. "There is no need in torturing yourself. Could you have prevented this . . . this calamity?"

"No," she said earnestly. "Oh no. Because if it was done, it was without my knowledge."

"What makes you think that it was done at all?"

"Well, someone died . . ."

He looked at her young anxious figure, leaning toward him in the half dark, so earnest and so troubled.

"Everything is fated," he reminded her. "Our lives must end, early or late. It is only natural that you are sad. But you must not blame yourself."

Abé looked at him more hopefully. Perhaps this must be so. "I will try," she said.

"Stay here a few days, read the service, offer yourself to the blessed Kannon, and you will soon feel better."

So she stayed in the little temple, though the room was rather dank and the sound of water falling constantly, the hollow toll of the bell was all very dreary. It is a sort of penance, she thought, though I have done no harm. But it is always good for the spirit to spend some time like this. And on the way home she was quite cheerful, keeping a running commentary as they passed the woodcutters' outlandish huts and the low farmhouses with their wattled gates.

They put up screens and picnicked near the river before they crossed it and rode into town. And her mood was such that she was able to make even Shihi laugh.

CHAPTER XV

Next year there were many earthquakes. On the first of the Fifth Month, during the hour of the Boar, suddenly there came a banging from the east like a sound of drums and a white light stood in the sky. Some said the islands beyond Isé had erupted and the sound of drumming was the noise that the gods made rearranging the land.

Then the earth jumped. And when people ran outside they were bounced about like grasshoppers and could neither stand nor lie down. Houses collapsed and fires started. Cracks opened in the streets.

Next day when the earth jumped again, the frame of the Great Buddha at Shigaraki toppled, raising dust. Shōmu was there and saw it go. He returned to Kuni with the thought that he must move the Court. Evil deeds had polluted his capital.

On the third day the quakes continued and people came running to the Palace with strange reports. The hot springs at Iyo had ceased to flow but at other places water spouted, both hot and cold. Abé wondered where to place the blame and thought again of Asaka and even of her baby brother, little Moto-Ō.

Shōmu read the Wisdom Sutra, specific against such calamities, but it did no good. And on the fourth day he called his Council to decide on the site of the capital. In the trembling room they reached consensus. All favored Nara.

Nevertheless the quakes continued, day after day, all day. Pagodas fell and shrines collapsed and sometimes the earth gaped. A wind with ashes in it raked the villages and the sea swallowed the poor fishermen's huts. To travel through such country was a terrifying thought, but the decision had been made. On the ninth day Tachibana Moroé went ahead to have the Nara palaces cleaned and swept, and on the eleventh day the Court moved there.

The earthquakes stopped.

They arrived in Nara in a state of exhaustion and spent the first night in the Palace Buddhist Center, far enough from the heavy roofs of the larger Palace buildings to be considered safe. At the last minute the Empress Dowager and her women were squeezed in with the rest of them so that the place was very cramped. It smelled unpleasantly of stale incense and the ashes of cooking fires, for the priests had not been able to use the Palace kitchens during the quakes.

Abé lay disconsolately in her traveling clothes, huddled behind a makeshift screen. Certainly this was not the homecoming she had longed for. When she had dreamed of Nara during the past four years it was of her childhood or of those early innocent days when she had Saisho for a friend.

It was with distaste amounting almost to disgust, therefore, that she saw the High Priest Gembō enter and bid them welcome. As ranking member of the clergy who had remained in Nara, he assumed the airs of host and made a long and complicated speech of welcome to which the Emperor replied politely, though he looked very ill.

Kōmyō, too, was gracious, allowing him to linger in their presence and conversing quite informally about the causes of the earth's upheavals and the effects on Nara and the palaces. It was as though they had all forgotten Saisho.

In the end it was the Empress Dowager who dismissed him. "Why doesn't he go?" she said quite loudly to her ladies, the words coming clearly from the dark corner where they were crowded. "He must know we are all deadly tired, after all."

Empress Gensho felt herself to be as devout as need be, but she didn't close her eyes to the wickedness she knew existed among many nuns and priests. As in her own reign when she had officially reprimanded the Buddhist hierarchy, she showed little patience with them.

When Gembō faltered, she spoke directly. "You may go." And to herself in a quite audible murmur, "Since the Emperor won't do it, then I must."

With a very dignified obeisance, Gembō withdrew. He knew he was on uneasy ground. While the Court was at Kuni he had taken it upon himself to preside over the almost empty Nara palaces and when courtiers had returned from time to time he treated them with lofty condescension. Word got back.

To Abé even the mention of his name was distasteful. Each time she heard it she thought of Saisho and of Hirotsugu and the way he died. She blamed the entire tragedy on the High Priest. So when the probable causes of the earthquakes were being studied and it was reported that the Imperial ordinance concerning the building of provincial temples had been neglected and that the local priests were often lax in reading the sutras that had been ordered for the national welfare, she spoke up, saying there had been laxity closer to home—scandals and outrageous behavior and neglect of the laws of Buddha.

She spoke quite passionately about this, and very often, until at last the Empress Dowager said, "It would seem we would all be better off without him here in the capital. I should think the Emperor might give him a task to perform . . . The Kanzeon-ji temple is in very bad repair . . ."

The Kanzeon-ji, which was in Dazaifu, had been built by the Old Empress herself in the very last year of her reign to fulfill a vow made by her grandfather more than half a century before.

"Your great-great-grandfather, Emperor Tenchi, made the vow," she reminded Abé, "when his sovereign mother, Saimei, died in Kyushu as she was on her way with her armies to help her allies in Korea. You remember that?" The old lady always looked for ways to assure herself that the *Kōtaishi* would remember the history and keep to the traditions as she had done.

Abé nodded and the Dowager paused to put a piece of dried

fish in her mouth, for she was fond of salty things. Then, ruminating, she went on. "I myself was never called upon to take up arms as Saimei was. I hope you will not be. But of course if that should happen, you must be forceful as she was."

Again Abé nodded, wondering how it would be. She knew nothing of war and battles.

"He vowed to have a temple built on behalf of his mother's soul. And I built it. I sent a priest down, very capable man. And now—it has been twenty years since then, and it is in disrepair . . ."

So Gembō was sent to Dazaifu to rebuild the Kanzeon-ji and his position as abbot of the Kofuku-ji was given to another. It was a form of exile, though they did not call it that, and some people thought this treatment very harsh. Abé saw nothing cruel in it. It was what he deserved, she said, though even her own ladies would have preferred her silence. "Let them call me hard," she retorted, turning away.

It was not so very long after that—early summer of the next year—that word came of Gembō's death. Abé was visiting her mother's rooms, enjoying a set of pictures that the Emperor had given her—the flowers of the seasons—and they had them rolled out on the floor when the news burst on them.

The senior lady who had received the message was weeping with excitement and the story came out slowly, interspersed with sobs: Gembō had died. So suddenly. A terrifying death. They had completed the reconstruction of the temple and he was being carried to the dedication ceremony when . . .

When what? When what? Abé, too, was weeping, whether with fear, with agitation, triumph, shock, she did not know.

In his palanquin. He was carried shoulder-high by many men. More a palanquin for a sacred shrine than for a man, they say.

And what?

Some people were enraged by this, they say. But some were awed. He was a priest of the highest station. With such powers! Some men worshiped him, they say. But some were afraid . . .

And died, did you say?

Yes, fell. As he was being carried in that high palanquin. When suddenly he screamed, they say. No one knows why. He screamed and then he toppled from that shrine, that palanquin. Called out! . . . the woman raised her hands on high as though to call herself . . . then fell. And died! And died! She was too overpowered to say more and brought her hands down covering her face.

How horrible, Abé thought. How horrible. The death of a high priest! Surely there was more to it than accident. Some malign spirit . . . She turned to her mother, whispering, "Send her away," and when everyone had gone she said, still whispering, "Hirotsugu."

Kōmyō, as she often did, pulled her close. She wished her daughter could be spared these memories and the terrors that they seemed to bring. She herself in recent years had turned her ambition more and more to a world beyond this one. Whatever had been done in the past, she said, was past, had vanished. Like the foam upon the water after a boat has gone. "So long ago," she said to Abé, trying to comfort her. "It was all so long ago."

"Long ago," Abé whispered. She was terrified. "But now, again!"

She knew that some people scoffed at such ideas as the power of vengeful ghosts. Nakamaro had said flatly that he did not believe . . . But how else account for these terrifying deaths? General Azumando, and now Gembō!

"What are we to do?"

Kōmyō was anxious to stop her daughter's weeping. "You mustn't be afraid," she said. "We will have the proper services read, and a repentance ceremony for his soul . . ."

"And there must be a temple," Abé said urgently. "To house his restless spirit. For he was driven to it, driven. Poor unfortunate man! [She had forgotten she had laughed at him.] And now his spirit is so angry there in exile . . ."

So a temple was erected in Hizen, not far from where he had

been captured, to house Hirotsugu's spirit and appease him. The Emperor appointed several local people to perform the priestly services, and when nothing more was heard from him, Abé regained her calm.

(They did not tell her, later, when the rumor circulated that Gembō's head had flown to Nara by itself and was seen in his old quarters in the Kofuku-ji. The Empress said it would be better to protect her from such shocks.)

Shōmu himself was far more concerned with the construction of his Great Buddha-image. He had tried repeatedly to build it in Shigaraki and had failed. No one could tell him why. He wondered if perhaps the site had not conformed to the laws of yin and yang or if there was some fault in himself. Perhaps he had placed too big a burden on the people to support it.

He thought uneasily of his first proclamation when he had urged his subjects to give all they could. "Even those who can donate no more than a twig or handful of earth," he had appealed, "come forward with an eager heart!"

He had not meant to press his people, only to share his dream. But perhaps it had resulted in too heavy taxes and forced labor. He would change that in this new location at the Todai-ji temple, and in deep humility he had gone to lend his own hand in the laying of the new foundation.

Before this time the giant blocks of stone had been fitted into place. Now, when the ramp had been made ready and the people cleared away, he descended from his royal palanquin and scooped up some of the sifted earth that was set aside for him and put it in his sleeve. Gravely proceeding to the high foundation stones, he opened up his arms and let the earth fall, a small stream of dust. The nobles and the priests who had accompanied him all bowed in unison. And Abé, watching from her palanquin, was deeply touched.

From the very beginning she had come often to this clearing by the hill. The Emperor came almost every day. He had a small pavilion built where he could rest and sometimes spend the night. It was his obsession.

They came in all seasons for the next three years. At first the clearing was still raw and smelled of cut timbers and warm earth. Small branches, twigs, and pine needles lay browning in the sun. At that time Rōben, who was now abbot of the Todai-ji, showed them the black ink sketch the master builder made: the Buddha seated on his lotus throne.

It was wonderful to Abé how he and the master builder could imagine the huge image from this simple sketch. She held the paper in her hand. The strokes were thick and strong, evoking the power of her father's dream. She raised her eyes to conjure up the Buddha as it would be and squinted intently till she saw its form against the hill—a shimmering figure—though it was composed of nothing more than dust motes and perhaps the quivering of her lashes.

Later she watched the carpenters build the huge wooden frame, and in midwinter brought a party from the Court to view its dark bulk looming through the falling snow. The patterned hemps of their hunting costumes and their quilted winter cloaks glowed in the rustic shelter of the construction sheds.

Rōben explained to them that when they had built an inner mold over this wooden frame they would smooth and shape and sculpt it and cover it with mica so that the outer mold would not adhere.

And after that?

And after that, when the outer mold had taken on the shape of the inner one, they would cut it into sections that a man could handle and take them down and harden them in the ovens. Then they would shave a layer from the inner mold so that when the sections were reassembled, row on row, there would be a space in which to pour the molten bronze.

Abé thought of the metal that her father had collected, the ore from the mountains and the things the people had brought forward as loving gifts—the bells, the coins, the precious artifacts. Such love!

During the last month of the following year the Emperor held a dedication ceremony in the Sangatsu-do so that the Empress Dowager might take part. The image was far from finished. Only the inner mold had been completed and all the more elaborate, hazardous, and time-consuming work of the outer mold and the casting was yet to be done. But he was afraid his aunt would not live long enough for that. She had suffered a stroke, and had to be carried to the ceremony wrapped in wadded robes like a cocoon and as stiff and silent. She was sixty-nine years old and until a few months earlier had been strong and active.

When they came down the hillside from the little hall they paused and Shōmu stood before the Buddha, looking up. It rose above him on its petaled throne, ten times higher than himself, the mica particles that covered it shining with many facets.

It was a bright and frosty morning with the sunshine glittering in a high pure sky, and the image sparkled with motes of silver and pale pinks and lavenders. For all its mass and power, it seemed to float. And through the haze that increasingly obscured his sight, it was to Shōmu as he had seen it in his dreams: Godhead of the Infinite Light and Source of all Being. In his dreams, however, it had been sheathed in gold. "I must have gold," he said aloud.

Abé felt a pang of compassion and saw the shadow of pity that passed over Rōben's face.

The problem of gold had pressed increasingly on Shōmu's mind. When he fell silent, those around him knew that he was thinking of the gold. And when he spoke, as often as not, it was about the gold again. There was enough copper for the bronze, thanks to the sacrifices of the people. But in all the land there was not enough gold to cover even the lowest petals of the lotus throne.

He sent a message to the shrine of Hachiman at Usa because the god had helped him in the past. But he was disconcerted when his ambassador returned with a message from the oracle:

"The yellow gold will come from this land itself. You must not send a request to the land of T'ang."

He had, in fact, already made his plans to send abroad for the gold. Now that the god had read his mind and advised against it, where was he to turn?

Meanwhile the old priest Gyōgi had been searching the land

and questioning the holy men who lived in the mountains and knew many secret things. They told him that a hermit of Mount Yoshino had had a dream of gold and he went there.

When he aroused the hermit he demanded, "Where is gold to be found?" He held him firmly by the sleeve, for the man was insubstantial and his clothing shook in the wind. "Tell me your dream."

The hermit's eyes rolled upward and he quivered gently as though vibrating to an unheard sound. But Gyōgi pressed him, "Where is the gold?"

And he answered softly, "Beneath my feet. Here in this mountain where we stand."

Then Gyōgi released him and he raised his hands. "But the gold that is hidden here in Yoshino cannot be taken out until the Buddha of the Future World appears at the end of time."

He turned and would have gone then, back into his cave, but Gyōgi grasped him once again and said, "What more?"

"If prayers are said to the merciful Kannon in a special place, the gold for the Great Buddha will be provided."

"Where? What place? Which temple? How shall we know?" There were hundreds of Kannon-images in every province.

The hermit closed his eyes, still quivering, and descended once again into his dream. His hands flew up around his ears and his heels knocked on the hard stone path as he recited in a high childish voice, perhaps the voice of the goddess issuing from his mouth: "On the stone seat of the old man who prays by the river."

"Where?"

"On the hillside above the Seta River. The stone seat."

Rōben was with the Emperor when word of this oracle was brought, and a sudden enthusiasm lit his pallid face. It struck him instantly that the old man who sat by the bank of the Seta River might well be the Old Man of the Mackerels who had planted the pole that was now blossoming beside the door of the Sangatsu Hall.

The Old Man had appeared, no one knew from where, selling mackerels that he carried on a pole. He had entered the hall without hesitation and mounted the pulpit and laid his mackerels on the sutra desk. There were eighty mackerels and instantly they were transformed into the eighty chapters of the Kegon Sutra. Then rapidly, with his old man's accents twittering over the Sanskrit words, he read the sutra and explained it and then, as suddenly as he had come, he disappeared. He left his pole stuck in the ground by the entrance steps and when they looked again it had become a tree with twigs and leaves.

Perhaps, Rōben thought, this holy man on the stone seat by the Seta River was the same. He would know him instantly if he saw him. So he started out full of curiosity and hope. But in the end he spent more than a year in the search. The hermit had said, "on the hillside above the Seta River," but the Seta ran through miles of countryside after it left Lake Biwa, and although he and others whom he sent had questioned everyone along the way, no one had heard of an old man—certainly not an old man with a string of mackerels—praying on a stone seat by the river.

In Nara Rōben consulted Gyōgi one more time. But the big priest was near the end of his long life and his mind was dim. To his friend's questioning he nodded, smiled, and closed his eyes. The two were seated on the polished floor of his little chapel room in the Gango-ji temple that was the seat of his authority. He was the only Chief High Priest in the country now, since Gembō's disgrace and death. But he lived simply in the vast complex of his wealthy temple as he had lived simply when he traveled among the poor.

The doors had been opened into the garden and they could look out into the warm sunlight. A young monk entered softly and placed a lacquered stand with a pyramid of small sweet oranges between them. Gyōgi leaned and gently pushed it in the direction of his guest. Then with his eyes closed once again he began to talk.

"I am remembering the holy man with whom I spoke on Mount Yoshino."

There was a long pause and a look of hurt hung on the corners of Rōben's mouth. Despite his placid face, he was a man of energy and large accomplishments. It pained him to be thwarted. "The hermit?" he said at last. "The hermit?"

Gyōgi nodded. His big head was strangely shrunken so that the bones of his temples stood out, leaving triangular hollows softly pulsing. "I am remembering him." He was reconstructing his conversation with the holy man. It had not occurred to him at the time—one year, two years ago was it—that he himself was surely older than the "old man" as he had thought of him: the hermit on the mountain. His recognition of his own mortality had struck him suddenly and late, for all his Buddhist teachings. He smiled again and nodded to himself.

The hermit's words came clearly to him with the scent of the wintry slope, though it was early autumn in the garden now with yellow star-shaped leaves on the raked pebbles. His voice had issued out on a mist of condensed air that floated from his mouth. "You must pray to the merciful Kannon on the stone seat of an old man by the river. Gold will be provided," were his words.

And he had asked him, "How?"

"An image must be made to the merciful Kannon. Prayers offered."

"Who shall make it? Where?"

"A high priest shall make it. On the stone seat . . ."

"Where?" (Perhaps he should have been more patient. Perhaps he should have asked him, What old man? But he had not. He had said, "Where?")

And the hermit, answering shortly as he had been asked, said: "On the banks of the Seta River." And he would have gone, then, shivering and twitching as he did, back up the steep path in the mist. But Gyōgi held him by the sleeve and repeated, "Where, where," until he spoke the name of the province: Ōmi, and the district: Shiga. But that was all.

Gyōgi opened his eyes again into the present. "The stone seat," he said abruptly. "It is the stone seat you want. No use chasing after a man. And you are to make the image."

There was a kind of grunt from Rōben as Gyōgi looked at him, still smiling his child's smile. "I should have thought of that before! I should have known that. It was quite clear at the time."

Rōben choked back anything he might have said. The High Priest was his superior, and he was very fond of him.

"He said it very clearly," Gyōgi nodded. "It was very clear." He kept on smiling, looking out across the garden, rubbing the bristles on the back of his bony head.

Rōben found the stone seat soon after that: great standing rocks that rose above the river just where it flowed out of the lake. He would have recognized it long ago if he had not been looking for a man. The stones themselves were like an old man, gray and gnarled. The trees were dense around them and the sound of water came from the freshets on the slopes. Rōben looked up and saw the bracken nodding in the crevices and felt sure. This was the place.

The wood he selected for the image was a section of cypress not quite three feet long. It had a sheen like gold: true spirit-wood containing a living soul. He sat before it many hours studying the grain and saw that out of its smooth length he would carve a Nyoirin Kannon seated in a pose of meditation, one knee raised. He would carve the entire figure out of the solid block except for one extended arm with the hand holding the wheel that grants all men's desires.

The work went quickly, as though the goddess, waiting to emerge, guided his hands, and late in the year the image was complete. Meantime the hillside had been cleared and a little temple balanced on a network of supports above the old man's stone.

Rōben unwrapped his statue and the perfume of the wood rose like the scent of incense in the room. The tung oil lamps sent flickering light across the translucent wood. The crimson lips glowed and the jewel in the Wheel of Men's Desires shot flames. Then Rōben solemnly brushed in the eyes, giving life to the wood.

He prayed before this image for three days. But in the end the Wheel of Men's Desires had not moved, and in despondence he returned to Nara.

Therefore he was amazed, when his carriage drew up at the

Palace gate, to find pandemonium in the Court. Gold had been discovered, he was told. Gold! In the far northern hills of Mutsu!

Loyal subjects digging in that distant frozen land so far from home, burrowing under hills of snow, under mountains of black earth, pushing the rocks aside, had found it! Gold!

Rōben was overcome by the news and found the Emperor transformed. Together they made plans to announce the find to the Great Buddha itself. They would go in vast procession to the Todai-ji site. They would have festive ceremony, music and dance.

Only a few, like Nakamaro who was uneasy with the growing priestly power, and Kibi no Makibi for more practical reasons of economy, were less enthusiastic. All the energies of the government, all the resources of the land and the labors of the people were being funneled into this undertaking, and they wondered if it was wise.

CHAPTER XVI

A new priest had come to the Kofuku-ji after Gembō's death. He was, like the Patriarch, a doctor-priest, but a younger man, a man from the provinces, less worldly and less highly placed. He had been in the capital before, however. In the Empress' palace. During the smallpox.

He was that Dōkyō of Yuge who, after a night of high excitement and of pain when he had immersed himself in the exalted person of the Crown Princess, had fled from his own daring and desire and had hidden himself in Kawachi Province all these years.

After his return he had tried to keep to the Kofuku-ji precincts but more and more his duties took him into the city and soon enough he found himself in the Palace grounds. The men from Mutsu who had discovered the gold had come to Nara to present it, and all the priests of standing were summoned to attend.

The delegation had arrived at the beginning of the Third Month, and shortly after the Peach Festival Shōmu received them with great honor. He assembled all the high Court nobles and leading prelates in the south garden of the Ceremonial Hall. He and the Empress took their seats on a dais placed on the steps and beside them, ranged to left and right, were the

Imperial Princes, who were the sons and grandsons of emperors, direct descendants of the August Ancestors.

Nakamaro, standing down below, took note of each of them, for it was possible that anyone of them might become Sovereign. The brothers Funado and Shioyaki stood solemnly side by side as though the thought of mischief had never crossed their minds. Too unpredictable, Nakamaro thought, too impulsive. On the other side stood Prince Shirakabe, already middle-aged. And next to him young Oi-Ō who with his look of innocence and small fat hands seemed hardly more than a child. There were more, and he looked at each of them, though nothing moved but his eyes.

The men from Mutsu had the gold in a special litter they had built for it. Though they were humble men, they brought it forward walking proudly between the rows of courtiers. When they set it down and backed away, Baromon Sojo, the High Priest from India, rose to his great height and proclaimed:

"As is widely known throughout the world, when a sage ruler rules his empire peacefully, extending his influence to all four quarters, heaven is responsive to him and the earth gives forth her treasures." He bowed his great bald yellowing head. And Abé, who had laughed when she first saw him, thought him magnificent.

Then the two Great Ministers came forward and lifted the litter, one at either end, and brought it to the steps of the high seat and set it down, and Shōmu took the golden nugget and unwrapped it and held it in his hand. The gold shone in his eyes like a warm heart, like a little sun, and his chest went tight with gratitude and wonder.

Rōben, as abbot of the Todai-ji, then rose to make the plea for an amnesty. "With our ears we have not heard," he said, "nor with our eyes seen such wonders as this gold that has appeared in response to our Sovereign's enlightened rule. We are bold to ask, therefore, for a general amnesty, so as to give joy to the hearts of the people."

It was, of course, the proper time to ask for an amnesty, and Shōmu was prepared to grant it. But it saddened him, for the priest who asked it should have been Gyōgi who in the past had spoken for the people.

But Gyōgi had died soon after the news of the gold had been received. He had been sitting in his usual small room enjoying the wintry garden when a young monk brought him the news from Mutsu and he was smiling, nodding his head with pleasure, while the blood rushed through the aging vessels of his brain and burst them.

The ritual in the south garden concluded with a Grand Obeisance and formal Congratulations performed by the Heir Apparent, and Abé rose, her long robes trailing and her fan before her face, and turned and bowed down very low before her father and then, rising, turned again and bowed and rose in the formal movements that were like a dance. How delicate she was!

From his place along the row of priests, Dōkyō stood staring. He stood with his ankles pressed together and his hands before him looped in his prayer beads. He stood very quietly, but his eyes as he followed the Princess glowed with such overflowing life, such speculation and desire, that his whole figure seemed to lean. It was as though his soul stepped forward from his body, leaving it still and stiff.

Abé finished the Obeisance and took her place before the Emperor to speak the Congratulations. "Because Your Majesty governs with serene virtue," she proclaimed, "gold has been found. And this gold shall serve as a sign that Your Majesty shall continue for a thousand autumns, for ten thousand years, to govern the Eight Great Islands of your realm . . ."

When he heard her voice, Dōkyō's soul came rushing back. It gave a shock to his body and the blood gushed in his face. She had spoken clearly, with great purity, but he had not heard the words. Only the voice itself, the sweetness, the forbidden lure.

But he was a man long trained in the denial of self. He commanded his blood to course more slowly and his breath to come evenly. He lowered his eyes so that he saw no more of the ceremony and set his mind on the final Reality and the nonexistence of things. It was a meditation in which he had had years of practice.

Nevertheless, when he returned to the Kofuku-ji his mind wandered back to the Princess, and he listened without belief or even too much interest to the strange report that the Patriarch Gembō's head had been seen again in the temple precincts—not once but several times. There was no body, the young monks said, the head floated free. And it was terrifying.

How could such a thing be true? Dōkyō had great respect for the High Priest Gembō. A man of such scholarship. As a small child he had felt the excitement that rippled even into the countryside when the Old Empress' embassy set sail. When the student-priests returned eighteen years later, and he was already a Buddhist priest himself by then, his admiration for the returning Gembō—the one Japanese whom the Emperor of the T'ang had ever granted the purple robes—amounted almost to reverence.

What he had heard since of Court scandals, overweening pride, the so-called exile and strange death he discounted as tales bred of jealousy. What counted was the learning, the brilliant lectures on the *Yuishiki* doctrine, the leadership in the Hossō school which Dōkyō followed.

The senior prelates at the Kofuku-ji were in a quandary whether to exorcise this unhappy spirit or wait and see what it would do. They did not want to call attention to so questionable a matter if it could be avoided.

"First we must determine if it is here. And if it *is* here, why." Dōkyō said this, smiling gently. He did not believe.

But the young monks were insistent. And of course . . . one often heard of such things in old stories . . .

In the old house in Kawachi when he was a boy his nurse had fed the children on such tales of ghosts and apparitions, fox spirits that appeared in many changing forms . . . and it could not be proven that they did not still exist . . .

"Let me watch for it," he said. "Where was it seen?"

They answered all at once: In the Eastern Golden Hall. Near the small pagoda late at night. In the bathhouse. Here.

He settled on the residence near the Golden Hall where Gembō had had his quarters and he himself now lived. The building was long and narrow and he chose for his vigil a gallery with latticed windows all along one side.

He had them set up a small shrine at the end of the corridor and sat there, waiting through the days and nights. His training in meditation had accustomed him to sitting for many hours—even to the state of trance—conscious only of his own consciousness, and he did not tire. Each morning he put fresh incense sticks into the censers and as the thread of smoke began to rise, he clasped his hands before him as he bowed and took his place again.

From time to time the little boys who studied at the temple peeked in to look at him. His profile was strangely white and pure against the smoke-stained wood, and they were affected by his beauty and the fragrant scent that came from him when he settled down again. They never laughed or nudged each other but stared solemnly.

For a long time nothing happened. Then in the third night when a spring haze filled the moonlit sky and the moon itself was furred, a sudden darkness fell upon the room. The air turned cold and a smell came, like the breath from a long-closed well. Dōkyō's eyes flew open and his head jerked up. Had he been sleeping? Was he sleeping still?

There in the corner, behind the shrine: a floating object like a drum with the long cords hanging, or like a dancer's mask. It kept to the shadows. He could not see. But he knew, he did not question, that it was the Patriarch.

It appeared as they described it—the head alone. And now by the latticed moonlight he could discern that the heavy-lidded eyes were closed and the mouth drawn down in pain. And to his horror he observed that the hair had grown from the shaven head in the long months since his death and hung below it in the dark like the trailing arms of a squid.

Quickly he turned his eyes away lest they affront the head, and made a slight obeisance to show respect. He would not speak, he thought, till it should speak to him.

"You know me?" The voice was Gembō's but unnaturally low. "You know what I have been and who I am?"

Dōkyō bowed again. "Your Reverence."

"No longer. I have descended." Then, as though choking back the tears, "How sad that I who once was proud have fallen low. Now I am less than the humblest of men. The very least and youngest run away when they see me, say their prayers and run . . ."

"Not I."

"How many honors came my way! And I fattened on them and was taken in by the world of illusion and impermanence. For that I am now on my way to the world of darkness. Pray for me."

"I will pray for your soul."

"For that I have come. But I have so little time. What time is it?"

"It is not yet dawn."

"I cannot linger here. But I must speak. I have come as an object, neither man nor ghost. I have come so that you may see what I have fallen to. And I was higher, far more powerful, than you."

"What do you have to say to me?"

"Pray for me, for my life in the worlds to come. And remember me. Remember."

"I will pray."

"Pray for the wreck of a man who lost himself in this transient world. Who sought honors, who loved women, who forgot the poor. For this I live in a cycle of unhappiness. What time is it now?"

"Near morning."

"I will go. But take my warning and remember me."

"I will."

"Remember."

And it faded, went away, while the morning light came seeping through the room with the sounds of waking birds.

The head did not appear again in the Kofuku-ji, nor elsewhere in this transient world. At least it was not seen. And Dōkyō, thinking heavily on what he'd heard—or dreamed perhaps, he was not sure—wondered if the warning had to do with his ambition for a higher post in the Buddhist hierarchy, his lust for power, or his lust—his mind veered at the thought—for the Princess.

In recent months the Emperor's thoughts had turned ever more longingly toward his retirement from the world. "Let me seek the way," he said to Rōben. "Let me seek the Pure Way, closing my eyes to the revolving sun . . ."

He was making preparations. Next month, in an unprecedented act of self-abasement, he knelt before the towering bronze Buddha and spoke of himself as servant, slave, while the Great Minister Moroé read the words of an edict Shōmu himself had written:

"In this land of Yamato since the beginning of time it was thought that gold did not exist. But now in the Province of Mutsu in this land which We rule, gold has been found . . .

"Hearing this We were astonished and rejoiced, and feeling that this is a gift bestowed upon Us by the blessing of the Roshana Buddha, We have joyfully received it and reverently accepted it and, not knowing whether to go forward or backward night and day, We have humbly reflected and are overcome with thankfulness because it has been manifested in Our time Who are unworthy and unskilled . . ."

The whole Court was there, and of course the Empress and the Crown Princess. Abé was transported by the scene and Kōmyō radiant. She had backed her husband in this undertaking with all the strength of her will and persuasiveness of her charm. Appealing for the help of the populace at the time of the dedication, she wrote forcefully:

Let the sound of the tools that are raising the image of Buddha
Reverberate in Heaven!
Let it rend the earth asunder
    For the sake of the fathers,
    For the sake of the mothers,
    For the sake of all mankind!

And, for the most part, they responded.

"I wonder how much His Majesty your father intends to lavish on this Buddha of the Todai-ji. The country is already depleted of its copper. And now the gold . . ."

Over the years Nakamaro had taken to speaking to Abé in this informal, almost disrespectful way, even of the Emperor. And when she frowned, he simply turned away.

Now it was dark enough so that he could not see her face. They were lying together in the curtained inner room of her pavilion on a warm May night of intermittent rain.

"The Buddha brings us peace in our hearts and a quiet land, Nakamaro. Don't forget the past." She spoke without much force or animosity. It was not a new discussion. But slightly irritated by the condescension of her voice, Nakamaro pursued it.

"There are more priests than I like to see . . ."

"There are priests and priests, as we have agreed before. There are good and bad. Surely there never was a man so good as Gyōgi. And the Indian prelate, very noble, and Rōben . . ." Her mind went wandering.

"Gembō, the High Priest, the Patriarch." His voice was scornful.

After a long pause she said, "Don't be unfair. There was a demon in Gembō, not a true priest."

"Maybe."

She moved a little restlessly and the sound of her sleeve passing over his was like a rustle in the grass. The rain started up again. "The rain is nice," she said. She didn't want to argue. "But I used to like it better as a child. Rain on cedar thatch. A special sound."

"Is it? I don't remember that I've heard it."

"In temples, surely."

"Yes, of course. But then, there's so often a waterfall or a river running by or some other sound. So many pilgrims." They were quiet again. "Or the priests with their drums and gongs and all that . . ."

"Why do you always speak that way about the priests? We have had this argument before. And yet you do it."

"And yet I do."

"You wouldn't dare to talk this way to my mother, would you?"

"No."

"And yet you do to me."

"Yes." He reached over in the dark, feeling for her face. "Yes," he repeated gently, his fingers groping. "I speak to you as I like, because you are mine."

It was true. She had become his, over the years, though she had not intended to. It was hard to remember what she had intended. Perhaps she did not really care for him. But what would her life be like without him? Surely it was better than the longing, the hunger she had felt. She thought for a time she might go mad. So long ago.

"You are mine and always will be." He was unfastening her belt.

Yes, she thought. Even when I am Sovereign. That is what he has in mind. But even this bitter thought had grown familiar. And the arousal of his touch, the warmth of her own response, swept over and obliterated every other thing. She closed her eyes and descended into the dark forgetful world of his scent.

CHAPTER XVII

The sovereign Ancestral Gods and Goddesses
Who divinely remain in the High Heavenly Plain
Spoke these words of entrusting:
    Our Sovereign Grandchild is to rule
    The Land of the Plentiful Reed Plain
    Tranquilly, as a peaceful land.

—from an ancient Shinto prayer

The next time the Emperor knelt before the Great Buddha it was to give gifts, make promotions, and announce his intention to abdicate.

With an even hand he granted rice lands both to the shrines of the Great Gods and to the Buddhist temples, gave gifts to the keepers of the August Tombs as well as to priests and nuns, and promised to raise monuments to those who served the state even as images were made for the temples.

As for promotions, he advanced Tachibana Moroé, his Great Minister of the Left, to the First Rank, first grade—the highest. And he named Fujiwara Toyonari his Great Minister of the Right. He granted favors to the children of princes, rewards to those of the Fifth Rank and up, promotions of one cap-grade to those of the Sixth and down (two to those who helped build the Buddha), and last, in keeping with his earnest nature:

"We will reward aged persons, and We will grant favors to poor persons.

"To persons of filial piety We will grant tax relief and bestow rice lands.

"We will pardon criminals, and We will reward learned men.

"We will reward those who found the gold and the officials of the province and the district down to the very peasants.

"All the peasants of the realm We will cherish and love."

However, it was not until the Seventh Month, when the rainy season ended, that a propitious day was found for his abdication and the elevation of his successor.

The day itself was clear and golden. New palaces had been built for the new Sovereign and the Hall of the Great Ministries shone with the purity of fresh wood in the midst of the old gardens. The great shields of the Ancestors were placed beside the doors and wooden tablets had been laid out on the floor to mark the places of the Court nobles.

The Crown Princess sat on the dais at the north end of the hall beside the retiring Emperor and Empress while the senior Shinto priest invoked the blessing of the gods. Then Shōmu, speaking through the voice of his Great Minister, announced his abdication and his intention to retire to the Yakushi-ji temple as a novice monk "because the tasks of government have grown too heavy and We must pass the burden on to Our beloved daughter."

Continuing, the Great Minister spoke the words of the Crown Princess as she with deep humility took up these tasks, calling upon the princes and Court nobles to assist her.

When he fell silent she was raised up and assisted to her place on the high seat, where she sat looking out above them all, a small imposing figure in her robes of state.

She wore a crown a goddess might have worn, a filigree of gold with golden beads and little jewels that played around her head. The rays of golden wire that sprang from the crystal sun trembled with pearls and amber stars and flowerets of jade, and chains of coral and colored glass hung down beside her cheeks.

The honorary chieftains of the ancient clans came and

bowed down to her to present the emblems of her sovereignty: the sacred Sword and Mirror of her ancestors and the Imperial seal. Then as they crawled and backed away, the nobles of her Court came forward to pay her homage. Rank after rank they stepped to their appointed places and clapped their hands, four double claps, and bowed. The princes of the Imperial line came first and she noted each of them. She knew of their ambitions. Then the senior men, her council of advisers, and then the others, rank on rank.

The sound of clapping fell on her like the sound of rain on leaves. The rhythmic patter, eight then eight, the slap of palm on palm, was light. It was the sound of affirmation, of respect, not heavy. And yet the repetition, the incessant sound—rank after rank—weighed on her at the same time that it lifted and exalted her. She lost herself in it.

Nakamaro, when his turn came, dared to glance up at her and note how she looked out from under the spangles of her crown with full authority. It gave him a twinge of doubt to see her, godlike, inaccessible, on the high throne. He had never known her to gaze so imperturbably upon the world. He clapped his hands, four double claps, and bowed. His Sovereign.

Then as others followed him and the sounds of their clapping beat around him and washed on to break upon that radiant jeweled figure, he reflected. This is what he had in mind, had worked for. She would do well in the high ceremonies—and she would need him. When the decisions of raw government, the appointments, the practicalities, arose, she would need him. That too he had worked for.

To Dōkyō, among the prelates clustered at the back, the new Empress was an indistinct bright figure impossibly far away. The colors of her robe glowed in the recesses of the hall, and the jewels in her crown were pricks of light.

He did not even dare remember what she had been to him. So close! It was past imagining. And the future? She was beyond him now, far far beyond. He did not even dare to hope they might meet in another world. For all his sage philosophy and detachment from earthly things, regret rose in him with such pain that he had to turn away.

As Empress, Abé took the sovereign title of Kōken, and in honor of her elevation the era-name was changed. The year was now the first of Tempyo-shoho, 749. She was thirty-two years old and never more radiant, never more calm. But very soon it was made clear to her that she would not rule alone. Although her father had retired to the Yakushi-ji temple and her mother to the Hokke-ji nunnery, there were no decisions made that they did not approve. Matters of state were handled by the Great Ministers Moroé, of the Left, and Toyonari, Right. And—after her mother's urging—she had appointed Nakamaro Minister of the Imperial Household.

For the first four months her duties were exclusively ceremonial. She presided at the Moon Viewing during the Eighth Month, and in the Ninth she sat in state to receive the annual reports on the condition of cultivated lands. (She did not read the reports; they were not intended for that.) And during the Chrysanthemum Festival, among other things, she received the tribute of small white trout that the Palace girls presented. It delighted her to see their charming faces, remembering herself.

But in the Eleventh Month her elevation was confirmed in the tasting of the first fruits by the Ancestral Gods at the time of the Great Food Festival of Enthronement. Then, in the sacred courtyard that was prepared for them behind rush fences where the torches flared, the gods descended and she honored them with gifts of silk and hemp and bark cloth and offered rice for the dark sake and for the light sake and dried fish and pickled vegetables on oak leaf plates as in the days of her forebears. Now, indeed, she was the Heavenly Sovereign of the Land of the Reed Plain.

However, when it came time at last for her first political decision, she quarreled with Nakamaro and it was her mother, in the end, who decided for her.

A priestess from the shrine of Hachiman at Usa had arrived in the capital seeking an audience. She was a woman of some rank and a Buddhist nun as well. But foremost she was a medium for the god's utterances. And although her cropped hair was covered by a decent cap and her nun's habit was seemly, there was something about her of the occult.

She approached the Empress crawling on her knees. She had been allowed into the Imperial presence only after having discussed her mission with the officers of the Ministry of Ceremonial and the Bureau of Divination as well as the Department of Shinto and with the Great Minister Toyonari himself.

Nakamaro was somewhat irritated that he had not been consulted and made sure he would be present when the audience was held. He looked on skeptically while the nun-priestess bowed, touching her forehead to the floor. Seeing this decorous woman with her prim closed lips, one would not have believed the wild contortions of the trance that had gripped her when the god spoke and she whirled upon her knees, bending her back so that her head knocked on her heels and rolling up her eyes.

When she was calm again, as she was now, and stretched out on the ground, the god had instructed her to say to the new Sovereign that he was pleased with the construction of a giant Buddha in the capital and would be honored by an invitation to go there and act as guardian for the image.

Abé was thrilled. But before she spoke, Nakamaro rose and in the guise of courtesy escorted the nun out.

When he returned the young Empress was already writing her mother: Such news! Such an extraordinary bright occurrence to mark the start of her reign! The God Hachiman to come to the Todai-ji! Please visit me and help me to rejoice . . .

"You can't believe her . . . ?" Nakamaro put on a sort of incredulity in order to flatten her enthusiasm and prepare her for argument.

"Believe?"

"That nun. She was put up to it."

"How do you dare speak that way!"

But Nakamaro had overcome his brief term of shyness with the Empress. She was to him as she had been, a woman to be guided. He looked at her as though to say he found her most attractive when she frowned.

At that she burst out angrily: "Who, 'put up to it'? What sort of scheme do you see now? Why should she be 'put up to it' as you say? I have no reason to doubt this woman. She is of excellent family . . ."

He smiled.

"You take me for a child!"

"Please. Please forgive me. But just let me say . . ." He paused and took another tack, his voice smooth and respectful. "You must know there are among the Buddhist priests some who would elevate themselves above their station. No, don't argue yet. I only want you to see it in this way, just for a moment, as I see it. If this God Hachiman of the Eight Great Banners, this native god of ours, comes in subservience to a Buddhist temple . . . who does this serve? Who profits?"

"Profits?"

"Who gains by it? Who dominates? To whom are more rice fields given—free of tax?"

But he had let the bitterness show in his voice and she turned away. "I know your prejudices, Nakamaro. I have heard you."

"You have heard. But do you understand? This is merely one more move on the part of the Buddhist hierarchy . . ."

"One more move?"

"One more attempt to bring people to their side—or under them. To convince us all that the gods support them and their growing power and . . . Surely you can see . . ."

"I can see that you resent what you cannot control!"

"It is not that, not that . . ."

But although the argument went on, it was not of real importance. The decision was not up to them. On the nun's first arrival in the capital, the Retired Empress had called her to the Hokke-ji and was already full of plans: A delegation of Court nobles, well-selected men, with a full escort of Imperial Guards would proceed to the foot of Mount Ikoma to greet the god's cart and welcome him to the city. Those chosen must drink no wine and eat no meat in preparation. The road must be prepared and swept, and in the name of the Retired Emperor the ceremony of releasing captive beings must be performed in all the provinces through which the god would pass.

She had come into her daughter's rooms with an entourage of nuns, and when the two met together, joining their long square sleeves, it was like the meeting of two birds, one brightly colored, one like a dove. Kōmyō was no longer the beauty she had been. She was forty-nine years old and the pure round face had softened and sagged around the mouth. When their two heads came together it was as though the brightness and the beauty that was hers had passed into her daughter so that the young Empress now had that pure, sweet quality, that grave expression and deeply shining eyes that had distinguished her mother.

The shrine-cart bearing the spirit of the god arrived as Kōmyō had planned, escorted by ten nobles of the Fifth Rank and twenty less distinguished, as well as one hundred officers of the Imperial Guard. It was the last month of the year and the frost sparkled under the horses' hooves.

A new hall had been built to receive him and forty priests were invited to perform the purification rites for seven days. Then, as the year ended, the spirit of the god went in a purple palanquin to worship the Great Buddha. Five hundred priests intoned the sutras and recited charms. The Empress announced the bestowal on the god of the cap of the First Rank and rewarded the nun his priestess with the Fourth Rank. To the Todai-ji temple at this time she granted four thousand households with one hundred male and female slaves. And after that a shrine was built in the temple lands so that the spirit of Hachiman could remain and protect the Buddha.

Later, when Kōmyō came again to her daughter's rooms (as she came often; the Hokke-ji adjoined the Palace grounds) they spoke of the quarrel with Nakamaro.

"He said that the priests of the Todai-ji planned the god's visit, that it was a scheme to enlarge their power!"

To her surprise her mother smiled as she said calmly, "No, I think not. In this case Nakamaro is mistaken."

"In this case?"

"In this case he has let suspicion get out of hand. But Nakamaro is a level-headed man, and observant. And the Great Minister Moroé has spoken to me also."

"About the god?"

"About the priests. He has complained of the men and women of low character—untrained, undisciplined—who are entering the temples and the nunneries with no better reason than to escape paying taxes."

"I have heard the charge. Of course. How often!" She was thinking of Nakamaro. "But is it true?"

"Oh yes. I do believe so."

How calm she was! "In the Hokke-ji?"

"No, not the Hokke-ji. But for a very long time I have been concerned—your father and I both."

Long ago, when Abé was still a child, they had sent an invitation to a famous Chinese priest by the name of Ganjin, a master of the Ritsu school of Buddhism that stressed the importance of monastic discipline and the correct transmission of Buddhist orders. They had asked him to come to Nara to erect an ordination platform and set standards for the priests and nuns, but delays, disasters, and the objections of his own superiors had hampered his attempts to leave.

Three times in secret he had sailed for Japan—once to run aground on the shoals of the estuary even before he left the Yangtze River, once to be shipwrecked on the rocky offshore islands, once to be blown far to the south to the island of Hainan, where he was detained for a year. But always he persisted.

Rumors of these attempts had come to Nara and the men and women of the Court had wept when the messengers recounted the tales of Ganjin's sufferings: the seas that boiled with snakes, the pirates, the terrifying storms.

"We think that you should send again for Ganjin and beg him to come."

"But he is old now, and Kibi no Makibi heard he has gone blind."

"Still, you must send for him. We must have a man of his

authority to establish our standards for us and initiate us properly into the holy orders."

"I will send Kibi, then. He will be so happy. He longs for China. And he knows the way."

The second great event in Abé's reign as Empress Kōken was the opening of the eyes of the Roshana Buddha. By now the Todai-ji precincts had grown to a vast parkland. Nearly ten miles of forest had been cleared and rice lands taken over. The shell of the mammoth Buddha-hall, the largest in the world, had been completed and behind it a cloistered quadrangle was taking form with a lecture hall and sutra library, dormitories and refectory and many storehouses. To the east and west of the towering main gate two seven-tiered pagodas rose in their own enclosures, and on the hillside leading to the old Sangatsu Hall the largest copper bell in the land hung in its bell tower.

In the hall the artisans still clustered around the great bronze image etching the scenes of the Buddha's paradise on the petals of his throne, and the last of the thousand snail-curls of his hair were still being cast. Nevertheless, it was time to brush the life into his eyes while the Retired Emperor still had strength to attend.

Shōmu had written to the Indian prelate, Baromon Sojo, asking him to preside. "Since I am very ill and weak and find it difficult even to stand, will you do us the great honor of presiding at our dedication ceremony and you yourself open the eyes of the Roshana Buddha . . ."

The date that was selected for the event was the Fourth Month, eighth day, the anniversary of the birth of Buddha.

CHAPTER XVIII

In the Todai-ji temple grounds the spring mist is rising. It is dawn, the hour of the Hare. Earlier, above the mist, the massive roof of the Great Buddha Hall had sailed like some dark softly outlined ship. But now the sun has touched it, sharpened it, and fired the gold curves of the kite-tail finials. Now in all its huge dimensions one can see it is a temple, largest in the world, the shelter for the great bronze statue of the Roshana Buddha.

The spirits of the eastern skies, the *Kami*, rising with the sun, look down on the Yamato Plain, the city of Nara, and the wide expanse of the Todai-ji grounds that stretch along the slope of Mount Mikasa. It is the birthday of the Buddha, April 752, and they are curious. They watch.

All through the city the white mist has lain along the ground. The roofs float over it, and to the east and west where the temples cluster the many-tiered pagodas rise into the sun. Little wind bells hang from the corners of their upturned eaves and catch the light.

The tiles of the palaces take on color with the day, blue-green. The blossoming cherry trees emerge in the shadowed gardens. And along the street called Sanjō from the Imperial Palace to the Todai-ji gate the brightly feathered screens that line the way look like a row of tiny flowerets far below.

Now the *Kami* watch as the figures of men appear, emerge

like bees from the dark hive of the Great Buddha Hall and from the maze of buildings out behind it. The sun has touched the ground and the smell of the warmed earth responds, carrying the scent of the leaning pine trees, dark against the sand.

Five little figures detach themselves and climb the steps up the steep slope to the bell tower and pull back the sounding-ram on its ropes and let it swing. Six times. The mellow sound echoes in the hills and drifts across the city.

Now men are swarming at the Palace too as the *Kami* watch. They are bursting out in a long procession like a trail of ants, but lively, bright, singing a thin fine music as they go. And in their midst the royal palanquin is like some iridescent beetle carried and pulled along. It sways and takes a half turn, sways again, as it is borne along in the great procession—for it is slow, majestic, though to the gods so small. A perfume of sandalwood and exotic foreign spices hovers over it. A strange scent in the eastern skies, but pleasant.

In the palanquin the Empress sat almost immobile, though she had to adjust the balance of her back and head as the broad floor swayed and tilted like the deck of a boat beneath her until her carriers grew accustomed to their task. They were not her ordinary bearers but selected officers from the Bureau of Imperial Attendants and although they had practiced diligently, some were still awkward. There were thirty-two of them.

The curtains had been tied back on all four sides and even the common people could have looked at her as she sat on the wide silk cushions in her full ceremonial robes, but no one dared even to glance. They fell down on their knees and bowed when the huge vehicle passed by in its crowd of men. Some of the high Court nobles walked beside it holding the cords, and the captains of the Inner Palace Guard served as escorts. But more than that, the sun itself seemed to flash from the golden roof and the phoenix bird that topped it.

Looking straight ahead, Abé watched the dancers who preceded her. Some wore enormous wooden masks—like buckets on their heads, she thought, until they turned around. They had chosen a very tall man to wear the mask of Brahma with its tubular nose and long earlobes. And the fierce green garuda bird, the lion with its great projecting eyes, the dark-skinned slave, she thought, must please the Buddha, being from his home country. They did not have such creatures in Japan.

She smiled within herself, remembering the visits she had made to the craftsmen's offices at the Todai-ji. There was an old man who was chiseling a mask, quite comical, and it had been pointed out to her that he also carved beautiful Buddha-images. When he turned the mask in his hands she saw that it was one of the servants of the Drunken Tartar King, and the craftsman rested one agile finger along the mask's low brow as though to call attention to the ludicrous blue eye. She smiled and she sensed that he smiled too, and it thrilled her to have this contact—this meeting of the souls, she thought—with one of the common people.

She enjoyed remembering this as the procession went along. They had left behind the tile-trimmed walls and high red gates of the wealthy mansions and had come into the low-lying area at the city's edge. It was here that they had put the feathered screens so that she could see nothing but the tops of trees above them and occasionally a roof. How well we planned it! There was nothing at all that could offend one's eyes.

When she thought "we planned it" she was aware, of course, that her father and Abbot Rōben had arranged the ceremony at the Great Buddha Hall and her mother had provided for the music and the feast. She herself, as Sovereign, was of course consulted, but it was Nakamaro—she must be honest—who attended to all the details. He had seen that these screens were made, for instance, and that the walls of the great mansions along the way were newly whitewashed and the street cleaned. He made sure that appropriate gifts were prepared for everyone, that the twenty carriages of her Court ladies were assigned to follow her palanquin in the correct order . . .

Though no one could look forward to the ceremony more devoutly than she did, she felt sure, still he had made her eyes glaze over with his long reports . . .

"The ministers and major counselors may ride in Chinese carriages," he had gone on, "and the princes of the Imperial line of course. The middle counselors, the major controllers, the senior secretaries who are too old to walk, some others [he had named them all] in lesser carriages. Some of the guards to go on horseback, some on foot . . ." And so on, down to the very servants with the decisions as to what each one must wear, where stand in the procession, how far to be allowed inside the temple grounds.

"But in the temple everything will be arranged by the abbot," she had said, to stop him.

But he had answered unconcernedly that he and Abbot Rōben had arranged it all between them: where the palanquin would stop, who was to help her out, how she was to cross the court and climb to the high platform, whether before or after the Retired Emperor . . .

And she had let him go on: managing, arranging, reporting everything to her. Although she told herself she was impatient, she found that she liked to watch him as he stood before her, his face so serious. He has grown handsome again, she thought. Or was it she who had changed? Of course he could make her angry sometimes, although at others, she must admit, he could give her pleasure.

But he could make her so angry! And he was ambitious. He had been after her to visit him at his residence, the Tamura palace, to show him honor as her father once had honored Moroé. But she would keep him waiting, she thought. He was too heavy-handed in his requests. He tried too much to dominate. But on the other hand, it was true that she could lean on him . . .

What a reverie on this important day! Where had her eyes been while she dwelt on Nakamaro? Here before her was the great gate and the clean expanse of the temple grounds.

It was like paradise, she thought, as they led her in. Five-colored curtains hung from the pavilions and bright banners flew in the wind. In the cloistered courtyard outside the Buddha-hall, dancers posed on high stages draped in grass-green cloth. Priests in their new bronze robes were everywhere, shaking their long ringed staffs and waving prayer flags. Nine thousand priests and nuns had come to worship the Roshana. Nine thousand, she thought, and another thousand courtiers and important people! And I at the heart of it!

When she followed her father and mother into the Great Hall she saw that the whole expanse of the vast floor was covered with crimson cloth and that banners of gilded copper hung from the pillars and reflected back the light from the pitch torches that blazed around the Buddha. Even the far corners of the cavernous hall were lit by a thousand earthen lamps. And when she had been helped to her high seat before the image, the reflected light on the gilded lotus buds and silver offering-stands, the incense burners and crystal ornaments around the base was dazzling.

At last she dared to look up into the face of the Roshana so far above. A kind of ladder like a scaffolding had been built to the height of the half-closed eyes. She went on staring upward while the members of her Court filed in and the high priests and the famous foreigners. The procession of the priests was very long; they filled the entire hall. How magnificent it was! she thought. Nowhere under heaven had there been such a day!

When the ceremony started, Baromon Sojo, the Indian High Priest, rose from his place and raised his hands together in a prayer. How tall and yellow he looked in the torchlight, and yet he was dwarfed by the dark bronze image. Slowly, with his assistants, he began to climb: to the knee, to the lap, to the outstretched palm of the hand that was like a little porch, and up.

One of his attendants carried in his arms the spotted bamboo brush with which the High Priest would paint in the eyes. It was more than two feet long and twelve silk cords were suspended from its ivory base. As the priests climbed, the cords unwound so that the ends could be held by the Imperial Family and ranking priests.

Abé held the end of her pale blue cord, feeling the gentle tug of it as the skein unwound. Now the priest stood at the very top, a miniature man, and she felt the cord jump and quiver as he took the brush in his hands. How she wanted to watch the

Buddha's eyes as they were painted in! But her own eyes filled with tears as she gazed upward and the thrill that the cord sent down to her, the wonder, made her breath come short. No need to cry, she thought. Better to give thanks. But her body trembled and something like sobs formed in her throat. How divine! she thought. How beautiful it is. He lives! He lives!

Whether she thought this first or the singing of the priests came first she did not know. Their voices rose in a hymn of praise as the censers were carried forward and the incense floated up, as though they sang aloud what was in her heart.

As the massed voices rose and fell, forty priests came forward to sprinkle purifying water and forty more to scatter flowers. Forty circled the image with candles of scented pine and others followed while they shook the rings in their long staffs.

Then Rōben led them in a service of the Kegon sect, turning the pages of the sutra and expounding on it. And although they had gently eased the cord out of Abé's hand after the Baromon Sojo had descended, she still sat with that feeling in her heart that she had felt transmitted from the living Buddha down that thin blue cord.

The ceremony and the dancing and the feast lasted two full days and when it was over she found that it had been decided, somehow, that they would go to Nakamaro's residence straight from the temple. Who had decided this she was not sure. Her soul was still exalted. If anyone had spoken to her of Nakamaro she had not heard. Nevertheless she went quite happily when her escort guided her small palanquin to his residence, the Tamura palace, and she saw that it was all ablaze to welcome her.

As in everything he did, Nakamaro had planned the entertainment for his Imperial guests with great attention to detail. Because the spring garden to the west of the main pavilion was at its height just now, he had the apartments on that side of the house redecorated. And knowing the warm affection that still bound the Retired Emperor and Empress, even though he now lived at the Yakushi-ji temple and she at her nunnery, he arranged the partitions and hanging screens so that they could come together without the bother of announcing their movements or rousing their attendants. This was to be a period of rest and quiet entertainment that they would remember with gratitude.

He escorted Abé to her rooms himself, showing her great deference, and when her ladies had arranged her cushions and her screen, he walked somewhat dramatically to the gallery and gave orders for the blinds to be rolled up.

The scene was truly breathtaking. In the light of flares set artfully around the lake, the cherry trees glowed with a youthful freshness and out on the water rustic fishing boats carried torches in their pointed prows. The fishermen, with white scarves bound around their heads, poled the small craft silently into the light and then far out again where their flares were like floating fireballs in the darkness. These were cormorant fishermen whom Nakamaro had brought from his country place and they had with them the sleek dark birds they used for fishing. But Nakamaro, mindful of the "Buddhistic principles" as he thought of them of the Imperial Family, instructed the men not to let their birds loose in the water. So they kept them perched beside them where the light shone on their long black necks with the metal rings around them.

When Abé took her eyes away she was amused to see that Nakamaro still stood at the very edge of the room in that attitude of deference. He is going to prove to me the delicacy of his tact, she thought. As if I did not know him! And when he saw that she was looking at him, he proved her right by bowing solemnly and asking leave to withdraw.

When he had gone the young women of his household brought her delicacies on fine lacquered trays. How very attractive and well mannered they were, she thought. They brought the trays and the dishes without affectation, simply and gracefully, and answered her questions in pleasant voices. Their little hands emerging from their turned-back sleeves were very deft.

She was astonished to discover that they were the daughters of the household, some Nakamaro's own and some the wives of his sons. To think that he had so large a family! Of course, if she had thought about it—but she had not. And this refinement of his family, this elegant simplicity of his house, made her feel strangely shy of him. How much of himself he had kept hidden!

Later the Retired Emperor and Empress joined her and there was a concert. "Nothing professional," Nakamaro said. "Just the simple playing of our guests and family. If it would amuse you."

So all the round lutes and the five-stringed lutes, the *koto* and the pipes and flutes belonging to the family were brought to the wide veranda where everyone assembled. Abé saw Prince Shioyaki in their midst and wished she could have had Fuwa with her, knowing of their betrothal. But of course that was impossible with her mother there. She had tried very hard to have her half sister as a friend and would have chosen her to attend her far more often, but Kōmyō would not allow it.

His brother Prince Funado joined him, and another of the princes, young Oi-Ō who was a grandson of Emperor Temmu and—this much Abé knew—was wildly in love with the child-like widow of one of Nakamaro's sons. The girl still lived in the household, so they said, and the rumor was that she was very pretty. And her connection with so powerful a minister as Nakamaro made her sought by many suitors. Oi-Ō himself, she learned, had taken to haunting the mansion almost every night.

Well, he is attractive enough, Abé thought, as though to say "in spite of." But she did not quite know in spite of what. For a time she watched his earnest face and his small plump hands as he beat time for the players. Why did she have the impulse to laugh when she looked at him? He seemed very serious.

Funado had taken the round-bodied lute and Shioyaki picked up a flute. They started to play a Chinese song, a "Song of Pure Happiness." Oi-Ō, after listening, dreaming up at the sky, suddenly took up the melody and sang in a high, clear voice:

"Her robe is a cloud, her face a flower,
Her balcony glimmers with the bright spring dew . . ."

He is not at all bad, Abé thought, despite his youth. Perhaps the girl is listening. She saw that the same thought had occurred to Shioyaki, for with the flute still to his lips he glanced at his brother and with a nod indicated Oi-Ō with his head. Funado laughed and the flute warbled shakily and trailed off in a breath. Everyone looked on smiling. How charming they are, Abé thought. She was sure that even in China one would not find more simple elegance or pure happiness. And when the lute was brought to her to play, she touched it with such delicacy and yet with strong emotion that even those who knew her wondered at the beauty.

When it was almost dawn Nakamaro sent around the great wine cup, and presently the Emperor began to speak, talking about his youth.

"When I was young I was considered somewhat frivolous. My father, as you know, died when I was still a small child and people wondered what would become of me. But it was my fate to become the Sovereign. So no matter what my attitude or actions, the gods led me forward. Of course I was made to study very hard, but never distinguished myself."

This was not true, of course, as everyone present knew, but they loved him for his humility.

"Though I loved music," he went on, "and could listen night after night, my fingers were never agile on the lute. And though I loved colors and a fine line and could see how the beauty of our Yamato should be portrayed or the figure of a bodhisattva or a Guardian God would look as it emerged from the wood, I could never make my brush or my chisel do as I wanted it to.

"I used to despair." He stopped to smile at his young self, remembering those trials. "But when I was elevated to Imperial power I knew what I should do. If I could not with my own hands make the Buddha-figures or produce the music, I could create a world in which these arts could grow. This was the way I could both entertain the gods and fulfill my longing . . .

"That was my intention. And you see," he smiled again, "incompetent as I was, I am, I have fulfilled that vow. Everywhere in our beloved land we have beautiful artifacts, wonders to behold. We have music and dancing at our ceremonies, and tonight—equally to be enjoyed—impromptu concerts, music and poetry among friends. These, I would say, are the offering of pure hearts . . ."

While he was talking the dawn light came up. The torches had long ago flared out and now along the far horizon the sky was faintly green. Across the lake the topmost branches of the flowering orchard caught the sun, and on the far shore the fishing boats rested silently on their reflections.

Most of the company had left to change into their morning clothes. Only Nakamaro still walked in the garden. Abé watched him stop beside the lake and gaze across it. How beautiful he is, after all, she thought. The silk of his cloak glowed rosy red in the pure light of the dawn. And for the first time the reservation that had lain in her heart—had lain there all these years—receded. The memory of the Hossō priest with his breathtaking profile and his secret-whispering voice, that poignant memory that had kept her heart stopped up and prevented her from feeling love—that memory, she thought, was nothing to her now, not any longer, it had vanished. Just a childish dream.

And watching Nakamaro with the blossoms falling, there in his exquisite garden, she thought: This is the true love. Now, for the first time, my eyes are opened.

CHAPTER XIX

For Emperor Shōmu it was as though, having accomplished all that was expected of him in this life, he set himself to die. Earlier when his health had flickered very low Empress Kōmyō had built a new temple to the Healing Buddha and he had recovered. And again, the arrival of the famous Ritsu priest from China had a great effect on him. Ganjin, himself a man of sixty-six, was travel-weary and stone blind, and yet he walked among them full of purpose and constructed an ordination platform in the Todai-ji grounds using as its base the sacred soil that he had brought from China—from the mountain of Wu-t'ai Shan—and checking the measurements as he paced around it by the length of his stride and his armspan.

Kibi no Makibi brought him to the Palace to present him to the Empress and Abé was overwhelmed by the aura of rectitude and the legends that surrounded this stubborn old man.

In April of that year she and her father, supported by two priests, and her mother—still beautiful in her nun's gray robe—were the first to step up to the ordination platform and take the initiation vow of the Ritsu order, the vow of the bodhisattvas. Surely this should make her father well, she thought.

However, during the next year he grew very weak and announced that his body was ill at ease in this world. He would be happy to let his soul depart for the next. Abé did everything in her power to save him. Not only were sutras read and services conducted in every temple, but she distributed alms and medicines to the old and the poor, the helpless and the sick. She granted amnesty to prisoners. She sent special offerings to the Grand Shrine at Isé and had one thousand decent men admitted to Buddhist orders—this despite the strict control that Ganjin had set up, but she was frantic. And finally she forbade the killing of all living beings for the entire year.

When Nakamaro remonstrated, she said, "If it imposes such a hardship on the fishermen, as you say, let them have rice from our government granaries."

"It isn't workable," he told her. "Such an order cannot be obeyed."

But she wept and wheedled as she sometimes did with Nakamaro now. She wanted him to approve of her, of everything she did. When she saw his closed face as he turned away from her she burst out, "But they love the Emperor, they love him! Surely they will obey."

"Of course, if you say so," he said coldly, calling her Your Majesty as he sometimes did. "Of course they love the Emperor . . ."

"But? You were going to say 'but.' "

"It is impossible," he said impatiently.

"Well. Well." She looked to one side and the other. "Well, just have the order written, Nakamaro, for my sake." She caught herself. "For the sake of the Emperor. Nakamaro."

"As you say."

It was indeed unworkable, but she was so preoccupied, so deaf to all the world, that she closed her mind to practicalities. Even when the Great Minister Tachibana Moroé came to tell her that he must retire—for he too was ill—she responded with polite vague words and let him go.

"It is with sincere regret, Your Majesty," he said. But, he assured her, the Great Minister of the Right would serve her just as faithfully. The government was in good hands. But he himself . . . too old . . . not well . . .

Yes, she thought absently, Toyonari could manage well enough. And Nakamaro.

But later the old minister came to her one more time. It was now the eighth year of her reign and it had been propitious, so she thought, with only her father's failing health to mar it. So she was surprised and somewhat shaken to hear him say that her father—dying now, as they must recognize—had summoned him to tell him that he had selected the next Crown Prince, the *Kōtaishi* who would rule the land after she herself retired. The man he had chosen was Prince Funado, son of the Imperial Prince Niitabe, grandson of Emperor Temmu.

Though Moroé had spoken in his usual stiff way, without any trace of humor, Abé suddenly laughed. Then seeing the way he gazed off as though angry she realized she had no cause to laugh. It was always understood, of course, that someday she would retire as her father had to pursue her Buddhist vows. It was only prudent, of course, to have her successor named. And why not Funado, after all? His lineage was of the highest. Why did she laugh?

Why did she laugh, she thought, when Moroé had gone. If Funado was her father's choice, surely he was worthy. Was it the suddenness? Was it that she herself, perhaps, might have chosen her successor? And why was she crying now about her laughter?

In the Sixth Month, on the third day, Shōmu died. The rainy season had come early and the cuckoo called through the silvery downpour from the sodden hills. The Headman of the Hill of Death, they said. But Abé with her mother in the Hokke-ji nunnery heard nothing but the dripping eaves and the sound of the nuns chanting.

They wept together, giving each other comfort in that way. Nevertheless they were both intensely, almost fiercely taken up with the mourning ceremonies. As soon as the death had been announced they saw to it that formal lamentation was begun in the Palace of temporary mourning and arranged that Buddhist feasts be offered in the solemn rites of repentance in all of the Nara Great Temples on the seventh day and on every seventh day to the forty-ninth. More than a thousand priests were fed at each of these ceremonies.

The funeral itself took place on the second seventh day. The body was borne in the Emperor's state palanquin to the place of cremation at the mausoleum on Saho hill. The procession stretched along the road for more than half a mile with Shōmu's chair and silk umbrellas, flags and flowers and incense burners going on before. More than a hundred honorary bearers walked by the palanquin and musicians playing somber tunes followed after it. Everyone in the long procession wore the rough cloth of mourning they had woven from wisteria bark, and over everything beneath the soggy sky the long white banners of bereavement floated.

They saw to everything: the sutra readings and the maigre feasts, the funeral procession and the eulogies. The eulogies went on for many months—by their arrangement—as men of all stations came to the mausoleum and read out their praise. And there could be no music, no entertainments, no sports contests or hunting expeditions all that time.

The rest of the year went by this way. But when the new year came she attempted to bring the Court life back to its normal course. Just then, however, there was a second blow. Tachibana Moroé died. Of course since his retirement they had not leaned on him as heavily as before, but with his death they realized what it had meant to have a man of such strength and rectitude to set their standards.

Only Nakamaro seemed less shaken, less sincerely grieved. And as soon as it was proper he came to her and said: "Do you know that the *Kōtaishi*, whom Moroé promoted, has acted heedlessly during the mourning period for your father?"

"Prince Funado?"

"I did not like to tell you at the time, to upset you."

"Acted heedlessly?" Nakamaro's face was so severe it made her tremble.

"Acted improperly, still acts improperly before the mourning period is over."

"Well, I shall warn him . . ."

"I have warned him."

"What did you say to him?"

"That if he expects to remain the Heir Apparent he must reform himself."

"And he?"

"He gave me a very short reply. I wish," Nakamaro turned his frowning look toward her, "you would give me more authority to handle such serious matters."

"Well, you know, Tachibana Moroé . . . and now Toyonari . . ." She meant that she had been taught that such authority lay with the Great Ministers. That was how her father ruled. And Nakamaro, though he had unquestioned power in her household affairs and was now the Supreme Military Officer of her government as well, had not been promoted to Great Minister.

Is that what he wants, she wondered, feeling afraid of him—afraid to lose him and yet afraid to put herself so wholly in his hands. Is that what makes him angry?

But Nakamaro's anger went no deeper than his scowl. He used it as an instrument to intimidate and influence the Empress. Since her elevation he dared not treat her as he had done before, controlling her through his sexual domination. Instead he alternated his approach between an almost excessive deference and blunt confrontations such as this.

"I doubt if Toyonari will say anything, he is so occupied with his position." Although Nakamaro and his brother had been close as boys, the jealousy of the younger one, the determination to catch up and excel, had muddied his feelings. He sincerely thought that Toyonari was not big enough to fill his post and should not have been Great Minister.

"Well, I shall speak . . ." How strangely young and weak she felt, confronted in this way. "I shall speak to Prince Funado and remind him . . ."

"Do."

However, though she gave the young Prince warning several times and each time he contritely said that he had meant no harm (indeed he was not sure what "heedless acts" she referred to), each time Nakamaro came again to complain of him. He had had music in his rooms. He and his brother had taken horses—there was no doubt at all that they meant to hunt. He had failed to prepare his eulogy properly on the anniversary.

Next Nakamaro began preparing edicts for her signature, announcing these transgressions publicly. And at last he presented her with the final proclamation concerning the Crown Prince:

Since the *Kōtaishi* had acted improperly throughout the mourning period and despite many warnings had failed to observe the restrictions, it was the Imperial decision that he must be removed from office and demoted.

Funado, not quite understanding, hiding his bitterness, accepted the sentence silently and moved from the Palace to his father's old mansion in the West Ward, where his friends gathered around.

Now it was necessary to choose a new Crown Prince. "As you are Sovereign, the choice should be yours alone," Nakamaro said. His mood was far more gentle when he spoke to her.

"Of course," she echoed. She had no firm opinion as to whom to choose. There were several princes of the Imperial line . . .

"But I suppose you will call a meeting of the Grand Council . . ."

His tone made her look up at him. Still strong, she thought, in his gentleness. "Perhaps I shall simply speak with the advisers. And I would be pleased to have you there."

"Very well." He looked into the garden. It was spring again. "How beautiful your garden is when the peach trees bloom." And after he had paused a long while, gazing away from her, he turned and smiled, saying, "Yes, how well you manage everything, so that the trees themselves bloom in your presence."

Again she trembled slightly at his words. What did he mean by them? Was he sincere? It was better when she had lain close to him and could feel by the warmth of his body and the way he turned what he was feeling.

"Whom do you favor?" he asked abruptly. "Whom do you choose as your successor among the princes?"

"Well, and you?"

"I? It is not for me . . ."

"Well, there is Shioyaki of course."

"Funado's brother?" his voice was incredulous.

"Yes. Oh no. Probably not." She was flustered and fell silent.

"And who else?"

"There is Ikeda, son of Toneri-Shinno."

"Yes, I have heard some people speak well of him. And certainly, if my advice were asked, I would favor a son of such a great man as Prince Toneri . . ."

"Should I suggest his name to the advisers, then? Would you say?" She added this last because he was gazing off again as though thinking hard.

"Such a great prince as Toneri was . . ." He spoke as though he had not heard her, as though his mind was occupied with something deep. "I have heard it said that he wished for a more filial son than Ikeda was. And I have observed myself that the honors due him since his death—the rites and observances—have not been attended to by his first son as he would have wished . . ."

"His soul has not been honored?" Abé was shocked.

"Someone else, I gather, rather than the first . . ."

"Another?"

"So I hear."

"Another son, you mean." Her voice took on a harder edge that told him she was not so easily led down this path as he had hoped. "You are speaking, then, of Oi-Ō, are you not? Your son-in-law." For that young Prince whom she had found so amusing had won the childlike widow after all and now lived as her husband in the Tamura mansion with Nakamaro.

"Hardly my son-in-law."

"The husband of your daughter-in-law. Let us be precise."

"It is up to you, of course. Choose whom you will."

"Yes," she said vaguely. "Yes, of course." She did not really care as deeply as, it seemed, he did. Why not Oi-Ō? He would grow up.

And when the advisers met in the Council Hall, gathered down below the Empress' high chair, and Great Minister Toyonari suggested Prince Shioyaki, she objected mildly that, as he was Prince Funado's brother, should they not think twice? And when others put forward Prince Ikeda she reminded them of the importance she placed on filial piety. (She need hardly have reminded them, since only recently she had decreed that every household in the land must keep a copy of Confucius' *Book of Filial Duty.*)

When everyone had sincerely given his thoughts and listened with respect to all the others, Nakamaro spoke, declining to name his choice. It would seem to him, he said, that since it was a matter of Imperial succession, the choice should be made by the Sovereign alone.

So it was left at that, and Abé chose Oi-Ō as she knew she would and his name was announced to the Court and the country as their prospective ruler.

"Well, he is young and innocent," Abé told her mother, "and no one yet has complained of him."

For two months the Court was calm.

But now it is the Sixth Month, sixteenth day, the hour of the Rat, and the signs are evil. It is dark, a night without a moon, and in the garden of the Great Council Hall six or seven men have gathered, maybe more. It is too dark to see. They are plotting the overthrow of the Sovereign—though their real target is Fujiwara Nakamaro. The ringleader is Tachibana Moroé's son, a strong-minded upright man like his father, but more fiery and without his stature.

With him are the brothers Shioyaki and Funado, Ōtomo Komaro who had gone as vice-envoy in the last embassy to China, Captain Ono of the Palace Guards, and several others.

They plan: "The Empress and the Retired Empress are at the Tamura mansion with the Household Minister once again."

Again.

"The Crown Prince stays with his mother here in the Palace."

A soft laugh.

"First to surround the Tamura palace and seek out Nakamaro." First things first. "Confront him."

But if the Empress is there?

If we lay hands on the Empress . . .

The Sovereign . . .

"We will wait until the Sovereign has returned to the Palace. But we must have Nakamaro."

Kill him?

"Kill him. And afterward, then, the Retired Empress. Do not speak!" (There had been a shifting of black figures, a hiss of breath.) "The Retired Empress holds the Imperial seal in her possession. She has held it since the Emperor died, handing the power of it into her keeping. We must have it if we are to raise an army. We must take it from her, and the power that she has . . ."

No.

"Those who cannot follow me, leave now. But I also have a mandate, from my father. He who held the government in his hands for nineteen years and served the Emperor truly. You see how Nakamaro waited until his death to take the succession of the Imperial line into his own hands and manipulate the Empress, putting his own man next in line. He has already stifled the Empress— I don't speak ill of her . . ."

Whose name, with awe . . .

"And he will control Prince Oi-Ō totally. You know that. He must go. And if we are to have authority over the guards and soldiers, we must have the seal."

And then?

"Then surround the Palace, drive out the Crown Prince . . ."

Kill him?

"He has done no harm."

"Summon the Great Minister of the Right, show him the Imperial seal, demonstrate our power. Through him we proclaim to the whole Court, the entire country, that the Empress has designated a new *Kōtaishi,* thrown out Oi-Ō, and that she herself is pleased to abdicate in order to devote herself to religion."

Again a movement, black on blackness, and the scent of sweat. If there were faces there they were masked. No sign of light showed until Tachibana stooped and lifted up an unglazed earthen bowl. Not a star was out, but in the blackness one could see the heavy rim of clay.

"All who agree to this, swear with me now," he said. And if

some black figures merged into the blackness of the heavy eaves and vanished, he was not aware. He only felt the breathing figures gathering close to him.

Fumbling, they took the bowl, one after the other, and drank the salty gruel. Then, by the four quarters of the heavens and earth they swore to secrecy and, on the second day of the Seventh Month—the first day of the Rat—to strike.

CHAPTER XX

"The Empress has returned to the Palace. Go to her. Go." Fuwa was speaking urgently to Shioyaki. Though their betrothal had long since been acknowledged, she still served her half sister as lady-in-waiting. Abé's attempts to make a friend of her had not succeeded but she kept her on out of pity—or perhaps envy and a kind of superstitious fear. As Fuwa had grown older she had lost some of her crystal beauty so that her flaws were magnified and there was, indeed, something frightening about her.

Now her eyes were wild as she grasped Shioyaki. "What foolhardy risks you take! You do not even know who was there. What if some informer . . ."

"Well," Shioyaki said quite easily, "we were all friends, you know."

"I do not know! And how do you know? All friends? Can you name them? Every one?"

"Of course, I told you, it was dark. I can name some, of course . . ."

Fuwa pushed her long hair back in a gesture of despair. She had let it fall loose during the long night, though they had not slept. "Go to her," she repeated, "before another does."

"How can I?" he smiled sheepishly. "You go."

"I have told you!" She was almost hissing now. "The Retired Empress is with her. I am not allowed." She smiled that soft and ugly smile she used as a defense. "I have been 'given to understand' that the 'bodhisattva' would be displeased to see me. My appearance might disturb her calm—make her ill, perhaps, the very sight of me, cast an evil spell . . ."

"Don't. Never mind." Shioyaki took her hands. "I will go, of course, if you say so."

Although the Tamura residence had become almost a second palace for the Empress, she and her mother always returned to the Imperial Palace for festivals and ceremonial occasions. Between these times, Kōmyō lived at her nunnery close by, performing her austerities and her charitable acts.

Just now, toward the end of the Sixth Month, they were in the Sovereign's residence hall going over plans for the Festival of the Weaver Maiden Star. It was, perhaps, Kōmyō's favorite fete, commemorating as it did undying love. The legend was that in the kingdom of heaven long ago the Weaver Maiden and the young Oxherd were so deeply in love that they neglected their work. In punishment the King of Heaven sent them to live on opposite sides of the River of Heaven, the Milky Way. One day only in each year—the seventh of the Seventh Month—they are allowed to meet when a flock of heavenly magpies forms a bridge for them.

"As far as the Bureau of Divination can foresee, it will *not* rain," Abé said. If it rained, and the heavens were clouded, it was presumed the two stars could not meet and the festival was postponed till the next year. And they were discussing the possibility of having a musical concert indoors in that event, and perhaps even the Magpie Dance, though by custom this was an outdoor festival and the dancing took place on the wide Pine Moor.

"In any case," she went on, "I have sent to Mount Ikoma for the most beautiful leaves to make our couch. And what do you think? Do you think we might have the Crown Prince take part in the Magpie Dance?"

"But that is a dance for young boys," Kōmyō smiled.

"Yes, but Oi-Ō is so innocent, so artless, isn't he? He is like a very young boy."

She had forced herself to this conclusion when she accepted the reality that someday she would retire. It was better if her successor was above reproach. But all in all, she thought, there was no reason why things should not go on as they were for many years. "Except for our great loss," she said to her mother, "things have gone well, haven't they?" She was thinking back to the auspicious visit of the God Hachiman, to the dedication of the Great Buddha and the glory of the Todai-ji, the presentation of the very first book of poems that had ever been collected, and of Kibi no Makibi's successful voyage and his return with such a famous Chinese priest, the rite of ordination . . .

And breathing in the warm air from the garden, she recited from that book of poetry that had so pleased her,

"Over the River of Heaven
I throw a jeweled bridge.
Across the lower shallows,
So that my lord may come over to me,
Failing me never,
Not wetting his skirt,
I throw a jeweled bridge."

"Madam." It was one of the servants speaking, bent in an attitude of deference till the Empress should acknowledge her. "Your Majesty." And when Abé turned to her: "Prince Shioyaki requests an audience."

"It is Shioyaki." She turned to her mother.

"Well, let us see him." Kōmyō decided to stay.

Shioyaki had hoped to deal with the Empress alone. Bad luck, he thought, when he saw that the Retired Empress was in the room as well. He put on his most charming manner, bowing low, apologizing for intruding on so beautiful a day.

It was indeed an almost perfect day, Abé thought, warm and hushed, so that the sounds of summer insects danced like sun motes in the quiet air.

"Well?" she said at last, for he remained silent, kneeling where he was.

"Your Majesty, I would like to report. I have to report . . ."

"Well, Prince, we are old friends, I think," she laughed. "What is this report that has you so tongue-tied?"

It occurred to him that this was a stupid thing to do. Why bring it up? Why announce it? Perhaps nothing would come of it anyway. In his experience, something always happened to counter his expectations, whether for good or bad. Then he thought of Fuwa's urgent face. Perhaps she is right. She has a feeling for such things, a second sight . . .

"Well?"

He wished he could say he had come on Fuwa's insistence, but with the old lady there . . .

"There has been an unfortunate . . . discussion . . ."

"Discussion?"

"Plot." What a fool I am, he thought.

"Plot?" She was still smiling, taking his strange discomfort lightly. This awkwardness was not true to his character, she thought, but rather charming all the same.

"Your Majesty, I have come to tell you that there has been talk—that several people have talked—have planned—made a pact—against you!"

"Prince Shioyaki," the Retired Empress spoke for the first time, her voice still small and gentle as it had been ever since she was a girl. "Prince, have you come to inform us of a plot against the Imperial Majesty? Are you speaking of rebellion?" Somehow her soft tone made it all seem trivial, quite understandable at least, nothing so dangerous as Fuwa had envisioned.

"Yes, my lady, a kind of plot."

"Well, I should think it was either a plot or not a plot, wouldn't you? It is difficult to envision a 'kind of plot.'"

"A plot, my lady."

"A plot to do what?" for he had offered nothing more. "Usually if there is a plot there is a plan. What was the plan, then? The scheme?"

"They were planning, my lady, to, uh, against Nakamaro.

That is, to replace Nakamaro, to depose him, change the designation of the *Kōtaishi*—with Her Majesty's approval, I need not say. But mainly the plan was to remove Nakamaro. That is, as I understand it."

"When you say, 'they were planning,' Prince Shioyaki, who is 'they'?"

"It is hard to say exactly who was involved." (Here he was prepared and knew what he would say.) "It was extremely dark in the garden where I heard them."

"How many?"

"It was extremely dark."

"Your brother Funado?"

"I did not see him." (This was true, though he had stood side by side with him and he had taken the bowl from his hands and heard him breathing hard.)

"But you know his voice."

"The one who spoke the most was Tachibana." (He had decided that if he had to throw one fish, as it were, to the cormorants, it would be this one.)

"He was the ringleader?"

"Yes."

"I want you to tell him to come to me, Shioyaki, and any of the others that you can name. I want only to talk to them. And I want to keep this quiet."

"If I can, my lady."

"You can, Shioyaki, because they will know—as you knew when you came to us—that those who carelessly plot treason, letting others know of their plans, have by their very talk precluded action. So they will come to me. Not here. They will come this evening to the Hokke-ji and I will arrange that no one sees them."

So Kōmyō took the matter out of her daughter's hands, and that evening in the long twilight, Shioyaki, Funado, and the young Tachibana came to the back garden of the Hokke-ji (for men were not allowed within) and Kōmyō sat behind her screens on the low porch and lectured them. She told them how the Emperor had left the Imperial seal in her hands as a symbol that he trusted her and passed his power on to her so that she would be obeyed. She said she regarded this as a family matter and felt herself to be at the very center, for Tachibana was of her sacred mother's blood and Nakamaro of her father's. As such, she would step in "like an old grandmother," and tell them to stop such talk. She smiled; she did not think of herself as old.

She spoke in a gentle, motherly way until she reminded them that although she and the Empress were faithful Buddhists, no one should be so foolish as to count on that, or Her Majesty's respect for life, to save them from punishment. The penalty for treason, as they knew, was death.

They looked very sober while she talked and bowed low when they left.

"What now?" Shioyaki asked, when they were out of earshot.

"Same as before."

"Same day?"

"Same time, same day. No more talk."

Nakamaro's reaction was quite different from his aunt's when an informer came to him, saying that through a friend . . . through a friend . . . through a friend (too tenuous to know the names) he had heard of that meeting in the Palace garden and the threats . . .

Even before consulting the Empress he called out the City Guard to defend the Tamura mansion and put the Palace Guard on the alert. Then, bursting in, ignoring protocol, he said to her, "I need to see you urgently. There is a plot. There has been talk of a rebellion."

How unlike him to breathe so heavily! she thought.

"I have had word. Just now. Young Tachibana is the ringleader. Ōtomo Komaro is implicated. Prince Funado. One of the Guards captains—Ono, I think. Who else? We must find out . . ."

She was ashamed to tell him that she knew, had known since yesterday, and hadn't told him. If she thought she could persuade him to her way of thinking she would have given him

Kōmyō's arguments: "Such things are best kept quiet. Calm talk and reasoning are better than attack." But he would be so angry if he knew she knew!

"Perhaps your . . . whoever told you . . . was making mischief. Surely, if there had been talk of rioting . . ."

"Not rioting. Rebellion. They mean to kill us."

"Kill?" Shioyaki had said nothing so violent. It was absurd to talk of killing when you knew the circumstances, foolish young men drinking salted gruel in the dark. They were not satisfied with Oi-Ō, that was all. "It was not like that in the least."

"Like what? What do you mean?"

"There has been no talk of killing."

"Let me tell you. I am telling you." The light shone on his pockmarked cheek so that the scars and little craters showed very clearly under the caked powder. He was surely angry and alarmed.

"They mean to kill. Depose. Overthrow. That is what rebellion means!" He checked himself, realizing that he was speaking far too roughly in her presence, and said more calmly, "I must have your permission to seek out and arrest the men involved so that we may question them. I assure you, this is serious . . . However, if there has been no conspiracy, as you suggest, then we shall know that too, when the men have spoken."

Captain Ono was the first man captured and the questioning was brief. It took no more than twenty strokes with the green bamboo as he struggled and jerked on the trestle to bring out the full story. A doctor was present to see that he stayed alive, but there was no need for him. Ono had not prepared his mental attitude—they gave him no time—and soon found himself screaming out the very words that he had sworn not to speak.

Thus Nakamaro, that very day, could report to the Empress: "The plot was this: On the second day of the Seventh Month they would surround the Tamura palace, take me, and kill me." Abé gasped. "Next they would seek out the Retired Empress and seize the Imperial seal from her, then strike her down."

"No!" Was this true? "Strike her down?" Strike down her mother! The idea was too grotesque. "It can't be."

"Then they would force Toyonari to read an edict in your name dismissing the Crown Prince and announcing your abdication."

"But that is absurd. Toyonari would not do such a thing. They are mad!"

"Perhaps he would not. Perhaps he would."

"If this is true . . . But then," her voice took on its pleading tone, "perhaps it is all lies."

"It is quite certain that they are gathering weapons and raising troops."

"Then we must act."

"With your permission I will call out the soldiers to bring in those whose names were mentioned and question them one by one."

"Yes, my permission. Do as you say. And I will call on the Grand Council." She had never before felt the full responsibility of her sovereignty. Decisions had been made for her, she realized . . . by Nakamaro, by her mother. If she appointed envoys or elevated priests, they had been first selected by her ministers or the high priests. She winced to think how small a voice she had. She knew, of course, that ceremony was what kept the land serene, and she had done well in that. But she had never known the actual use of power.

Now she was confronted in her very sanctum. The lives of those she held most dear were threatened. "I hope you will be forceful as she was," her great-aunt's voice was in her ears, "if you are forced to take up arms."

The Grand Council met on the fourteenth day and listened while she repeated what was already known to them: that base and treacherous men, leading a band of rebels, had plotted treason against the throne and threatened the lives of the Retired Empress, the Crown Prince, and the Supreme Commander. "The punishment for such treason should be death, as we know. We have heard your words." (For most of the ministers, having examined the evidence for themselves, were in favor of the death sentence.) "But it is the law of the Buddha to be merciful—even in such a case of these evil and mutinous men—and we must therefore be merciful ourselves, following these precepts . . ."

She went on speaking, imposing her will on them for the first time, detailing the places of banishment for each of the accused, the insulting names by which they would be known as they were stripped of their identities in this life and the next, and the disposition of their families and slaves.

She was unaware, as she spoke of mercy in this way, that already most of them had died under torture.

When Nakamaro received a summons from the Empress, he called for his wife to bring him his Court cloak and to scent it properly the way it pleased him. She was his second wife, not so beautiful nor delicately high-born as his first, but the one who always knew his needs and always supported him. They seldom spoke, but understood each other very well—at a distance, as it were.

She crouched on a cushion in his private inner room, running the censer through the long plum-colored sleeves as he paced restlessly before her. He was in his pongee under robe, barefoot and with his trousers bound at the knee. An imposing figure in any garment, she thought, glancing up.

"This summons. Is Her Majesty angry?" she asked. It was clear that he was nervous.

"Yes. I believe so. We have not spoken."

"For how long?"

"Long enough." He did not like to be questioned. The fact was, he had stayed away from the Palace as long as he dared, using every excuse of illness and taboos: Someone had died in the house and he was afraid he might pollute the Palace; the Palace was in a forbidden direction for him on the days of this month when his household god was in that quarter; according to his yin-yang calendar it was essential for him to stay indoors . . .

He had hoped to prolong the time before he must face her, but this summons had been imperious. "Haven't you finished?"

She rose quickly, putting the censer aside and holding up the robe so that he could slip his arms through.

"And my belt."

He finished dressing while she moved expertly around him, seeing that everything was in proper order. Then he turned and walked out, grunting his thanks.

His wife had calmed him, but even as he strode through the outer rooms of the Empress' residence he began to feel uneasy. He hoped—he almost prayed—that the Retired Empress would not be there.

He was announced.

She kept him waiting.

Then he saw the long slim figure of her half sister, Princess Fuwa, gliding along the corridor and quickly caught up with her, hoping to find out from her the Empress' disposition these past days. She should be grateful to me, he thought, for Shioyaki had been spared. He did not know that it was Fuwa herself who managed that escape, for she had the kind of foresight—a sensitivity to the future keen as any expert's in the Bureau of Divination—that told her what fate had in store for the rebels. And she had sent Shioyaki, dressed in her own clothes, to the villa of a friend till it was safe.

She knew she had no reason to be grateful to Nakamaro. Nevertheless she answered his questions as though thoughtful, this man of power, feeding his self-esteem. In fact, she did not tell him anything and he could feel the sweat start as he entered the Imperial hall.

"Well, Nakamaro." She spoke without preamble. "So you have put a blot on my reign and then thought that you could hide from me."

He had decided that he would be humble. He was prepared even to apologize. He could have denied all responsibility: "It was done by the soldiers against my orders," perhaps. But the ultimate responsibility was his. And there was pride.

"You have known very well that my policy has been to practice compassion for the protection of the land." Her tone was still that of her mother's, outwardly calm. "You know as well as I that it is only through a sovereign's forbearance and acts of virtue that the Seven Great Calamities can be averted. You know that it was my father's policy to follow the Buddha in this virtuous path, and that it has been mine. And yet," her voice was rising, "and yet you have gone against these sacred teachings to the ruin of us all. How could you go against me in this brutal fashion?"

He said nothing, bowing his head, and she burst out: "You yourself should be the one under such torture! You knew my will. I told you very plainly I was merciful. You disobeyed me, disobeyed."

He still said nothing.

"Deliberately disobeyed. You listened to what I had to say, your Sovereign. And then deliberately went against my will. From my very presence," she slapped her palm on the armrest and her body shook. "From my very presence, where you have been *privileged* to be. You left and countervened my orders. Didn't you?"

"It was not my intention . . ." he said softly.

"Not your intention! You as Supreme Commander have no authority over your soldiers? Your soldiers did it in spite of your 'intention'? In that case you are not fit to hold the post. I shall have to appoint another."

"You did not let me finish." He still spoke humbly. "If I may . . ."

"Yes, finish. Finish by all means! Explain. Explain to me how the men on whom I had pronounced Imperial mercy were killed under your command. Explain it, please. And tell me how to undo the damage done . . . in this world . . . in the next. Tell me how to guard against the catastrophes that will follow. Well, explain!"

"If you will let me."

She turned her head away as though in disgust. He could see the movement behind her curtain and even feel the surge of her emotion, almost like a bitter scent emanating from her. Anger, rage, frustration. Yes, frustration. The realization came to him, a sudden, almost happy thought: Yes, she is frustrated, she is trapped. She spoke of replacing him as Supreme Commander. Yes, she could do that. It was within her power. Nominally. But who was there to take his place? Who knew the situation as he did? She spoke of catastrophes . . .

"Please forgive me," he said quietly. "But you speak of some disastrous consequence of the justice that was carried out . . . Let me go on." For she had raised her hand.

"Disastrous consequence of what was done. And I take full responsibility." (He knew his ground now.) "And it may be, as you say, that there will be wrath in heaven or some such. But wait. Let me tell you the consequence of letting such men live. A man who has plotted treason may never again be trusted. No matter in what corner of the land he lives, on what bare island, he will always plot. And you may say to yourself, 'Oh, just a few young men,' 'my cousins,' or some such. Wait." For she had actually risen behind her curtain at the tone of his voice.

"You are speaking to your Sovereign, Nakamaro!" (How frustrating, how demeaning, that tears should make her sight swim now when she wanted to be firmest. She could even hear them in her throat, making her voice tremble.)

"Yes. I am speaking to my Sovereign, whose life I guard. Do you suppose I kill for pleasure? I put my own life in jeopardy—and my future life, for how many aeons, who can tell—because it is my responsibility to the sovereign line, to you. I have never, at any moment, no matter what we may have been to each other, ever gone against your will, deliberately disobeyed you as you say, for anything less than to save your very life."

"Oh, you are very eloquent!"

"But do you know," he was beginning to lose patience. "Do you know that in the north the Ezo have been making trouble? Oh yes, they think that there is weakness in the capital, and the border guards have paid for it. Men have died there, loyal men, far more than those few who so concern you.

"And do you know that since the great rebellion against the T'ang in China, the Kingdom of Silla which the T'ang supported is now vulnerable? So that we must strengthen our defenses in Dazaifu once again." (It was in his heart, actually, to mount an expedition against the Korean kingdom, but he did not mention that.)

"And while we are so vulnerable to these threats on our north and west, here in our very heart false men rise up against us. Who knows with whom they might have been in league . . ."

She was still standing, but she was listening. Nevertheless, when he said this last she interjected coldly, "If they had lived, we might have asked them."

He checked himself. He must not lose patience. "You can dismiss me, take my rank and title from me if you like. But I swear to you that whatever I have done, I did for the safety and honor of Your Majesty." Then, changing tone, as though inquiring, almost informally: "With whom will you replace me? Who is it that you trust?"

"I trust Toyonari." She could hear his grunt.

Then for a long time there was silence. Nakamaro was wondering whether to attack his brother openly now. It was in his plans to do so when the time was right. Was this too soon? Would it anger her beyond control? Or was it exactly now, just now, when her rage had unbalanced her, that he could be most persuasive? He took the risk.

"You trust Toyonari." There was a vague suggestion of unbelief or a sad wonderment.

"Yes." She was seated again, but there was that slight quaver in her voice, though she had wanted to make it a strong affirmation.

"And yet Toyonari's name was spoken repeatedly . . ." He did not mention torture, but the picture was clear enough.

"Someone . . . They spoke of Toyonari?"

"He is my brother and the Great Minister. Do not ask me to indict him."

"How was he involved? In what way?"

"Oh no. He was never one of the plotters. Please don't believe such a thing of him. It is out of the question that he would have met with them in the Council garden. I will never believe it. But of course there was a great deal of pressure brought on him. These murderers, with weapons in their hands, demanding that he acquiesce . . ."

"To what?"

"How am I to know? I will not question him, my own brother."

"You told me that they wanted him to read a proclamation."

"And what could he do . . ."

She heard the false note in his voice. Nakamaro never did lie expertly. Was he lying now? Where was the truth, she wondered. Whom could she trust?

"Nakamaro," she said. "Nakamaro." She spoke the name like a statement, not reprimanding, not entreating. But in it, in the calm, tired way she said it, the almost loving way—the undertone of sadness and yet the faint suggestion of a trembling laughter—was the whole history of their lives together.

He realized that she understood him through and through. "I only said this," he blustered, "because it was reported to me."

"I know," she said. "I know. I will speak to the Retired Empress and we shall see."

CHAPTER XXI

On the first day of the Eighth Month the appointment was announced of the Great Minister of the Right Fujiwara Toyonari to the post of Assistant Governor-General of the Government Headquarters in Dazaifu. It was exile, and the term was indefinite.

It had been learned, the announcement said, that the Great Minister was implicated in the late rebellion, and his appointment, though a severe demotion, was a demonstration of Imperial clemency. After his departure the affairs of government were largely in the hands of his brother, the Household Minister.

Of course the Empress reigned and the Grand Council met, but it was not as it had been before the rebellion, with advice from many quarters and decisions made in concert. When a senior secretary or a major counselor complained of the people's unrest, Nakamaro as Supreme Commander warned them of uprisings among the Ezo or threats of invasion from abroad. We must stand together, he said, in these times of peril.

For her part, Abé ordered every provincial temple to make copies of the Diamond Cutter Sutra and to have them read aloud on the eighth day of every month for the "repose of the Court," as she dictated, and the "great peace of the realm." If the priests and nuns could learn but four lines of this sutra (as she had) and understand and explain them (as she undertook to do) an endless stock of merit would benefit the land.

She had chosen for herself four lines on which to meditate and had copied them on strong hemp paper in the precise fine characters that were so like her father's:

> Stars, dark, a lamp,
> A phantom, dew, a bubble,
> A dream, a flash of lightning, a cloud.
> Thus we should look on all that is made.

She tried with all her heart to understand this and to rise above herself and rule wisely, but she could not help but be aware of her own earthbound preoccupations and that the land was not at ease.

Kibi no Makibi, her old tutor whom she had promoted through the years, requested an audience. He thought he could explain to her where he felt the problem lay: It lay in these grants of rice fields to the temples; in these lavish gifts of precious cloth and other goods from the tax levy; in this commandeering of all the metals in the land for Buddha-images and temple bells. It was this spending of the country's riches that was making the land poor.

"But enriching it, surely, in the eyes of heaven?"

"The government is spending more than the revenue brings in."

"But this has been so for many years." She knew that the cost of building the Nara temples—and the palaces as well—and furnishing and maintaining them, conducting the ceremonies in the proper way, was greater than the worth of the goods and services that came from the land tax and work levies. But there was always more land to be cleared, and the land belonged to the crown. It seemed unlikely that this limitless expanse of field and forest and mountainside could be exhausted, but she put the question to him anyway, smiling as she said, "Is there no more land to annex?"

"The system is breaking down," he said bluntly. He presumed on his position as her teacher to speak his mind. As she well knew, the "system" as he put it was based on that of

T'ang China, where all the land belonged to the Sovereign and where every farmer was allotted fields to cultivate according to the number of mouths he had to feed. And in return he sent to the government a portion of the produce of his land and his able-bodied sons as unpaid laborers for their allotted years. To Abé this was the natural routine of government, though in essence it was uncongenial to her countrymen.

"But it has never 'broken down' as you say, for as long as I can remember—for more than a hundred years," she laughed. "Since Emperor Tenchi's reign." For it was then, at the time of the Great Reform, that the Emperor had taken over ownership of all the land.

"But I must warn you." Kibi's look was stern. But in his heart he felt both warmth and sympathy, for he knew that she was dominated and kept in ignorance by her Household Minister. He knew her brain to be equal to, perhaps even better than Nakamaro's, but it was a matter of assertiveness, of will, he thought. She had been kept like a plant in the dark, so well cared for and admired for its very fragility. And he wondered fleetingly what would happen to her if she were ever set free, set out in the sunlight to flourish on her own.

"I must warn you that the burden is falling so heavily on those least able to pay that men are selling themselves into slavery to escape their taxes and others, of course, have been entering the monasteries for the same reason."

"But the Ritsu priest has corrected that. Our rules for initiation are very strict."

"Still, some escape their taxes in this way," he dared to contradict. "And others by pushing north into the wilderness, where they hope the government cannot reach. And still others by misrepresenting to the census, for they are desperate."

She found this very sobering, for she had done what she could to make the country prosper and the life of the people easy. She had promoted the most elaborate customs of the Court and perfected their use of Chinese etiquette as well as observing every Buddhist rite and Shinto ceremony to the point of utter exhaustion.

But the truth was that throughout her great-aunt's reign, her father's, and her own, so many tax exemptions had been granted that the burden on the poor had become too heavy. No one of the Eighth Rank or above was taxed, nor were priests or nuns, nor doctors, scribes, or master artisans or artists. Furthermore great tracts of good rice land were granted free of tax to support the government offices and as rewards to various high Court nobles as well as to the Shinto shrines and the Buddhist temples.

Every year, as the Court expenses rose, the need for more taxable land grew more acute. But already in Shōmu's time the hardship and expense of clearing the wilderness and carving out rice fields with their complicated dikes and irrigation streams had grown so burdensome that those who undertook the job were compensated with such tax exemptions that there were never any revenues from these new lands.

"What are we to do, then," she said, more as a statement than a question, for it seemed to her a cycle that she could not break. With the people unhappy and rebellion in the Court, she had tried the remedies of her ancestors: ceremony, music, and rewards—the tools with which a wise and compassionate sovereign could bring harmony to heaven, earth, and man. And as her father had taught her by his example, she had given lands to the temples and commissioned images to be made in order to win the Buddha's protection for the state. But these things, too, meant a loss of revenue.

When she said, What are we to do, she did not expect a practical answer from her old tutor. Scholars held a special place in her mind, not related to practicalities. So he surprised her when he said, "I believe the expenditures of your Supreme Military Officer are an unnecessary burden on your treasury. Though he seems to be gathering forces on Kyushu, I can see no threat whatsoever from abroad."

She looked at him more closely, this face she knew so well, this familiar lively countenance that sometimes wrinkled and came alive with his enthusiasms and then again grew flat and calm in his contemplations, almost as though bored. Was he not aware of the danger of challenging Nakamaro? Was he not frightened? Yes, she observed, he knew the danger and was bored by it. She felt a rush of admiration for him, this wise man.

"I have spoken to Nakamaro," she said, "but he assures me that these moves against the Ezo and in Kyushu, as you mention, are vital to our defense . . ."

Kibi heard her voice go soft and realized that she was looking at the question from her minister's point of view. Perhaps she learned the lessons that he had taught her all too well, he thought, for he had spoken over and over again of the Superior Person who was one who could see a question from all sides, without bias. But this problem of vast military expenditures on top of the deficit needed a firm decision, even a biased one.

"The land is yours," he said, "not your Household Minister's. Heaven and earth hold you responsible, not him."

"Yes, I have spoken to him," she said once again, "but he has explained to me the dangers . . . and of course he is very wise in these matters . . ."

"'We must not mistake cunning for wisdom,'" Kibi murmured, falling into his old habit of quoting the Master. It was his way of putting off responsibility, as she did through her vacillation, "seeing the question from all sides." And he backed away from the subject, then, and they talked of other things.

When he had left, Abé went to the Hokke-ji to consult her mother. Kōmyō's influence in her daughter's Court was as pervasive as it had been in her husband's, and it was she who had tipped the scales against Toyonari. For whether or not he had entered the conspiracy, she reasoned, his opposition to his younger brother brought an air of discord to the Court. And harmony, above all, was the aim of a wise sovereign.

In the interest of harmony she had spent much of her time since the Emperor's death in her nunnery caring for the sick and poor—not for the accumulation of merits for herself but in appreciation of the works of her ancestors and as her contribution to the world treasury of moral good. She was busy, as the nuns said, with the practices of a bodhisattva, but she was always available to her daughter and went often to the Palace to advise her.

This time, however, Abé went herself to the nunnery and

found her mother in the bathhouse, where she was bathing the poor. Although she had seen her mother this way often enough, the sight was still amazing to her, and very moving, for Kōmyō stood with the skirts of her habit tucked up and her sleeves rolled back holding the wooden dipper in both hands as she leaned over the crouching, shivering old woman whom she was bathing.

Abé saw again with a pang how very weary her mother's figure looked with her arms and legs grown very thin and her body in the bulky apron disproportionately thick. Her face—so concentrated now on the work that she was doing—had grown rather heavy with age although her expression, when she turned to glance around, was still very sweet.

She filled the dipper a second time and, stepping back and leaning forward, poured the silvery water over the scrawny, uncomprehending, indigent old woman while two of the younger nuns, their faces set against the splash, held her by the arms.

When this was finished and the woman was led away, Kōmyō turned to Abé, holding her arms out at her sides and shaking her wet hands in a smiling, rueful way. I do my best, she seemed to say, but it is never good enough. Two of her attendants hurried up to dry her hands and feet. How I love her, Abé thought, and how truly good she is!

Among the lovely things that Kōmyō had done was to give to the Todai-ji temple all of Emperor Shōmu's personal belongings—all the beautiful artifacts and instruments he loved—keeping nothing for herself. The list of her gifts was like a catalogue of Shōmu's taste: his lute of sapanwood inlaid with mother-of-pearl; his chalcedony flute, his Persian ewer and his Chinese porcelains; his swords and bows with arrows set with colored insect wings; his ivory scepters and his crowns. There were more than a thousand articles including his mirrors backed with silver and intricate cloisonné, his feathered screens and patterned rugs and ceremonial robes, his jewels and white jade cups and magical vessels of rhinoceros horn and bundles of medicines, and of course many Buddhist sutras in their woven wrappings and cases of chased gold. So many precious beautiful things, almost beyond counting.

But Kōmyō had counted and listed all of them, and she wrote a dedication when she gave them to the priests: "His virtue filled the universe, his wisdom was as clear as the sun and moon. His fame reached far and wide, and priests of the purest virtue and deepest learning came to his empire from afar. Heaven was partial in the blessings it bestowed on him, and the earth produced its rarest treasures. To his people he was indeed a saint . . ." She had given these gifts to the temple, she explained, for the sake of his spirit, "to help its progress to the Lotus World."

This she had done soon after Shōmu's death and since then had spent her time in the Hokke-ji, caring for the sick who came to the infirmary, attending prayers, copying the Lotus Sutra which she honored most, and molding the little clay dogs from the ash of the holy fires to make charms against evil spirits—for her hands were never idle. But far more important, she continued, as she always had, to visit the Palace almost daily and to permeate every nuance of her daughter's life.

Now as she stepped carefully along the soaking boards in her bare feet, her shoulders sagged a little and she seemed to lean quite heavily on her attendants. To Abé, waiting at the door, she suddenly seemed old. The beautiful mother who had made her world was for an instant gone and an aged woman, drawn and heavy, came toward her. It was as though some other had crept up behind her and inhabited her figure and peered from her face with anxious eyes, her cheeks grown puffy and the color drained away.

When she came closer that dreadful look of age was gone and she glanced up from the corner of her eyes in that familiar winning way. With great relief, Abé reached out to her, her beautiful mother. But she had seen the warning and felt panic in her heart. It shouldn't have come as such a shock, she told herself, this revelation of passing time and what the years can do. All things, she knew, were transient and without substance. A phantom, she repeated to herself, dew, a bubble . . .

She struggled with this thought, not only then but over the months that followed, but she could not perceive her mother in this way, Kōmyō who was always young, always strong.

It was Lady Shihi who saw more clearly that it was not age alone that was draining her mistress' energy. "Shall I call the doctors?" she said more than once. But Kōmyō laughed at her. "Do I look so old?"

"Not at all, not at all." Shihi's face showed plainly that she did. "Only tired, perhaps. You have grown so thin."

It was not until the next summer when the warm wet rains from the southern seas fell so heavily upon their spirits day after day that she admitted that she was not herself. Although she had risen at her usual hour before dawn, she did not go to the bathhouse or the infirmary at all that day. And long before the evening bell, when the watery light still shone through the dripping rain from the eaves, she retired to her bed with the mild excuse that she would "rest for a minute."

"Are you ill?"

"Only tired." But she looked very worn.

"Shall I call the doctors?"

"No." But after a pause as she lay back looking at the canopy, contemplating it as though it might tell her something, seeming to listen, she added in a calm small voice, "but perhaps the Empress . . ."

She had been listening, in fact, to her own body, and it had told her of its weariness, its exhaustion—and the little pains beginning.

Abé needed hardly more than to see Shihi's face when a sense of panic so overtook her that she hurried to the Hokke-ji without any ceremony or prior warning. The nuns were taken aback to see her in their midst before they could prepare the rooms and arrange her screens, but she ran to her mother without noticing.

The doctors had no word for Kōmyō's illness. If a spirit had inhabited her body it was very quiet, for she never cried out or tossed in her sleep. But they were deeply moved to see how very tired she was and how patiently she bore her illness. Certainly a lady of such high position and good works and character would not be burdened with the body of a woman in her next life, they assured themselves. And when she was reborn a man she would be on the very threshold of Buddhahood.

When they said this Abé knew that they had lost hope for a cure. But she would not give up so easily. While they chanted their spells and administered their needles, she arranged for a special life-prolonging service at the Yakushi-ji temple, going herself to join the priests in their circumambulation of the Healing Buddha. It was the hour of the Dog, after sunset, but the sanctuary had been lit by a thousand earthen lamps of incensed oil and the light that poured through the door as she approached was as though the sun itself was rising in the room.

Inside, she bowed and touched her right knee to the ground as the priests had done, and then together with them in a long procession made her slow circuit of the image. She knew that in order for this ceremony to be effective she must remain throughout it full of peace, compassionate toward every living thing, ready to sacrifice herself, uplifted.

Full of peace, she told herself as she walked in the scented, smoky light round and round the image. Full of peace. But in spite of her words, her heart was anxious and her thoughts stayed with her mother.

Afterward, when Kōmyō remained the same, sleeping and waking to smile faintly at her and then sleep again, she arranged for a general amnesty and then, in a kind of desperation, freed all the male and female slaves throughout the country (although, on Nakamaro's insistence, she excepted those belonging to the Imperial Court) and forbade the killing of all living things as she had done for her father.

"For how long?" Nakamaro asked, for such proclamations were handled by his office now.

"Till the end of the year, why not?" She spoke in an abrupt and challenging voice, as she often did these days, and he was silent, for he too was desperately concerned. All through his young ambitious years he had had his aunt's support, and he was aware of her importance to him now.

"Perhaps," he said slowly, "you should stay by her, tend her, till she is well again."

"But I am, I do, I intend to . . ."

"In the Hokke-ji."

"To move there?" She did not understand him. "Live there? Leave?"

"Do you trust me to carry on for you?"

"How, 'carry on'?"

"To govern as best I can for you—for you and the Retired Empress. As I have tried to do."

"Well, yes. As you have done." She still was not aware of his full meaning until he said, "And Prince Oi-Ō can attend the ceremonies and perform the rites."

"Oi-Ō?"

"In your place, while you attend Her Majesty your mother . . ." And seeing that she was still hesitant (for he had not had time to prepare her properly) he added, "for she needs you. It is her life that most concerns us now."

"Yes. I see. I see your meaning." It was clear now. Nakamaro would be the central government and Oi-Ō his Emperor. Oi-Ō to do whatever his minister thought best.

"I only propose this for your mother's sake."

"Of course." Her voice was very low, even in her own ears, as she spoke.

When she said nothing more, he prodded a little. "The people are not in harmony, the land is not at ease. A change . . ."

"You mean for me to abdicate, to retire." He could not read her voice.

"I felt, because of the Retired Empress' health. And your own stated wish . . ."

Yes, she had often spoken of her plan to retire as her father had, to leave the world for the quiet of her mother's nunnery. But to be pushed like this!

"You may leave me."

He was surprised to hear the steel in her voice and did not linger.

When he was gone she called in Kibi once again and two advisers whom she trusted, the cautious Fujiwara Nagate and his cousin Momokawa.

"Nakamaro advises me to abdicate," she said abruptly.

They were silent. The cousins felt as Kibi did that the government was weak and that her expenditures were damaging the land. But they put more blame on her Household Minister than on the Empress herself, and they knew that Prince Oi-Ō would have even less control than she.

"Well?" What did this silence mean?

"What reason did he give for his advice?" Kibi asked.

"A change. He said a change is needed. The land is not at ease."

They could not argue with the truth of that. But a change to the weak young Heir Apparent—in Nakamaro's power?

"It would be better to change the Household Minister," Momokawa said, "if a change is needed."

Replace Nakamaro? But she had never ruled without him. The thought frightened her. "And my mother's health. I am needed in the Hokke-ji, to be beside her."

There was a silence once again. It was clear she would not bring herself to dismiss the Household Minister. She had been dominated by him—and by her mother—for too long a time.

"And the Retired Empress, does she agree?" Kibi said at last.

"I do not intend to abdicate! I called you here to inform you of that—if it was in your minds."

"It was not in our minds, not in our minds," Momokawa said. In fact the thought had shocked him.

"But I will consult the Retired Empress, as you suggest," she said to Kibi. And looking off, and weakening: "I will not neglect my filial duty."

"You are the Sovereign," Kibi said, reminding her. It had pleased him—pleased them all—to hear the determination in her voice. "You are the Sovereign, not Nakamaro." He would like to have added, Not your mother, but he did not dare.

"Well, I have told you," she said, dismissing them. "I will not abdicate. Unless the Retired Empress truly needs me and requests it . . ."

And later, after Kōmyō had gently said how happy she would be to have her daughter with her at the Hokke-ji, she called in Nakamaro for the last time.

"I have decided that since my mother needs me I will retire to be by her side and comfort her . . ." Her voice trailed off.

After a long time he said softly, "No one could do more than you have done. The love and gratitude of all your people shall be eternal. And I, what shall I do when I can no longer sit by your screen, hear your wise counsel, your commands . . ."

"Never mind," she cut in. "You were right to remind me. I have often said I longed to leave this world. Therefore," she straightened and her voice grew firm, "you will have the Central Ministry draw up my proclamation."

"Now?"

"Yes, now. Are you surprised? You have said yourself that the country is not calm, the people upset. A new emperor—even though it be Oi-Ō—will bring a change, as you say. A change."

CHAPTER XXII

After her abdication Abé no longer used the Imperial name of Kōken-Tennō but was known as the Retired Empress Takano. Her mother was now referred to as the Empress Dowager.

For a long time Kōmyō lay almost in a coma, then inexplicably she began to move, to sit up, even to drink some broth. Abé held the cup for her while Shihi supported her with cushions. The old doctor poked his head right through the curtains.

They will take any kind of liberty, Abé thought. With her mother's returning strength she found she was growing restless and somewhat irritable, regretting her decision and wondering how it had come about. Was she really needed in the Hokke-ji every minute as Nakamaro had said? And what was her role now?

"We were afraid you might be leaving us," the doctor said.

It was indeed very irritating to have him smiling and nodding in this way, his face and the long hairs of his beard so close. Even though he was a learned priest and the doctor in charge, such intimacy was offensive. Abé frowned.

"But I see you are feeling better," he went on nodding. And Kōmyō, though she was too tired to smile, gave him a grateful look.

Gradually, over the months, she seemed to recover, but she remained quite weak and there was no flesh at all on her arms.

Shihi coaxed and scolded. "Take a little of this bean soup. Try the abalone, just a bite." But it was almost as though her throat had closed and she could not eat. However, at last she was able to be up and about again—although she did not do half as much as she had done before—and because the quarters in the Hokke-ji were very cramped, Abé moved back to the Palace.

Oi-Ō had put his mother in the Empress' rooms, so she chose the old pavilion where she had lived as a girl. "It is quite large enough for me," she said. She did not intend to have much of a court, but to watch quietly what the young Emperor would do.

The state of the nation was no better, she observed, than it had been in her reign. Though the ceremonies of the seasons were observed, they were beginning to neglect the Buddhist rites. That was Nakamaro's influence, she felt sure. He was Great Minister of the Right, at last, as well as Supreme Military Commander. Everything was in his hands.

Sometimes he came to consult her, sitting beside her screen as in the old days, gazing out into her little garden, taking his ease. The willow tree had been replaced and bamboo grew by the pond. It saddened her, but she felt she had got over her longing for the past. Perhaps there were still some tender feelings deep in her heart, she thought, but with her responsibilities—with age—she had plastered them over. Even Nakamaro accused her of being hard (and he is an expert, she thought wryly). Perhaps it was this very "hardness" that brought him to consult her—though she did not think he meant to follow her advice.

"Perhaps he is sincere," her mother said when she mentioned this.

"Perhaps."

"You have not trusted Nakamaro as you might have. He was my choice for you."

She felt her mother's judgment was unfailing and this accusation stung. It was true, she had not put her whole trust in him. She could not. And she had begun seriously to doubt the soundness of his policies. He was far too concerned with those imagined threats from abroad and the stirrings of the Ezo in the north.

Even before she abdicated—and over her strong protest—he had sent the slaves of the rebels' households to reinforce the northern palisades and rounded up more than a thousand vagrants for the same purpose. And now he had ordered every province to provide two thousand more. Weapons were being stored in all the fortresses. She could hardly think his actions were defensive and she told him so. He intended to open up the war there and push north—at what cost in lives? she asked him. At what cost?

It was not until much later, when she was too preoccupied to care, that he plunged into his campaign against Silla, strengthening the fortifications of Dazaifu and ordering the commanders there to prepare for the movement of unnumbered troops. He had appointed Kibi no Makibi to be military instructor there—whether to utilize his knowledge of Chinese practices or simply to be rid of him, she could not be sure.

Toward the end of the year he sent instructions to the provinces along the coast to build and equip five hundred warships and afterward staged a grand review of four hundred of these vessels and nearly fifty thousand troops. It might have been that this display was as much to impress his own countrymen as to intimidate the Silla King. But Abé was unaware of it in any case for by that time she was in deep mourning for her mother.

Kōmyō had seemed quite well for many months and then, on the seventh day of the Fifth Month, when the iris were in bloom and the leaves were newly green on the tips of the young branches in the Hokke-ji garden, she woke in the early morning and could not rise.

She waited patiently for her waiting women or for Shihi to come. I am very ill, she thought, but I am not afraid. However, of course, fear has a life of its own, and when it invaded her it made her body sicken and sweat form on her brow.

By the time that Abé could run to her, the priests had already been summoned. She sent off messages for services to be held in all the Nara temples while the old doctor called for the exorcists.

While the drums and the noise of their loud praying started up again, as they had those months ago, Abé sat quietly beside her, praying with all her heart. "Let her have a little longer in this world," she prayed. " 'Though life be nothing but a transient morning mist, though it vanish like the wake of a ship, though it be smoke,' " she quoted. But she could not bring herself to believe that her mother's life could be over so soon, could vanish without a trace. "Like smoke," she said, and was aware of the thick black smoke that rose from the altars of the exorcists. Someone brought her a breakfast tray but she did not touch it, and all day long she sat there gazing at the drawn remote face on the pillows.

Kōmyō was absorbed in her own body, in the pain that came and went, and in the contemplation of her sins. The exorcists were hoping to determine if a spirit had possessed her so that they could call it by its name and bring it out and transfer it into the body of a medium. But she showed no signs of possession, and the little girl whom they had put into a trance lay still behind her curtain.

The doctor tried every kind of medicine, from ginseng to rhubarb to petrified dragon bones, but nothing brought her relief. Week after week Abé sat beside her, taking the cold limp hand in hers or stroking the forehead where the short cut hair had grown a pitiful gray fringe.

"How beautiful you are," she encouraged her. "How beautiful you are to me." Then tears would stop her and she would sit silent, gazing at the shrunken, frightened face, until she could pull herself together enough to say, "You must think of encouraging and optimistic things. It is when we worry and expect the worst that we grow ill. You have always taught me to be calm in my heart and mind, to look for the best in things . . ." And she would try to smile but when her lips parted they turned down like a little child's.

Kōmyō watched her with unchanging face, week after week while the summer went by, until one time toward the end of the Sixth Month, when the heat had been oppressive and Abé was wiping her forehead with a cloth dipped in shredded ice, she suddenly woke and sat up straight as though in anger, clutching her throat and indicating that she could not stand the smell of the smoke from the little altars. Her eyes were wild as she grasped her throat with one hand and with the other pointed accusingly.

The doctor, hearing this movement, poked his head between the curtains as it was his habit to do, and when Abé turned she saw that his face was suddenly alight.

"There is something possessing her," he said. Then, almost triumphantly, "At last."

He withdrew to tell the exorcists to renew their spells. "There is something there," he assured them. "You will surely conquer." And, as he predicted, the little medium began to moan.

Abé became aware of this transfer as she watched her mother's face. It was no longer rigid as it had been all these weeks, but seemed to relax a bit, and she stretched her body slightly and moved her head.

Outside the curtain Abé could hear the medium moan. Then, as the priests increased their chanting, making their voices roar, the child began to writhe and shriek. "Let me alone," she cried in a voice like a young boy. "Let me alone! I meant no harm!"

"Who sent you?" the doctor roared. "Tell me your name."

"My father sent me. I meant no harm. Please don't torment me so with your charms. Let me alone."

"Tell me your name and you may go," the doctor said. He had to shout above the terrible noise the exorcists were making, and Abé turned to peer through the curtain at this terrifying scene.

Presumably the child had answered, for at that moment the doctor smiled, and taking a large paper handkerchief from his sleeve he wiped his face and beard.

What had the child said, Abé wondered. Perhaps it was just a name. She had heard the voice very faintly under the roar of the priests. Kazuragi, Kagitori, some such thing as that. But it meant nothing to her and she turned back to her mother.

Kōmyō lay as she had lain all through these summer months, but her eyes looked out quite clearly, full of intelligence, and her face was not so drawn. In her expression there seemed to be a marvelous relief.

She died about ten days later, on the eve of the Weaver Maiden Festival that she had loved so much. And Shihi took Abé by the shoulders, pulling her away, and her women led her blind with weeping to her old childhood rooms.

When she remained where they had put her, saying nothing and not moving through the days and nights, they worried that she might attempt to do away with herself. But she knew she had not the strength for that. Perhaps from childhood she had always drawn what strength she had from her mother. Or from Nakamaro, who for so long had had a hold on her. But he had let it slip. Now she had no one and it meant nothing to her whether she lived or died.

She lay in darkness and her soul wandered. She lost her sense of time and place and thought she was a child again and in her mother's rooms and looked up happily—only to see her ladies in deep mourning and feel her heart plunge down again into the dark. How many hours, days, had she been lying lost in this fog of grief with her mind spiraling?

Lady Shihi said, "You must eat something."

She looked up. She was back in her old pavilion, the familiar rooms. They brought a lamp and placed a tray before her.

"Take a sip," Shihi said. She lifted the lid from the bowl and the steam drifted after her hand.

Like the mist of an autumn field, she thought. Aloud in a faltering voice she began the poem, "In the loneliness of my heart . . ."

At the cremation she had seen the pale smoke rising, fading and disappearing into the bland sky. The thought that this was her mother's life was almost unbearable and she saw her own life, so ephemeral, so vague . . .

"You must eat to keep up your strength," Shihi said sharply. But she could not.

There was no room for all the priests, and her ladies were crowded into back corners. With Nakamaro's help they persuaded the Emperor's mother to take up residence in the Imperial quarters, and Abé was moved into her mother's old pavilion where the priests could set up their altars and the women have some privacy.

Here again her memory was stirred. She looked out across the lake, the bridge. It was rather worn, she saw, with the paint peeling. How often she had looked out on that bridge. How often she had crossed it. Little red carp had lived under it. They are old now, she thought, even older than I.

So many years of growing up, growing old. She closed her eyes. Suddenly she saw Nakamaro coming toward her across the bridge as it had been. After thirty years the picture came to her! And that was I, that child. It seemed to her she could feel that little girl within her, the little slender limbs lying doll-like within her own, the quick pulsebeat in her throat. That little body, so light, so tender—that was I. And that was Nakamaro coming at me, walking so steadily, stamping his feet on the boards.

Now, here, in this emptiness that had descended on her since her mother's death, the sudden picture of the young Nakamaro sprang at her. How well she had come to know him since that time. And here he appeared in her mind's eye, a young man in spring green. She saw his face again, although the faces he had shown her in later times slid over it like shadows on a pond. He was frowning. Well, she had seen him frown since then!

He had gone on to speak to her mother. Why did the memory trouble her so? Had she followed him in? She remembered how she had slipped behind the deer screen. Ah, the deer screen, how she had loved it. Her refuge when things went badly . . .

Her mother was talking, speaking of death. One way to die, another way. Fall from a cliff, eaten by animals. Demons. Was it because of her brother's death just then? Little Moto-Ō? It had been so puzzling, and her mother's voice so sad, so soft, so full of anger underneath . . .

"Where is the deer screen?" She had to say it twice before Shihi understood.

"The deer screen?"

"The deer screen that stood by the door. The little sister deer."

"Sister deer!" Shihi tossed a little smile over her shoulder. But when she looked again at those questioning, troubled eyes, her face grew somber. "My lady, you have been dreaming. That screen was given to the Todai-ji treasure-house with all your father's fine possessions, you must remember."

She looked around. It had grown dark. The room was shadowy beyond the circle of the lamp where the lamplight threw a filigreed pattern on the floor. "Where is Nakamaro?"

"Why, he is here, my lady!" She spoke as if he had come here many times.

And indeed, she saw him standing just beyond the light. He seemed to be weeping and she was aware that a very strong emotion must have brought him here, braving the contamination of a death so close to her, for she would still be in a state of defilement for some time.

"Please try to do as Shihi asks," he said, "for we all need you. You must eat something and grow strong again." His voice was thick with sincerity and she was touched. She did not speak, however, and he went on. "Remember, you are not alone in your sorrow . . ."

It seemed he could not speak any more and she roused herself enough to feel pity for him. Heavy responsibilities, she thought, looking up again at the bulk of his figure, there beyond the light. But she did not feel any inclination to share his burden or comfort him. I will soon be gone, she thought, so it does not matter.

On the forty-ninth day, when her mother's soul would find another home, Rōben held a ceremony of national mourning for the relief of suffering souls and prayed that the Empress Dowager might be forgiven any human crimes, any defilements in her previous lives, and that her soul might be reborn into Amida's sun-bright land.

But her mother had been good and pure, Abé thought. There were no sins for her to take into another life. She had gone to the Todai-ji for the ceremony and had sunk into a reverie while the sutra was being read and the charms chanted. But afterward, when she was home again, suddenly her mother's form appeared before her—but so changed! She was creeping through dusty, ruined streets, threadbare, forlorn. Where had she ever seen such streets as these? There were no such streets in the Palace grounds, not in all of Nara.

Ah, it was from the time of the earthquakes when they had been borne through the countryside and seen the villages with their charred and broken houses, the ragged people wailing. It was the time that Asaka had died . . . that beautiful young Prince . . . and she was so terrified . . .

Now, in her dream, her mother turned. Oh, mother! She was misshapen like the hungry ghosts painted on the screens of hell in the Buddhist Center, her stomach swollen but her neck so thin! She was searching ravenously through the filth and rubble, but her mouth was no bigger than a needle's eye! "The roots of your mother's crime are deep and complicated," a voice re-echoing. Mother! It is not true!

She spoke aloud, starting herself awake. Her heart was pounding wildly in her throat as though she had been running somewhere—through the halls or through the countryside. Absurd. Her heart was beating and yet she could hardly move. Had she cried out? She heard some of the younger women murmuring beside her curtain . . . Is she well? Should we speak to her . . . ? They are afraid of me, she thought. And I, too, am so afraid.

With a great effort she moved a hand, then lifted it to her throat. And by the time Shihi came through the curtain and crouched close to her she was able to speak and to assure her, "Nothing. It was nothing."

After that for many months she lived in torment for her mother, and on the anniversary of her death she had a special hall built in a corner of the Palace grounds next to the Hokke-ji with a sixteen-foot image of the Amida Buddha and four guardian gods. Also, she took to going frequently into the little alcove room where Lady Tachibana's shrine still stood. She had not been there since that night—that special, that extraordinary night, that night unlike any other—so many years ago, so many, when she was still a girl and had unwarily slid back the door . . .

But now when she went down that corridor her mind was filled with her mother and the welfare of her soul, her heart still terrified by her dream.

Perhaps when she first peered into the room the semblance of a thought did cross her mind: It was here I saw him. But that was all. It was so long ago. It was here I saw him. And then she looked at the Buddha and sank down, and her mother came to fill her prayers.

Sometimes her women found her there, exhausted and asleep. How very delicate she looked, how beautiful. Since her mother's death she had taken on an almost transparent quality, her skin so pure and her eyes so luminous.

"Lady, lady, death comes to everyone," they said. "And now the mourning period is over."

It was true. The year had come and gone. Now they laid out colorful clothes for her, and once again music . . .

Now sometimes she approached the shrine with a small guilt stirring. There was that time when she had felt alive. So much pain, confusion, sensations of all kinds—but alive. Now she allowed her mind to brush obliquely over the scene: the light falling on the beautiful bare head, the voice, the hand that held her. She did not let his name come boldly to her mind, fearing that to think it, much less to speak it, would evoke too much.

Later, when she had become accustomed to this journey—this visit to the shrine room and to the past—she allowed herself to dwell awhile in that memory. She did not yet pronounce the name. She felt it would be a kind of desecration, a despoilment of that sacred place where she had hidden it, so deep within her heart, so many years. But she thought it, and she thought of him, and of herself.

It can do no harm, she told herself. She was so young then, although she had not realized it. We think of ourselves as fully grown at every age. Young and unaware of time, of endings and impossibilities. It had seemed to her that there would be another time presented to her, another opportunity, another chance meeting. Somehow, at some unexpected moment . . .

How heedless she had been of passing time, of lost opportunities! Her life was passing like the wheels of a carriage seen through a crack in the fence, and she was unaware. She had healed the pain, or smothered it, thinking: There will be a time.

She wondered if her mother knew, if she had seen her turmoil and how she had come searchingly into every room, and understood. Perhaps, later on, that was why she had sent Nakamaro to her, someone to occupy her nights . . .

Recently Nakamaro had been coming to her pavilion, bringing his problems to her. But it was beyond her power now, beyond her strength, to respond. What did he want of her, she wondered. He had the Emperor in his hand.

"I feel that your life is not happy," he once said to her. He spoke very tenderly. "And we, you and I, have meant so much to each other over the years, it hurts me to see you sad . . ."

She found it hard to respond to this. She truly felt nothing for him, not since her mother's death. Perhaps it was only her mother's wish, after all, that had bound them all those years . . .

"I am only waiting for my life to end," she finally brought out. "There is nothing more for me."

"You must not speak like that. I know it must be dreary for you here. I'm afraid the Emperor has let things go a bit, and I have been preoccupied." He did not mention his intention to invade the neighboring peninsula and the difficulty he was having rallying support. He would have liked to have her on his side. "It has been on my mind to move you to the Tamura palace, where things are more orderly and there is more life." And before she could object he went on hurriedly, "These Palace halls must be rebuilt, you must admit. You cannot stay here with your porch sagging as it is, and the pillars home for insects."

The Emperor's residences too were in terrible disrepair, and water came into the Bureau of Books each time it rained. Some of the gardens were disgracefully overgrown. When Nakamaro spoke of this she could not help remarking, perhaps with some satisfaction, that if the Emperor was incapable of managing his own household, one wondered about the state of the whole nation. He had not even kept the alternate compound to the east prepared, so he had no choice but to move away completely while everything was rebuilt.

"Well, I have arranged for him to go to the new Hora Palace in Ōmi. It will be cool near the river these early autumn months. And the carpenters will have a free hand here."

Perhaps that is the place for me as well, she thought. Away from this Palace, away from Nara. The Hora Palace had been built not far from that miraculous temple Rōben had built above the stone seat of the holy man on the banks of the Seta River. She had often thought of that and the gift of gold that rewarded her father's reign.

If she could no longer stay here in the darkness of her rooms, going from day to night along the corridor and from night to day from the shrine to her bed-space once again, she would go far away. The thought of daylight frightened her, of moving about, of seeing people—having them see her! But better to make the long journey to the river Palace than to display herself to Nakamaro's family at the Tamura.

"You will be more comfortable with me," Nakamaro said. But his voice had less of the soft command it once had, less power to move her, and she did not answer.

CHAPTER XXIII

Even before they reached the bridge at Uji she began to regret her decision. Their departure had been delayed, time after time, by the young Emperor's indecision, for it seemed he had great difficulty making up his mind. They had spent their first night in one of the old palaces at Kuni, empty, echoing, and full of memories . . . "a happy place where the rivers meet," she thought sardonically of the old poem. It was no longer a happy place but cold and desolate.

It was already the middle of the Eleventh Month, and at Uji where they crossed the bridge the turbulent waters thundered under them. A dark gray mist hid the mountains they must travel through and she wondered, almost in panic, if she might turn back. But it was too late for that and she let her bearers carry her on, following the Emperor's long procession.

Before they reached the Hora Palace, high on the banks of the Seta, it had begun to rain. They had traveled most of the night. Without Nakamaro, it would seem, even so simple a thing as a journey could not be arranged capably. And as she dragged her skirts up the steep steps, small and wet and weary under the towering trees, it was anger and impatience with Oi-Ō that kept her from breaking down.

Fuwa walked beside her—for her half sister had become her friend again in recent months—and her men held lanterns for her, revealing sodden leaves on the steps. What an outlandish place for a palace, perched on the side of a hill! She could see nothing of the lake or the view that they said was so famous, though she could hear the rush of the river and the high wind in the trees.

It was no wonder that in the following weeks she fell ill again, sinking into the same depression that had gripped her when her mother died. Sometimes her sense of all reality seemed to drift away and she spoke to Fuwa as though she were her mother and to the doctors as to demons. Then in her lucid moments she gripped Fuwa by the hands and stared into her face as though to force a promise by the strength of her gaze: "I do not want the old doctor! He brings death. I do not want his old face inside my curtains. You must promise me!"

Fuwa said nothing, seeming to absorb the fierce look and the hissing words in her own receptive pose. And seeing this, some of the others said it was a blessing that Lady Shihi was not well and could not be in attendance. Shihi would have argued, scoffed, called in what doctors she thought best. Fuwa said nothing, and that seemed to bring a calming influence into the little room.

The arrangements for their living had not been well thought out. Shihi, for instance, with some of the older women was in a small pavilion reached by a flight of steps. Abé and her other attendants were in a hall set on the edge of a clearing known as the Cypress Court, while Oi-Ō, who kept his mother close to him, had set up his Court in a cluster of pavilions overlooking the lake.

Though he sometimes called for his advisers to come from the capital and held conferences on minor matters, there was little for him to do in the way of governing. Before he left Nara he had conferred on Nakamaro the highest Court position (First Rank, senior grade) and had appointed him Prime Minister. He was now known as the Grand Preceptor and had been granted a million sheaves of rice (the produce of six thousand acres of rice fields) as well as three thousand households with their services on top of his other income. In actual power he outweighed the Emperor manyfold.

When she heard of these latest gifts, Abé laughed. "He sees himself as a warrior now, in splendid armor! He will make a splendid warrior against the Silla King. A champion!" When she laughed it was almost as disturbing as the anxious whisperings of her depression.

"It will never come about," Fuwa said. She was not so much soothing her sister as stating a fact as she foresaw it, for Fuwa more than anyone else in the whole Court intuitively knew what was to happen and—when she was asked—could tell it. It was rare, as now, that she volunteered her foresight, but it pleased her to see Nakamaro fail—after so many successes, after destroying Prince Funado and her other friends.

Fuwa's girlhood had been lived in a household strictly regulated by taboos and omens. The roots of her character were steeped in magic and she received messages from other worlds. When her mother, the susceptible young Lady Hiro, was pushed aside by the Emperor's consort, she developed a jealous spirit that took possession of her and ruled her life.

Fuwa could remember dimly that as a tiny child she had known sunny days when her mother caught her up and played with her, laughed at her baby words, at the words of the nurses too, even the song of the birds. Those were the times when the Emperor sent word that he would visit. But increasingly there were long dark puzzling periods when her nurses would not let her go to her mother and sometimes she heard wails, even screams, coming from her rooms.

Relegated as they were to a small detached palace in the second ward, they were seldom visited by people of interest, and after Asaka was born the Emperor never came at all. As her life grew lonelier, Lady Hiro often sat all day in tears. Her people warned her that if she could not keep a calm and cheerful spirit, even in this sad state of neglect, she would surely succumb to some evil influence.

As a result they took even more than the usual precautions: If someone forgot to close a shutter for the night, leaving an entry for some wandering spirit, it was not enough simply to scatter a little rice. No, the exorcists were called. Every sixteenth day, on the day of the Monkey, the entire household had to stay awake from dusk to dawn prepared to fight off the demons that were most active on those nights. Fuwa was not allowed to cut her nails except on the day of the Ox or to have her hair washed on any one of a long list of taboo days that her mother could recite. And during the whole of her sixteenth year she was forbidden to make a move toward the northwest because the elements ascendant at the time of her birth made that direction taboo for her that year. It was then that she developed her abnormal interest in occult spirits, in magic, and in her way of prophesying through the *Book of Changes.*

Of course everyone at Court was familiar with the *Book of Changes.* The Masters of Yin and Yang at the Bureau of Divination were always consulted by the Grand Council and were quite obliging with their advice to anyone who consulted them through the proper channels, but few untrained people could read the moving lines with the deep understanding that Fuwa had.

When she first saw her mother take the yarrow stalks between her thin white fingers, she was so small that the jumbled piles of twigs seemed to her mere playthings. But she had learned—oh, at a very early age—to toss them, count them out, and hold them expertly in her little fist. And very soon afterward the images and the lines in the *Book* had come alive for her.

What struck her most deeply, at that sensitive age when she first became aware of herself and her position as the daughter of a discarded second wife, abandoned (for the Emperor had never formally acknowledged her) and unprotected, was the relationship of the primordial family that was represented in those lines.

There were eight, like the eight points of the compass, but Fuwa concentrated on the ones she knew: *Father: Creative,* with the attributes *heaven, jade, deep red, the Prince.* All true. *Mother: Receptive, earth, a cow with a calf.* True also, for at that time Asaka was a baby, a little calf.

Attributes of the younger daughter—that was herself: *Joyous.* She smiled at that, and the smile, even on her still-plump childish face, mocked what should have been her primary attribute.

She was anything but joyous. But further the *Book* said: *The lake, a sorceress. It means smashing and breaking apart. It means dropping and bursting open.* That she liked.

Attributes of the elder daughter—that was the Crown Princess: *Wood, wind. It is the white, the high. It is advance and retreat, the undecided. It is the sign of vehemence.*

How often she had pondered those qualities! She had never seen the Crown Princess, the elder sister, and what she heard of her came filtering through the malice of her mother's ladies. For her they spelled evil.

But now it was almost twenty years since she had entered the Princess' court and she had become indebted to her in many ways. It was she, when she was Empress, who had sponsored Fuwa's marriage to Prince Shioyaki, she who had forgiven him his part in the rebellion and, since the death of the Empress Dowager, had shown them both such favor that in order to fulfill her obligation Fuwa had left her husband and young son to accompany her to this Hora Palace.

Thus, over the years, those frightening qualities she had attributed to the "elder daughter," that vision she had of the Princess' double character and vehemence, had softened. She saw instead the indecision of a person always under another's influence and the vehemence as simple outbursts of frustration. Now she could even pity her—alone as she was, and in her turn abandoned.

She offered to look into the future for her, casting the yarrow stalks. "Ask what you like," she said.

They had been sitting looking out into the rain. It fell past the rustic porch of the pavilion, past the flat brown earth of the Cypress Court, down past the roots of the tall red trees, down to the churning river and wet rocks below. It formed a curtain all around them, dark and gray and so dreary that no one had the heart for music or for games and now had ceased even to talk.

There is no going through it, Abé thought, no way of going around. And, after Fuwa's question, What should she ask for in this dark place? What could there be to comfort her, alone and growing old? And yet she would like to know . . .

When Kibi no Makibi had begun her studies in the *Book of Changes* he had said: "Whoever knows the tao of the moving lines knows the action of the gods." And: " 'The nature of the yarrow stalks is round and spiritual, the nature of the lines is square and wise. The lines move and the meaning changes in order to answer the question.' "

What question?

"The Superior Man when he consults the *Changes* does so in words. The *Book* takes up the question like an echo. Neither far nor near nor dark nor deep exist for it. Thus he learns the things of the future."

Fuwa was waiting.

"What will become of me?" she said aloud, her own voice strange in her ears.

Fuwa handed her the yarrow stalks and she tossed them down, discarded one, and began to count them, placing them between her fingers, four by four. It was something she was not accustomed to and Fuwa helped her. When she had cast them six times and the six lines were determined, Fuwa consulted the *Book* and told her, "The hexagram is *Kou: Coming to Meet.*"

"What does it mean?"

"The image is, *Under heaven, the wind.* That is the way the Prince sends out his commands—*as the wind blows to the four quarters.*" And when there was silence she read further, "*Heaven is far from the things of the earth, but it stirs them by means of the wind . . .*"

"And *Coming to Meet?*"

Fuwa was confused. The question, What will become of me?, had not been properly phrased. But as these words were the first to be spoken in so long a time, she had proceeded. Now she hazarded an answer: "You will command the Grand Preceptor. *Coming to Meet.*"

"Nakamaro?" It was the last thing she could wish. Summon Nakamaro? She wondered if he would even listen. Never obey. Especially as she had spurned his invitation to the Tamura palace. She would never call him and he would never come. "Nakamaro?" She raised her eyes to contemplate Fuwa's smooth bent head. "Summon the Preceptor?"

Absorbed in reading the moving lines, Fuwa did not answer. "Nine in the second place," she said, "means *There is a fish in the tank.* This is a symbol of darkness, yin . . . Nine in the fifth, again the yin: A *melon covered by leaves.*

"You are in darkness," she said, glancing up. And then, continuing: "Nine at the top, *He comes to meet.*"

"Who comes?"

But because of the darkness Fuwa could not tell. Instead she went on to the next. "It says, *No blame.* But there is humiliation."

"Yes." And after a long pause, "Is there more?"

"Much more." But at that time Fuwa did not pursue all the comments and interpretations that the Sages had written. It was not until afterward, when she was drawn to the sound of a vibrant voice and had seen the doctor-priest, that she went back to the hexagram—and not until years later did she realize what had been done.

Standing in the shadows, watching the priest, she had had a premonition and gone back to the *Book:* Six at the beginning, a divided line, not moving. She had not given it her full attention. Now she read: "Six at the beginning means: *It must be checked with a brake of bronze.*" How to interpret that? She read the Sages carefully. "*Coming to Meet: The dark principle advances and encounters the light . . . An inferior man insinuates himself into high places. If his influence is not checked misfortune is bound to result.*"

When Abé asked the question the phrase that she uttered was "What will become of me?", but in her mind were the words: "What am I to do?" It was important, she knew, to approach the *Book* in a positive way so that a decision could be made—so that as one advanced into the future one could act appropriately with the help of its wisdom. But she had said, "What will become of me?", and Fuwa was misled and made that preposterous suggestion about Nakamaro.

Coming to Meet. Why did the hexagram say that? And why

did the lines tell her that the Prince sends out his word like the wind? What shall I do? *Send out to the four quarters . . .*

While she pondered this, the image of that beautiful young priest came surfacing to her mind. Why should that be? Certainly she could not deny that she had often wondered where in the four quarters he might be and whether alive or not. Of course it would be quite possible to send out word . . .

"*Coming to Meet* . . . there is humiliation . . . *No blame* . . ."

At the New Year she fell ill again. The young Emperor observed the ceremonies that were necessary but it was pitiful, she thought, when Fuwa described to her the first-day Congratulations when those few nobles who were here in this forsaken place paid their respects to the Sovereign. Only two departments of the government had been transferred here—the Household Ministry and the Guards. The rest remained in Nara, where Nakamaro had taken on yet another title. He was now Guardian-in-the-Sovereign's-Absence! She could picture the brilliant ceremony at the Tamura palace.

There was nothing at all for her to do. The Emperor had made the Grand Obeisance to the August Ancestors and his mother had honored his small Court with a banquet and Chinese music, but making an excuse of her illness she did not attend.

Shihi, herself very thin and weak, insisted on calling the doctors. When they came she informed them that the illness was difficult, very mysterious, and deep. They agreed that the case was hard to diagnose; there were no real symptoms, and yet the patient never felt well. They prescribed a number of tonics and arranged for services to be held, but nothing relieved her. The illness was, in fact, simply one of ennui, of inaction, a surfeit of leisure, and they did not recognize the malady.

"We must call in the exorcists," Shihi said.

It was then that Abé said aloud for the first time the name of the man who had grown in her mind from a memory to a dream to a secret preoccupation.

"There is a doctor-priest," she told Fuwa in a small shamed voice, "a priest of the Hossō sect." And after a long pause, with her head turned away, "I believe he could cure me, if that is to be my fate . . ." And again, with painful hesitations, "If I am not to be allowed to die . . . as I would like . . ."

Fuwa, wisely, did not speak.

And so at last she said the name, bringing it to her lips with a rush of feeling such as she had not had since her youth. "Yuge no Dōkyō. A Hossō priest." And then, rather quickly spoken as though mere matter of fact: "He is a man of good reputation, I am told. I am sure if anyone can help me it would be such a man."

The word went out "to the four quarters" and very soon the doctor, Dōkyō of Yuge, was located at a small temple on Mount Katsuragi where, as was well known—for he was indeed a man of reputation in Buddhist circles—he had been spending the past year in meditation.

In the years since he had last seen the Princess—at the time of her enthronement—he had followed a career of meditation, study, and discourse that had brought him respect in his field but no outstanding fame. When Abé learned that he had not been more than a long day's journey from Nara she was amazed that he could have been so close and she be unaware. But over the years he had often been in her vicinity, living in various Nara temples, even visiting the Palace, though he had never again been called to attend the Imperial Family.

In his boyhood in Kawachi he had studied medicine and divination. But after he had come to Nara as a very young man and been accepted as a pupil of Rōben, who was then the disciple of the great Hossō teacher Gien, he plunged into the study of the Hossō school of thought, which teaches that while all phenomenal things are merely illusion, there is one reality, and that is consciousness. The Absolute, the one existent thing, he learned, is Mind. And he had gone on to immerse himself in the seven kinds of perception that might lead him to ultimate inner consciousness.

As usually happens with attractive people, he was singled out for praise and in three years was ordained. But when the Master Gien died he returned to his home in Kawachi and continued his study of medicine, mastering the techniques of the six pulses, and of acupuncture and moxabustion.

What brought him to the capital once again was the arrival of the famous Chinese priests who came with the returning embassy of 734. They had passed through his home and he had seen the tall priest Gembō and his own ambition was stirred. So he had followed them to the capital and in time had obtained a position in the Palace Buddhist Center and attended the ladies of the Empress' pavilion during the year of the smallpox.

Although he had never really thought of it that way and never regretted it, his encounter with the Imperial Princess in the shrine room put an end to the ambitions he had had to be rich and famous. At twenty-six, when others were making their ascent through the hierarchy, he left Nara with scant explanation and retired to a mountain fastness where others had gone to meditate before him.

There on Mount Katsuragi where giant bamboo groves enclosed him from the world, he resumed his long and painful meditations, sitting erect by the north window, counting his breaths in order to concentrate his heart. At first, sometimes, slipping from his concentration, he thought of the Princess and that amazing night. But as the years passed he remembered less and less until it could have been said that the incident did not exist for him at all.

Indeed, the world itself, the activities of men and women, the concepts of time as past and future, and all phenomena of every sort ceased to exist, in his belief, except as an idea in the transcendent mind. The Sanron priests whose work he had studied proclaimed the theory of the Void, of nothingness: Nothing exists. But he had been taught by Gien—and his own meditations had confirmed—that consciousness itself is real, exists. It is the central element from which all things derive and radiate. In thought alone is the existence of all creation. All else is illusion.

After six years of isolation he returned to Nara and was caught up in the affairs of his profession as a doctor-teacher-priest. The Court was then at Kuni, but when the Emperor returned and he saw the Princess from a distance he was able to tell himself that there was no reality there.

Thus he had lived, one of many hundreds of priests, first at the Kofuku-ji, then at the Gango-ji, performing his duties, teaching the student-priests, sometimes called to treat the families of the high Court nobles in their residences. For the past few years he had been on the medical faculty of Chancellor Kibi no Makibi's university, but it was clear to him that he would rise no further.

As a boy he had dreamed of fame, of becoming a high priest, of a position in Court. When his career was broken, as it had been that fatal night, he turned himself to philosophy and meditation. Now, as he approached his fiftieth year, a Master of Buddhism and a Learned Scholar, it seemed to him it was time to turn once more to the discipline of meditation and its eventual reward.

So he had gone again to the mountains and had been there this past year. The summons to the Hora Palace disturbed his concentration and he was reluctant to go. But they had said "someone of importance" . . .

Once when she was a young girl Abé had gone on a moon-viewing picnic on a warm August night. She had sat on a small embankment at the river's edge and looked at the bright water. The weather had been dry and the embankment under her looked crumbly to the touch. Spiky tufts of grass grew out over the edge. She remembered seeing a grain of sand clinging to a blade and she had reached out in the harsh whiteness of the moon to nudge it with her finger and dislodge it.

After the grain had fallen, rolling down among its fellow grains, the bank was quiet. Then, as though made restless under the black shadow of the grass, a second grain rolled down, and after that a few more followed it as though to find a brighter, or perhaps more comfortable place to lie. Leaning forward she watched for the next, though she did not put her hand out a second time.

A tiny rill, a little ripple in the silver sand moved down the slope and stopped. And in a little while another. Then another, and a slide, almost an avalanche with the grains grouping, rushing together, until there was a movement of the whole bank under her and someone snatched her back.

Long afterward she remembered that little avalanche with the minute clarity of a dream and thought of what she had touched off when she said, "What will become of me?"

Her first meeting with the doctor-priest (she did not say his name) left her so quiet, so exhausted, that some of her ladies said he had done more harm than good. He had come into the room—Fuwa brought him—and she struggled with herself to raise her head, lift her eyes, to look in his direction.

Through the fabric of her screen she could see his figure: dim, composed, erect. He was moving quietly, seemingly with assurance, and all at once it struck her forcibly that he was a stranger. What of that dream that she had nurtured, that familiar presence that she knew so well? The frightening realization struck her that she had stored the memory of that man very deep in her consciousness as a sort of bulwark against the depression of her loneliness, against those menacing waves of hopelessness that swelled and poised themselves in the background of her existence. Would that collapse now? Would the waves rush in?

He moved forward to the cushion they had put down for him and sat, tucking the skirts of his habit under his knees. So composed! It gave her strength to look more closely, though she drew back far into the shadows and held her sleeves before her. His face was as she remembered it, very little changed. Extraordinary! It was more square, perhaps, more set, the mouth a little firmer. She did not see the eyes.

What left her exhausted were the quiet emanations that came from his presence. More than the scent of his skin and clothing, the outline of his figure, or the tone of his voice, they were the vibrations of his whole personality. They had not changed.

She wondered desperately if he remembered. What had he thought of her? What did he think now? Nothing that he said or did gave any indication.

Seated beside her screen, he had asked her how she felt. So prosaic! Shihi had answered for her that she was weak, had no appetite, was sometimes out of temper . . .

What medicines had been given? (This time he questioned Shihi directly. Perhaps he thought her stupid?)

An elixir of apricot kernels, the "compound of seven vapors," wild rhubarb . . .

He suggested ginseng. So banal! And did little more, it seemed to her, before he rose and left. But his visit had exhausted her . . . Perhaps he had sensed this? Though he had not looked in her direction, perhaps he had felt her fear, the silly trembling of her expectations? Perhaps the very turbulence of her soul had reached him and he had left so that she might calm herself and reassure herself that he meant to help. Perhaps he had felt her very essence as she had felt his.

Next time he came he spoke more directly, questioning her at length, and she answered him through Fuwa, not trusting her own voice.

Had she any pains?

"Only the headaches"—whispered to Fuwa.

"Headache," Fuwa said. (She was thankful it was not Shihi speaking with her embellishments and opinions.)

Any tightness in the throat, constrictions in the chest, sensation of breathlessness? Any rush of heat to her head and face? Any chills?

"No."

"None."

Any dreams?

"Sometimes." It seemed to her that she lived in a world of dreams and often was not aware when a dream ended and her waking state began.

"Yes."

How often?

"Often," she whispered.

"Every night." Fuwa was aware of the dreaming because she heard the restlessness beyond the bed-curtains, the sighing, the small noises that a nightmare scream produces, and in the morning the frightened recitations, the relivings.

"Tell me about your dreams," he said, still not looking toward her. She had seen men approach skittish horses with this same nonchalance.

The quiet questioning went on like this over the space of a month. Sometimes, for Shihi's sake, he prescribed some medicine and once, to appease her, he called in exorcists, though he told her quite frankly that he did not suspect possession. Also for Shihi and the other ladies—and for the beauty of it too, which he enjoyed—he began opening his daily sessions with a reading from the Yakushi Sutra and chanting some of the spells. He knew quite well that his voice was strong and that women found it enthralling and he was gratified when his audience increased every day. Even some of the ladies from the Emperor's pavilions took to coming over.

Later he found it irritating. How could he hope to reach his patient in this public atmosphere? And gradually, tactfully, he trimmed the daily service and cleared the room. The visiting ladies complained to the Emperor's mother, but he was firm.

"How are your headaches now?" he asked one day.

"Better," Fuwa said.

"I think you could speak for yourself, now. You are no longer afraid."

How did he know that? She was surprised. For it was true that her lethargy and terrors seemed to have left her and she felt alive. What, indeed, had she been afraid of? "Yes, they are gone," she said. It was the first time he had heard her voice.

"Then I think we can begin the cure."

"Am I not well?"

"There are degrees. If a teacher can instruct an ignorant boy, can he not make even better progress with one who has learned a little?"

"You do not think me an ignorant boy, then?"

"Hardly that!" he laughed. He was delighted with this progress when it had seemed for so long that it was hopeless. He would like to probe her mind and the state of her soul.

So began a series of conversations that lasted through early spring while the weather cleared and the mountain mists drifted away, while the wild camellia blossomed on the slopes and down below the fishermen mended their brushwood weirs, and as yet they had not so much as glanced into each other's eyes nor had even their fingers touched.

During that time he made himself a member of her household so that he came and went informally and she often sat or stood beside him talking casually as though unaware of the vibrancy that filled the space between them.

Then at the start of the Fourth Month on the day they changed into summer clothes and put fresh hangings in the airy room, he actually helped her ladies hang the summer curtains. It was a clear pure day and the glimpses of the lake striped blue and lavender between the trees, the scent of sun on cypress wood and of freshly laundered clothes seemed to turn their heads.

Somehow the ladies began to laugh at all kinds of little things and the young ones played tricks on one another. Two of the servants who had hearty voices chanted an old work tune while they rolled up the winter hangings, and even Shihi shuffled her feet in time.

The dancing and the singing and the teasing laughter went on all around. And in the midst of this, in the swirl of sun-dried hangings, he caught her sleeve and held it, and they stopped amid the laughter and stood still.

CHAPTER XXIV

The young Emperor and his mother were very close. She had felt free to complain to him when the new priest excluded her ladies from his services—although at the time he had not felt he could interfere in the Retired Empress' affairs—and now she came to him with a report of truly scandalous misdoings.

It was not that she was so fastidious or that she didn't know the ways of the world, but she had a deep reverence for the Heavenly Sun-line into which she had married and felt the Retired Empress was demeaning her ancestors.

Besides that, she told her son, it was repulsive to her to see a woman of her age indulge in the passions of youth. She herself—who was, as it happened, exactly the ex-Empress' age, which was forty-four—had grown quite plump and matronly in recent years while Abé, in this pastoral summer, glowed like a girl.

"What do you advise?" he asked fretfully. He knew his mother would ask him to take some action that would embarrass him.

"Speak to her."

But the prospect made him too uncomfortable. He was above all an ingratiating young man, always intent on having others like him. And he was aware that although he owed his elevation to the ex-Empress, they were not on very good terms.

It was awkward enough for him as it was without confronting her . . .

"Tell her that her behavior is causing talk."

The thought of such an interview appalled him.

"Tell her that as her Sovereign you feel a responsibility."

"Perhaps a note of some sort . . ." though that too seemed hideously awkward.

Leaning forward, his mother looked directly into his eyes. Son and mother were surprisingly alike with their round appealing faces and plump hands. There was an air about them of some soft and innocent small animal, although the mother's tone was sharp.

"Simply go to her," she insisted. "Or rather, summon her." Her small round lips were pursed as she said these words.

He sat a long time open-eyed resisting her pressure—so long, indeed he thought that he might cry—and then said hopefully, "Surely it is something that the Grand Preceptor is more fit to handle?"

When Nakamaro's letter arrived there was some dismay among the servants because the Retired Empress and the doctor-priest had left the Palace for the day—not an unusual excursion for so beautiful a season, but in this case rather delicate to explain, especially to a messenger from the Grand Preceptor.

The messenger himself was an imposing man—a Guards captain of the Fifth Rank senior grade—and the attendants were not certain how to welcome him or what to say. He had dismounted and without a word had seated himself on the veranda while his grooms led the horses down the path to the stabling area. And when he took out his fan and began to wave it about before his sweating face, they were afraid he would demand an audience.

"It is not my responsibility," they whispered to one another. And one crept out to a corner of the Cypress Court where he could look down through the cross-hatching of green branches to the bridge across the Seta far below. He saw that the little party had left the central island where the bridge was anchored and were coming back this way. He could see their little shadows on the rough wood planking and the top of the great round parasol moving along.

He watched them pause a moment by the railing and then the figure of the Empress—he was sure it must be she—step out from the shelter of the parasol and lean against the railing. Beside her the bronze silk of the priest's robe glinted in the sun. He turned and skirted the dry ground of the courtyard and went up the steps to Lady Shihi's rooms, where he told the women on duty that a messenger had come from the capital, that the Retired Empress and her ladies were on the bridge (he did not mention the doctor; he did not have to), and that it was not his responsibility.

On the bridge Abé stopped to look into the water. They had gone to see the mountain wisteria that grew wild among the trees on the farther bank and were bringing home some of the long trailing branches. When she stepped to the railing it was to hold a spray of the small lavender blooms out over the water.

> "Clear is the bottom of the lake
> That mirrors the wisteria blooms . . ."

she recited.

But below her the waters of the Seta raced along and the glassy surface mirrored only the glancing sun. She drew back, laughing, holding the drooping blossoms in her arms, and the merry, mock-rueful look she gave him over the fading flowers was like a charming girl's.

Dōkyō was struck again by the recent change in her. When he was first allowed to sit beside her screen she had seemed so fragile—hardly able to support herself against the armrest. And now, as she glanced around at him in the open sunlight, she radiated life. The corners of his mouth turned up in a small and bemused smile, a look compounded of delight and incredulity—and a tinge of self-satisfaction. It was an expression that had settled on his face almost like a mask since the day, nearly two months before, when he had caught her sleeve and felt the current pass between them as it had so irresistibly that night outside the shrine room so long ago.

He had been aware in his deepest mind from the moment he walked into the darkened rooms of this strange mountain palace and felt her silent presence there behind her screen that all his medical and psychic treatments, all their conversations, were leading them to this. He had not consciously designed it. Indeed, he had held back. But a force beyond his reason and his will seemed to propel him.

During the years when he had practiced meditation he had sometimes dared to think that perhaps his soul was progressing to an elevation where he might hope for the oblivion of paradise after this life or the next. But when he sat attending the invalid, chanting the scripture outside her screen and later helping her toward an understanding of herself, he had felt himself dragged back. Even while he explained away her fears in the light of the ineffable compassion of Buddha's love, he felt less sure of the desirability of oblivion.

He had tried at first to resist this, then to regret it, but in the end he could not bring himself to feel sorry for this new and delicious tie to the world. It excited him even while the magnitude of this adventure stunned him.

For her, the transformation was one of waking from a long paralysis. How long had she peered out at life through the black mist of depression? She had lost all sense of time since her mother's death and sometimes in her melancholy the tears flowed for no reason but the vague conviction that she had lost her way.

With his very first appearance—although she did not speak—she began her slow awakening. And as the clarity of thought returned, she began to wonder what her former lives could have been, first to elevate her to the very highest—Sovereign of the Heavenly Sun-line—and then to plunge her into the timeless anguish of her depression. And thinking this, she marveled also at the bond of fate that had drawn her to this doctor—this one out of all the myriad men who shared this world with her! Surely some karma from their past lives made their meetings preordained. How many previous lives they must have shared!

And with relief she gave way to her growing passion, telling herself, It is my karma, it is inevitable.

So she had listened, floating on his words while he sat beside her screen those first dark weeks and spoke to her of suffering so that she could understand it. Was she unaware that all of life was suffering—the suffering of birth, of parting, of longing unfulfilled, of hatred encountered, of the transience of all attachments? She herself had suffered the pain of loss, of illness, had she not? And what of the awareness of the passing years, of age? The fear of death? Had she forgotten the first Great Truth of the Buddha, the Truth of Suffering?

He did not teach her anything she did not know. But before now she had valued the Buddhist rites and teachings for their magic value rather than their philosophy. It is his voice, she thought, that makes it clear, especially when he speaks of the compassion of the Infinite One who understands the suffering of mortals and teaches us how to overcome it. "The root of all suffering is desire . . ." For a little while she managed to convince herself that she was free of desire.

As her mind cleared and the days grew lighter, she followed his discourse along the Eightfold Path that leads to the end of suffering: correct understanding, correct thought, correct speech and action and so on to the ultimate correct meditation. But with her impulsive nature and intuitive turn of thought, this sort of discipline was really not congenial. Rather, she snatched up little morsels from his words and ran off to make a feast of them, as it were, in her imagination.

For his part, he felt that she had a true bodhisattva nature, far above the common run as she was, and that he could help her to attain perfect enlightenment. He felt this not only because of her high station (he believed that he himself was among the favored classes of mankind who could hope for Buddhahood) but because of the sympathetic quality of her listening. She seemed to hear and understand him even before he spoke. This made him an eager teacher, more inspired than he had ever been, rushing along too fast, perhaps, for anyone to follow.

"You must understand," he said, "the essence of our

thought." He was speaking about the core of the Hossō doctrine. "While we reject, of course, the primitive belief in the reality of things . . . [he said "of course" as though the concept of the unreality of the material world were elementary] . . . we do not fall into the extreme of nihilism, saying 'nothing exists; all is illusion.' No, we understand that although the world exists through our ideas of it, and nothing exists outside the mind, the overarching Thought itself, the Absolute, is real."

How marvelous! she thought. How wonderful! But what thrilled her were not the words or even the ideas but the sincerity, the awe and inner excitement of his voice. A sense of well-being surged in her heart and made her smile.

So he had gone on talking earnestly day after day. And in a few weeks, when he felt she was up to it, he began his questioning. She answered as best she could, and since she had a quick bright mind, made it sound as if she understood. But she had not the training for this kind of abstract thinking, nor the repose of soul.

He spoke of the "stored consciousness" of all the universe, the infinite cosmos—"like a great store of seeds," he said. But right away a picture of stored seeds came to her mind: those rush baskets and clay pots of the Great Food Festival at the time of her elevation. There were so many! All different kinds of rice. And millet too . . .

"All phenomena," he went on, "are nothing other than the revelations of this stored consciousness. We are all part of it. As the saying is, 'One man is all men; all men are one.' And when we understand this, feel it in our hearts, then it leads us to an infinite compassion for all living things . . ."

Yes, yes, she thought, as he went on. I have certainly practiced that. Freed prisoners and liberated sentient beings. She had forbidden killing for the space of nearly a year—in spite of Nakamaro, she thought triumphantly.

So she had floated on the surface of his words and on his voice, happy as she had ever been, until one day they stood together amid the housekeeping and acknowledged their true feelings.

That night when he first pushed his way inside her curtains she was startled and ashamed. What would her mother think? Then she remembered she was alone now and responsible for herself. She could do as she liked! And they came together as two halves of a whole, perfectly fitting.

After that there was less talk of the ineffable and more of the mysterious bond between them. "Surely we have known each other through many lives," he said. "But never could you have been as beautiful as you are now."

And she had thought of herself as old and ugly! Could she be so changed?

When they came laughing up the steps trailing their flowers on the day they went to pick the wild wisteria, they found Shihi waiting in the anteroom, a letter in her hands. She looked so disapproving that Abé felt a twinge of guilt—though, why? she asked herself. She had done nothing wrong.

She took the letter. "Very official indeed," she said for Dōkyō's benefit, and went into her inner room to read it.

"We have had word here in the capital of some involvement with a doctor-priest," she read. "I must tell you, with due reverence, that when scandal touches your person it is very painful for me as well as harmful to the nation. I feel it my duty, because of my loyalty to your exalted parents—and my continued devotion to yourself—to warn you against this ill-considered attachment.

"I am afraid it is no mere gossip," the letter went on to say, for it was a very long letter as well as arrogant, she noted, her anger beginning to rise. "The Emperor himself has written me that both he and his mother have been made uncomfortable by your light behavior.

"Relationships between men and women, as you well know, should not be entered into carelessly, with a light mind, or through passion, for these relationships are not limited to this world alone . . ."

Preaching! Preaching to me! Her hands were trembling and she shook the paper to steady it.

"Through the virtue accumulated in past lives you rose to the highest, most exalted place in the world. For this reason if for no other you must guard your soul against contamination."

"Oh, he is so concerned for my soul all at once!" she said aloud, although there was no one with her. She shook the paper again as though to sharpen the blurred characters, for tears of anger filled her eyes.

"You must beware of opportunistic people who would play on your susceptibilities and take advantage of your position . . ."

She flung the letter down. "And who is he," she said, again aloud, "to use such a tone with me? He with his worldly ambition and unscrupulous . . . unscrupulous . . ." Her mind went back in a quick angry glance over their long relationship, touching down like a stone skipped over water on the incidents to his discredit and skimming over the deep involvement of the years. "He takes me too lightly," she said angrily. But her even sharper fury and disdain were for that impudent young man, the Emperor.

She called to Shihi, who was lingering by her screen. "I would like to send to the Emperor to request an audience. Or he can come to me!"

Shihi had guessed what was in Nakamaro's letter and approved of it. She had been against this scandalous arrangement from the very first. So she said nothing, pretending she did not understand.

"Please bring me my writing things."

Shihi stood still.

Abé glanced up, her eyes still blurred with tears, and realized how very old and brittle Shihi had become. She had hardly seen her these past months, or if she had she had not noticed. She had been oblivious to many people and things. But I have been moving in a new world! she thought. Others do not belong.

What she needed now, she realized, was not Shihi or those others. She needed *him*—to have him comfort her and advise her what to do.

She watched him while he read the letter through, his face

very still, only his fine eyes moving up and down along the characters. Then he sat silent for a while, then spoke, although he did not take his eyes away from the paper.

"I am dismayed by the lack of respect for you," he said slowly. (His eyes had seen the word "opportunist" at the first glance and he wanted very much to tackle that. But he held it back until they could speak more calmly.) "And I wonder if you should even stoop to answer." (Opportunist! How could that be? I came to this Palace not even knowing who would be here.)

"If I don't answer, he will write again. I know him."

"Perhaps if you explain he has misread, misunderstood, His Majesty's report . . ."

"His Majesty. A stupid boy!"

He looked up, startled by the vehemence of her reaction. This was blasphemy. But the look of unaccustomed rage in her sweet face and the sparkle of tears in her eyes made him feel tender toward her, and protective. He had heard, of course, of her liaison with the Household Minister but he had not known the quality of their relationship. Certainly the letter showed great freedom. (But opportunist! That was not true at all. That was a wild thrust and a lie. He felt some anger of his own begin to rise.)

"It was I who elevated him." She was going on about the Emperor. "And he does not know the first thing. He is like a baby when it comes to governing. And in spite of that he dares to criticize. He and his mother. 'Scandal'!" She picked the letter up. " 'Made uncomfortable.' " Her eyes raced down, looking for other phrases to fling out.

She will come to "opportunist," he thought. But she tossed the letter down. "What are we to do?"

He was glad that she included him. "We." But already he knew, as his mind began to handle this, that whatever he did—unless it was to disappear entirely—would put him in the wrong. If he stayed here with her as if nothing had changed, or if he returned with her to Nara to face the accusations, or if the two of them together went to some distant temple and vanished from the world, as they sometimes spoke of doing—if he did any of these things he would damage her forever. And he himself, too, though he did not like to think of that.

"I think that I should leave," he said at last.

"Leave?"

"Yes. That would put a stop to these accusations, this unpleasantness."

Unpleasantness, she thought. A strange word. The letter had been insulting, yes. And furthermore it showed very clearly the young Emperor's dependence on his mother and the vacuum he had left in the government for his Great Minister to fill. Ever since she abdicated, Nakamaro had been usurping power. And now—as though he were her own superior—he dared to criticize! She would deal with him!

"But there is no need for you to leave," she said to Dōkyō. She knew the letter went far deeper than a mere degrading reference to her private life. Since she and the Emperor had both retired here to Ōmi there had been no brake at all on the Great Minister's presumption.

"Can I remain?" Dōkyō said. "Can we do nothing, in the face of such a letter?"

"I will respond to it," she said. "I will respond!"

At one time she had not had strength, or even the desire, to curb Nakamaro. Now, when his letter jolted her, she found she had. She turned to Dōkyō, her face still stern. "Do you know," she said, "that when I came here to the Hora Palace I was so weak in both my body and soul that I could barely drag myself from one spot to another. I think the life had nearly gone out of me . . ."

Still earnest, she looked at him more tenderly. "And then you came."

He put his hand out to her face and she held it there.

"And then you came. You healed my body and taught my soul and made me well again. And let me tell you . . ." for he had gently run his thumb across her lips. "Let me tell you what you have done for me, a beaten, tired, old, discarded woman . . ."

He smiled at that, and she took his hand from her face and held it, clasping it almost fiercely as she said, "You have restored me. No. More than that. You have given me a life I never had. You have given me strength . . ."

He saw that she was making up her mind. "What do you intend?" he asked. And then as she said nothing, clutching his hand and looking at his face as though to devour him, "I see. You will go away from me. It is you who will leave. I see that." And then quietly, "And I shall return to Katsuragi and wait there."

"Shall I really leave you?" She drew away, still staring at him, and put the flats of her hands against her temples in that old gesture, pressing against the pain while tears flowed from her eyes.

He too was weeping. "Everything passes," he said.

"Our love too?"

Seeing her pitiable look he could not bear to remind her of the roots of suffering. But as his own defense against the pain, he tried to disassociate himself from the delusions of his own ego. All is illusion, he repeated silently, there is no substance to this scene, to this destructive yearning, to the two of us caught as we are in the false concept of passing time . . . He tried, but his throat ached terribly and such a mournful feeling filled his chest that he groaned.

"No, that will live," he said at last, "until we can be born again," he tried to smile, "two souls together on one lotus bud in the bright Tusita Heaven." Could this be true? He had thought that he was on the path to true oblivion when he was living the austere life on Mount Katsuragi. He had put the world behind him. That was peace. Was it true that the attachment of their souls in some past life could really hold him back? Surely this ache was real.

I have failed once more, he thought. I will go back and try again. But he knew that in this life at least he was bound up with her. She would not let him go.

"That will live," he said again.

She put her hands out, feeling the contours of his face with her palms and fingers like a blind woman. "Comfort me," she whispered. "Comfort me."

During her journey home the long summer rains began. Even before they had crossed the hills the oxen's hides had been soaked black and the grooms in their straw raincoats walked ankle-deep in mud. There was no beauty in the scene, she thought, nothing to distract her or entice her to look out. She did not even notice the rough swaying or the sudden jolts of her ride. She was lost in her anger, carried along by it, and by the bitterness of parting.

In Nara she went directly to the Hokke-ji and called upon the abbess. "I would like to renounce the world," she said. "I have made my preparations."

"But these things cannot be done so hastily!" the old nun said.

"I would like to do as my mother did." She had hardly heard the remonstrance.

"Your mother the Empress Dowager was well prepared."

"And I too. I have made all the preparations that are necessary with the priests at the Hora Palace."

The nuns had heard nothing of the scandal, even though they were so close to the Palace. Since the death of Kōmyō they had had very few visitors, and in any case their innocence was not receptive to sly rumors. Nevertheless this sudden appearance and abrupt request of the Retired Empress unnerved them. Perhaps she might consult with the high priests?

"You forget that I received my first initiation from the holy Chinese priest Ganjin himself."

Strange how calm the Retired Empress was, the nuns said to one another. She was not like this in the past.

"So if it can be arranged for tomorrow," she said. "And please no tears."

To oblige the abbess she submitted to the preliminaries and the questioning. Then on the third day, rather hastily, the rite was performed and her hair clipped short. Now I am like him, she thought.

The young nuns helped her don the habit, dark against the pallor of her skin. The clipped ends of her glossy hair falling beside her temples gave her a youthful, almost boyish look. She is more beautiful than ever before, they thought.

But the abbess was troubled by the stubborn, almost worldly look she wore even as she took her vows. It was as though she were re-entering the world rather than leaving it, she thought, for she had last seen her during the long mourning period when they were afraid that she might follow after her mother.

And Abé, alone again in her mother's rooms, felt a kind of blending in herself of her mother's cool determination and the strength—the faith in herself—that Dōkyō had given her. I can do anything now, she thought. There is no one who can stop me.

"I will make this my palace," she told the abbess. And she sent word to the Fujiwara cousins Nagate and Momokawa whom she knew were jealous of Nakamaro's overriding power, and to Sakanoue Karitamaro whom she thought of as "the Chinese warrior" because of his ancestry and fierce temperament, and Kibi no Makibi whom she trusted, and some others. And with their help drew up a proclamation.

Then, on the twenty-eighth day, she summoned all the Court officials from the Fifth Rank upward to hear her words. Momokawa read the edict in his high Court voice: "*Hearken to the words of the Retired Sovereign, Manifest Deity of the Yamato line . . .*"

And he read the words they had composed: that she, direct descendant of Emperor Tenchi's line (whose name he spoke with awe) daughter of Shōmu (likewise) had reigned for nine bright prosperous years and on her abdication had chosen a new Emperor to rule after her.

It is the duty of a succeeding Emperor to respect the former, he went on. But this new Emperor had not done what is right and proper.

"*When I was at the Hora Palace*" (here he used the Empress' own words) "*this Emperor spoke ill of me and mentioned publicly what should have been left unsaid.*

"*In my heart I am innocent. However, there is undoubtedly some lack of virtue in me to encourage such a charge, and I must regard this incident as a manifestation of the Divine Law encouraging in me a more devout disposition.*

"Therefore I have forsaken every worldly tie and have shaved my head and taken up my residence in this holy nunnery."

And dropping again into the more formal phrases of their composition, Momokawa continued: that because the Retired Empress had become a nun, however, it did not indicate that she would shirk her duty.

Since the present Emperor had shown himself to be incompetent, from now on he would confine himself to matters of ceremony and sacred festivals while she would conduct affairs of state, including rewards and punishments.

CHAPTER XXV

When Nakamaro came to the Hokke-ji he hoped that he might be able to reassert his old influence or, if not that, come to a reasonable understanding. She had taken an unprecedented step and might be eager now to smooth things over. He decided to approach her formally, as befitted her new position, but without undue reverence. However, the little nuns who greeted him, speaking in small whispery voices and bending, bowing almost to the ground, formed a sort of barrier, like a stand of wavering gray sedge grass, that blocked his way until the old nun who was the abbess could come out.

"Men are not allowed in the Hokke-ji."

She said it in so soft a voice, like a pleasant summer greeting, that he could not take offense. Nevertheless, he could see them walking along the colonnades around the cloister in their short robes and *kesas* and shaven heads like eggs.

The Empress, she said, was waiting for him in the garden house, a small pavilion like a moon-viewing hut away from the main buildings. Would he be pleased to come this way?

He saw the pale gray of her summer screen—nun's color—and wondered how she might look with her hair cut off. Then the abbess left him and he stepped up onto the low porch and settled himself by the screen. When he spoke it was an attempt to establish their old footing.

"So you found the Emperor incompetent?"

"Perhaps we were both mistaken in his character." She had not forgiven him his letter but thought it best not to provoke him needlessly. Her edict must have made him very angry.

"I will do my best to follow your wishes, as I have in the past." He did not know to what extent she had committed herself to the priest. Perhaps the affair was over, as she had announced, but he doubted it. He was aware also that his cousins Nagate and Momokawa had advised her against him, no doubt because he had failed to see to their promotions. It was true that the young Emperor had not been a help to him in that sort of thing. Obviously Momokawa had put his brush to the proclamation; he could tell by watching him read it out. A stubborn man, full of strong opinions. He had misjudged him as a boy. "So let us not take sides against each other."

"Why do you say that?"

"I felt, on hearing your proclamation, that you were angry with me." And when she did not reply, "You do understand, of course, I had only your welfare in mind when I wrote you."

He shifted slightly and the silk of his trousers made a little hissing sound. "We are such old friends. I hope you didn't feel it was too much of a liberty?"

How awkward for him, she smiled to herself. So occupied with his grand plans and his invasions, he hardly gave a thought to insulting his Sovereign!

"Of course your decision was wise," he continued heavily. "The Emperor is young and inexperienced."

Again she said nothing, and when at last he rose to leave, he made a rather elaborate ceremony of his departure.

She thought this conversation over. How did they stand now? The Emperor had returned to Nara—he and his mother—as soon as they realized that she had left the Hora Palace. But before he could think of anything to do, the proclamation had been read and he found no one to support him. He had taken up residence in the pavilions of the women's palace, where repairs had been completed. Since a great deal of construction was still going on, they could not have been comfortable. And obviously Nakamaro did not mean to make an effort for him.

All this should have been pleasing. But she had been so happy there at the Hora Palace, and was now so lonely, so burdened with memory and longing, that she could not laugh.

She wrote one of her many letters to Mount Katsuragi keeping Dōkyō abreast of all the news and ending with the poem:

> Looking at our changing lives,
> Transient as the wind,
> Ceaseless as the flowing stream
> I cannot stop my tears . . .

His answering letter echoed hers:

> Even the trees that flower in spring
> In autumn shed yellow leaves . . .
> This transitory world!

She had wondered how long they must remain apart and why he could not come to the capital, but he did not answer her questions. Better to wait.

She wrote him that she had consulted the High Priest, Rōben. "The High Priest comes to my nunnery to advise me, and every day there are many priests and doctor-priests in attendance." Why could he not come?

> But for the hope of seeing you
> How could I live through this life
> Day after day?

But he too had consulted Rōben. "Concentrate on your studies and your meditation," the High Priest wrote. "The scandal is too fresh."

So he stayed away, although he wrote her almost daily and she kept the letters tucked in the sleeve of her habit:

> So loud the deer cries, calling to its mate,
> That the answering echo
> Resounds through the mountains
> Where I am alone.

And:

Rather than suffer this endless longing
Would I might be transmuted
Into a tree or a stone
Free from these pangs of love . . .

And later:

How I waste and waste away
With love—
I, who thought myself
A strong man.

But he did not come.

At the end of the year Nakamaro came again to report that although there had been some setbacks to his plans because of the stubborn resistance of the northern barbarians, he would soon be ready to launch his expedition against the Silla kingdom.

"Well, that is a matter for the Grand Council, isn't it?"

"I had hoped for your support." He wanted to say, "more active support" or perhaps even that she refrain from deterring him, but he had to be careful with her. He found it frustrating, but he had learned to deal with that, and had counted up his past mistakes with some humility. Had he not been so preoccupied with his military preparations he might have intervened in the demotion of the young Emperor before it was too late. And he might have acted more decisively when Kibi no Makibi, whom he had placed in charge of military training in the Kyushu region, repeatedly returned to the capital on other business. As it was, the lack of cooperation—the jealousy perhaps—of his other officers had forced him to take over personal command of the training exercises all along the coast. And these delays were ominous, he thought.

"If you seek the blessing of the gods, then you should go to the Emperor."

"Yes, of course," he said. "But more than that . . ."

More than that, she thought, he wants me to supply him

with the enthusiastic backing of Momokawa, Nagate, and the others. And he wants the support of the Buddhist hierarchy too. How strange that he should come to her for that! He must know of the constant correspondence back and forth to Mount Katsuragi, not only between herself and Dōkyō but between Rōben and his pupil. Could he guess that the letters, full of love as before, had begun to advise her in decisions of government? Could he possibly understand that he was dealing with a man as strong as himself—but unlike him, oh totally!—a man of peace and gentleness, a true bodhisattva with an infinite compassion for all living beings?

"Is it necessary," he had written her, "to take the sons of farmers from their homes and the support of their parents and transport them to a foreign land to kill and be killed? Surely it is not these innocent boys whose 'corpses, lost at sea, should steep in the water; or on the hills rot in the grass,' " he admonished, quoting the warrior's code, "when it is not the protection of our Sovereign that they die for, but one man's ambition."

Before this she had not objected to Nakamaro's plans on these grounds. Her ancestors had once conquered the peninsula's southern tip after all, and she often thought of Empress Saimei who had died in Kyushu on her way to another conquest there. She had once been tempted to join Nakamaro and his generals and give heart to the army. Now she was glad she had kept that thought to herself, not only because it would have given Nakamaro a certain hold on her but, more important, Dōkyō would have seen that side of her character.

To Nakamaro she said, "What do you want of me?" and the way she said it made him want to groan. He had been so careless to let her slip away, he who was never careless, never left a thing to chance. He wondered how he might reach her. Through ambition perhaps? Through an appeal to her heart? How beautiful she had grown in recent months—not like her mother, no, whose beauty he had thought supreme among women—but so delicate in her gray habit, and yet so radiant. He supposed it was the effect of that love affair which she denied.

"I want, primarily, your good will toward me. I need your encouragement. After all, what is it that we seek together but the glory of this Realm-Under-Heaven" (he paused, wondering how far to go) "to fulfill our destiny?" And when this got no answer: "I look back on the years in which you were pleased to direct your government through me, when you trusted my judgment . . ." This was a mistake.

"I trusted your judgment," she said mildly, "and selected Oi-Ō as Heir Apparent."

I have come at the wrong time, he thought. Everything is cold between us. And he tried to think how he could reach her . . . by what strategy . . . through whom . . .

At the time of promotions and rewards during the New Year celebrations the Empress announced the advancement of those men on whom she counted: Momokawa, Nagate, the warrior Sakanoue. Although undoubtedly she would have done this on her own—she was no stranger, after all, to the network of debts and loyalties that made up the Court—it was Dōkyō who advised, or perhaps reminded, her.

She was mildly surprised by this worldly understanding on his part, and even displeased. She did not like to think of him in this role. But he had taken advantage of an offering she made to appoint him Junior Assistant High Priest of Buddhism—a very honored position—to write her (while declining) with the suggestion that instead she shore up her own position with such appointments as would strengthen her hand. "For I see the opposition growing between the ambition of the Grand Preceptor and your peaceful guidance of the Realm." And he went on even to name names: "Fujiwara Nagate, a prudent adviser; Momokawa, a strong man and tenacious; Sakanoue Karitamaro with his military background . . . good to have a man of his experience on your side . . ."

She read on, wondering at his understanding and, too, at the bluntness—almost the crudity—of his words. She herself understood these matters and their complexity almost by instinct and had grown up watching the delicacy with which her mother had manipulated them in her own reign and, yes, even her father's.

She found the letter slightly distasteful. But then, he had declined promotion for himself, she thought, and had written only with her in mind. How far above the others he was in his character! How pure his understanding of this passing world, how far above it!

"You wonder at my interest in mundane affairs," he wrote, as though he read her mind. "But although I have tried to leave the world behind, I am bound to it by this love we did not seek but which has united our souls forever into one.

"Should the time come
When heaven and earth shall perish,
Then only should we cease to meet.

"And even more than that, you have raised a hope in my heart—a dazzling vision—that through your divine guidance this ancient Realm-Under-Heaven may one day become a true and practicing Buddha-land!"

She had never known him to write so beautifully. Beauty of mind, she thought, as well as feature! She answered with many words of her appreciation, her hopes for the future, and her love.

If it were death to love
I should have died—
And died again
One thousand times over.

From then on his letters often carried his advice, but it was not until the end of the year that he accepted the next promotion that she offered: "I have decided to remove the present Senior Assistant High Priest from his office," she wrote, "and I beg of you to accept . . ."

He had not refused the first promotion simply because it was not high enough, he told himself. He had sincerely tried to live the ascetic life, there in the mountains. But now: Senior Assistant High Priest! There was only one superior in all the hierarchy, and that was Rōben himself. And he could be useful, he told himself, he could be useful. The land was drifting into conflict. Nakamaro still at the helm. In all compassion, he told himself, for the sake of all sentient beings . . .

He came to Nara in the second winter month, the Month of Frosts, and on an early morning rode across the city from the Kofuku-ji to her nunnery beside the Palace. How beautiful it was with the empty streets still white with the night's chill. Above the frosted roof tiles of the long low walls the maple leaves were blurred.

In the Hokke-ji garden the chrysanthemums were withering into pale gold colors, ochers and browns—more beautiful, he thought, as they confronted death than in the brilliance of their flowering. Looking at them he recalled the verse, "frail as flowers are the lives of men, passing phantoms of this world . . ." But despite this sobering reflection he felt as alive and youthful as he ever had, and his lips were smiling.

She received him openly and he was gratified to see that she was as beautiful as ever and when she turned her head he saw how charmingly the short-cropped hair revealed the lobes of her ears. It was as though a day had passed rather than a year, and their faces were absorbed, alight, as they came together without uttering a word.

Although he took up residence at the Kofuku-ji, he came daily to be by her side and gradually became familiar with the affairs of government that were reported to her: the allotment of taxes, the relief of the poor, the inspection of conditions in the countryside, the reception of foreign missions . . .

In the previous spring an envoy from the Silla kingdom had arrived with tribute and she would have received him, but on Nakamaro's instructions he was detained at the port and then sent back without ever coming to the capital. Now, in the autumn of this new year, the envoy came again and again Nakamaro, still intent on his expedition, sent him away.

She was in tears of rage. "He will explain this to me! He will apologize!" She did not say aloud the thing that rankled most: that he treated her as he had treated her in bed—as though she were not fully sentient, less than human, like some creature without a brain—an inferior! She remembered his hands on her and his careless manner. "He will come here and apologize! He will explain!"

"Dear heart," Dōkyō said softly, "do not demean yourself. No need to confront him. So painful."

"Then what?" She spoke with the tears still streaming on her face and her mouth sagging.

Another instance of her indecision, he thought, for he had studied her attitudes and actions these past months and felt that although she understood the workings of her government she was not really practiced in the forceful moves of power; she was not aggressive. Only once since he had come to know her had she acted decisively, he realized, and that was when she had returned to Nara to challenge the Emperor.

Mistakenly, he had thought her strong, even combative, because of that precipitous decision and its momentous results. He had not been aware how much her victory was actually the working of men like Momokawa who had seized the opportunity to thwart the Grand Preceptor. Since he had been close to her, here in Nara, he had begun to realize that that was a single uncharacteristic move. She had been held in check for so many years, he theorized, that her instincts were those of the powerless: persuasion and manipulation. All she needed, he thought, was encouragement to act boldly at the proper times. It hurt and even irritated him to see her weeping in this childlike rage when there were courses of action open.

When she turned to him that way, saying "Then what?" in that quivering voice, he acted on these ideas that had been growing, even though Rōben had warned him never to interfere. "Then what?" he echoed gently. "Why, that is up to you, for you are the one who makes decisions. You are the one who holds the power here."

He watched a change come over her face as her mouth grew firm. "You have the power to reward and punish," he continued. "You have the power to promote and dismiss."

"You are thinking," she said, "that I should dismiss Nakamaro." She was looking off, away from him, as though to hide her face.

"I understand he appointed himself to the position of Military Instructor in the coastal regions. Perhaps it was in that capacity that he presumed to spurn and insult an envoy to your Court . . ."

"It was of course the Emperor who made the appointment," she corrected him. Again she was made uneasy by this obvious advice so bluntly spoken.

"And since then, you have relieved the Emperor of those functions?"

"Yes. Of course."

He heard the asperity in her voice. And he did not want anything less than full unity with her. And yet, how could he not remind her of this opportunity? It seemed so clear to him who did not know the subtleties of her relationship with the Grand Preceptor since early childhood. He said nothing, but his thoughts were forceful and they showed plainly in his face.

"I have the power, it is my position, to admonish him, if that's what you are saying."

"Then, I may say . . . if I may say . . . It is an opportunity, an opportunity to dismiss him from this post through which he has presumed to thwart you . . ."

"As you say." She knew that the course he suggested was an obvious one. And she had often asked for his advice. Now that he gave it, why did she draw away? Perhaps, she thought, it is because his interests, his concerns, had always been on a far loftier plane. She had somehow felt—though she did not bring these feelings to the surface of her mind—that because of his lofty spirit, whatever they might have done, the two of them, could not be wrong. "But there are many considerations."

Nevertheless, soon after that she summoned her advisers and together, after some deliberation, they sent notification to the Grand Preceptor of his dismissal from the post of Coastal Military Instructor.

And Dōkyō, when he saw that she had taken his advice and seized the opportunity, was troubled by that word, opportunity, and its companion: opportunist.

When Nakamaro received his notice of dismissal he burst out laughing. His rage was terrible. He did not show the messengers the deep red flush of his face but thanked them formally and let them go. Then he walked carefully around the room, his body trembling.

It says something for him that he did not strike out thoughtlessly at the Retired Empress and "that priest with whom she dallies" as he put it, nor take his revenge vicariously on his wife or servants or his daughters-in-law as would be natural. Instead he laughed and laughed and walked around the room, trying to think soberly and plan his moves.

Nakamaro was now fifty-four years old. He had become, not fat, but heavy in the chest, and that trudging walk of his was almost stately. He had grown large with the power he acquired, year after steady year—the one among the many cousins who reached the very top: First Rank, first grade. The Grand Preceptor.

Walking and thinking, the smile now dead on his face, he reviewed the situation: where he was strong, where weak, what men he could command by loyalty, which ones were in his debt. How to maneuver that priest out of her Court. How to win her back . . .

The Emperor was of no use to him. Yes, they had made a mistake. And of the advisers: He had made an enemy of Momokawa long ago, when he was still a boy. Nagate, so many years out of the capital, owed him nothing; he had no hold there. She had pre-empted the loyalty of the soldier Sakanoue who should have served the Emperor . . .

On the other hand, there was Kibi no Makibi. Although relations were not always good between them—indeed he had often treated him as an adversary—the old scholar was in his debt. And he was often at the Hokke-ji, "that ruling nunnery" as he thought sardonically, and enjoyed a special privilege there.

He called for him and when they had gone through the formalities he said abruptly, "That priest is advising her, isn't he? How many priests has she got now, swarming around her?"

Kibi smiled and waved his hand as if to say, Who can count? He had no intention of giving comfort or advice to the Grand Preceptor, whom he opposed in so many of his maneuvers. So he remained noncommittal with that wave of his hand.

(Actually, the number of Buddhist doctor-priests and sutra readers, reciters, exorcists, and dream interpreters installed in the Palace Buddhist Center or coming frequently to the Hokke-ji had increased quite startlingly since her return to Nara. Surely, Kibi thought, there were more than a hundred of them and half as many nuns.)

"Perhaps it is not important what the number is," Nakamaro went on, "as long as they do not attempt to govern. I have nothing against priests. There should be no enmity." But Kibi noticed that he had folded the ribbed fan he held and was jabbing the end of it on the floor.

Then, taking up the fan again, he looked at it absently, away from Kibi, and said carefully: "I am a blunt man. I say what is on my mind. I hope I have the right to speak openly . . ."

Kibi understood. The Grand Preceptor—whom he knew to be acute, even devious sometimes, and far from blunt—was saying that he had a right to speak as he wished to Kibi and make demands on him because he, Kibi, was in his debt for his appointment as the overseer of military training on Kyushu.

It was an appointment Kibi had not sought, and uncongenial to him, but it had been a tremendous step in his career, he had to admit, this position of such practical influence given an old professor. Until Nakamaro had chosen him from among a great many more experienced men, he had been thought of solely as a teacher-diplomat. Now he might rise—if the years allowed; he was seventy-one this year—to a very high position in government. He nodded, hoping that the demand would not be too hard to meet.

"The Retired Empress, as you know, has relieved me of my position in charge of preparing the troops and crewmen along the coasts . . ."

Kibi fixed his face as though to say "regrettable" but he did not speak.

"Is she speaking, or is it the priest who speaks?"

"I believe it is the Empress herself."

"Retired Empress," Nakamaro murmured, nodding as though in agreement. He did not want to put too much emphasis on the correction.

"I believe that in the matter of rewards and . . . so forth . . . the Retired Empress speaks for herself."

"I think I should have an audience with her, with her alone."

Kibi kept surprise out of his face. Was the Grand Preceptor saying that he needed to go through him, who was far from a sympathetic friend—through anyone, indeed—for such an interview? Did he feel himself so cut off, so isolated?

"And before such an audience, it would be well to call together the Grand Council."

But I have no place on the Grand Council! Kibi thought. Then, glancing hastily at Nakamaro's profile as he sat gazing off: But this man is by no means stupid.

"Of course, of course," he murmured, thinking: Ah, he is asking me to call in all my debts for him, to use my influence with such men as have been my students or whose careers I have helped. With them, and with those loyal to himself, he gambles that he can override the Empress. Well, perhaps. But she has many ministers and experienced commanders who would be happy to see this big man fall . . .

And Nakamaro at the same time, gazing off, thought Kibi's thoughts for him and came to the same end: They would be happy to see me fall.

"But you know," he turned on Kibi, calling him "master" in deference to his teaching but staring him full in the face, "you know what is at stake. The men are gathered and the ships nearly complete. But we need training, training, toughening the men. We cannot call off the exercises! All of our energies and resources have gone into this! There is no going back now. Surely she understands this? What is she thinking of, under this priestly guidance?"

Kibi kept his eyes fixed on his knees. "We must have patience," he said.

"Patience? Patience? I have been patient, silent, like a dumb man, all this year!"

"Well then, a little longer." Kibi smiled at his knees. " 'Small impatiences can confound great projects!' "

But Nakamaro, never having been one of Kibi's students, was not impressed by the sayings of the Master.

He decided to go directly to the Hokke-ji one more time. He would not send word ahead until the last minute. Let me find her just as she is, he thought. He did not want to give the priests time to prepare. Meanwhile he took ample time over his own approach.

He would first speak once again of their long relationship and how fate had placed the two of them together so many years ago and how her mother had rejoiced in that. He would remind her how her beloved father the Emperor at the time of his most radiant achievement had brought her to his (Nakamaro's) humble dwelling the Tamura palace and how he had been honored to entertain her there, how he had served her and the cause of the Yamato line, unwavering over the years. And then, perhaps (excusing his boldness), he would recount the glories of her ancestors and of the "Heavenly Task" of which the ancient records spoke that was given to Emperor Jimmu at the dawn of time to extend the power of the empire "so that its glory should fill all the universe." (Here he would touch upon the present expedition that he was—he would say "they were"—preparing in obedience to that Task.) And after that he would hear her answers and proceed from there.

When he arrived, however, eluding the little nuns and stepping directly up to a side door, he peered into the dusky rooms and thought he saw the figure of a man, a priest. He was walking softly but as though he knew the way—swiftly crossing past the sliding doors with their ghostly paintings and out by the far veranda.

It is he, he thought. He has been with her again. And the picture leapt into his mind of the two of them together, intertwined. They had taken the position called "the unicorn shows its horn" and she was smiling. And now her naked body turned and twisted and he was teaching her how "the phoenix saunters in the crimson cave."

He found his mouth was loose and he sucked in his saliva. Why had *he* not taught the Princess to do such things? His nights with her, as he remembered them, were tame. A sense of duty had hung over them. Now, as he pictured her with this handsome priest, she was shrieking and writhing as he mounted her. She had never shrieked with him.

It was appalling to him suddenly to hear her voice. She had appeared behind the lattice screen and was speaking in that calm superior way she had spoken in their last interview. Hadn't this life of debauchery changed her at all? The pictures were still vivid in his mind, and yet her voice—so cool! It was like her mother's!

"You asked to see me," she said again.

"Yes." But he found it difficult to speak. "I came here . . ."

After a long pause. "For a reason?"

"Yes." And while she listened silently he told her all that he had planned to tell—about their long relationship, about her parents, about her ancestors. But none of it seemed persuasive, even to himself.

CHAPTER XXVI

From the Hokke-ji, Nakamaro went directly to the Palace to seek out the Emperor—that young man, he thought, whom he had elevated to the very heights but who had seemed since then merely to float there doing nothing! Many things had angered him in the Empress' proclamation, but the statement that she had selected her own successor had made him laugh. He himself had done it—as she well knew—and he was the one who had to live with it.

His Majesty was in the Festival Hall and greeted his Grand Preceptor happily. It was an auspicious day for him, he said. (Nakamaro had forgotten.) The governor of Settsu Province was presenting him with a white copper-pheasant that a man had caught, and after the presentation ceremony and the announcement of rewards he planned a night of music and a dance performance. "You see how beautifully the hall has been prepared."

Most of the Palace buildings had been rebuilt by now, but the Emperor still used the women's pavilions as his residence until everything should be complete.

"I am really anxious to see the propitious bird. A pure white pheasant! I think it is an omen of success for all our plans."

Nakamaro looked at him. Still the same boy that he had selected to marry his son's widow—but he had expected that the young Prince would mature. If only he had it to do over again . . .

"I must ask your indulgence, but I cannot attend . . ." And when he saw the disappointment on the innocent round face, "As you know—as only you can fully understand—we are rather pressed by the necessities of our foreign obligations." He often spoke to the Emperor in vague terms such as this, implying that the young man not only understood but had actually instigated the Grand Preceptor's moves.

Also, he realized that what he was about to ask might seem extreme, even unprecedented, but he had no time to explain. "It will be necessary," he went on, "for me to take over the full military command of all the inner provinces and the six barriers."

He might have gone on to explain, but the Emperor merely said, "Oh. Yes?" And he heard no troubling doubts in his voice, no questions. Nothing unusual, he seemed to say.

"At once."

"Of course."

In this way the Grand Preceptor gave himself control of the five home provinces surrounding the capital. On Kōmyō's death the Imperial seal had passed into the keeping of the Emperor. Now Nakamaro had the use of it to stamp his military orders as well as the official bell-tokens as safe passage for his messengers. And he prepared to send to each provincial governor a request from the Emperor for six hundred healthy men, well equipped.

But it is very hard to keep a secret among scribes. In the office of the Controlling Board where these orders were being copied, the men who bent over their agile brushes murmured as they wrote: "Six hundred men from Kawachi, hm." "Six hundred men from Settsu." "Six hundred . . . that's quite a number." "Six hundred . . ."

A Sage named Ōtsu Ōura, who acted as diviner for Nakamaro, had not been consulted. Indeed, for many months the Grand Preceptor had ignored his divinations and made light of his advice. He was a proud, ambitious man, and it was through him that news of some sort of plot—for plot it surely was—reached the Retired Empress that very day.

"Does he have the authority to do this?" Dōkyō asked.

"He has used the Imperial seal and the bell-tokens. That is his authority."

"He has them in his own keeping?"

"The Imperial seal is held by the Emperor!" She was frequently surprised by his ignorance of the simplest Court matters. "It is not for everyone to use!"

"But he uses it?"

"By the Emperor's authority."

"And why is the Emperor bringing soldiers, so many troops, into the capital?"

"It is on the Emperor's authority that the troops are raised, but it is not the Emperor who raises them. The Emperor stands by."

"And Nakamaro?"

"He plans to use them for our overthrow."

They were both smiling as they talked, simply because they often smiled when they were together, but she knew that the matter was very grave, although Dōkyō, who was not yet versed in plots and counterplots, was slow to understand.

Once more, to his amazement and delight, she acted swiftly and with precision. She sent word to Fujiwara Nagate, her adviser whom already she planned to name Great Minister of the Right, and to his cousin Momokawa, that because of the Emperor's carelessness—his lack of responsibility—the Imperial seal had fallen into the hands of her enemies. And she requested that an edict be drawn up officially placing the seal and bell-tokens under her jurisdiction, and at the same time she dispatched the warrior Sakanoue directly to the Palace to take them from the Emperor and bring them without delay.

But just as scribes may sometimes talk, so novice nuns amuse themselves sometimes with harmless chatter. And that day the news reached Nakamaro of the Empress' intent. At the time he was talking with his wife in the Tamura palace, pacing about the unscreened room that overlooked the back garden. She was arranging large black mushrooms in a shallow tray and she spoke with her back turned toward him. "Shouldn't you go to the Emperor yourself?"

He found it distasteful to see her hands crawling around the tray, and the way she spoke with her back to him was offensive, he thought, like an insult. If she had not spoken, he might have gone. Instead he said in a careless tone, "I will send Kuzumaro."

"Not Materu?"

"No." (Materu was the youngest, the quick and aggressive one, and if she had not said his name in that rising, questioning voice, he might have selected him. But he had said Kuzumaro and would not change, even though he, the elder, was cautious to a fault. It was her hands, he thought afterward when he sought to place the blame, the way they fingered the mushrooms, and the way her back was turned.)

When Kuzumaro stood before him it was as he knew it would be. Every step of the errand had to be explained before he would make a move. What reason should he give, he asked, for appearing before the Emperor when he had not been summoned and was not even on duty? How should he dress, in his Court robe? Did they think he should take a guard? And by what right was he to say—what precedent was there for it—that a man like himself, Fifth Rank junior grade, could enter the Palace unannounced and demand the Imperial seal? The eyebrows in his clean young face went up. An amazing thing, he seemed to say, you are asking me to do! But still he stood respectfully, waiting his father's answers.

Must I justify myself to my own son? Nakamaro thought. Must I explain to this young man whom I have raised and sheltered, but somehow failed to teach, the drive and dream of my being and the thrust of my whole life?

"Rather than affront the Emperor and seize Imperial property," Kuzumaro suggested, "mightn't it be better to wait and see?"

"Wait and see and you will wait too long!" His stepmother rose from her mushrooms with a look of scorn for him.

(And she was right, of course, for at the moment General Sakanoue with some fifteen men, his spindle-wood bow slung across his back and his sword strapped to his side, was riding through the busy streets toward the Palace's western gates.)

"No, there's no time," Nakamaro said. But he spoke gently to this thoughtful son—quietly in contrast to his wife's sharp tone. "There is no time to wait to assess the threat. You must go now."

And at that Kuzumaro would have gone, obedient if doubtful. But Nakamaro felt again that need for justification. "Son, you must keep in mind, in every circumstance, your duty to your Sovereign. This does not mean a blind obedience. It means service. Why are we proudly called the Fujiwara family?"

The son knew but the father carried on, gravely speaking while they stood there, ready to part but waiting. (While Sakanoue rode through the Palace gate and deployed his men in the grounds.)

"This name," Nakamaro said, "that Emperor Tenchi granted your great-great-grandfather when they took the government in their strong hands and built a modern nation; this name that your great-grandfather Fuhito glorified through the reigns of five sovereigns, serving with pure bright heart; this name that I have borne, remembering our past, while under two sovereigns I served as minister . . ."

And he went on to justify his warlike preparations, his plan to spread the glory of this empire over all the world, and to explain the role that he, Kuzumaro, must play. He might indeed have launched on a description of the Emperor's character and the influence Kuzumaro might have on him, but his wife, who had not stayed to listen to these long words, returned.

"Go now," she said, holding out a sword. "Take this and go quickly."

How easy it had been for Sakanoue! He had chosen to enter the gate between the Bureau of Horses and the Artisans' Hall where there were no armed guards, and he had ridden openly across the wide parade ground to the Emperor's Treasure Hall and there, in the name of Her Imperial Majesty, demanded and received from the frightened custodians the seal and the bell-tokens. The Emperor had not said yes or no.

Riding back under the autumn foliage on Nijō Street, seemingly at ease in the saddle and as unobtrusive as so large a man could be, he was confronted suddenly by a young gentleman with a stern, clean face and a look of doubt in his eyes. Kuzumaro knew General Sakanoue to be the Empress' man. But what was his errand, armed as he was and with an escort larger than his own? And if he had been sent for the Imperial seal, why was he riding away from the Palace grounds?

Best to approach him. But before he could, Sakanoue pulled up to him and spoke. "May I ask your name?" he said, though he knew it very well. "For I see you wear a sword, as I do, in the peaceful streets. And where are you bound for?" though he was sure he knew.

"Sir, I am Kuzumaro, of the Fujiwara family, and I am on official business to the Palace."

"Does your official business have to do with this?" Sakanoue tapped a package wrapped in blue print cloth that he cradled in front of him.

Kuzumaro wondered if he should ask him, Is that the seal? Where are the bell-tokens? But he felt he would look foolish. So he kept silence and his young face did not change. Inside he was thinking desperately, What would Father do?

"So you had better turn around again," Sakanoue went on. "Tell your father that he is too late."

But Kuzumaro could not do that. Return to tell his father? To see his stepmother's face?

He backed his horse up, putting his hand to his sword.

Instantly Sakanoue straightened as though he had been struck, and the faces of the men behind him stilled, their eyelids lowered over watchful eyes. They were trained men and experienced, and in spite of their fierce whiskers and rough coats that gave them the look of brigands, they were disciplined and loyal.

The men with Kuzumaro were the guards of his father's palace, proud of their livery and eager to show off. Seeing Kuzumaro put his hand to his sword, they drew theirs. And seeing the general pull back, they rode forward.

Even the simple bystanders shrinking against the walls could have said what was sure to happen if these two sides clashed. Nevertheless, when Kuzumaro saw his guards advance he felt it was his duty to make a move. Sakanoue still backed his horse, his hand on the blue cloth packet, and Kuzumaro eased up close to him. Should he try to seize it?

Too late he realized that his guards had been forced back. Soldiers surrounded him and he sat there alone. So foolish. What should he do now? Desperately he reached out for the package as the general moved away. He never saw the soldier who pressed next to him and rose up in his stirrups with his sword held high, gripped in both hands, before in a terrible voice he shouted, "Ya!" It was like a bark. And the sword slashed down so swiftly and with such sure aim that the others cried, "A stroke! A stroke!" and a scream went up from the crowd.

They had a name for it, that stroke. They called it "the priest's robe" because of the way the cut sliced down from the neck and across the breast. It severed the body cleanly, leaving the bones exposed even while the nerves and muscles continued with life's work. Kuzumaro's legs still rode his horse with his trunk and left arm flailing while his other arm and shoulder and grimacing young head rolled in the street below him, spilling blood.

Into the hush that followed, Sakanoue spoke. "Pick up your dead. Go home. And show him to his father." Then he went with his men down Nijō Street on his way to the nunnery.

From then on things moved swiftly. Nakamaro dared not waste time in mourning. Taking the final risk, he called in Prince Shioyaki and said to him: "I will make you Emperor."

Are not two enough? Shioyaki thought. He was still capable of such lighthearted response although things had not gone well for him since that failed rebellion.

"I would have chosen you at the time the Empress selected her successor, but she would not be persuaded."

Shioyaki smiled. He knew the history.

"And now it is my responsibility, I must have my way. We drift between a weak young Sovereign and a dissolute priest."

Shioyaki nodded. Was this possible? True, the Emperor was not very forceful. And true, the Retired Empress was strongly influenced by the priests. But was it in the power of the Grand Preceptor to raise up yet another prince (himself) to the High Seat? Perhaps it was. So, smilingly, he asked him: "How do we proceed?"

"Through the Grand Council," Nakamaro said. He was thinking that he might still raise sufficient men—men he had trained for foreign duty but who could serve at home as well, men who could convince the ministers of the Grand Council.

It is a temptation, Shioyaki thought. I will ask my wife, for he relied on Fuwa to read the future. And Fuwa, who had come home to him from the Hora Palace, consulted the *Book of Changes* and found the image: *Fire in the Lake* (that is revolution) and the words, *supreme success.* Reading further she had also found, *the younger daughter is above.* So he agreed.

Abé exclaimed when she heard it: "Ah, he has gone too far!" And together with Dōkyō and her advisers she issued a decree: *"The Grand Preceptor, guilty of traitorous acts, is stripped of the honor of bearing the Fujiwara name, deprived of his rank, dispossessed of his lands, and ordered to come before the Court of the Grand Council."*

"Of course he will not come," Dōkyō murmured.

"Then we will fetch him."

On the night of the tenth day of the Tenth Month—that Month When the Gods Are Absent—thirty men under General Sakanoue were sent to surround the Tamura palace. The men wore scarves across their mouths and the horses' hooves were muffled. In silence they seized the watch at the gate and pushed open the heavy doors. Under a high and brilliant moon the courtyard shone like metal.

There was no sign in the darkened halls that far in a back pavilion Nakamaro crouched by a lamp consulting with his captains: How many troops do we have in Kawachi? How many in Yamashiro? Have they seized the armory at Hegura, and when will the weapons arrive?

A boy ran in. "There are men at the gate!"

He knew they had come for him. He had made his plans and briefed his men and prepared his family. He sent a squad of his strongest guards to hold them off at the gate and summoned the women from their rooms and called his son to him.

Materu was his favorite, the child of his second wife, and he was even more precious now that Kuzumaro was gone. "I place the women in your charge," he said. "And I will send a guard of fifty men to protect you. Captain Yezeka will command them. If for some reason I am delayed and do not overtake you, go straight to Echizen and I will meet you there."

Echizen lay on the coast, far above Lake Biwa, but Nakamaro's eldest son was governor of that province and he planned to join forces with him against the Empress' army.

"Yes, sir," Materu said. He was very quick and bold. "We will start at once."

"Don't go hastily. Take it calmly," his father said, stretching a hand to detain him. And when the young man felt the touch he turned again and looked into his father's face with eager shining eyes. Nakamaro clasped him in a strong embrace and then stepped back and took his shoulders, shaking him gently, this young favorite.

After a moment he resumed, "You will have to go slowly with the girls"—as he called his daughters and his daughters-in-law. "But your mother will be a help to you." His wife, he knew, would ride like a man as she had since she was a girl. The others, who were more delicate, would have to be carried in light palanquins.

"Make straight for the Uji bridge, no stopping. That is the first place they will try to cut you off. Then cross the hills, keep going, no matter how tired the girls may be, till you reach the Seta River where the long bridge is. There is a temple there where they may rest. Keep clear of the Hora Palace. There may be spies . . ."

He might have gone on and on with fresh instructions, guiding his son through every possible contingency as he thrust him in his mind's eye through a possible ambush at the Uji bridge, through the mountain forests in the dark of night, across the long bridge at Seta, and up the road that ran along Lake Biwa's eastern shore, but there was a noise outside and he paused to listen. The women had gathered on the back veranda and were quarreling. There would be no room for ladies-in-waiting or even the old nurses on whom the house relied. Then he heard his wife demanding silence and knew that she was aware—as he was, though his words and actions seemed so deliberate—that the men at the gate could not hold out very long.

"Go now," he said to Materu. "Get your horses and go quickly, and I will follow."

Materu bowed and would have left, but Nakamaro went on talking as though loath to see him go: "If it should happen that for some reason I do not join you at Seta, cross the bridge yourselves and head for the Ōmi fort. It is not far." He intended to take the fort at Ōmi and gather more troops there before continuing north.

And again, as Materu stepped away: "Or if I am stopped, if there is an end for me, press on to Echizen and tell your brother all that has happened."

When the boy had left he stood listening to the horses and the carriers departing, then to the sounds at the front gate as they grew louder. He had already sent the rest of his captains with a contingent of his guard to take his horses and his armor and the weapons he would need to wait for him at Shijō Street near the Toshodai-ji temple. Those who could disengage from the skirmish at the gate would meet there too.

Therefore, alone he slipped from a side door and out a broken place in the back wall. Keeping in the shadows that striped the moonlit streets and the overhang of vines by the fenced alleys, he made his way across the city to his rendezvous behind the temple.

When it was reported to General Sakanoue that Nakamaro's wives and daughters with an escort of fifty men had left the mansion, he gave orders to hold back. "But follow and report to me where they are headed."

"No need, sir. They were easily overheard. They hope to outrun us to the Uji bridge, cross it, and make straight for Seta, where the Grand Preceptor plans to join them and go north."

It would have been a simple matter for Sakanoue to send some men to cut them off at the Uji bridge, or to ambush them on the dark mountain road, or come upon them from behind when they waited there at Seta, but it was not his way to make war on women, and the ugly memory of the young Kuzumaro split in half was still in his mind. Nevertheless, he knew the need for haste, and he went immediately to the Hokke-ji to report.

There, still in the dark of night, they made their strategy. "He must be stopped before he gathers up the forces he has trained in the near provinces," the Empress said.

"Let them get past Uji," Dōkyō said. "Let Nakamaro be drawn up to them. But cut the Seta bridge and trap him when he is encumbered and before he can bring up more troops."

They were surprised to hear a priest talk thus of military tactics. But it was Kibi who thought further—up to Echizen and the real battle. "What is important is the son at Echizen," he said. "And the key to Echizen is not nearby, at the Uji bridge or at Seta. It is the barrier at the Arachi pass, the gateway to the province."

The Arachi pass led through the mountains at the north of the lake, a long ride from Seta.

"Nevertheless we should cut the Seta bridge," Dōkyō said.

"Yes, 'we,'" Kibi murmured, looking hard at him. "We should." But it was Kibi's troops alone who started out that night at a full gallop while the others planned.

CHAPTER XXVII

When Nakamaro came at last to the Arachi pass and saw the enemy arrayed against him his face showed something very close to despair. Until then he had not revealed his weariness and concern, although he had had cause to many times in the past few days.

Much earlier, at the end of the first long day and night of his escape, when he had looked down on the Seta bridge, his face showed nothing. But that was at the beginning.

He had joined Shioyaki at the Prince's residence behind the Toshodai-ji temple. And when, in the gray edge of dawn, he had counted the armed men who stood in the stabling area he had asked, "Are these your men? Are these all?" And Shioyaki, who had little property or influence since the failed Tachibana insurrection and his brother's death, said, "These are all—unless we can pull down some from their eminence," and he gestured toward the bulk of the Toshodai-ji that crowded his own small house, for the temple had been his father's residence and his own home as a boy, but it had been given to the Chinese Ritsu priest and many of the old retainers were now Buddhist priests themselves.

"Well," Nakamaro said at last, making the best of it, "we will have more men when we reach Ōmi," for he meant to take the Ōmi fortress and gather his trained men from that province before continuing north. "And in Echizen there will be Asakari's troops, well armed," for he knew his son to be a competent soldier as well as governor.

So they had ridden through the dawn and the long windy morning and had been relieved to find the Uji bridge intact and to be told that the women and their escort had passed over it in safety. Ah, he thought, the gods are with me. He had waited, then, hoping for reinforcements, but none had come, and at nightfall, when he could wait no longer, he had crossed the mountains with his men, picking his way through the dark trees, and at dawn had come upon Materu standing in the trail.

The young man stepped from the shelter of a grove of maples where the first light was turning them pale pink and stood in the open path, a golden boy. Nakamaro reined, looking down at him. He had ridden without stopping, hoping to overtake his family, and at first his heart lifted to see Materu before him. They were safe. Then he saw his son's face with the brows drawn down and knew that there was something wrong.

"They have cut the bridge," Materu said as he stood by his father's stirrup.

"Where are the others?"

"There in the woods." They had drawn back when they saw the bridge and hidden themselves from any enemies that might be waiting.

Nakamaro trusted his son, but still he did not believe. Who could have done it? Who would dare? Or how had Imperial troops got there before him? Of course if they had spies in his house . . . and anyone could outrace the women's train with the baggage . . . and he himself had stopped at Uji that long time . . .

But to cut the bridge? "Show me," he said.

Together they crept forward to the crest and looked down. There indeed was the long bridge spanning the river where it left the lake, and there were the broken timbers in the midst of it, the charred planks, and the water rushing under the empty space.

He stayed a long time looking down, one heavy hand on the surface of a rock beside him—staring, staring down at the wreck of his plans as though he gazed into the future with a set face. Then they crept back again.

The women were sitting in the forest, where they had spread the robes from the palanquins. The grooms and carriers lay in the trees at a distance, sleeping and trustful that they would be protected. And around them Captain Yezeka had stationed his men, keeping the horses picketed far back where they would not be heard.

Yezeka reported that they had encountered no one and heard nothing, only seen the bridge. The nearest fording place was many miles away, and he had waited for the general, he said, as he was instructed.

Nakamaro called for his wife. "Comfort the girls," he said. "We will go by the western route."

She nodded without comment, but the young women, sitting in the forest where they had sat so long, so silently, picking at the twigs that stuck in their clothing and their long hair, questioned her: "Where will we go 'by the western route'? Where will we rest?"

"We will go to Echizen, of course. And you will ride." No longer the luxury of the palanquins. "Tie up your hair and bind your trousers to the knee."

"Is it far?" they asked.

"It is far." But she did not soften.

It was Nakamaro, in the end, who softened, not because—when he sent back to ask—his daughters whimpered or complained of their exhaustion, but because they did not. And he had other reasons, too, for turning from the shore road when they reached Takashima. He had sent word ahead that they would stop at the house of a local dignitary who was in his debt and he hoped that night he might gather troops from the district.

It was during that night that he named Prince Shioyaki Emperor, using his own seal as Grand Preceptor. And word went flying back to the capital—as it had from Kibi's captains when they passed over the Seta bridge and cut it, and from spies along the way.

"How many men has he now?" the Empress asked.

"Some hundred or perhaps less. And he is hampered in his progress by his family."

"He threatens to raise more in Takashima? Will they join him?"

"We do not know."

"My force is swift but small," Kibi said, speaking of the fifty hard-riding men he had sent galloping to Seta and on to the barrier at the Arachi pass.

"How many men have we in the capital to send after him?"

"Many. But arms are scarce." For five years Nakamaro had been gathering weapons and sending them to the northern provinces to be stored for his coming war against the Ezo or to the coast for the soldiers of his warships.

"Send to the priest-in-charge at the Todai-ji and request the arms and armor that were my father's, that my mother gave to the temple. They will lend them."

How many were there? They did not know.

"Bring me the list that the Empress Dowager drew up." And when it was brought she read, in the dear characters: "Ninety scale armor with lacings of silk cord; ten plate armor of iron metal; eighty-nine bows of spindle-wood, twenty-four bows of catalpa wood (the best); eighty bundles of arrows; same number of wrist guards; thirty-three halberds . . ." She read on.

"How many shall we send for?"

"Take them all!"

And when the priests had taken them from the great storehouse she sent a hundred men thus armored, and many more, to take the road along Lake Biwa's western shore after the rebels.

This was the fourth day of Nakamaro's flight and he was pressing on toward Echizen with Shioyaki's men and his own riding briskly with the guards and the women following. He had waited for reinforcements in Takashima but none had come.

It was a clear autumn afternoon with a high sky and the mountain foliage bright as a brocade sleeve. But to the east, across the lake, the clouds were gathering.

Nakamaro hoped to enter the Arachi pass before nightfall and urged his men forward at a quicker pace. The women and the baggage could come up with them when they had prepared a camp. And they had left the lake and started the climb to the pass when suddenly they looked up to see a horseman, fully armed, before them.

Nakamaro stopped and stared. Was this a messenger sent from Echizen to escort them? Then why the armor? Or was this, then, an enemy set in his path? He ordered Captain Yezeka to ride up and demand the man's identity.

"By what name are you called?" Yezeka asked, reining before the warrior. "Tell me so that we may know who sent you."

"First tell me yours," the man replied, "for I am a person of no importance and no interest to you, unless you intend to take the pass by force."

"Then I will tell you, I am a captain in the service of the Grand Preceptor and Supreme Commander, and we will ride peaceably to the pass tonight and on into Echizen tomorrow."

The man moved sideways on his horse. "The barrier is closed."

"In whose name is the barrier closed?" Yezeka demanded.

"In the name of the Great Minister Kibi no Makibi."

Yezeka rode back to Nakamaro, and while he did more men appeared behind the first, all armed.

"Bring me my armor," Nakamaro called. And to the others, "Arm yourselves!"

It was a confrontation he would not have chosen, even though he guessed that such a company, sent up from Nara by the Great Minister, could not be large. He was tired, he had ridden hard that day. And evening was coming, dark with storm clouds sweeping across the lake.

Nevertheless the challenge must be met, and when he was

armed he rode back—not trusting any other—to where the women were. "Move back to the lakeside," he instructed them, "and I will send word to you when you can come forward."

Nakamaro was magnificent in his full armor. Watching him, the women thought, "He cannot lose." His armor-robe was water-blue dyed deeper at the hem and his trousers were embroidered with cresting waves. His leather-covered breastplate was tooled in gilt. Crimson cords laced the metal scales of his corselet and thigh guards.

When he had spoken he put his helmet on and turned away. The flaring metal neck-guard shaded his shoulders and darkly feathered arrows rose from the quiver on his back. But the flat gilded antlers that rose above his head and the copper tenons of his seven-foot bow gleamed in the long rays of the setting sun.

There is no champion to match him, his wife thought, and would have followed him, even into battle, but her duty was to the others and they withdrew.

When Nakamaro left them to gallop up the road he was prepared to challenge any champion they might put forward. But Captain Yezeka, taunted by his foe, had already loosed his arrows and was riding forward into close combat. Nakamaro saw the other leap from his wounded horse and draw his sword, flashing it in the zigzag manner so that it sang. Yezeka leapt after him, but the loose stones of the mountain road rolled beneath his feet. Nakamaro saw him go down, saw the other poise above him and then strike.

There was shouting all around them, and Nakamaro took his eyes from the fallen Yezeka and saw horsemen on the embankments that bracketed the road. His men surged forward and now arrows fell upon them from both sides. The enemy horsemen followed, their big mounts snorting and sliding on the dirt and little tufts of foliage they trampled. Dust rose, even in the damp air with the storm impending, and men and horses were entangled in the murk.

Where was their leader? Whom could he challenge and turn the tide? He made his horse go forward toward the thick of it and called out in a loud voice: "I am here! I, Fujiwara Nakamaro, Commanding General and Grand Preceptor . . ." and he called his titles out, the lengthy string of them, each one. "Let anyone who dares to challenge me come forward. I am here!"

But no champion appeared to answer him and, spurning the others, knocking them back from him with his fists alone, he rode in among the fighting men. Next to him someone lifted up Captain Yezeka's severed head, and he drew his sword while he still sat in the saddle and struck the man and felled him and rode on.

They pressed so close he could not draw his bow, and yet above him on the banks ever more of Kibi's men appeared and poured down their arrows. Nakamaro turned and turned in the melee, seeking their leader, but his teeth were clenched in his set face and he did not call out again. It is hopeless, he thought, caught by this rabble, as he saw his men go down.

They fought till dark, an early dark, for the rain clouds were upon them, and then they faltered, turned. He saw his men go by him, weeping in their despair, and he opened his mouth once more to shout his challenge, but no one answered.

He was alone in the rocky road, dark horsemen confronting him. He stared at them a moment, breathing hard, and then he turned his back to them and galloped away.

He brushed off the women's questions. "A rabble," he said. "A trap." He scorned to meet them once again. "We will go around them," he said.

"How shall we go around?" they asked.

"By boat, to the eastern shore. We can cross in an hour, for the lake is narrow here."

By midnight he had commandeered five fairly sturdy boats but they lay so low in the water when they had crowded in that the waves ran over the gunwales and they were slow. An hour out—they were midway—the storm broke over them. In the black low-lying sky the thunder rolled. Snakes of lightning danced upon the lake. A strong wind blew in their faces, rising to a gale until they lost control and made no headway.

The gods are against me, Nakamaro thought. We must go back. He shouted an order and, when the oarsmen paused, the boats turned sideways and the water sloshed. Then suddenly the rain began, sharp against their backs, and they turned and scudded before the wind till they jolted on the shore.

What now, the women wondered, though they did not ask. But Nakamaro answered what was in their minds: "We will turn south again," he said. "We will go to the Mio Fort. We will rest there and repair ourselves [for many men were wounded] and gather the reinforcements that are on their way."

The Mio Fort was on the lake, many miles to the south. They had not passed it when they had ridden north because they left the shore road to go up through Takashima.

The Mio Fort. Is it not held?

"We will take it if it is."

But some wondered—standing mutely in their sodden clothes, the cold rain falling and their hearts dismayed—some wondered if they had the strength. Perhaps they could find some shelter in the trees and send up prayers?

"We cannot stop here," Nakamaro said. He did not know if Kibi's forces might come after them.

So in the darkness they started out, feeling their way, till after a while the rain stopped and they came upon a village and found food in the granaries. They pulled down the rush fences to make fires to warm themselves, and before they left they took the fence posts to make torches for the road. By dawn their spirits had lifted. Perhaps their luck had turned.

The fort, when they reached it, was only lightly held. Nakamaro took it easily from the Provincial Guard. He did not hold the men, but in a lordly spirit sent them away. He wanted only those whom he could trust to the very end. The place had not been used as a fort for many years, but the ditch and low earth wall surrounding it were unbroken and the stake fence, though it had rotted in some places, could be defended. There were towers at the corners and he posted sentries there, and had the bearers sweep out the soundest hut for the women's comfort.

Late in the hour of the Horse, when the sun was high, the sentry saw a company from Kibi's little army riding down from the hills. Nakamaro sent his own best men to meet them and they fought. Although the fighting was less fierce this time, less bloody, it was a lengthy and exhausting combat between tired men. It was not until the hour of the Cock, when the sun had lost its force, that Kibi's men withdrew again into the hills.

Nakamaro went to the women's hut. It was bare but clean, and a spray of crimson maple leaves stood upright in one corner. He looked at the women, feigning confidence, and saw on the tender faces of the younger ones an expression of hopefulness and trust. What could he offer them? What comfort? There was no priest to send up prayers. He stood before them and recited solemnly:

"The Land of Yamato is a land
Where matters fall as the gods will
Without the lifted words of men.
It is so.
Yet I do lift up words . . ."

Outside they heard the playing of a flute. It was Prince Shioyaki, who had brought his favorite instrument, wearing it close to him, even under his armor when he fought. So they were silent, listening in the long late afternoon while Shioyaki's music brought them to tears.

The Empress' army crossed the Uji bridge at midday, one hundred mounted men in Imperial trappings. They brought a sound from the wooden planks that was like rolling thunder. They galloped, and a trail of dust rose after them like a long yellow banner over the mountain roads. They topped the ridge above the Mio Fort and looked down upon it in the setting sun. They paused to settle their armor and let the horses breathe. Then they swept down.

For the last remainder of the day Nakamaro's bowmen held off the attack. If one man fell he thrust another in his place until at last there were too few to hold. Wounded, exhausted, even dying men stood by the palisades, and by dusk each of the women, too, held a long sword in her hands. Shioyaki could not be contained but rode out from the gate and was struck down.

Nakamaro left his post and called out to his wife, "Take the girls, and when it has grown dark go out by the small north gate. I will send Materu with you and ten men. You must get to the shore and find a boat. Cross over. The lake is calm. Go quickly."

But she would not go. "I will stay here by you."

While they stood panting, arguing, Materu came up to them. The Empress' men had crossed the ditch and were scrambling up the wall. Now they were putting torches to the wooden fence. The light leapt up. Nakamaro shouted, "We cannot wait. Come! Now!" And they crowded to the small back gate, the women dragged by the men, and raced across the sloping ground to the road and then the shore. They found a boat and pushed it out. For a moment they were safe.

But they had been seen and were followed. The fires lit the beach. Men on foot and horsemen came shouting after them. They pulled at the oars, they crouched and dodged, but the arrows found them out and those who were struck let their oars fall. Others plunged overboard. The boat lost its momentum and rocked in the lapping waves.

Nakamaro stood and braced himself and stared back at the fort. Smoke billowed from the watchtowers and yellow flames shot up. The Empress' soldiers following him were black against the light. An arrow struck him but he felt no pain. He pulled it out and looked at it and tossed it in the waves. He heard a cry and saw Materu jump from the rocking boat and stand waist-deep in the water with his young wife by his side. He saw him lift her with one arm, his sword in the other hand, and in the firelight glimpsed the arrow lodged in her slender neck. He watched the foremost soldiers come wading out to them and saw Materu flailing, flailing and going down.

Then he heard the shrieks of the others and the plunge and grunts of his men and turning saw his own wife in the midst of them. She was wading forward grimly, dragging a heavy sword. And she stopped before them and raised it, gripped in both her hands, and held it high above her head while they stood back. But they had seen that she was old and the sword too heavy for her, and how her face contorted and her arms shook. Slowly her wrists began to give. The wavering sword descended until it dangled harmlessly as though broken off by the water.

A soldier laughed. Nakamaro heard. Rage and anguish blinded him, and he leapt from the boat to kill them. But he too seemed old. The water dragged at his feet and thighs. The mud sucked at his shoes. Floundering, falling, slashing, he made an easy prey, and they closed around him shouting and thrusting with their swords. They struck and cut and hacked at him. And still he stood, till, probing the great barrel of his chest, they found his heart.

The men who brought the news to the Empress expected a reward. They came and crouched before her and kept their eyes on the floor, though they let triumphant smiles play on their faces while they talked. And when they finished they waited for her praise.

"And that is how he died," they said. "Pierced through." They had respect for him and the manner of his losing. But they were proud as well.

"Pierced through." She felt a stab at her own heart and made a little sound. Then there was silence . . .

They wondered if they should go, just back away on hands and knees as though they had been dismissed. Who could tell what she might do next, who had ordered them to kill and now sat moaning? They crouched there with their heads to the floor and the sweat crawling until at last a nun came out and told them they could leave. The Empress had withdrawn long since.

In the scented shadows of her bed-space she sat alone. So he is gone, she thought. It had to be. There was no other way. Only there were so few, now, to whom she could say, Remember? Remember when you brought me a cricket you had caught? When you were a big boy and I a child? And I soon lost the little cage and was so sorry . . .

Remember when you came to tell us about the embassy, that night when the fireflies were so bright . . . and you lay on the porch and tried to watch us, peeking around the curtain . . . and Saisho pinched me so that we wouldn't laugh . . .

She smiled and tears came to her eyes and she began to sob. Oh, Saisho, that foolish Saisho. And now you . . .

She stayed there, thinking and remembering, refusing to speak, refusing to eat. It took her three days to mourn her past. Then she put it away forever, so she thought, and buried her memories.

When she emerged she was very pale but composed and the first thing she did was to send for Toyonari, who had returned from exile, and they talked together soberly, placating his brother's ghost.

"Ambition overcame him," Toyonari said. "But I remember the days . . ."

After a little while, when calm had returned and all of Nakamaro's properties were disposed of, she said again to Toyonari that although she had left the world and lived in a nunnery, she perceived her duty to resume the throne that she had left—was forced to leave—six years ago. "The young Emperor is unfit to govern. That is clear to all. Even Nakamaro acknowledged that when he tried to raise up Prince Shioyaki . . ."

Poor Shioyaki, that gay young man. She was sorry for his death, sorry for Fuwa, widowed now, and for the children.

"And when I take up my responsibilities, I shall rely on you once more as my Great Minister of the Right." First, however, there was the problem of the discredited young Emperor.

"What is to be done with him?" she asked Dōkyō when they were discussing her resumption of the throne. She thought that if it were not for his mother he might agree to abdicate, go quietly, perhaps return to the Hora Palace and bother no one.

"But don't you suppose," Dōkyō said, "there are those who are loyal to him?"

"Yes. You are right." She saw the danger. There would always be some disaffected people to make trouble.

"Was he helpful to Nakamaro? In his plot and plans, I mean?"

"Perhaps he was. Yes, surely."

"He seemed quite willing to give over the Imperial seal had not General Sakanoue prevented him."

"Yes, yes, it is surely true. He conspired in the whole rebellion, played his part. Why should others suffer and he go free? He is not above punishment. You are quite right."

Dōkyō looked doubtful. He was not yet accustomed to high power and did not like the feel of another's life put into his hands this way. "Perhaps he did not conspire. Only a dupe."

"No. I know him. So incompetent—and yet so crafty. Secretly they plotted together. He must pay for it."

"All life is sacred."

"Yes. Of course. Of course he will not be harmed."

Next month was the Month of Frosts and the mountains blazed, but it was a cruel month for the young Emperor. At dusk on the fifth day, after the evening drum, a servant dared to report to him that a troop of soldiers had crossed the Palace grounds and surrounded his residence. He still lived with his mother in the women's quarters; why should soldiers come there?

"What do they want of me?" he asked. "And where are the Household Guards?"

The servant, seated below him on the frosty ground, was not prepared to answer, for he knew that he was one of only three out of all the Palace attendants who had not run away.

That night his mother urged him to slip out in the dark and flee to Yamashiro where her family was, and there find help, but he could not make up his mind to do it until it was too late. At dawn, when the sky was very red, they came for him.

At first they spoke respectfully, requesting him to come out. But he clung to his bed and refused to dress and dared them to touch his Person, until at last, mid-morning, two of his princely half brothers strode into his inner room, to his bed, reached in, and pulled him out.

"Wait, I will put my clothes on."

"We have waited too long already."

"Let me find my shoes."

"Too late." And they held him by the arms and brought him out.

On the porch he saw that his mother was already standing there, small and bewildered among the men and the horses stamping the ground.

"Let me put my shoes on."

"Come this way."

And he walked between his brothers, the frost cold on his feet, out through the gardens to the north and past the storehouses to a small graveled courtyard behind the Bureau of Books. And there while he stood beneath the horsemen, holding back his tears, he was forced to hear their charges and his sentence of banishment:

"For his incompetence as Emperor, for his weak nature, but most of all for his complicity with the traitor Nakamaro in his plot to overthrow Us, the former Imperial Prince Oi-Ō is deprived of the rank of Sovereign and granted the rank of Prince. And he shall be banished to the Isle of Awaji where he will live out his days and henceforth shall be known only as Lord of Awaji."

"Here, put the Lord of Awaji on his horse," they said, lifting him to the saddle.

He was weeping openly and would have hid his face, but they bound his arms behind him, and bound his mother's too, and led them out of the Servants' Gate and along the road to the coast.

Later, during the enthronement ceremony, when she took the Imperial name of Shōtoku, the Empress proclaimed that although she had cut her hair and donned the habit of a nun she felt her responsibility to her Ancestors and to the people to carry on the government. And it was fitting, under these circumstances, to include Buddhist priests among her close advisers. Therefore she was awarding Yuge no Dōkyō the special title of Minister of State as well as Master of Buddhist Meditation.

This was the first of many appointments that gave rise to a growing hierarchy of priests and nuns that soon became a third branch of her government, advising and persuading her in their own interests alongside the Great Council of State and the Department of Shinto.

CHAPTER XXVIII

The golden crow lights on the western huts;
Evening drums beat out the shortness of life.
There are no inns on the road to the grave—
Whose is the house I go to tonight?

—Prince Ōtsu on the eve of his execution, 687. From the *Kaifūsō*

She had said, "He will not be harmed." But who was to pay for the misery, the loss? Nakamaro gone. Shioyaki gone. And the land distracted. There had been drought all year and the value of rice had doubled. She had had to open the granaries to the poor. The Emperor must take responsibility.

And yet . . . She turned her head away from the picture of the poor fat young thing with his bare feet in the snow (for his brothers had been quite graphic in their report) and brushed the fringe of hair from her forehead in that gesture from her childhood, brushing bad things away.

They will call me hard, she thought. But they do not understand.

Early in the new year she moved back to the Palace. The renovations were complete at last, and she wandered through the rooms her father once had occupied, savoring the grandeur.

Before the curtained platform of her inner room stood two large porcelain figures: a roaring lion and a Korean lion-dog. And above it hung two copper mirrors to frighten demons from her bed.

A fine clear scent of lakawood rose from the censing braziers and she felt the spirit of her father lingered here. His purity and devotion. And such wide spaces after the hushed corridors of the Hokke-ji! Such vistas looking out across the wide flat gardens with their ponds and stepping stones. A fresh snow lay on the branches of the pines and along the dark curve of the water.

She hoped for a propitious reign this time. She prayed for it. But already her advisers pressed her for the name of her successor. And at the same time she heard rumors of attempts to rescue Oi-Ō.

She wrote the governor of Awaji:

"We have heard the rumors. A criminal is preparing to escape. Men have been going to the place where he is kept pretending to be merchants. (We have heard this also.) You have not realized the importance of this matter; it should have been reported to Us. You must know that visitors are not permitted to this person in your charge."

And in closing, ominously: "You will do well to report to Us every detail of what your prisoner is doing."

Some time later she said to Dōkyō, "It is certain that some dissatisfied people will bring ruin to our land." He had not seen such a frowning look on her face before. Impatient, he thought, almost vindictive. It was as though on mounting the High Seat she had taken on a kind of godlike wrath. Could she have looked like this when she reigned before, he wondered, she who had been so tender, delicate, even fragile when they were together there at the Hora Palace?

It was his impulse to mention this, to talk to her as he used to from the heart and remind her of the futility of these concerns. Had she forgotten all his teachings and the progress they had made toward their souls' rest? It seemed to him she was bound and tangled in a web that she had made of her own preoccupations. And as he drew away and looked at her with clear dispassionate eyes, it was as though he saw these ties of duty, rights, and obligations—all the trappings of her position and the Court—like visible strings and nets.

But am I any better? he thought suddenly. Advising and encouraging—plotting and scheming. And in shame he thought of his own determination to live a sinless life, to practice charity and mediation and to obtain that holy calm he once had made his goal.

So when he spoke it was not from his heart, but only to soothe and gratify: She must not worry, the people loved her, even as he did.

For a moment she looked at him, a hungry, almost consuming look. How I love you, she seemed to say. How I depend on you. But right away she frowned again. "My ministers are pressing me to name an Heir Apparent."

"The decision must be yours." (They had been over this ground many times before.)

"They come at me." She sounded pitiful, but she would never weaken. She knew from her own experience that once an Heir Apparent has been named the factions form in opposition, and she added in a changed voice, almost triumphantly: "But I will not be caught in that trap again, not that particular trap!"

He smiled. "Perhaps you should notify them formally and put an end to it."

"Yes! I will tell them."

And with his help she drew up an edict to be read to all the Court: a warning not to promote their favorites among the princes because she herself, in her own time, would make her own decision. And further, to those misguided people who would bring back the person who was on Awaji, they were proposing ruin, for he was of weak intellect and flawed character and totally unfit to govern.

From the sea the island of Awaji rises green against the sky. The steep hills are gentle, and the young Emperor (deposed) looked from the deck of the small ship and thought that he could live there. I am a simple man, he thought, I can get along with little. It was only the thought of his mother's suffering that brought the tears to his eyes and made the sharp lines of the shore go blurred.

That was in the Month of Frosts, the second month of winter. Since that time he had lived to see the snow fall on the deep green ocean—fall and melt as it touched the water, a most wonderful sight—for during that first winter of his exile he was allowed to walk about quite freely. He had seen the blossoming of the wild plums from the courtyard of the mansion where he had been housed—for in the early spring he was still permitted to go out of doors, if not beyond the fence. In early summer he talked to his last visitor. And in the rainy reason, when they would have had to stay indoors in any case, the governor of the island spoke to him for the last time: He was obliged to ask the Emperor to stay in his quarters from now on.

The "quarters" where he and his mother lived was one small mud-walled room. There was no shutter on the window, and no screens, their beds were mats. When winter came again they shivered. And they were hungry.

"You take it, I have no need for food," his mother said.

This made him want to cry. She had never denied herself in all those years that she was the precious daughter in her father's house, the honored first wife of her husband. She had been ambitious for her son and coveted honors for herself as the Imperial mother. The best was always hers, by right.

He might have thought, therefore, that when the food was pushed to them—a wooden bowl of rice—she would accept it. Surely she was hungry, as he was. Surely starving. It caused him pain to look at her, she had shrunk down so thin.

He could not see himself grown gaunt, which was fortunate. What a strange appearance! The fat young face had melted down to the shape of the bones with the childish eyes looking out bewildered from the flat ridge of their sockets. If he had been charming as a boy—as many thought he was—it was the charm of rosy cheeks and the gleam of healthy skin. Now even his own mother merely glanced at him when she spoke, and quickly looked away.

"I have no need," she had said. But it had been so many days since they had been offered more than one bowl of rice—or rice of some sort mixed with millet as it seemed to be. It was something neither had tasted in their lives before.

"Perhaps this is what the people eat?" he had asked his mother when it first was handed them.

"Not hungry . . ." But she was starving! She is starving, he thought, and she will die. But in fact what was killing her was despair. She had exhausted all her efforts for her son, but his fate was failure. From birth, from very birth he had failed her and she could do no more.

At first he had said nothing when she refused the food. But at last he could not stand it any more—eating so guiltily (though he did intend to save a half for her, always one half, until somehow it was gone) while she lay in her many wrappings in the dark. (It struck him also how these mannish clothes had changed her, she who had loved the Chinese silks and golden colors and the jewels and scents reserved for an emperor's mother. The clothes she wore now were beneath her station, plain and dark, but they had been accepted thankfully: the hunting cloaks that sympathetic men had left them when they had been allowed those visitors so long ago.)

The daily meal had come and as he always did he looked across to the dark bundle in the corner of the room, that silent heap of clothing that was his mother. He went to her and put the bowl beside her on the floor and touched her shoulder, pushing on it gently, nudging. "Mother."

He pushed again, more wildly, using both his hands, till she was rolling on the floor and the covering clothes fell back. He saw—what he had known already—that she was dead.

He whimpered as he drew the garments back across her face, but he did not cry out. I must think very clearly, he thought, how to protect her. First, I must eat this food as though we both had eaten, so they will never know. He thought his mind was clear and calm, but it was then his nightmares started.

At first, when the face came looming at him, anguished, accusing, he thought it was her ghost. But it changed so often, sometimes young, sometimes with horns like a snail's horns growing from her head—or was it her hair ornaments as she bent over him, demanding, demanding. What? Be a man! Be a man! But he was so small, his body shivering . . .

Or again, the accusing eyes, so wide and staring and surprised. Demanding. Those wide eyes like the round eyes of a cat staring at him, questioning—his young wife asking more than he could give. "But I can't!" he cried out, and half woke.

No, he had not been sleeping, but he was half mad with fear. And even awake, the face loomed over him, dark and featureless like a gourd but still demanding. "What do you want? What do you want?" he whispered. But he knew. The woman bending over him was the Empress, and he knew what she demanded. It was his death.

I must plan, he thought. They must not know that I am alone. And he crept to the window craftily and peered out with one eye. I will wait for the guard to pass, he thought. But no guard came.

Fool that I am! To have lain here all this time, these days and nights and days and nights—and no one guarding! Fool that I am, just as they all have said. He could have wept.

Tonight, he thought, when the moon has set and before the sun has risen, I will leave and go. No one will stop me, and there will be a boat. He pictured the boat waiting for him there on the green water, and the snowflakes slowly drifting—though it was far too early in the winter yet for snow.

There will be a palace where I can go, and they will serve me. Red bean soup. The childish soup he loved more than all the delicacies they had brought him on their green ceramic dishes, their flower-shaped bowls. "Thank you, I want no more than soup," he whispered, staring through the window into the night.

He thought he heard his mother stir behind him and his hair pricked on his skin. He sidled to the door. Still locked. But the window . . .

Outside they watched him, how his hands emerged through the dark hole, how they felt around like crabs and grasped the wooden bars, then how his face, moon-white, pressed up against them . . . "He is restless," they said. "Something has changed."

That was the way they knew the lady must have died. She never let him press against the window, never allowed the whimpering. But they had not expected the smell when they entered, and stepped back in fear. Pollution! Someone else, whose job it was, was called to remove the body. And when he whimpered at them where they stood beside the door, they backed away.

That night they watched him, first at the window. They said nothing. Then at the door. They had not locked it, and they watched. And in the dark between the moonset and the dawn they saw him come. Bent and trembling he crept out, crossed the yard, made for the earth embankment and the rough rush wall. They caught him, hands in the thorny hedge, and pulled him back.

"Attempting to escape," they told the governor.

"Where is he now?"

They were surprised. "In the room."

When the governor frowned they understood and nodded.

Next night they tried to lure him out again. "The door is not locked," they told each other loudly. "Yes, the bolt is missing." But he would not come.

So they walked in at last, reluctant but obedient. And when he looked up at them he knew why they had come. He saw sweat on their faces and smelled their fear.

"We regret to disturb you," one said, but his voice was thick in his throat.

"Why are you trembling?" he asked them.

"It is being in Your Majesty's presence; I am overcome with awe."

"Why do your faces glisten?" He was standing now.

"It is warm," one murmured. But the other simply moved.

They crouched as they approached him, one on either side, and slipped the noose around his neck. It was easy. But somehow he got his fingers under the taut cord so that they had to fight with him around the dirty room, one working at those clutching hands, the other twisting the cord, while his body thrashed between them and his legs kicked the walls.

Far away, across the court and garden and behind closed blinds, the governor heard the noise. Like the scrabbling of rats, he thought, and his stomach heaved. He was a tender man, and the guards knew it, so that when they made their report they were very careful.

"The person in the small room has departed."

"How? Not escaped?"

"Not escaped. He is dead."

"He died?"

"Yes, died."

"He was well cared for, wasn't he?"

"Yes, very well."

"Then I must hear from you how he died. So suddenly."

"Yes, suddenly. But peacefully, in his sleep."

The news arrived in Nara at an awkward time, just as they were preparing for the Great Food Festival, that most sacred of all Shinto rites when the gods give sanction to a Sovereign's enthronement during the first year of his reign: the Great Thanksgiving Festival for the Treading of the Succession of Heavenly Light.

The shock was specially severe to those of the high Court nobles who had been asking whether the Retired Emperor ought not be present, along with the Heir Apparent—if the Empress would only choose one!

Some even wondered if the ceremony should take place at all —a Buddhist nun at the center of this ancient Shinto rite? And Kibi no Makibi suggested to her that the security of her position did not depend on this particular rite but on her own wise and compassionate rule, but she did not listen.

Her own shock was more personal—and more ambivalent. It was as though she had taken a knife and, after staring at it in her hand, after holding it against some ugly wart or blemish on her own skin, had suddenly cut—and been surprised and horrified at the blood, yet somehow gratified.

. . . though I did not will it, she told herself. I did not wish him dead . . . it was simply a matter of his destiny . . .

The fact that he died so young only goes to prove his weakness and inadequacy, she thought. But I am sorry for it, truly sorry.

"Poor young man," she said to Dōkyō. "They say he was alone." (They had told her he died peacefully, but when she questioned them about it they had revealed that his mother had died before him.)

"Poor man," Dōkyō agreed. (In his dealings with the Emperor he had not thought him so young.)

"I wonder if he suffered. He must have suffered."

"Surely."

"Poor young man!"

"But you have forgotten the basic truth: All life is suffering!" He smiled and his voice was gentle, as if he spoke to a child.

"But so alone!" She certainly had not meant, when she wrote the governor, that he should be kept alone.

"Truly in this world a man is born alone and dies alone, and there is no one who can share his suffering in this life or the next." He meant to reassure her, although he continued gravely, "The law is universal; each man must carry his own burden and go alone to his retribution."

She turned away from him and hung her head. "I am truly sorry." She could barely speak.

"But the same law applies to our good deeds, remember that." He was full of love and encouragement. "A life of sympathy and kindness will bring its reward . . ."

"You know these things," she said, still looking away, "because of your own kindness and good deeds. You are not like the rest of us, so selfish."

"But you are never selfish," he protested.

"I am."

"Never with me."

"No. Never." (She would, indeed, have given him anything he asked for, and because he did not ask she gave him all the more.) She turned to give him a soft, glistening look. "And now you have comforted me."

In this way they disposed of the late Emperor, though of course she had the proper rites performed for his spirit and his mother's. But ahead of them they had the matter of the Great Food Festival to discuss.

Some time before this, when the murmurings first began, he had brought up the subject so as to prepare her for any opposition.

"Do you know," he had told her, as though amazed, "some people seem to be saying that the gods will be offended . . ."

"Offended? Why?"

"That you, an Initiate in the Order of Bodhisattvas and a follower of the Law . . ."

"Well, what?"

"Might be displeasing to the gods . . ."

She smiled. "Who can speak for the gods if not I?"

"Yes. True." This was the answer that he wanted, and yet it was so delicate a subject for him, this matter of her divinity, that he skirted it when he could. But he could not let this opportunity go by, this chance to demonstrate the power of Buddha and the strength of the Buddhists in her Court. "Truly, no one can know better than you the Way of the Gods."

"But some disgruntled people, or some troublemakers?"

"They do not understand that there is no longer any reason why priests and nuns should not take part in these sacred rites. They are not evil people. They simply do not understand, because they have not studied the sutras. We who have understanding know that the gods are willing protectors of the Law which they reverence. But these people are in the dark, and have short memories. They have even forgotten how the great God Hachiman requested to be brought to Nara to worship the Great Buddha of the Todai-ji. And since then, many more . . ."

"It is true," she murmured in wonderment.

"Since you have taken your Buddhist vows," he continued strongly, "you are not *less*, as they imply, but *more!* As a Buddhist on the path to enlightenment, surely you can worship the gods even more effectively and serve your people with a greater love!"

He spoke with more than his usual animation and she agreed with everything he said. How eloquent he was!

"Surely," she echoed him, "a Buddhist can take part in the sacred rites of the gods, and the gods can worship and serve Buddha!"

He smiled and nodded but said nothing more. The conversation had gone as he wanted it to. However, he was not sure that these arguments would persuade the various powerful men among her advisers. And it was difficult to know, just now, who did hold power. There was no Nakamaro with his web of relationships—so many men in his debt—and his history of victories ever since childhood. (For it was not until he failed in love, or the pretense of it, that he began to lose. A lesson well taken.)

Toyonari, her only Great Minister, was severely ill. His cousin Nagate had a strong family following but the Empress did not like him, and Momokawa, though he had very definite opinions, seldom spoke. Of course there was the scholar Kibi no Makibi, who had that special relationship, but there was no powerful family backing in that case any more than in his own. (He was aware that although he had the strength of the Buddhist hierarchy behind him, his real power lay in his closeness to the Empress—the very fact that made him also vulnerable.)

Nevertheless they proceeded with preparations for the great festival. Long before this time, the diviners had heated the sacred tortoise shells and reported what they read in the cracks: "The provinces of Izumi and Mino shall be honored to supply the rice for the gods' sake. Izumi for the dark sake; Mino for the light." And after that, in each of the provinces, the governors had gone with their diviners into the hills to worship the Mountain Gods and select the trees for the gates of the ritual grounds and others had gone to the marshlands to pray to the Gods of the Moors and bring in the rushes for the fences. Offerings had been sent to the August Ancestress in the Grand Shrine at Isé, and instructions to the Shinto priests in every district to prepare their sacred compounds for a great purification.

Kibi no Makibi requested an audience with the Empress,

and even while she talked with him she was preparing a message to the chief of the Hayato, far off in the south province of Kyushu, reminding him of the obligation of his tribe to dance for the entertainment of the gods during the great enthronement festival and to make haste to start their journey, for the date had been fixed for the twenty-third day of the Eleventh Month.

She sat with her inlaid writing box beside her and the screen at her side was decorated with chrysanthemums sprinkled over with gold powder. The sliding doors to the garden had been opened, and in the autumn evening sun the leaves were falling like a golden rain.

Kibi had been selected as a spokesman for the others. He would be able to speak to her as no other dared. And he had agreed, at the risk of his own standing, because he too feared the influence of the Buddhists in her government and mistrusted her handsome favorite, the chancellor-priest.

When he had been escorted into her presence and sat overlooking the veranda below her chair, he turned to catch a glimpse of her against the chrysanthemum screen. She had not changed as much as one might have thought, though the quality of wistfulness that he had noted so long ago and the slender line of her shoulders had hardened into a regal and somewhat static pose.

All this made him pause a long time before he spoke, even though her greeting had been warm. And even when she indicated she would hear him, he still hesitated while he sought the exact approach that would influence and not offend her. Of course the immediate question was the propriety of inviting the gods themselves to honor the enthronement of a Buddhist nun. But his true concern was not so much that she herself was a Buddhist—so had her father been—but that she was so strongly influenced by a particular prelate.

At last he began, rather hesitantly, tipping his head to one side: "I am aware that in the service of one's Prince, repeated scoldings can only lead to loss of favor . . ."

He was quoting Confucius, as in the old days, and she understood him well enough to know that this meant he was anxious. So when she spoke it was in a gentle voice, though her words might seem abrupt.

"Are you seeking the appointment of an Heir Apparent? Once again?"

"No, no," he smiled. "I will not trouble you with that. It is the matter of the Great Thanksgiving Festival . . ." He stopped. Dōkyō had come into the room, walking easily and softly in his priestly robes. He bowed to Kibi and greeted him with that quiet, radiant glance that had so captivated men and women all his life. It was as though he were saying to each one: You above all others are the very one I am most pleased to see.

Kibi rose and bowed. Then as the priest, after making his obeisance to the Empress, still stood beside him amiably, he realized that they must settle down together side by side. How disconcerting!

"My two dear friends!" the Empress' voice was vibrant. She gazed down at them and then past their seated figures—so very different!—to the golden trees.

There was a silence until Kibi said, "I have disturbed you," and would have asked to leave, but she stopped him and said to Dōkyō: "The subject has come up, again, of the Great Thanksgiving and the Treading of the Succession . . ."

And when again there was silence—very long, while Dōkyō sat calmly gazing at his hands and Kibi fidgeted—she broke it only to call attention to the garden and the translucent falling leaves, and then, rather abruptly, while she still looked out at the garden, "I know there are some who think that the gods should be kept distinct from the Buddha. But if they will examine the scriptures they will see that it is proper for the gods to revere the Law . . ." She paused. "I am well aware that formerly it was thought that Buddhists and non-Buddhists should not mix together, but that is no longer true. We are all one people."

She waited for Kibi's answer until at last he said, "You speak of the people, yes. People can be induced to follow your reasoning; they cannot always be persuaded to agree."

"We will explain it to them. They will understand."

And on the following day she had the scribes draw up an Imperial proclamation wherein she vowed ever to serve the Three Treasures of her Buddhist faith, to worship her Ancestors, and always to cherish her people.

So it was that on the Second Day of the Hare in the Eleventh Month of the first year of her reign as Empress Shōtoku, during the dark hour of the Dog when the gloom clung to the thatched roofs of the August Communion Halls, she walked in exquisitely slow procession past the great shields standing at the gate to the sacred precincts and across the hard ground lit by the torches and the courtyard fires toward the halls and the Great Food Offering set out for the gods.

Before her two vice-ministers unrolled a fine leaf-matting and behind her two major counselors stooped to roll it up. Two high Court nobles went beside her, one on either hand, holding the cords to her sedge umbrella and progressing on their knees.

It is true that there were Buddhist priests among the ranks of courtiers who stepped forward to clap their hands. But the spirit of Buddha was not there. The gods were. It was to them the prayers were offered and the music played, the dancers postured in the firelight and the Hayato stamped. For them the sacred kitchens had been built and the food prepared: the cooked rice and the fresh fish and the fruits . . . the dried foods, the seaweed pickle sauce, the abalone soup . . . the dark sake and the light.

Dōkyō felt some loss of confidence as he watched the princes and the ministers step forward to clap their hands. His own position was equal to these men's, but he was aware of his lack of training in the Court etiquette of these high ceremonies, in this formal worship of the gods, even as he too advanced to his allotted place and clapped his hands before those rustic buildings where the diviners stood with their bamboo wands and their sleeves bound up in bark cloth.

Afterward, when the four days of the solemn ceremonies had been completed, the last of the dancers stilled and the ancient instruments put away, when the time of abstinence was over and the feasting done, when the fragile buildings and communion halls had been dismantled, the fences and the gates removed and the post holes filled, he came once more into her presence.

He found her in her audience hall with her ladies gathered around and other members of her Court conversing in the outer rooms. There were so many that they overflowed into the outer corridors and the verandas. Kibi no Makibi was there with the others and greeted him politely but Dōkyō thought his smile seemed sly.

He felt there was a special aura in the room when he approached her curtain, and when she spoke he could hear her solemn exaltation. She had not come down from the company of the gods. It frightened him to lose her in this way, but there were too many people in her hall, too many sidewise glances and little smiles, so that he dared not ask when they might be alone. His handsome face took on that diffident friendliness that he used on such occasions as he bowed to the gentlemen he passed and retreated to the porch.

Kibi, watching him, made the observation: "'When the Superior Man is at Court his manner is friendly and affable to those below him, restrained and formal to those above, and when the Ruler is present, he is wary but not cramped.'"

"You seem to approve of him," his neighbor said.

"No, I am merely observing. He is a man to watch."

CHAPTER XXIX

Among the many priests at the Kofuku-ji temple was a man named Kishin. He had attended the Great Festival for the first time and had been made uneasy by that slow procession through the firelit courtyard, the shouting and stamping when the Hayato danced, those offerings in earthen vessels and leaf plates—the whole overwhelming presence of the gods.

Only some time later was he able to shake this awe. Then he declared to his friends and fellow priests, "The power of the Buddha is far greater than the power of the gods."

One day in the autumn season Kishin went by himself to the small Buddha-hall that marked the northeast corner of the greater Palace grounds next to the Hokke-ji. When he made sure that no one was around he went inside and found there, hidden in a wooden image of a guardian god, a wonderful small box made of painted ivory. A light came from it, so he later said, that outshone even the bright sunlight streaming in the door. In the back garden the cicada's shrilling filled the air, but inside, so he said, there was an awesome silence while he crept toward the light. Even the dust motes ceased to dance.

It was the light that led him to the sacred image and to the small hole in the base. And he felt commanded to reach inside to where the box was hidden and draw it forth and open it and find—a sacred relic of Buddha!

It was like the ashes that are left in the crematory fire, but not like the ashes of an ordinary man. They were shining, radiant, marvelous to see. They were like jewels, he said, like pearls, like lustrous glass beads!

When these ashes were presented to the Empress she was overcome. Trembling, she leaned over the little box. Her whole face was shining. She was like a child. "How wonderful!" she said. "How wonderful!"

She thought that she did not deserve to have such a miracle take place in her own Palace, during her own reign, and her sense of awe and gratitude nearly overwhelmed her. She thought of her shortcomings and her failures and the bad things she had done and she bowed her head over her clasped hands and shut her eyes.

Afterward it occurred to her that this miraculous discovery must have been brought about not by any actions of her own but by the accumulated goodness of others before her. So much merit had been stored, she reflected, by her father and mother through the years. And now the purity and good deeds of the Great Minister of State had added to the store!

She was swept by relief and gratitude, and next month wrote an edict proclaiming the great merit of her minister-priest and promoting him to the new rank of Chancellor of the Realm with the title King of the Buddhist Law, a dignity that had been reserved until now for retired emperors. (The priest Kishin she promoted also, to the even greater consternation of her Grand Council, making him an adviser in her Buddhist Council and alloting him permanent escort of eight military men.)

When some of her counselors murmured that the Great Minister's promotion seemed excessive, she exclaimed that such a miracle, such a beautiful and radiant gift, such a sign of Buddha's favor, surely required a reward! Besides, she felt such an extraordinary sense of well-being and such a joy in her heart each day that no gift was too much.

At the turn of the year a series of luminous banner clouds appeared in Mikawa Province in the eastern sky. They grew and multiplied till they were flying overhead and all the people wondered. This was reported to the Empress as a lucky omen and she changed the year-name to Felicitous Cloud. It is such a happy time, she thought, my reign shall be propitious.

She began to add color and ornament to her nun's costume and demanded that all the New Year ceremonies be scrupulously followed. Between the showing of the blue horses and the tasting of the full-moon gruel, she invited the high priests from all the Nara temples to expound the Sutra of the Sovereign Kings while she listened and questioned them. "It will assure us seasonable weather and good crops," she said, "and happiness for the people."

At the poetry reading on the sixteenth day she wore her Imperial headdress and long winding scarf that circled her shoulders and trailed down across her sleeves. It was like the scarf of the Kannon image that had recently been carved for the new temple she was building on the city's western edge, the Saidai-ji. (It would complement Rōben's powerful Todai-ji on the east, she said, though she meant counterbalance.)

At the reading one of the verses pleased her very much and she had the poet repeat it:

"Lasting as the fir trees
on the green mountains,
Endless as the pine tree's roots,
Our Sovereign, our goddess
(May she rule the land for ages
in the Imperial city of Nara)
This day holds a banquet
Out of her godlike will . . ."

On the day of the promotions she announced that—Fujiwara Toyonari having died the previous year—she had chosen his cousin Nagate as her Great Minister of the Left and the eminent scholar and diplomat Kibi no Makibi as Great Minister of the Right.

Now the year began to go ever faster for her and it seemed she was in an almost constant state of delight. Nothing was beyond her power nor less than exquisite.

During the Third Month, at the Festival of Winding Water,

she sat by the little sparkling stream in the garden of the women's palaces where the peach trees were exceptionally fine and floated her cup in the shallows. It had been intended that she do no more than watch from the steps of the water pavilion, but at the last minute she had gone down impulsively to sit on the young grass. Seeing this, Dōkyō followed her and sat a few steps below.

When the little cup came floating to her hand she picked it up and sipped the wine and set it down again. How the cold water tingled on her fingertips! "In my spring garden the peach blossoms glow," she recited. She was smiling. How would he link the verse? Behind him the pale blossoms set off the elegance of his figure. How beautiful he was. The little cup went spinning gently to his hand and he reached out for it: "And on the flower-lit path beneath," he said, "Lo! a maiden!" He caught the cup and raised it, lifting his eyes to hers. How she loved him!

Again, in the Fifth Month, during the Iris Festival, they sat together on the high steps of the Festival Palace to watch the archery contest on the parade ground below . . . and in the Seventh Month, on the dais of the old Shinto Hall for the sumo wrestling . . . at the moon viewing in the Eighth Month . . . for the court dances during the Chrysanthemum Festival in the Ninth. Always he placed himself behind and a little away from her, but no one was deceived. She had made him her equal.

She had never been very interested in her mirror, and since taking her vows she had tried to refrain from looking into it at all. But it became important to her now as she was approaching fifty. It was Dōkyō's insistence on her charm that made her wonder. Am I really so beautiful?

"Oh yes, Your Majesty. Beautiful!" her women said. But they were young, she thought. They had not seen her mother.

Nevertheless, at the time of the Chrysanthemum Festival when she sipped the tea brewed with the petals, as others did, for long life, she also took the silk floss that was used to protect the blossoms through the frosty nights and pressed it against her face, for they had told her, "It will keep you youthful."

Why am I doing this, who have given myself to Buddha, she reproved herself. But when she said "Buddha" she thought "Dōkyō." And then, in an effort to say first what she feared other people might be saying, she took her brush and inkstone and copied out:

Old old woman that I am,
How could I have sunk so deep in love
Like a helpless child!

Later Dōkyō found the paper and it made him laugh—he who so seldom lost his grave composure. "So you have grown old," he said. "So very old!"

"Not young." She hid her face.

"So. Perhaps you can teach me something out of your ancient wisdom."

She too smiled slightly. She was ashamed. "You know I cannot teach you, who are my teacher."

"But you are nearer to paradise now than when you were young, I suppose." His voice was teasing. "While I am trapped in perpetual immaturity, neither here nor there." He was watching the side of her cheek as she turned away—still fresh, or skillfully powdered, he did not know—and the tender little ear. "And need to be taught to grow ancient, as you have, and wise."

"I was only thinking old for love."

"Are we too old for love?" He was grave now.

"Are we?" Her mouth was trembling as she turned to him.

How brave she is, he thought, seeing the little sagging lines of her face and her pleading eyes. And he smiled again as he assured her, "Never too old."

That winter she had the main hall of the western compound rebuilt and refurnished and herself designed the garden with a stream and waterfall and distant vistas planted with groves of trees and had them bring some deer from the Kofuku-ji grounds to wander there, and in the spring, when it was finished, gave it to Dōkyō as a palace for the King of the Buddhist Law.

After that she concentrated on the Saidai-ji temple, where

now the Image Hall and Lecture Hall had been completed and the foundations were being laid for two pagodas. She planned to make it more extensive even than the Todai-ji with all its halls and colonnades and gates and storehouses.

The ministers of the Grand Council, meeting privately, selected Kibi no Makibi as the one most able to remonstrate with her about the cost of all this building. Her expenditures far exceeded her resources.

"Oh, they are concerned again about the power of the temples," she replied. "That is not new. They complained in this way even in my father's time." And she gave orders that the Palace Shinto Hall be rebuilt with a roof of lapis lazuli and painted with lavish pictures, "So they cannot say that I always favor the Buddhists."

After that she embarked on a totally new palace complex built on the grand scale. As there had been a detached Imperial Palace at Kuni in her father's time, and the Hora Palace in Ōmi, she would build her own in Kawachi near the Yuge family center where Dōkyō had been born, and she would call it the Yuge Palace in his honor. No one could stop her.

In fact, she was growing irritable as the months went by, resenting even the mildest counsel and bridling at advice. She said the days went by too fast for her to stop and listen. She was often breathless and she did not sleep. Sometimes at Palace entertainments she grew almost boisterous and at the service for the anniversary of her father's death she suddenly stood up while the priests were intoning and began to talk in a loud voice.

Dōkyō had special rites performed for her health, though he dared not tell her. But her ladies said what she needed was the soothing company of someone her own sex, someone she could confide in—like a sister. So they suggested timidly that she send for Fuwa and were relieved when she agreed. It had been three years since Shioyaki's death, after all, and surely any bitterness must be gone by now. It was not the Empress' fault that he had joined Nakamaro. She could not be blamed.

Fuwa had been living with her little children since her husband's death in the small house that had been left to him outside the temple grounds. She had no relatives among the powerful to support her and the house had gone without repairs, the garden was desolate. Sometimes the moonlight came through the broken roof and she sat in a dead-white pool of it and watched her sleeping son. Grandson of the Imperial Prince Niitabe, great-grandson of Emperor Temmu—and on her own side grandson of Emperor Shōmu, although she had not been recognized. There he lay, the little Prince, in a worn garment of her own and she alone to protect him. So when she received the summons to the Palace she went gladly.

The Empress was entranced by the little boy who looked so like his father with his finely marked eyebrows and black merry eyes. She often called for him to come and play in her garden and arranged for several little boys of his own age to keep him company. She liked to watch them running through the trees in their bright silk jackets. And when she called them and they stood before her panting with their cheeks ablaze, their glossy hair bound up in loops beside their ears and their eyes shining, she found them wonderfully charming and lavished such gifts on them that her ladies gasped.

One day she said to Fuwa, "You think that I have everything, but you have him." Quite suddenly she began to weep and Fuwa thought: Perhaps she will make him Heir Apparent. But she said nothing.

When the boy was five she arranged for tutors to begin his education. "He shall have the best," she said to Fuwa. "He is bright, and so active!" The child was running from tree to tree rolling a ball before him. "First he shall learn to play football properly!" she laughed.

There was a young man, Waké Kiyomaro, who was a distinguished hunter and loved sports of every kind. His sister Hōkin was a nun who had served her at the Hokke-ji, and whom she trusted. "I shall have Kiyomaro teach him." So toward the end of the Third Month she instructed Kiyomaro to set out the trees for the football field—the pine and willow and maple and flowering cherry in their tubs at the four corners—and dress the little boys in their brightest costumes and instruct them in the art of kicking the ball with their insteps and keeping it aloft.

Watching them as she sat among her courtiers she was again entranced. She thought the shrill cries of the boys were like the piping of birds, and Kiyomaro looked very handsome in his bright green tunic and his trousers laced to the knees. Fuwa's little Prince was the best of them all, she thought, as he leapt about on his sturdy young legs and managed to kick the ball.

She turned to Fuwa, full of delight. "He is surely the best," she said.

"If you think so," Fuwa said carefully. She hoped this might be the time. "If you think so, perhaps you will honor him."

"In what way?"

The question was rather absent, so Fuwa went on more quickly. "He is the grandson of the Imperial Prince Niitabe . . ."

The Empress abruptly turned away and leaned forward as though to watch the game. However, Fuwa had consulted the *Book* when she planned this conversation and it had foretold this "*difficulty at the beginning*" (as a young plant struggles with difficulty out of the hard earth) but later promised "*supreme success*." So she went on, "He is bright and active, as you so graciously have said, and can be educated here in your own household, under your own direction . . ." She hated the tone in her own voice . . . "So what more fitting than if he were to be the *Kōtaishi* . . ."

"I do not want to hear any more about it!" The voice was cold and she stopped as though the conversation might end there. But in a moment she went on: "They have been pestering me to name the Heir Apparent ever since I took the throne! Perhaps you did not know, perhaps I should forgive your ignorance. But how am I to forgive your presumption? Because you are my father's daughter, does that give you the right?"

She made no pretense of looking at the play in the garden but spoke as to the treetops, pale with anger. "They are merely waiting for my death when they ask about my successor. They do not care for me or for the land. No. Each has his protégé, his prince, whom he controls. Oh, I understand them very well with their concern about a successor. Successors are named on the deathbed, they know that!"

She was silent for a long time but she was breathing hard. Fuwa could see the rise and fall of her stiff silk robe, she could even hear the rustle of it and the sound of her breathing.

"And now you come to me, under my protection, in the guise of a sister, and say, 'I have a son who would mount the High Seat after you—and I hope it will be soon!' Oh, you will deny it. You did not ask how soon. But that is of no importance in any case. Your son will never be in line for the succession."

She turned abruptly to look at Fuwa, who sat with her head bowed as though ashamed. "Yes, you have a charming son—grandson of Prince Niitabe, as you remind me. But could you think that I would so offend my mother's spirit? Do you think me so unfilial? No, the boy will never be *Kōtaishi*. Never!"

Her voice had risen so that others turned to look and she stopped and said more quietly, but still with vehemence, "In any case I shall not be fool enough to choose a successor now, just yet! Let them wait for the time you are all waiting for, when I lie on my deathbed and you gather around!"

If one could judge by words and soft expression, one would have said that Fuwa was contrite. It was as though she had made it her life's aim to please. When she was in attendance on the Empress she acted as her mirror, laughing when she laughed or frowning solemnly at appropriate times. Indeed, sometimes she actually held the mirror when the Empress was made ready for the day.

"You hair is still so lustrous, so beautiful," she said one early morning.

"Oh no," brushing at it quickly with her hand, "it has grown long again. I must have it clipped."

"What a pity! What a pity!" Fuwa cried. "Exceptions should be made for exceptional beauty. The gardener does not cut down the loveliest flowers while they are in bloom. It would be a crime to do so."

"But I must not take pride in it!"

"Perhaps not for yourself. But is it wrong to offer beauty for others to enjoy?"

"It is not that beautiful, surely?" peering in the mirror.

"But we all say so!" Fuwa cried, while the others nodded.

"Then indeed I must have it clipped. No, no, I must keep my vows . . ."

So the little ceremony was performed, as it was periodically, and Fuwa was present to take up a lock and slip it in her sleeve.

What was the purpose of this lock of hair? Fuwa took it and wrapped it in her scarf and kept it hidden while she went to find the sorceress who lived behind the temple in her old neighborhood. The sorceress was a deceptive woman, small and round, who sold rice dumplings in the West Market, but her powers were formidable. She was adept at unearthing hidden treasure and had studied the art of flying about at will. When they were neighbors she and Fuwa had sometimes pooled their strengths and worked some things together—finding lost pins or straying husbands, speaking with the dead. They had never harmed anyone and never would (these were the sorceress' words) but sometimes they supplied the small wooden images and the nails and gave instructions how they should be fixed to a tree in the shrine courtyard at the hour of the Ox.

Fuwa went to her and said, "I need a skull."

"A skull is hard to come by, dear. There are not many about. Will the skull of a dog do?"

"I need a human skull."

"Well, it might cost you something. A good deal." They were in her kitchen and she had dumplings in a bamboo steamer. The steam was rising, dampening the cloth, and she was impatient to leave for the market. "It would hardly be worth it, I should think. A skull is so costly these days, isn't it."

"I need it."

"Well then. When?"

"I should like to have it the next time the moon is new."

"That'll be the Second Day of the Hare, isn't it? And where

shall I bring it? Oh." The thought had struck her that her old neighbor was a lady in the Palace now, a place she herself could not enter.

"I will come here. And you must go with me to the river near the Sanjō bridge where the bank dips down to the water's edge, I have seen it."

So, in the hour of the Ox when the night was darkest and the moon no more than the thinnest eyebrow on the dome of the sky (the Second Day of the Hare, as the sorceress had said) the two of them went groping down the riverbank, feeling the muddy sand with their feet till they reached the water and squatted down. Fuwa had with her the lock of hair, still wrapped up in her scarf, and the sorceress carried a woven basket that usually carried dumplings but now held a skull.

"Give me the skull," Fuwa whispered, unfolding the scarf. And when it was taken from the basket she examined it and nodded and placed it on the scarf beside the hair.

"Whose is it?" the sorceress whispered. She meant the hair.

But Fuwa did not seem to hear her as she took up the skull again and then the little lock and pressed it against the shadowy dome and then by the brow and then above the black hole that was the temple.

The sorceress watched her. She did not know this style. "You have brought very little," still in a whisper. "Is that all you could find?" And when Fuwa was silent, still holding up the skull and staring at it, pressing the hair against it here and there, "That is not at all the way to do it. You have not brought enough." And again, with some impatience, "How will you fix it on? You must be able to make a wig of it, you should have known!" She was growing cold.

"I will bind it with my scarf," Fuwa said in her normal voice.

"Shh, be quiet!"

Fuwa's scarf indeed had magic properties. Simply by waving it she could clear a room of insects, or by tying a knot in it remember what she had never known. Now she wound it carefully around the skull. (As though it had the toothache, the sorceress thought. She was disgusted.) And tucked the lock of hair beneath it and began her spell.

"Karite kitte mamane mane manye anye . . ."

The sorceress recognized the foreign words—a spell from India! "That is a Buddhist spell," she hissed. It was a kind of magic she did not know.

"I tell it backwards," Fuwa snapped. The spell was broken and she had to go back again to the beginning.

"Karite kitte mamane mane manye anye." Then a pause. "Muktatame mukte sante samitavi . . ."

"What was that noise?"

The City Guard had found them and scrambled down the bank. They looked at the skull with horror and then took them in.

After a lengthy hearing the sorceress was absolved of actions threatening the realm. She had not known Fuwa's intention nor that it was the Empress' hair that she had stolen. (She was absolved, but her license to sell dumplings was revoked.) And Fuwa, through the gracious intervention of Her Majesty, was allowed to live. She was merely banished from the capital and her son was exiled to a different place—in the land of Tosa, far away.

As for the Empress herself, the incantation, although it was interrupted, seemed to have some effect. She felt cold all over and complained of exhaustion for many months, and often she said in a quiet voice, "I did not know how she hated me. I did not know she hated me so much."

That was not the only blow the Empress took that year. In the Ninth Month, not long after Fuwa's banishment and just two years after the miraculous discovery of the relic of Buddha, she heard two of her ladies talking with a young minor counselor.

"Do you mean glass, really glass?"

"Oh yes, it was nothing more than a hoax, you know."

"A hoax?"

"I have suspected it all along . . ."

The Empress called for Dōkyō.

"They say it was a hoax!" She was so agitated that her voice rose high and broke over the word.

He paused a long time before he chose his answer. Then he said soberly, "I have heard so."

"I cannot believe it. So magnificent! So beautiful! And they said glass."

"So I heard."

"You believe it? You?"

"Well, I have never trusted Kishin." And when she was silent, "He is a man of questionable character. In fact," he took a breath, "I was doubtful from the first."

"So you thought, Let them make a fool of her," she burst out. "Let them play tricks on her!"

He said nothing.

"I suppose you laughed with the rest?"

"No. Never. But you seemed so happy."

"Yes, I was happy. Prattling over a handful of glass beads! Exclaiming! Clapping my hands! A spectacle!"

"No, not that. We were pleased for you."

"We?"

"Those who rejoiced with you. Perhaps it was really true—a miracle. I truly hoped so, for your sake."

"You hoped so," she was calmer. "But you doubted."

"Yes."

"And now you can say quite casually, 'They are glass.'"

"Yes. In fact," he paused. "I have questioned Kishin."

"And he admitted it—a hoax perpetrated on his Sovereign?"

"Not a hoax exactly. A proof of the Buddha's favor, which is true enough. And to please you."

After a long time she said, "I am not pleased." And then, "Before you go, I commission you to punish him. I do not want to hear that he remains in the capital. I do not want to hear of him again, or of this matter."

"Before I go?" He tried to smile. "Are you dismissing me also?"

"Oh, I am so weary," she said, turning away, and he knew she had not dismissed him. She had not mentioned how he had benefited from the miracle—perhaps it had not occurred to her?—and he felt the tension leave him in relief.

After a little while he was able to say, in his most gentle tones, "You are weary. Let me help you."

"Yes, help me, help me." She turned, holding out her hands.

He took them and was her comforter and helper, sharing her burdens. And when the new year came, while she rested, he held court in the palace of the King of the Buddhist Law, and all the high Court nobles and priests of the Nara temples came there instead of to her Court to bring their congratulations, as to an emperor.

CHAPTER XXX

Next summer the Chancellor used the seal of the King of the Buddhist Law for the first time. He said it had the authority of the Imperial seal and the Empress upheld him.

"He has gone too far," Momokawa said. He was speaking to Kibi no Makibi and they were alarmed. "What is to stop him?"

Kibi nodded. "I am afraid it is a case of the ivory chopsticks." And when Momokawa stared rather blankly at him, he expounded: "In ancient times in China, King Chou ordered a pair of chopsticks made of ivory, and when Chi Tzu the Good heard about this he was disturbed and said:

" 'Once the king has ivory chopsticks he will not be content with ordinary bowls;
He will want cups of rhinoceros horn and jade.
Instead of beans and vegetables he will ask for delicacies like elephant's tail and baby leopard.
He will demand embroidered robes and splendid mansions. His greed will have no end.' "

"And so it transpired. The King became a tyrant, tortured his subjects with hot irons and caroused in a lake of wine."

Momokawa's way of listening was to keep his concentration on his own thoughts. "I believe he has his eye on the throne.

Incredible. Of course it is impossible. But what is to stop him?"

"In order to stop him we must think back to where he started," Kibi said, tipping his head sideways. He felt that this was pertinent, but Momokawa only repeated heavily, "When he uses his seal for Imperial documents, he has gone too far."

"I think," Kibi repeated, "we must remember where he started, who he is, and where his power lies." And when Momokawa did not answer, answered himself: "He started as a doctor-priest, one of many. I am not saying he was not well schooled, not devout, not able, has not gathered a powerful second government around him. I am saying only that he rose to where he is through the Empress' promotions."

Momokawa looked at him as though to say, Of course. He was still thinking, What is to stop him, without going further to seek an answer.

Kibi went on with his analysis: "So that is where he has come from and where he is. And what is important now is how he stands in her eyes. She has made him Chancellor of the Realm, she has given him a palace as King of the Buddhist Law, she allows him to accept the New Year greetings. All these things. Does she ever think, I wonder, that he will ask for more?"

"What more is there to ask for?"

"Who is to say? My point is that the important thing is how the Empress thinks and feels—how she perceives him."

It was beyond the realm of Momokawa's mind to harbor thoughts against the Empress. Far beneath thought, however, in his innermost being, he assumed that she was wholly under the influence of her favorite and the other Buddhist priests. He stared at the old scholar and said nothing.

Kibi could read him very well, however. "She has a very good mind of her own, you must realize," he said. "Delicate but precise. She can make decisions. It is only a matter of reaching her, of persuading . . ." He paused.

"No, not persuading. She must be shown. She must see this priest, this man, as she has not seen before. Yes. It must come upon her suddenly, like a great light, so that she sees quite clearly how he is using her."

Momokawa was slightly shocked by this conversation. He felt it was not respectful to the Sovereign. Besides, he thought, how was one to shine such a light on the Chancellor? Fantastic.

"There are many sides to her character," Kibi went on, feeling his way. "She is of exceptional filial piety and always observes the rites. Her manner and bearing at the Great Thanksgiving Festival—you saw it—were exemplary. Even the ancients who laid down the ritual would have approved . . .

"Yes, she has great respect for the gods, great respect. She is especially attentive to the God Hachiman . . ." He paused, head to one side, eyes squinting. "The God Hachiman whom she brought to the capital in her first reign . . ."

"Yes," Momokawa said, when he grew tired of waiting. "I remember it."

"That message from Hachiman . . . that oracle . . . was brought up from Usa by a nun, a priestess . . ."

"Yes."

"And the Empress was deeply moved. She was exalted . . ."

Next month, which was the Eighth and very hot, the nun Hōkin was granted an audience. The night was stifling and the Empress' ladies had set a little mountain of chopped ice on a tray beside her. She sat with one hand resting on the edge of the tray and with the other slowly waving a large fan. Her thin summer garment was unfastened to reveal her breast and her whole attitude was unguarded.

Even so, when Hōkin bowed and then looked up and saw her in the yellow light of the lamp, she seemed almost too regal to approach. Her impulse was to remain there silently in her low bow, or to retreat. But Kibi had said it was for the Empress' own sake they must awaken her, for the sake of the whole empire. So she came forward.

When they had finished with small talk about the heat, their health, and the affairs of the nunnery, Hōkin said: "Word has been received of an oracle. A message from the Head Shinto Priest of Dazaifu." Hōkin herself had once served with the

Buddhist nuns attached to the shrine at Usa and knew the Head Priest from those days. It was quite possible that the message should come to her.

"An oracle?"

"A message from the Hachiman shrine. Or that is the report." She did not want to appear too credulous if the Empress should sense duplicity.

"This message came to you?" It was not improbable.

"It was received today. Only this evening."

"Well?"

"The oracle, as it was reported to me, dealt with the Chancellor of the Realm."

"The Chancellor?" Her voice took on more animation and she straightened a little and drew her garment closed.

"Yes, he."

"And the oracle?"

Hōkin gazed at the lumps of ice that were melting on the tray. "The god has said, according to his priestess, that he would be pleased, would rejoice indeed, if the Chancellor were to be Sovereign."

"Sovereign?" She was shocked.

"That the land would prosper and there would be peace among all people, high and low . . ."

If he were to be Sovereign! What did it mean? She recalled how often she had dreamed of a true Buddha-land here on this earth. Her father spoke of it too. Was this, then, the way?

Hōkin saw the eager light that flushed her face. She is going to believe, she thought. "The oracle was quite clear—as it was reported."

The Empress stared at her. "But he is not of the Imperial line!"

Hōkin said nothing.

"This message. How did it come to you?"

"From the Head Shinto Priest, Sunge Asamaro . . ."

"A letter? Let me see it."

"Word came. But not written. It was a message, brought by a messenger from Dazaifu . . ."

"But from the shrine at Usa, from the god?" It was possible.

She remembered the arrival of the god's cart and the great procession into Nara and how he had supported her reign, how he had helped her father to find gold for the Great Buddha. The priests at Usa were faithful men . . . But could they have been mistaken? How could a man born of the people—no matter how good, how gifted—inherit the godhead of the Heavenly Line? And yet . . .

"The ice is melting. Take it away," she said to her ladies. And to Hōkin, gazing at her for a long time while the nun kept her eyes respectfully lowered, "I will see about it. This is very grave. I will see."

For the next few days she did nothing, while Hōkin reported to the ministers that she had done as they had asked but could not tell what would come of it.

"Did she believe?"

"I cannot say."

"Did the news dismay her? Make her sad?"

"Neither sad nor happy, though she wondered at it."

"Who is to get word to the Chancellor?"

"He has been told," Kibi said.

When at last the Empress called for him, Dōkyō was prepared. He had been surprised by the message, so unexpected. He had thought for a moment that the old scholar was making some sort of joke. But Kibi had appeared very solemn and spoke quite openly. "I do not approve of it," he had said. "It would upset the relationships of Sovereign to subject and of the Buddhist hierarchy to the Court. But of course the word of the god must not be taken lightly."

"I am overwhelmed," Dōkyō had said.

And Kibi thought: He is hooked.

So when the Empress told him and he seemed not surprised, she knew that he had been told.

Yes, he had heard, he said. And he marveled.

"You think there could not have been a mistake? It has seemed to me unlikely that the god, who has been so strong a support of my family, should suggest an end to it."

"But need there be an end? Not soon at any rate. The oracle did not say that your reign should be shortened. You must rule as you have, of course, until you tire. As I see it, it is then, when you come to the time that you choose to leave the world, that the oracle suggests . . ."

"I did not hear that part." Her voice was dry.

"Please. We must not quarrel."

"From Amaterasu's time, at the birth of the world," she said, her voice suddenly grown strong, "from the time of Emperor Jimmu when our history began, from Sovereign to Sovereign through the years, the line has not been broken . . ."

"Please do not think . . ."

"Sovereign to Sovereign of that line. And I am the forty-eighth!"

"Please do not think that I presume . . ."

After a time she said very softly, "I would give you anything." And he knew that she was crying.

He waited, willing her to listen, before he said in his most gentle manner, "We have often spoken, you and I, of building a true Buddha-land here on these sacred islands."

"And you think . . ." He could hardly hear her. "And you think that a Buddhist priest as Sovereign would bring this about?"

"I think—and, you know, we have often agreed on this—that all the world should be governed by the True Law."

"And do you think," she stopped to clear her throat, "and do you think you are the man?"

"No, no. Not I. I know my shortcomings," he recovered himself. And even as he spoke the words he knew the truth of them. How far he had descended from the purity of his meditations! How worldly he had become, grasping at these transient things. For a moment he saw himself with clarity and loathed how he had fallen . . .

And yet. And yet. Who could deny that he was better able to rule wisely than she was who had seemed so hesitant this past year and who leaned so heavily on his advice? Courtiers complained of his promotions, he knew that, but he deserved them. He was not ashamed. He had served her and she rewarded him no more than was his due. Of course there was her love for him, he was aware of that. And he was bound to her as well. Affection, love, he pondered. What was the reality of that?

He must not be seduced again by those properties of the six senses. The truth, he knew, was not in them but in the Absolute. He must beware of the knowledge that corrupts the mind, that arises from the idea of self.

All is illusion. He winced to think he had to remind himself of that—so busy he had been with worldly preoccupations. All, everything, outside the true reality of the universal Mind of the True Spirit, is but illusion.

Against this teaching in which he had steeped himself, the world of the gods and the history of the August Ancestors seemed wanting, and he thought again of the oracle—whether true or false. In any case, might it not be a call, he thought, an opportunity to lead the nation out of its illusions into the pure land of Enlightenment?

His face had taken on an otherworldly glow with this thought, and she was watching him. He felt her eyes and looked up.

"Every man has his shortcomings," she said. "But yours are of a different sort. You live above the rest of us, in a higher world."

Gratitude flooded him for her trust. He would serve her and serve the people. They needed him.

And indeed, even now when there was pressing business to attend to, it was he who was called to go.

When he had left she went alone to the bed-space of her inner room and lay as she had often lain before when life oppressed her, stretched on her back with her eyes unseeing on the canopy above.

What more had she to give him? She would give him her life, she thought. She would give him anything at all. But this?

She closed her eyes and for a long time thought of nothing but the darkness that pressed down on her, the oppression. And when at last she opened her eyes again she sighed so deeply it was like a groan.

She would give him her life. But this that he wanted was not hers to give! She sat up restlessly and turned and lay down again. Perhaps it was true: If he were Sovereign the land would become the Buddha-land she had dreamed of. The oracle had said the country would prosper. Perhaps the god had really spoken as Hōkin reported. Hachiman had always supported her, her father and herself. It was not impossible. Her heart lightened.

But a man of common background? Could that be? To enter the Heavenly Line of her ancestors? To inherit her father's place on the High Seat? Could such a man pray to the gods, could he manage the seasons and the hearts of the people, bringing peace and order as her father had—as she had tried to do? Was it possible?

She sat again and put her cold hands to her cheeks. Whom could she ask for help? Who was a friend whose confidence and wisdom she could trust? She longed for her mother, even for Shihi from the olden days. Fuwa had betrayed her, and now perhaps Hōkin, who could tell? Should she bring the matter to her advisers? Kibi no Makibi? Kibi she could trust. But then, she knew what he would say.

I am alone in this, she thought. As always, I am alone. Without Dōkyō I am a poor creature, worthless and alone.

Although she wept some in the night and felt the pain of loneliness like a stone in her chest, and let her mind go back and forth in torment, aimlessly, by morning she had decided. She would send a messenger herself, a man whom she could trust, and ask again of Hachiman the words of his oracle.

The man she selected was Kiyomaro. He is young, she thought, but loyal. And while he knelt by the garden steps below her—for he was still of the lowest of the Court ranks—she told him of the mission she had in mind for him:

"I had a dream last night," she said, "a dream that a messenger from Hachiman of Usa approached me." She watched his sturdy figure kneeling respectfully, his head bent while he waited. "The messenger said that the god requested that I send Hōkin to his shrine to receive an oracle." Again she waited, but there was no sign that he had heard of this. "But Hōkin is no longer young. So you will go to Usa for me, telling no one, and bring the god's words to me as they are told to you."

Then Kiyomaro bowed very low and left her and arranged for horses for his trip. But before he left the capital he went to the Hokke-ji to see his sister and was amazed to find she knew already of the Empress' dream. And while he lingered there—for she pampered him, her younger brother—the adviser Momokawa came, and then the scholar Kibi no Makibi, Great Minister of the Right. They too knew of the Empress' dream and of the mission he was sent upon.

"You know what word to bring back," Momokawa said.

He did not know.

"But I have told you," Hōkin said. And to the others, "He is a good man and will do what is right and good."

Then Kibi lectured him: "Remember, goodness cannot be obtained until what is difficult has been duly done. Only he who does what is difficult may be called truly good."

Kiyomaro wondered if it could be good if, even though difficult, it was not right. Should he not simply ask for the message from the Head Priest and report it back?

"Yes, yes," Kibi nodded. "Ask for the message and report it dutifully, that is what is right."

And Momokawa: "Hōkin can tell you what the message is. But go to the Head Priest, as you say. The Empress expects it. The Head Priest will tell you." And when he saw the look of doubt on Kiyomaro's face, "Just do as you have been told to do. We will protect you."

So he started off, but had not gone beyond the turning to the Yakushi-ji when a man ran up and stopped him and asked him to come aside to where a carriage waited behind the temple wall. "A matter of grave importance to the Empress."

The carriage was of the ordinary kind used by members of the Court, drawn by a pair of oxen and with only two attendants standing by, and Kiyomaro, when he had dismounted and approached, was surprised to see the Chancellor of the Realm lean out and extend his hand. He greeted him by rank and name and begged his pardon for intruding on his time. "You are starting off on a long journey? And you go alone?"

"Yes." Kiyomaro was uneasy. What did the Chancellor want?

"To Dazaifu? To the shrine at Usa?"

"Yes."

"Please, sit by me," Dōkyō invited. "Do not stand on rank."

The carriage was large but rather dark, austere. Curtains were drawn across the split bamboo and it smelled of sandalwood when he stepped into it. The Chancellor was full of grace as he moved to make room for him.

"You hold the Fifth Rank junior grade?"

Kiyomaro nodded.

"But a young man of your accomplishments could rise much higher." And: "You go to receive a message from the god." It was not a question and Kiyomaro felt he need not answer. "And perhaps that message has been given to you—even before you arrive at Usa, even before you leave Nara?" He paused. "That would be carrying a lie, wouldn't it? Even a sacrilege. To put the wishes of a human being, no matter how sincere, into the mouth of a god?

"I suggest you go instead with an open mind. Consult the priestess of the shrine. Let her hear the words of the god when she enters her trance. Then let her give the message as she receives it.

"And I suggest to you—" His voice was firm, persuasive, and his face seemed to loom very large as he leaned to the young man. "I suggest to you that the message that was received before—the dream the Empress dreamed," he smiled, though there was no mirth in it, no friendliness at all, "was true, was the true message sent by the god from Usa."

"I do not know," Kiyomaro faltered. "I am sent to find out."

"No." Again the Chancellor's voice was firm, almost threatening. "You were not sent for that, but to bring back a falsehood." And then, softening, "I do not mean to frighten you." He put his hand on Kiyomaro's arm. "There is no need to be afraid. You must trust me, as the Empress does. You must keep in mind the welfare of your Sovereign and of the state. You have seen how the country has prospered since she made me

Chancellor of the Realm, since I have taken charge from the palace of the King of the Buddhist Law . . ."

He drew back, smiling once again. "These are merely titles. But they enable me to lift up those who are deserving. Just as the Empress could make a king out of a doctor-priest," he made a little gesture, self-deprecating, "so can I now make major counselors out of worthy young men, be they even of the Fifth Rank junior grade!" His smile was frank.

But Kiyomaro did not smile in return. He sat so still beside the Chancellor it was as though he squirmed.

Dōkyō sighed. "I will give you some advice. Men of wisdom do not tamper with the gods. The fury of a god, should you cross him and ignore his words, is even greater than the fury of men. I should not tempt either, if I were you. You are a peaceful man, I know. But perhaps you have enemies you are not aware of? You are a brave man, I am sure. But have you foreseen the danger? Do you love your life?"

When Kiyomaro did not answer, Dōkyō heard his own voice echoing and his own words hanging there in the dark, and he drew away from the young man and sat back. His face was tense, drawn in, and suddenly in the confines of the carriage there was an aura of hatred.

Why does he hate me, Kiyomaro thought. And then, when he dared to look into the Chancellor's face, wondered if the hate was inward. It was terrible to see.

He was so shaken that he had ridden down the length of the city and into the fields before he freed himself of that thick atmosphere of loathing that had filled the carriage and the sound of a voice—so pleasing and yet so threatening—that had enthralled him.

Next month, the Ninth, on the twenty-fourth day, Kiyomaro returned from Usa. He had spoken to the Head Shinto Priest and visited the shrine. All the way back he had thought about the things he had been told.

At the news of his arrival Dōkyō hastened to the Palace to be by the Empress' side. He saw the nun Hōkin sitting with the Empress' ladies by their separate screens, but he had made sure the young man should be met as he passed the barrier and had given orders that he should speak to no one on the way.

Now Kiyomaro, still in his traveling clothes, stood in the garden beside the steps and was aware of the Chancellor beside the Empress and of the others all around—the whole Court gathered, dead still and listening.

"Well, Kiyomaro, welcome home," the Empress said. And the Chancellor, without waiting, "What message do you bring?"

Kiyomaro had thought deeply on his long journey home. He loved the Empress and he loved the land. He had seen the people of the countryside, such men and women as he had never known: her people, the Sovereign's. It was the time of year the farmers called White Dew and he had seen the rice fields gleam in the rising sun. How beautiful the land was, loved by the gods!

He heard the Empress speaking, her voice high and thin. "Yes, Kiyomaro, speak to us. What is the message that you bring from Usa?"

Kiyomaro closed his eyes. The words of the Head Priest had been derisive. He had been shocked. But the truth of the message that he brought he had learned by himself on his long ride, the message from the land.

"Since this Land of the Reed Plain has existed," he said slowly in his strong young voice, "the distinction between the Sovereign and his subjects has been clear. An Emperor ought always to be chosen from the Imperial Family of the Line of the Sun. No ordinary mortal ever has been Emperor, and none shall ever be."

Then in a lower voice, as though he faltered, "Those are the words of the god."

After the Empress withdrew to her own pavilion the atmosphere in the Great Hall became triumphant—or so Dōkyō felt—almost exultant. It was as though the whole room laughed, though there was utter silence. He left and hurried after her. He did not know what she would do.

He found her standing by a painted screen in her inner room, her hand resting on the frame. How thin she looked, how fragile! And there was a lassitude about her as she turned and crept into her bed-space like a child. Or an old woman, he thought suddenly. It frightened him. He was afraid she might escape once more into illness and oblivion as she had done when her mother died. He sat beside her and tried to rouse her into anger.

"They must be punished! An insult to the throne!"

"The throne? It was not aimed at me."

"Why, their whole purpose was to deceive you with that false oracle so as to give themselves more standing in your eyes."

"But you, I think, believed it."

"I am not important. It is the deception, the low trick they played upon their Sovereign that must be punished."

She turned, almost smiling, though her face was drawn. "But I knew that she was lying all along."

"You must punish them."

"I must punish Hōkin and that young man?" She put her hand across her eyes. "You think that they alone devised the scheme?"

"They and their conspirators. They must be punished."

"And you too?" She took her hand away and looked at him. Strange that the force of her gaze could be so strong, upward from where she lay.

"And I?" He felt his face flush.

"Yes. And you. What was the purpose of their scheme but to show me your ambition."

"No. In what way? In what way?"

"In what way?" She was still looking at him very hard. "In what way did I observe your secret thoughts, your ambition? Why, in the way your face lighted at the suggestion. You would be Sovereign! Ruler of the Heavenly Sun-line! You, of the Yuge family. From the provinces!"

"No. Never. I did not seek it. I thought it was an offering

from the god." And pausing, more softly: "Is it extraordinary that I believed it, or half believed? I was never schooled in treachery. Who would have dreamed that they would lie, would *dupe* their Sovereign? It is *that* that is unbelievable. What was my choice but to believe the god had sent some message of that sort?"

"But you are not a child. Intrigues abound at Court."

"Intrigues, yes. But insults to the throne?"

"I have been insulted and made light of before now. I have been intrigued against and threatened and deceived . . ." She had closed her eyes and tears were coming from under the pale lids.

"But this must not go unpunished. It is not only you and your sacred person, but the Sovereignty itself. And I too, and my position. They hate the Buddhist Law."

"Well, do as you like then," still with her eyes closed. "Make a proclamation so that the people may hear it. Only say," she put her hand out, groping for him, "only say that I could easily tell that she was lying. I could easily guess from her face and the way she spoke."

"I will say it."

"You may make a proclamation in my name, and say it, and you may punish them if you like, the sister and brother. But say that we know this false report was not made by them alone but by others as well, and we know who the others are. But we will not punish them because we are merciful . . ."

"Yes."

"But they must change themselves and their attitude and be always faithful, because of the mercy I have shown."

"I will do everything you say." His voice was very low, as in a sickroom, and she nodded, still with her eyes closed, slipping away.

Word spread that the Empress was ill and there was panic among the princes, for she had not named her successor and no one dared approach her with the question.

Her proclamation was read out in Court, including the punishments: Hōkin was given the name of a worm and banished to the west. And Kiyomaro was stripped of his rank and sent to Osumi where the Hayato lived and his name was altered to mean "dirty" when it had meant "pure."

"I promised to look out for him," Momokawa said, and sent an escort of twenty men to protect him on the way. "I do not trust the priest."

But Kibi was more concerned with the Empress. It seemed she still did not understand the danger, even after all their effort to expose it. What more could he do, he wondered, to convince her. Even a child should recognize that if a man use his seal of office as the Imperial seal it usurps the royal power and reverses the order of things.

Good government results when the ruler is ruler and the minister minister, he thought with a kind of rising irritation and perplexity. He had certainly taught her that! High should be high, low should be low. To ignore this threatens the whole edifice of the state. It presages disaster!

And yet, he thought almost in despair, she continues to uphold this man and speaks of honoring him once again, taking her Court to the Yuge palace that she had built for him there in his birthplace. He felt that he had failed as her teacher in those formative years. He would be bold enough to try again, and when she was well enough he asked for an audience.

She received him in her private residence, in an alcove where she kept some books and where an ancient panel of calligraphy hung above the window. Now, in the Eleventh Month, the sky outside was blank and the world was cold, but a brazier stood between them and when he stretched his hands to it he remembered earlier times. He spoke to her in the familiar tones of teacher to apt pupil, and when he had finished she said softly—but in such a tired voice!—that she understood. "You mean the Chancellor has no love for me but would use me and the throne itself for his own ends."

"Something like that."

"And you think," she went on, still in that tired voice, "that this is new to me, that I have no experience in such things?"

He looked up startled but he did not speak as her voice began to rise. "Oh no, you are wrong, quite wrong, my friend. I learned very early what it is to love more than I am loved. That is my history. There are some whose quality is to be loved. But that is not my fate—though I have tried!" She sounded almost gay. "Oh, I have tried!"

He saw that she was weeping and was dismayed by this exposure of her private anguish. He had not meant to hurt her.

She made an effort and began again. "You and I have known each other many years, Great Minister. You must have followed the turnings of my life, how all along I have been falsely flattered, lied to, bullied, *utilized* . . ."

She sat so long gazing out the window at the iron sky that he thought she had lost the thread of her thought, but without moving she began again, quite harshly.

"The Chancellor is ambitious. Was that unknown to me? You think I am incapable of judging men? No. You and your clique of schemers told one another, 'She is so ignorant . . .' "

Kibi's beard was trembling as he shook his head, but she went on.

" 'She is so childish in her ignorance, our Sovereign, that we must play a trick on her to open up her eyes.' "

"It was not our intention . . ." Kibi started, but he found it hard to speak.

"So you had Hōkin lie to me. I understand. But aren't you the very man who taught me the first rule of life: Honor thy parents, and serve the Emperor and revere him."

And when he was silent: "Tell me, my old teacher, isn't it the duty of a Sovereign's subjects to obey the Sovereign with respect?"

Kibi said nothing and she was unaware that tears were choking him, that old man.

"But if the balance is disturbed, and the respect withheld, who is at fault? I have often thought of this and wondered. No, I have done more than wonder." She was talking to herself. "I have examined the question and I know. It is the Sovereign who is at fault." She turned away from the bleak window restlessly. "All my August Ancestors, and my Imperial parents, too, like gods, accumulated happiness among the people and amassed glory for the Court and are revered. But I, though I have kept the rites and ceremonies faithfully, and fostered justice and relieved the poor . . ." Her mind went running on over all the efforts she had made to rule as her father had . . . "And I have had temples built, and sacred images carved and molded, and how many times have I had sutras read? and feasts and fastings for the priests? and rites of repentance and thanksgivings? And shown mercy?" she was almost fierce.

"I shall show mercy to you all," she turned at last to Kibi. "You need not be afraid. And I will go to Yuge, to the Yuge palace, to be away from you. And you and the Grand Council will remain here."

Kibi was dismissed. He bowed his head over his hands, still trembling, and retreated from her presence on his hands and knees as he had been taught to do in China long ago.

The ladies who had overheard this talk were weeping in sympathy. They did not know how to comfort her. Long after the old minister had left she sat by the brazier under the cold window, gazing out, and did not hear them when they spoke to her. Finally they took her up between them—she was very light—and led her to her inner room and called the doctors.

Dōkyō came running through the corridors and knelt beside her but she would not even turn her head to look at him. Her skin was pale against the darkness of the clove-dyed robe they had thrown over her.

"What is it, what has happened?" he asked her ladies, but they were weeping and distracted and could only tell him that she seemed tired.

"She does not speak to me!"

"No, she does not speak."

When the herbalists came with their medicines he hurried off to give instructions for special services in all the Nara temples and for the Healing Sutra to be read in every province. But when he returned she was no better and he had her ladies fix a bed for him close to her own and stayed there through the nights and days of her decline.

There were no alarming symptoms but she refused to eat,

and although she lay with her eyes closed she did not sleep. The herbalists and the exorcists did all they could, but he knew this illness was one of the soul. He had diagnosed it long ago when he came to the Hora Palace and found her alone and grieving for her mother.

"But I am here. You are not alone," he told her, often repeating it, "not alone." But she was inconsolable, it seemed, and turned away.

After a few days she revived a little and complained of dreams. "I thought I saw Oi-Ō," she said one time in a bemused faint voice. "He had a string around his neck and was playing with it in his little hands. He looked afraid, but in my dream I scolded him and told him to go away."

Another time she groaned and started up.

"If you would only let me comfort you," he said.

After a few weeks she grew stronger, strong enough to move, and early in the Twelfth Month—which is the time for sweeping out the old—they started for the Yuge palace across the hills.

The day was cold and windy, though the sky was clear, and those who had followed the Imperial cortege from the Palace gate down the great avenue and through the Rajōmon stood with their hands tucked in their sleeves and their skirts blowing off to one side.

Kibi no Makibi stood among them when the palanquin passed by and remained there with his arm raised, waving his long sleeve, even after the others had taken shelter in the gate.

He watched the slow procession as it went down the road, the oxcarts swaying in the ruts, the banners fluttering, the curtains of the carriages billowing in the wind, until it had gone a long way through the winter fields toward Mount Ikoma.

One of his former students standing near feared for his health. But when he respectfully approached to urge him to take shelter he was amazed (he reported afterward) that although there were a thousand wrinkles in the old scholar's face, he was crying like a child.

EPILOGUE

In the Eighth Month of the following year, which was the first of *Hoki* (A.D. 770) the Empress died. She had held sovereignty under the names of Kōken-Tennō and later Shōtoku-Tennō, and this was the sixth year of her second reign. She was fifty-two years old.

One of her last acts was to present to each of her old advisers a purple brocade scarf with the word "merciful" written in gold powder at each end, and her last Imperial edict instructed the priests of every temple to read the powerful sutra, the *Daihan-nya-kyo*, by the page-turning method "in order to avert calamities and counteract evil omens by the power of Wisdom and Compassion."

Shortly before her death, the one million miniature wooden pagodas that she had ordered carved for the protection of the realm at the time of Fujiwara Nakamaro's rebellion were distributed. (The charms contained in each of these little pagodas are the oldest examples of printing in existence.)

She died in the Yuge palace in Kawachi and was cremated and her ashes placed in a small pavilion on the palace grounds during the first funeral rites and while Dōkyō, her Chancellor of the Realm, assigned six thousand workers to prepare a tomb for her on the slopes of Mount Ikoma west of Nara.

When it was finished her ashes were taken there and Dōkyō

built a small hut on the hillside and lived there, praying for her soul, until rumors started that he was plotting again and he was exiled to the far north.

When she was dying, Fujiwara Nagate, Kibi no Makibi, Fujiwara Momokawa, and several others consulted about the appointment of a successor. Momokawa, who was more stubborn than the rest, succeeded in having the Imperial Prince Shirakabe named *Kōtaishi.* The Prince was sixty-two years old and suffering from neuralgia, but his son was a strong, well-educated man and Momokawa had his eye on him.

Ironically, Shirakabe, who became Emperor Konin on the Empress' death, wanted to appoint his daughter, rather than this son, as his own successor, but the ministers and advisers, almost to a man, said: No more women. (They considered them too easily influenced by Buddhist priests.) And Momokawa stood outside the Palace in mute demonstration for forty days until the Emperor gave in.

In 781, Emperor Konin abdicated in favor of his son, who took the name of Kammu and became one of the few of the one hundred and twenty-four sovereigns in the annals of Japan whom historians consider strong and able rulers in their own right.

However, at this time the city of Nara was still surrounded by great wealthy temples with their communities of influential priests whose power rivaled that of the Court itself. And in 784, Emperor Kammu solved that problem by picking up his capital and removing it to a new site at Nagaoka over the hills. All the palaces and mansions of the rich, the marketplaces, and the houses of the citizens were carefully dismantled, loaded on carts, and hauled away. Behind them they left vast empty fields where gradually grass grew and farmers moved in and planted rice and at last a little town grew up off to one side. The great Nara temples—the Todai-ji and the Kofuku-ji, the Saidai-ji and Toshodai-ji and Yakushi-ji and Gango-ji, and the little Shin-Yakushi-ji that Empress Kōmyō had built for the health of her husband's eyes, and the Hokke-ji nunnery and others—stood in a ring around those empty fields where the remnants of them stand today, bracketing modern Nara.

The site at Nagaoka proved unlucky, and it is interesting that it was Waké Kiyomaro, back from exile and with his name restored and his rank elevated, who, when he was out hunting one day, came on a secluded valley intersected by streams and with an imposing mountain to protect it in the northeast. He reported to the Emperor this promising location for a new capital and in 793 the Court and all the city moved there. They called it the capital of peace and tranquillity, and as Kyoto it remained the seat of Imperial government for more than a thousand years.

In all that time, only two women were elevated to the sovereignty and their power was minimal. However, in the course of that time, there were plenty of personal intrigues, scandals, and political plots. Warrior monks attacked the capital, and there were quarrels of succession, civil wars, religious persecutions, and military rule. Later there were foreign wars, aggressions, holocaust, defeat—and all such acts of statesmanship that men of power are adept at.